THE IRISHMAN'S DAUGHTER

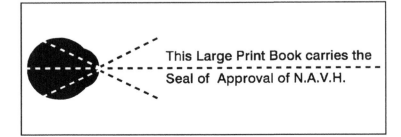

THE IRISHMAN'S DAUGHTER

V. S. ALEXANDER

KENNEBEC LARGE PRINT
A part of Gale, a Cengage Company

Farmington Hills, Mich • San Francisco • New York • Waterville, Maine
Meriden, Conn • Mason, Ohio • Chicago

Copyright © 2019 by Michael Meeske.
Kennebec Large Print, a part of Gale, a Cengage Company.

Kennebec Large Print® Superior Collection.
The text of this Large Print edition is unabridged.
Other aspects of the book may vary from the original edition.
Set in 16 pt. Plantin.

LIBRARY OF CONGRESS CIP DATA ON FILE.
CATALOGUING IN PUBLICATION FOR THIS BOOK
IS AVAILABLE FROM THE LIBRARY OF CONGRESS

ISBN-13: 978-1-4328-6307-4 (softcover alk. paper)

Published in 2019 by arrangement with Kensington Books, an imprint of Kensington Publishing Corp.

Printed in the United States of America
1 2 3 4 5 6 7 23 22 21 20 19

To the tribe — for showing me the way

PROLOGUE

And bring back the features that joy used
   to wear
Long, long be my heart with such
   memories fill'd —
                    — Thomas Moore (1779–1852)

September 1845

The boggy lane to Lear House had been tamped to a hard surface by years of use by people, carriages, horses, and donkeys. The path veered down from the high hill above Broadhaven Bay to the crescent curve of land that abutted the water. Gulls soared silently on the winds over Rinroe Point, the narrow promontory that thrust into the bay. The home stood like an imposing gray fortress rising up from the land, surrounded by checkered patches of tenant farms, as solid a manor house as there was in Ireland.

On a perfect day no country was more beautiful than Ireland, Daniel Quinn believed with all his heart, although he knew little of the world other than what he had been told. He dreamed of England and France on occasion and had seen etchings of those countries in books but, like others in his position, doubted he would ever travel from his native land. As he walked to Lear House, the brisk air skimming off the Atlantic fortified his lungs, cleared his brain. The crisp feel of it deep in his body eased the task of delivering unpleasant news.

Savoring the beautiful late September day, Daniel took his time. He expected Brian Walsh, the agent of Englishman Sir Thomas Blakely, to be at home, either in the manor or in the adjoining cottage where he and his family lived. If Brian couldn't be found, he would spend the night in the shed with the horses. It didn't matter — one way or the other Daniel would deliver what he had to say. He owed Brian the favor, for the man had been kind to him on many occasions.

Sir Thomas had inherited the estate through his English lineage. Lear House was bordered on its east and west sides by tenant farms. Rows of sod homes stood on the acreage that had been divided and then subdivided to accommodate the growing tenant population. Brian had once told Daniel that more than three hundred people made their living on Lear House lands.

Beyond the house to the north, the land rose in boggy hills that undulated across the landscape like waves. The higher a person climbed to the west, the more the wild Atlantic came into view. The hills ended at precipitous cliffs that stood as ancient guards against the sea. If one looked south from Lear House, the waters of Broadhaven Bay stretched out in a gentle half circle along the line of sand dunes. Lear House, on its solid foundation, had stood unfettered for a century, weathering Atlantic squalls and storms, political insurrections, and any manner of upheaval cast upon it.

Daniel Quinn walked past the sod homes — many belching smoke from the hole in their roofs — capturing the eyes of some tenants working in the fields and, finally, arrived at the rocky circular path that led up to the manor steps. He took off his broadbrimmed hat at the door and lifted the iron knocker. It was a molded ram's head, heavy with age but coated with a sheen of animal oil to keep it from rusting. After no answer, he knocked again.

Soon, the door swung open in a measured gait. Brian, wearing gray breeches, a white shirt and red vest, stood before him. Recognizing his visitor, the agent's face brightened with a smile.

"Danny," Brian said, and extended his hand. "It's been so long since you've paid a visit. I was beginning to wonder if you were still in County Mayo."

Daniel returned the smile. "You'll not be rid of me so easily." He waited, hat in hand, for an invitation, but then looked down at his bare feet to see if they were fit to enter the house. They seemed passable: The rocks had scraped away the mud from his skin. He swiped at some of the dirt on the legs of his breeches.

"Oh, my manners," Brian said. "Please come in. I've no liquor to offer, but maybe a smoke will suit you."

"Just fine," Daniel said, patting his vest pocket where his pipe lay. "I appreciate your hospitality." The entrance to Lear House was light and airy with high plastered ceilings decorated with egg-and-dart molding. The sun's rays had shifted in the afternoon, but the foyer still glowed like a fire-lit room on a winter's night.

Brian led him to the large sitting room on the front of the house. "Now, let me find that tobacco. I was in need of a break from my bookkeeping."

Daniel sat while Brian disappeared down the hall. He looked through the wide windows at the green lawn with its unbroken vista to the bay. On either side of the manor, the fields were fractured by rectangular walls constructed of brush and stone. The tenant farmers lived on these plots. Verdant potato ridges, lush with green leaves, cut across their tracts. The homes shone black, mostly mud and stone, a few braced by wooden lintels. *What luxury,* Daniel thought. How wonderful it must be to live in your own home, no matter how modest. How sublime not to sleep on the dirt floor in the back of a public house or in a shed with livestock. Lear House, even the crude homes that surrounded it, were like castles compared to his usual accommodations.

Brian reappeared with a pewter ashtray and a thick plug of tobacco, one that promised more than a night of good smoking. The agent lit Daniel's white pipe and then his own, a meerschaum with a dog's head bowl stained black from use.

"Always an honor to have Mayo's finest poet in the house," Brian said. "What news do you bring?"

Daniel didn't want to jump headfirst into what he dreaded, so he recounted versions of his various travels during the summer, including tales of nights in Newport, Mulranny, and Westport filled with too much liquor, tomfoolery, and song.

Brian, always up for good stories, listened intently while puffing his pipe, his hands planted on his thighs.

"How are your daughters?" Daniel asked, still avoiding his task. He could not delay much longer. The afternoon was growing short. Soon dusk would overtake the day and he would need shelter for the night.

"My dear Lucinda is spending the fall and winter in England tutoring three children — a family acquaintance of Sir Thomas." He puffed on his pipe. "My lovely Briana is either preparing supper at the cottage or sneaking off to see Rory Caulfield. Like most children, she thinks I have no eyes or ears." He laughed, and a stream of gray smoke spilled from his lips.

Daniel removed the pipe from his mouth and tapped the ashes into the tray. His forehead tensed. "I've come because I have an unpleasant matter to discuss."

Brian gave him a quizzical look. "An unpleasant matter?"

"I feel you should know what I've heard. By all accounts, it will affect the parish. As the biggest agent in the barony, and a friend, I came to you first."

Brian's gray eyes flickered in apprehension. "Go on. . . ."

"In Westport I met a man from France who was taken with my songs — a level-headed wanderer who touches neither drink nor tobacco — and he showed me a drawing." Daniel remembered the picture as clearly as the day he had seen it. "The Frenchman knew a smattering of English and Irish and he described the flowing charcoal lines he had drawn. Black lumps of wilted leaves. Withered vines. Rot. Decay. It has happened in his homeland and has spread far — to England and beyond. A plague will soon be here."

Brian leaned forward, pointing his pipe stem at him. "A plague! Surely, you don't mean the sickness that visited Wallachia not so long ago."

"No. It thrives upon the land — in fact, upon the crop that fills our very stomachs."

"The tubers?" Brian asked.

"Yes. It turns them black as night, transforms them into a vile, stinking mush that neither man nor beast can eat." Daniel read the look of mild concern on the landlord's face.

"This man — the one who told you — you believe him?" Brian asked. "I've not heard of any plague upon the crop." He returned the pipe to his lips. "Besides, there have been other blights on our land. We've survived them."

"He had no reason to lie."

Brian pointed to the window. "But you saw the fields. The crop is luxurious."

Daniel nodded. "Yes, but this plague strikes overnight and spreads like fire. We can pray that the Frenchman is wrong."

The manor door opened, and Briana strolled into the room. Many seasons had passed since Daniel had seen her. She was a young woman now, probably eighteen if his memory served him, with round, feminine features and long, dark brown hair. She was no longer the gangly adolescent he remembered from previous visits. A hint of recognition passed across her face. He remembered singing to her when she was a child on many nights before he had taken to his bed of straw behind the cottage, where he listened to the wind until he fell asleep under the stars. How peaceful the night, how calm the sleep.

"The poet." Her youthful face brightened. "Won't you dine with us?"

Brian nodded and looked out at the pink light slanting across the lawn. "The day is slipping away."

"I won't decline an invitation from such gracious company." Daniel rose and kissed Briana's hand.

He and Brian gathered their pipes and followed Briana out of Lear House into the dusk. Company was one thing, but the prospect of a good meal was another. He rubbed his suddenly growling stomach.

As Briana opened the cottage door, the rich, milky smell of potato stew wafted out the door. The sight of a table with oat bread on it, a turf fire with the steaming pot hung over it, was like heaven to him. He counted his blessings as Brian took his place across from him. Briana served the meal in heaping bowls, and they prayed over them.

He looked up after the prayer at their smiling faces and thought, if only this heaven would last.

■ ■ ■ ■

PART ONE:
COUNTY MAYO

■ ■ ■ ■

CHAPTER 1

October 1845

Briana Walsh descended the steps of Lear House and breathed in the brisk Atlantic air. She had taken in its crispness all of her life. The air comforted her, filled her with joy, and always deepened her sense of security, no matter the time of year or the weather. The solid structure of the manor cheered her, although she owned not one of its stones. It stood behind her like an austere guardian, rising from the sloping green and brown heath, surrounded by the hamlet of tenant farms. Along with her family, these farmers were the people she loved, and she could imagine no other home on earth than these lands.

She considered Lear House her second home, the first being the adjoining cottage, the site of her birth. Sir Thomas Blakely, the English owner who spent most summer months in County Mayo, when he could divorce himself from his textile business in Manchester, also called it home.

This evening, Briana had been to the manor, in her father's stead, to make sure everything was locked for the night. With its rock façade, climbing ivy, and slate roof, Lear House retained its regality in the dying light. Briana knew every nook and cranny of the manor, the history of every oil painting, the provenance of every object displayed upon its shelves. She had touched each book in its ample library and read many of them except for those — the most academically stuffy — that held no interest for her.

She and her father lived in the tidy cottage that rested just to the west of the house, adjacent to the western farms and the cliffs that ended at the sea. She gazed at the cottage as well, which was infused with a buttery glow from oil lamps. At this hour, after supper, Brian would be smoking his pipe and reading.

The sun, obscured except for occasional splits in the leaden clouds, was beginning its descent into the Atlantic beyond the western cliffs. The pallid rays, when they did appear, cast streaks of purple across the lawn. Behind her, to the north, the land rose to the plateau and bluffs overlooking

Benwee Head and the Stags of Broadhaven — the rocky, jagged islands rising like shark's teeth from the sea.

As she walked from Lear House to the farthest eastern tracts on the manor acreage, a foul odor wafted into her nostrils. There, on the last remaining lands before slanting to the bay's shifting dunes, Rory Caulfield and his brother made their homes. He had claimed his corner on the far border of the manor holdings. It looked out to the sandy bay and the distant hillocks to the south.

Rory had sent her a message through his brother's son asking her to come to his land. Something was wrong, and she only had to breathe to know it.

The poet and her father had told her weeks ago at supper about rumors of potato crop failures on the Continent, but she had wondered if the story might be part of Quinn's own flair for the dramatic — she had always felt there was something theatrical, bordering on artifice, about his personality — tales embellished by too much poteen.

But tonight, judging from the urgent message conveyed by the boy, the nervous apprehension that filled her body, and the putrid odor, something was indeed wrong.

She wondered how the smell could be so overpowering that it could dominate the wind rushing in from the Atlantic.

She tightened her mother's red shawl about her shoulders, covering her nose and mouth. The faint odor of wisteria water, a gift long ago from her father to her mother, blotted out the terrible stench.

She walked in the center of the pebbled lane, avoiding the carriage ruts carved into the path, lifting the hem of her scarlet petticoats as she bounded over puddles. An excursion up or down the drive was always a challenge by carriage. Often she preferred to be let out on the hilltop road to walk down to the house, even in the foulest weather. The middle of the path also held its dangers — rocks dislodged by the horses, indentations made by the power of hooves, that could easily cause a sprained ankle or fall.

The estate was separated by irregular lines of brush and stone fences, some hundreds of years old and others built much later as the tenant population bore children and expanded its claim. Many of the homes had thatched roofs, but most were little more than mud huts with a vent so the turf-fire smoke could escape. The estate seemed to grow every month with a new fence and the wail of a newborn.

Soon she neared Rory's small acreage where he tended his potato crop, in addition to the oats and rye he farmed on land higher up the hill. He sold the oats and rye, as did the other tenants, to pay in kind for his rent. The lane led her past the larger parcels, some as sizeable as an acre, down to the quarter acres owned by Rory and his brother.

Rory leaned casually against the corner of his cabin. He was clad in dark breeches, a white shirt, and a green jacket; he, like her, wore no shoes. Tobacco smoke twirled through his nose and mouth as he inhaled deeply from his clay pipe. His reddish hair glowed auburn in the sunset. Near his cabin, a pig snuffled in the turf. Rory, like other tenants, kept the animal inside at night for safety and warmth.

She stopped a few paces away, her body kept to a respectable distance by the social views of her father. "A woman should save herself until her marriage night," he had told her years after her mother had died. His words only echoed those she was sure her mother would have spoken had she lived. Tonight, the plans she dreamed of sharing with Rory, the whispered words of love she wanted to say, would wait for another day. No matter that they had known each other since they were children and their affection had grown over the years. The time to show it hardly ever seemed to present itself because of their duties with the manor and farm. But their marriage was coming soon. Rory had told her so.

Rory pointed to the potato ridges that weren't far up the sloping land.

She stared at the blackened leaves and pressed the shawl tighter against her mouth.

Rory beckoned her closer, stooped, and touched one of the dark leaves. It melted into a viscous goo in his hand. "See," he said, "this is what the poet predicted would happen. Look." He grabbed a nearby spade and thrust it into the ground. He dug quickly, turning over the moist earth at the top of the ridge. The potatoes were planted there for maximum drainage. He reached into the earth, grasped the potatoes and lifted them for her to see.

He crushed one with his hand, and a slimy mush dripped from his fingers. His hand opened in the feeble light, revealing the moldy, black and gray meat inside them, gangrenous in appearance.

She would never have suspected that the crop, lush, bright and green as of yesterday, could change to rot in less than a day. She stepped back. "Are they all gone?"

"All that I've checked," Rory answered. He threw the rotten potatoes on the ground and rubbed his hand across the furrow to rid his fingers of the putrefaction. "Even my pig has the sense not to touch them."

"The 'plague' Daniel Quinn predicted. And we don't know why?"

Rory nodded. "The summer was mild and wet, excellent for growing potatoes. Even the fall has been good. Some will say this curse came from rain and wind, others insects, but what I fear most are those who will claim it comes from God."

"Even after Daniel Quinn departed, Father said it was silly to worry about such things," Briana said. " 'Providence will provide,' he told me."

The wooden door to Rory's brother's cabin creaked open. Jarlath stretched his arms, lit his pipe and then nodded to Briana. She shifted on her feet and bowed slightly to him.

Looking back to Rory, Briana asked, "Is every row like this?"

"Yes, this crop is ruined. We'll have to start over for the spring. I don't know whether we can salvage seed potatoes."

The poet's words about the "plague" came rushing back to her. A number of horrifying thoughts struck her as she stared at the plants, including one that crept slowly in from the back of her mind, of not having enough to eat — starvation, plainly put. All the farmers, even her family, depended upon the potato for their daily meals. To lose the crop would mean they would have only seed potatoes to eat, and those wouldn't last forever. A disturbing picture flashed through her mind as she imagined children begging for food as they lifted their empty bowls.

"What will the people eat. . . . What will *we* eat?"

Rory looked toward the gray waves of Broadhaven Bay. "Maybe a herring, if Jarlath can fish the waters. Seaweed? Birds' eggs? A frog now and then." He chuckled at the thought.

Briana didn't think his musings were funny. Few men ventured out in their small canoes, their *curraghs,* on the ragged ocean, and they knew the risks when they did. She had seen the bodies of several drowned men. The ocean currents were powerful, the tides swift, the waves treacherous on most days, and only the most skilled among them could navigate the Atlantic waters.

Rory looked again at the rotted plants lying putrid on the ridges, and his voice turned somber. "Without food, the people won't have the strength to farm. How will we pay the rent if we have to eat our oats and rye?"

Briana hadn't thought that far ahead, and his question jolted her. "I don't know," she said after a few moments. "The crops have to be sold." She wanted a solution, but the immensity of what she had seen was too much to take in. "I have to tell Father," she said, and walked toward the lane. "He doesn't even know — he's been working inside all day."

Rory followed a few steps behind. "Will I see you tomorrow?" he asked in a wistful voice.

She turned, well aware that they both would have liked to have met under more pleasant circumstances. "Tomorrow."

He took her in his arms and kissed her. She didn't mind that Jarlath, still outside smoking his pipe, was a witness, for he would never speak of their affection to her father. Besides, everyone on Lear House grounds knew, or at least suspected, that one day they would be married.

She left him standing at his cabin. The deepening indigo sky retained its swaths of red. The wind licked against her, and she folded her arms against her chest. Fear lapped at her as well, as the images of the rotted plants floated through her mind. Only one question offered some hope. Was there anything her father could do? She was filled with doubt. In less than an hour, her world had shifted.

Rinroe Point beckoned, with its broad view of the ever-shifting Atlantic, but the walk was long and treacherous at night. Sitting by the cliffs, watching the stars shift in and out of the clouds, would be so much easier than telling her father about what she had seen.

He might be reading in his chair near the turf fire or, by now, have fallen asleep. The cottage would be cozy and warm inside. "You saw Rory, didn't you?" she imagined he would ask with slight disdain. "You can do better." It wasn't that he didn't like or respect Rory, or perhaps hold some love for him in his heart — but she understood that her father, in his love, wished for her a better life than a tenant farmer might have to offer. A life like her sister, Lucinda, might construct.

She arrived at the circular lane in front of Lear House. The house was as black as her mood. No light burned in any window, and the ivy clung like strangling, dark fingers over the stone face.

She shivered and darted toward the cottage door.

Her father had read *King Lear* to her years before. He loved Shakespeare and had imparted that love to his daughters. The playwright was one of the reasons he had learned English and then taught the language to Lucinda and to her.

She thought of Rory and how much she longed to be with him as she clutched the latch. Lines from the play came into her head.

So we'll live, and pray, and sing, and tell
    old tales, and laugh
At gilded butterflies, and hear poor
    rogues
Talk of court news; and we'll talk with
    them too . . .

Any sense of happiness of singing and telling tales was blotted out as she thought about the crop. Without potatoes there would be nothing to eat. Her father would be placed in the difficult position of collecting rents he couldn't gather. And she knew from his bookkeeping troubles that many of the tenants were already in arrears. This failure would put them further in debt.

A hopeful thought struck her as she stood

outside. She would write to Lucinda informing her of the blight and ask her to intercede with Sir Thomas on the family's behalf as well as the tenants'. Those words, asking for forgiveness of debt, might fall upon the unsympathetic ears of the landlord, but it was the best plan she could think of. Her sister, after all, was in close contact with the Englishman through the family she worked for.

She decided not to tell her father of her scheme. Of course he would raise a strong objection to her interference in a business matter. It would be better if he didn't know.

Her mind shifted back to Rory and the crop failure and then to her family's situation. What of the food stored in Lear House? How long would it last? The questions made her head spin.

She stepped inside and greeted her father, who looked up from his reading, closed his book, and smiled.

Her stomach quivered as she spoke. "I saw Rory this evening."

His smile faded into a look of thoughtful reflection. "I thought you must be with him. It took you longer than usual to check on the house." The light from the oil lamps and the turf fire cast flickering shadows across the room. Her father lowered the book to the floor.

"You've not been outside today, have you?" she asked.

"Other than to run from Lear House to the cottage," he replied. "Why?"

"Did you smell it in the air?"

His nose crinkled. "What? I noticed nothing unusual. The wind was strong off the bay."

That explained it. The wind would have swept the odor up the hill toward the farms and then on toward the village of Carrowteige. It had now shifted more from the Atlantic. "The potato crop has failed — rotted."

Her father smiled again, as if she had told him some kind of perverse joke. "We've been through these before — it can't be as bad as you imagine."

Briana sat in a chair across from him. "Rory says all the ridges have failed. There's nothing left. Daniel Quinn told us it would happen."

He scoffed. "The poet isn't right about everything. I'll check in the morning. Now I'm going to bed." He rose from his chair.

"Perhaps Sir Thomas should be notified that the tenants may fall into more debt," she said without mentioning her plan.

Her father turned, his face flushed. "I

would never do such a thing!" He lifted his book and tossed it on the chair. "I'm working very hard to keep Lear House solvent. Sir Thomas need not be burdened with an additional worry." He started for his bed and then stopped. "And don't get any grand ideas in your head. You should stay out of my business, and that includes any meddling from Rory Caulfield."

"Well, you've made your feelings clear." Briana got up. "I'm headed to bed as well."

"Daughter," Brian said with a tone of reconciliation, "let's not panic. The tenants have had many troubles over the years, and this is one more — that we will get through *together.*"

She admired her father for not panicking despite the stress he was under. She kissed him on the forehead and retired to her room as he extinguished the oil lamps. The cottage still glowed from the smoldering turf fire.

Despite what her father instructed, she couldn't let go of her plan to write Lucinda. What could it hurt? It would be a friendly note to her sister with one addition. . . . She undressed and said her prayers. She was grateful for the firelight because it made her feel that she and Lear House were safe — at least for the moment.

CHAPTER 2

April 1846

"By all that's blessed in heaven, I don't know what we're going to do," Brian Walsh said as he peered out the drawing room window of Lear House. He threw back the curtains, sending a stream of dust whirling into the air.

She was getting taller, or her father was shrinking. But the crop failure, the threat of starvation, the necessity to collect rents from families they had known for years — many of them friends — had taken a toll on him since October. He was forty-two but looked older. Deep creases lined his cheeks, and his forehead was furrowed with ridges. His gray hair fell in wild wisps from his temples, while the top of his head, lacking in locks, reflected the light shining on his balding pate. Briana worried about his health and what the situation in Mayo was doing to his constitution. He spent long hours over the ledger books, muttering to himself, thinking about ways to keep Lear House from falling into bankruptcy.

Her father swiped at the air, scattering the dust in the breeze. Even the suspenders that pulled at his breeches couldn't correct the slight stoop in his posture.

Briana wiped the black smudges off a silver candlestick and then removed the dust covers from three high-backed chairs. She was excited at the prospect of reuniting with her older sister. Lucinda's arrival was a celebration of sorts, yet her feelings were tempered by the harsh realities surrounding Lear House. Her father, despite his troubles, had insisted on opening the drawing room to his oldest daughter. He was taking liberties that wouldn't be afforded others, and he was only doing it for Lucinda, whom Briana suspected had come to expect such treatment.

Briana threw her polishing rag upon the sideboard as her anger toward Sir Thomas rose to the surface. Her letter asking for a temporary exemption from debt had been ignored. The only posts she and her father had received in the months since October had been those of salutations and greetings from Lucinda, talking of the dull English weather and offering holiday cheer.

The long-time cook and hired man had been dismissed early in the year as a result of Blakely's wishes. The Englishman's reasons, as her father had reported them, had been vague as far as Briana was concerned, but her father had not raised a fuss, preferring to remain silent and accepting of Blakely's opaque explanation rather than risk their own livelihoods.

"I don't want you to think you're a serving girl," her father said as he paced in light made dull by rain. "You do enough now, but we'll all have to do more if times don't change."

Briana appreciated his concern, but he depended upon her housekeeping now that the help had been dismissed. For years she had helped Margaret in the kitchen and even assisted Edmond when needed. Lucinda was too concerned with her books and studying to learn how to cook a proper meal — her culinary skills were only enough to keep her alive. Briana supposed her sister longed for the day when cooks and maids would be preparing and serving her food.

Drops from the misty clouds splattered the window.

"Where is the damn carriage?" Brian pushed a hand through the few strands of hair that remained on top of his head.

"Probably delayed by weather," Briana replied. "I can't imagine the terrible shape of the road from Belmullet after the winter we've had." Lucinda was sailing into the port village on a ship from Liverpool, the passage paid for by Sir Thomas. The carriage journey to Lear House was many miles from the port — but one that could be accomplished in much less than a day in good weather. Briana knew her sister had no affinity for arriving at the small store on Broadhaven Bay that sold goods. The ships landing there were small and uncomfortable.

Her father turned a chair toward the window and took a seat. Briana stood behind him and looked out upon the wide lawn. Through the mist she could see the store far below.

"I wouldn't have believed the crop could be destroyed had I not seen it with my own eyes," Brian said. He rubbed his palms together and formed a steeple with his fingers. His hands were hardened into strong instruments of work, tight flesh, sinew and bone, molded by long hours in the fields before Sir Thomas had hired him as agent.

Briana put her hands on his shoulders. "No need to worry, Da. Everything will work out." No sooner had the words left her lips than she doubted their truth. They had a hollow ring, a platitude that anyone could express. No sentiment could blunt the dread that filled people now. Rumors had spread through the tenant farms of evictions, homes destroyed, whole families living in holes in the earth, their only protection being a crude roof of branches and sod. Rory had told her of "ejectment" atrocities in Galway. Her stomach had churned when she'd heard these stories because she knew they were true.

She preferred to remember the happier days of growing up in the cottage, on the grounds surrounding Lear House. Carefree, taking in the wonders of life — Briana had sparred with her older sister but grew close to her father after her mother had died. She had learned to milk goats, at first afraid to pull the teats but then getting her hands upon them, as practiced as any milkmaid. She fed livestock, collected water from the spring, and learned how to cook. Markets, fairs, and county celebrations made up her life. And there was Rory, whom she admired for his strong spirit and handsome face and body. Their friendship, which turned to courtship over the years, had filled the sparse time they could find together with walks along the bay, along the cliffs, reveling in all that nature had to offer. Rory had stolen several kisses at Rinroe Point when she was fifteen and he was sixteen. The innocent act had taken her breath away, and the feeling of his lips upon hers had lingered for days, leaving her cheeks flushed and her hands tingling.

On the other hand, her sister had, over the years, stretched out in the cottage during the winter and on the grass in summer, content to read textbooks on various subjects and romantic novels, and dream of a life far away from Mayo. Her father spent what little spare time he had watching sporting races and fights. He had even sparred once, much to the consternation of Briana and her sister. Both cried when he took them to the makeshift ring in the village. He left victorious, but with a broken and bloody nose.

But never far from the good times past were the funerals and the keening women. Briana could never forget the sound — a cry like a wounded animal that wound through the air in spirals as ancient and primal as the stars. This was the sound she had heard when the men had drowned. Recently, not sure of her ears, she believed she had heard the plaintive call drifting over the silent fields like an echo on the wind. She feared there would be many more such cries to come.

Briana walked to the window and looked out. The land had changed over the years as the tenant farms expanded around the manor, except on the sloping farm lands to the north. She supposed it was called progress, a use of the land for the greater good. It was certainly all she knew. But now she wondered about progress: She had seen the ravages of the blight herself, touched the wilted leaves, seen the concerned looks of the women as the food diminished, witnessed the exasperation of her father as he failed to collect the rents.

The clop of horses' hooves jogged Brian from his chair. The square form of the jaunting car, covered in oilcloth to protect its passenger, bounced into view in the circular lane. The driver, clad in a tan overcoat splotched with water, held the reins in his left and a whip in his right. He guided the horse up the lane, the light carriage quivering in the ruts.

Her father rushed to the door. Briana followed him down the steps to the lathering horse.

"Thank you for safely delivering my daughter," Brian told the driver. "Can I offer you a cup?"

"No, thank you," the man replied, pressing the rain from his coat. "I must water my horse and return to Belmullet." Brian directed him to the cistern in back of the house where he could find a bucket, ample water, and patches of grass. The driver thanked him again, telling Brian he wanted to take advantage of the daylight for his journey back. He descended from his wooden perch and unloaded Lucinda's large trunk on the wet landing.

Briana peered under the oilcloth and saw her sister. Lucinda was twenty, two years older but a woman Briana thought more mature because of her worldly knowledge. She always harbored some jealousy for her sister's travels, but those thoughts were short-lived when she reflected on her own love of her native land.

Brian peeled back the cloth. A leg covered by an open silk cape and fine satin dress lowered toward the carriage step. Lucinda, smiling, shifted her body, allowing her father to lift her in a graceful sweep to the slate landing of Lear House. At least her sister's white-buttoned shoes would not get soiled by the damp.

Brian patted the driver's back. "Let me get your payment."

Lucinda kissed her father's cheek and shook her head. "No need, Father. Sir Thomas has taken care of everything." She spoke in English.

Briana had heard her sister speak English since they were children, but Lucinda's tone and accent had changed in the past year. Her words held a snobbish affectation that had developed since her sojourns abroad.

The driver snapped the reins. The horse snorted and headed around the pebbled lane to the back of the house. Briana moved closer to her sister. Lucinda's pale yellow dress, crosshatched with squares and stripes and patterned with white periwinkles within the geometric shapes, blossomed under her black cape. Her matching bonnet was secured to her head by a pale green bow knotted under her strong chin. Her gloves matched the color of the bow. The dress was not brocaded with ruffles in the manner of the highest fashion; in that respect it was simple — a dress in which to travel. But any Irish woman of breeding, let alone the wife of a tenant farmer, would have coveted such an outfit. Briana looked down at her simple, deep yellow skirt; brown bodice; and worn black shoes and felt inadequate in her sister's suddenly imposing shadow.

Lucinda leaned in and pecked her on the

cheek, hesitated for a moment, but then pulled Briana to her waist with a heartfelt squeeze. "It's so good to see you again, my dear sister. How I've missed you, but England was so exciting —"

"Let's not stand in this weather like we're daft," Brian chided. "It's much more comfortable inside." He grabbed Lucinda's trunk by the straps and dragged it up the steps. Briana opened the door for her sister, who stepped inside with the air of an entitled owner.

Lucinda doffed her bonnet and gloves, depositing them on the mahogany entrance table. Like a dutiful father, Brian removed her cape and hung it on the hall tree. Lucinda, her dress buoyed by petticoats, appeared to float across the floor. They followed her into the drawing room, where the ancestral portraits of Blakely's family hung on the mustard-colored, flowered walls.

"Much better," Brian said. "I'll light a fire to keep out the damp."

Lucinda sank into a chair. "Thank you, Papa. I'm rather tired after my journey. Maybe Margaret can make us some tea."

Brian looked puzzled. "Didn't you get my letter?"

Lucinda nodded. "The most recent, a month ago." She appeared equally puzzled.

"Is something wrong?"

He walked to the fireplace and placed several ash logs on the grate. "Apparently, you've been shielded from what's going on. Haven't you heard?"

Lucinda's eyes widened as alarm spread across her face. "I've heard nothing. Where is Margaret?" She scrutinized the room with narrowed eyes. "And where's Edmond?"

"Sir Thomas has kept you under a rock," Briana said impatiently. "Both are gone. Let go, after kind consideration from Mr. Blakely. Father can explain better than I. While he does, I'll make tea." She left the drawing room and considered that Lucinda had not received the letter about pardoning the tenants' debts. That explained why there was no response from her sister. She suspected Sir Thomas must have intercepted the family posts, only to deliver those of the most innocuous nature. Still, she wanted to make no mention of her attempt to sway the landlord for fear of upsetting her father.

Briana walked through the dim hall to the kitchen on the back of the house. With Margaret and Edmond gone since January — a cruel time for anyone to lose their income, especially considering the blight — the manor had taken on an added air of melancholy without their presence. Briana considered Lear House to be most inviting in the spring and summer, when on warm, sunny days the doors and windows could be flung open. Then, light filled the drawing room and the dining room on the opposite side of the hall. Despite that, two rooms remained in darkness on the ground floor: The library was always left in subdued light to protect its books, and the kitchen received little sun through its north windows. On the upper story, Blakely's bedroom; the Master's bath, as her father called it; and the guest rooms were also pleasant when opened during the summer. If the owner's guests were in a festive mood, Lear House could be especially cheerful in its season.

Of the two doors inside the kitchen, the one farthest to the north opened to the sloping hill rising from the back of the house; the other, now chained and padlocked, had served as the entrance to the cramped quarters of the cook and hired man. Those rooms were even more austere than the adjoining cottage where Briana and her family lived.

Dust coated the windows as well as the large oak table in the center of the room. The long iron stove looked equally forlorn having been denied the tender attentions of Margaret. Briana placed several logs on the grate below the cooking rack and scattered them with twigs and loose bark. The airtight metal box containing the Congreve matches sat nearby. She opened it, and a soft whoosh poured from its interior. She struck a match against the sandpaper. It flared in a smoky haze, and the smell of phosphorous filled her nose. The flame ignited the bark.

Through the small window she saw the jaunting car headed up the hill to the village of Carrowteige, returning to Belmullet. She filled an iron kettle from the cistern and returned to the kitchen. In a few minutes the steamy smell of boiling water filled the room. The tea, teacups, and serving tray were in the oak cupboard. For a moment, she resented her role as "serving girl," the one her father had spoken of. However, it was a duty thrust upon her, and she couldn't depend upon her sister to make tea or keep house.

When Briana returned to the drawing room, her father had lit the fire and moved a small table between the three chairs. She placed the tray on the table and waited for the tea to steep. Lucinda was silent, her attention diverted to the window. The afternoon light faded in the deepening overcast. Gloom settled over the room.

"I had no idea," Lucinda finally said. "Sir Thomas said nothing of this to me — the dismissal of Margaret and Edmond, the blight . . . However, he's not required to keep me informed of events in Ireland." She stopped and pondered for a moment. "He certainly wouldn't withhold your letters."

"Wouldn't he?" Briana asked. "I wrote to you concerning matters here — with no response. You don't know the half of what has happened." Briana hated the stiffness of her tone, but Lucinda needed to know the truth. She poured the tea. "No one seems to know what's causing the potato crop to fail. Mr. Caulfield told me that three hundred smallholders were evicted from Ballinlass in Galway last month so the tenant's land could be turned into pasture. Perhaps it had nothing to do with the crop, but the Infantry was called in and homes were demolished. Mr. Caulfield has told me of other incidents as well, of struggles in Tipperary. The blight seems to be happening everywhere in Ireland. I fear the worst is yet to come."

"Rory would know," her father said. "He appears to have a keen interest in the state of the government."

Lucinda raised an eyebrow. "Yes . . . more than he should." She looked at Briana.

"London was so bright and gay when Sir Thomas and his friends were there, even on the dullest days. No one in our circle could have imagined such goings-on here."

Briana sipped her tea and brushed off the slight to Rory. It amazed her that her sister could have heard nothing of the suffering that had overtaken County Mayo since the fall. But, on reflection, perhaps Lucinda was not as heartless as she imagined. Could the letters have been lost in the post even though she took great care in addressing them? She suspected Sir Thomas was to blame. After all, her sister was fulfilling her duties as a governess to the children of a family friend of the owner. Unmarried, Blakely had no children himself, but he did look out for his close acquaintances, particularly those in high places, as her father had pointed out. Blakely needn't have looked further than to Lucinda and her bookish ways for the right candidate for a governess. She imagined that her sister spent her days with pampered children near Manchester or on trips to London with the family. On the nights she could socialize, her sister could draw the attentions of those with greater breeding than found in Mayo. Lucinda may have been a flower against the wall in her position as governess, but her perfumes extended well into the room.

For the next hour, they sipped tea while Lucinda regaled them with stories of her time in Manchester and London. She had met some important people in the government courtesy of Sir Thomas. Frankly, Briana found herself envious of the maturity and connections her sister had garnered during her time there. Lucinda's stories left her feeling inadequate and lackluster.

Lucinda lifted her teacup. Her lips narrowed in a slight quiver.

Briana was adept at translating her father's and sister's movements. Formerly, Lucinda would have jerked her head toward the window like a schoolgirl at someone's arrival. Now she simply gave a refined look, one that Briana knew consisted of fifty percent disdain.

"It seems *your* Mr. Caulfield is about to pay a visit."

Briana glimpsed Rory striding up the circular lane. He would be a harsh judge of her sister, even more caustic than she. He had no use for Lucinda's English ways — he considered them a cultural extension of an uncaring government. In fact, he had never expressed any interest in Lucinda other than his dislike for her slights to his social standing and the social obligations he was required to render.

By her own admission, Lucinda had never been the beauty in the family. She was not ugly or maladroit by any means, but her face was more severe than Briana's, even under her layers of powder and color. She had inherited the masculine chin and forehead of their father and the equally dark hair and brows of his younger figure. Briana took after their deceased mother. Her features were lighter, softer, rounder, more feminine, and more likely to draw the attention of men. This reality predisposed Lucinda to try harder with the opposite sex, particularly when it came to Sir Thomas. But looks had never been a rancorous issue between them in childhood. Both had been reared by their father after the death of their mother when Briana was two and Lucinda four. As a loving father, Brian had never favored one over the other, except to give Lucinda dispensations from housework when her studious moods struck.

Rory knocked and Briana rose to answer. She pulled it open to find him holding his hat and smiling. The rain pattered around him and glistened in his soft, reddish hair. He brushed the drops from his shoulders and stepped inside. She sighed in relief when she found he was wearing boots, even though they were spattered with mud.

For an instant, she wished she could go back three years before the rot had struck, when every visit to the manor or cottage, mostly secretive and childishly innocent, was cheerful and not indicative of doom. The times he'd visited the house took her breath away and stirred heated feelings in her young heart. He was but a year older than she, a year younger than her sister. In those past times of sun and laughter she appreciated the wide, green lawn; the slope to Broadhaven Bay; and the dusky mountains beyond. Even the ever-increasing patchwork of tenant farms held their own rustic beauty. Now, despite Rory's smile, she suspected he bore some news of importance considering the lateness of the afternoon.

"Come say hello to my sister," Briana said in Irish as she closed the door. "Don't irritate her by speaking our native tongue. You'll be thanking my father for teaching you some English."

Rory scowled. "I'd rather bite off my tongue than speak that language."

"It's necessary." She put her lips close to his ear and whispered, "Come." The earthy scent of turf rose from his jacket. Briana found the smell primal, invigorating, an anchor to the land she loved. She led him to the drawing room.

Lucinda extended her hand. "Mr. Caulfield . . . so good to see you again." She spoke in English like Briana knew she would.

Rory gripped her hand somewhat awkwardly and then made his way to Brian, who offered him his seat. "No, no," Rory said. "Keep your place. I'll only be here a few minutes."

"In England, a gentleman kisses a lady's hand when it's offered," Lucinda said, and smiled deviously.

"Lu!" Briana blushed at her sister's forward manner.

"This isn't England," Rory shot back.

"What's your business?" Brian asked, attempting to defuse the situation between his daughters. Pouting, Lucinda sank in her chair and stared out the window.

"I'd like you to come with me, sir, on the morrow, to Westport. My brother has been told that an English steamer is arriving. The landlord's agent might . . . what's the word?" Rory raised his right hand, still holding his hat, and scratched his temple.

"What's on board?" Brian asked.

"Indian corn — for the people."

"Yes, yes," Brian said. "So the landlord or

his agent can . . . arrange . . . lobby . . . ask for?"

Rory lowered his hand. "Arrange is the word I'm looking for, I think. You might make an *arrangement* for a portion of the cargo to go to Lear House and the tenants rather than being stored for later use."

"Do you feel it's come to that?" Brian asked.

"Yes, sir, I do."

"I didn't see anyone starving when I left Belmullet," Lucinda said. "There were no beggars along the road."

Rory turned to Lucinda. "You probably didn't see them because you were huddled comfortably in your carriage under the oilcloth. *Scalps* are common now. You'd think the people are no better than rabbits."

Lucinda folded her hands in her lap. "What are scalps, unless you mean those taken in ancient warfare?"

Rory glared at her. "*Sceilp,* in our tongue."

"A hole in the ground?" Lucinda asked derisively. "Surely you can't mean that people are living in burrows."

"It's true," Briana said. "The tenants have heard of the horrible conditions, some have even seen it." She looked to her sister for a reaction, but there was none. "It's the only shelter they have. A hole covered by a roof of branches, sod if they're lucky."

Rory directed his words to Lucinda. "You probably sailed past them outside of Belmullet, past Glencastle, not noticing them when the road turns north before Glenamoy. All those you passed remained silent. Our people have been silent for too long, too willing to bow to others. The time has come for change, but with no food in our stomachs how can we be expected to fight for what is ours?"

Brian clapped his hands to hush them. "Fight? I don't want to hear the word." He shook his head at Rory. "We were able to make it through the winter, despite the blight at Lear House, and, I think, we will be fine through the summer. But we have to think of the future." He looked at Rory. "I have correspondence to attend to, but if you feel it's important, I can push it off."

"Soon we'll have nothing left," Rory said. "It won't be long before we . . ." His voice trailed off, and he lowered his head.

"May I come too, Da?" Briana asked in Irish.

Settling into a forceful stare, her father turned his attention to Lucinda. "I suppose — if your sister agrees to handle any matters that come up at the estate."

Irritation flashed in Lucinda's eyes, but

the look was momentary. "It's not something I planned to do, but if it's necessary, Father . . . if I can command the attention of three young English boys, I can certainly manage subservient tenants."

Briana wondered if her sister knew that the thirty families who now lived on the lands surrounding Lear House had continued to propagate through division and subdivision of the acreage, until even her father wasn't certain how many people now lived on the estate. A census would have to be taken to ascertain the true figure.

"England has treated you well, Lucinda," Rory said as he eyed her from head to toe. He bowed slightly to Brian. "I'll come by at five tomorrow morning with the horses after I've had a chance to eat and to feed my pig."

Lucinda sniggered. "Pearls before swine. I'm so glad to be home."

"And we're happy too," her father said flatly. He looked up at Rory. "If I were you, I'd get rid of that ribbon before we travel to Westport."

Rory flushed and grappled with the green ribbon that hung from a buttonhole in his jacket. "Yes, sir. I forgot it was there." He finally captured it and shoved it in his pocket.

"That's a good man," Brian said.

Rory backed out of the drawing room. "I'll let myself out. I wish you all a good evening."

"What was this business about the ribbon?" Lucinda asked after the door closed. She shot Brian a quizzical look. "I hope that doesn't mean he —"

"You must be famished," Briana said to Lucinda, cutting off her question. "I'm hungry too. Since the stove is fired up, I'll cook here."

"I'll explain later," Brian said. "I've been meaning to talk to Rory. Lucinda, please help your sister."

Lucinda stood up. "Not in this dress, I won't. I'll change. After we eat, I'm off to bed." She walked to the hall and opened her trunk. Soon Lucinda was headed upstairs with a dress draped over her arms, her white-buttoned shoes clicking against the wood.

Brian's back bent into a bow. He covered his face with his hands and massaged his graying temples.

Briana knew that he was distressed about the future of Lear House, and at the green ribbon threaded through Rory's jacket. It was a symbol that Rory had only recently begun to wear, and it made Briana uneasy as well. She had heard of the Ribbonmen in songs and tales passed on through families. Although the group's aim was noble, as described by Rory — a secret society of Catholics who stood up for tenants' rights — clashes had erupted for many years with Protestants.

She looked at her father still bent in his chair. What saddened her most were the tales and songs that told of the Ribbonmen's history — of bloody battles fought on Irish soil between Irishmen. She wanted no part of death and destruction, and she hoped she could talk Rory out of his allegiance to the group. But that might be like fighting the waves that crashed upon the Stags of Broadhaven. One might as well try to tame the wild ocean.

She closed her eyes and tried to think of thoughts less disturbing than religious turmoil and hunger. Was Rory saying that everyone was going to starve, the Walshes included, if they couldn't get food in Westport?

She patted her father's back. He looked up, his lips stretched in a thin smile. Their world had become much more fragile.

CHAPTER 3

True to his word, Rory arrived early the next morning with his supplies, ready for the journey. The sunless sky, still harboring its misty stars, hung over Briana as she stood in the chilly wind. She held a full pouch containing soda bread, potato scones, and cheese. Her father, puffing on his pipe, stood next to her, holding additional bags of food and water. The burning tobacco glowed red. Ashes sputtered into the air in orange arcs and fell in black specks on the dew-slickened steps.

Once they had gathered, they walked to the stable on the northeast side of the house and loaded their supplies on the three ponies selected to make the trip. Her father called them "bog trotters" because they were good horses to ride on the open heath. The animals instinctively knew how to avoid the brambles, the furze, and the watery stretches of bog by stepping from tussock to tussock, the high mounds of dry grass that dotted the heath. Briana had been around horses since childhood and had learned to ride at an early age. At one time, Sir Thomas had been proud to call Lear House home to more than fifteen of the animals. But over the years, as costs increased and revenues decreased, a good number of the horses had been sold or traded. Only five remained — the three trotters and two working animals.

They struck off down the lane that led to the village road. Briana wrapped her shawl around her head and shoulders and eased into the rhythm of the horse. The tenants' homes slipped past them. Candlelight flickered in the few cabins that had windows. White smoke from the turf fires whirled from the openings cut into the structures.

A long two-day journey to Westport lay ahead. It would have been easier for them to travel to Belmullet and then take a ship to their destination, but Rory said he knew of no ships in the harbor since the one carrying Lucinda had departed.

Briana looked back as Lear House, dark and imposing, fell away. The quiet cottage where Lucinda still slept, after a promise from her father not to wake her, faded from view as well. She and her father had eaten a breakfast of oats and buttermilk, taken from the manor stores. Supplies, once abundant, were running low. Many grains, even though stored in jars with lids, were under attack from insects and mice as if the lowly creatures hadn't enough to eat as well. Margaret would never have allowed such unpleasant incidents to occur.

"It's too bad we couldn't take Ariel and a wagon," Rory shouted back at her. Ariel was Jarlath's donkey, but hauling three people over the rough roads would be arduous for the animal.

They would start on the high bog lands near Carrowteige and descend to a river crossing. The road would take them past the east side of Carrowmore Lake, crossing the bridge at Bangor, past Ballycroy, skirting the valley below the green and rusty hues of the Nephin Beg Mountains. The final miles would lead them through the expansive hills that bordered the coastal towns of Mulranny and Newport before they finally arrived in Westport.

After forty-five minutes on the horses, a bruised purple light scattered across the eastern horizon. Rory led the way, Briana in the middle, and her father bringing up the rear. The heath dropped away into a black cut in the land. Rory slowed his pony and looked for the shallow point of the river that allowed the crossing. He shielded his eyes as the sun rose, its rays infusing the sky with yellow and pink.

Majestic swathes of blue encircled the coursing, patchy clouds. Briana was lost in the splendor of the bracing air, the clean scent of the water, when something startled her horse. The animal pitched sideways, nearly knocking her from her saddle.

A man's bony hand, all withered skin and sinew, knuckles protruding, grasped for her leg. He shouted at her, and at first she couldn't understand what he was saying. Rory and her father circled around as the horses trotted to a stop.

"Do you have food?" He repeated the question several times, his voice piteous, raspy, in its pleading.

Rory gave a knowing look to Briana, a signal to keep her mouth shut. "We have no food. We're on our way to Westport to see what might be done for our own families."

The bearded man's jacket was coated with mud, his breeches shredded near the ankles, his naked feet slopped with muck. His clothing shivered on him like rags in the wind. If a man of Rory's strength squeezed him too hard, he might break in half.

"Please, please . . . have mercy," the man begged.

Briana dismounted from her pony.

"Daughter!" Brian rose on his horse.

The man's mouth wrenched into a frown.

"My wife, my children," he pleaded. "We have nothing to eat."

When she peered deep into the brush that lined the swift water, the family appeared. There, as if animals hidden by the branches, a woman and two children crouched in a hole by the bank. The thatched boughs that formed a crude roof over their heads shadowed their faces. She walked toward them as six piteous eyes stared at her. Their hollow gazes seemed an exact measurement of their despondency, their bodies devoid of joy. Anguish stung her heart. Never had she seen such suffering.

"What can we do?" she called to Rory. Her gaze shifted to the provisions strapped to the side of the horse by straw ropes.

His eyes followed hers. "At the moment, nothing," he said with little emotion. He jumped from his horse and walked toward the *sceilp.* "Where are you from?"

The man tottered on his feet. "Clanwilliam."

"Evicted?" Rory asked.

The man nodded.

"How long has it been since you or your family have eaten?" Briana asked.

"My wife and children last ate two days ago. I've had nothing going on four."

"My God," Briana said to Rory. "We must give them food."

He took her arm, turned her away from the man, and walked a few yards along the bank. "I understand your sympathy and I feel bad as well, but think of what you're offering. If we help every beggar, soon we'll have nothing of our own."

"Beggar?" She looked at him with fresh eyes, questioning his charity to his fellow men. This was a part of him she'd never seen. She stepped away, quelling her rising anger. "This family is from Mayo. They deserve better. We would do it for anyone who lived on the estate."

Brian walked up from behind and heard Briana's words. "Be cautious, daughter. These are bad times."

She understood what Rory and her father were saying, but she couldn't ignore the pathetic state of the family who stood before them. "We can go back — get something. . . ."

"No," her father replied in a soft but firm tone. "We're more than an hour from Lear House. We might as well forget getting to

Westport in time to meet the ship if we turn back."

"Anything . . . anything you can give us," the man shouted in his hoarse voice. "We would be in your debt." He was like a sad apparition, watching them with sunken eyes from his spot near the river.

"Yes, *I can* give you something." She went to her pony and lifted the cover of the pouch. Rory sighed behind her as she turned to see her father's frown. She pulled out two scones, two slices of soda bread, and a small hunk of cheese.

She was about to give the food to the man when Rory stopped her. "No!"

"Why not?" she asked, irritated by his command.

"Let me." He took the food and handed it to the starving man.

"Thank you," the man said. Tears welled in his eyes. He took the bundle, staggered toward his starving family, and collapsed in the *sceilp.* Briana saw the man's wife question him as he tore the food into small bits. The woman's voice was so weak Briana could not hear her, but she appeared defeated, on the verge of fainting.

Rory scrubbed his hands in the river before mounting his horse. His eyes narrowed as he approached Briana. "That was a mistake."

He helped her back on the pony. "It was no mistake. It was the right thing to do. We can't let them starve."

"What if *we* have nothing to give?" Rory asked. "What will we do then?"

One of the man's small sons had crawled from the hole and, with his dirty thumb stuck in his mouth, stood on the side of the river staring at them. "Look at him, will you," Briana said. She flushed with anger at the sight of the child, his face and neck sunken, his skin flattened against his skull like a wizened old man. The boy shifted in the sun and she noticed something that horrified her. The top of his head was nearly bald, but a coating of fine hair covered his face, as if he were changing into an animal, a wolf of sorts. She looked at Rory for an explanation. "Why did you stop me from handing over the food?"

Rory turned and waved to the boy, then mounted his pony. Before he shook the reins he said to Briana, "Look at that child. I'm sure the hair on his face comes from starvation. We'll see more like him now that food is scarce." He paused. "Something was crawling over that man's skin. I couldn't let you touch him." He urged his horse onward. "You don't know how desperate I feel. I want to do something . . . anything that will make things better. But *I won't* sacrifice my family for others."

Her father gave Rory an understanding look as the horses trotted off together.

A flush rose on Rory's neck. "I'm sorry. I've spoken out of place. I'm not part of your family . . . but that man, and the others like him, are why I wear the green ribbon. We'll stop on the way back if we have more to give."

Rory's voice was filled with an urgency that Briana had never heard, and she realized he had protected her and her father despite her irritation with him. Many years ago in Westport, she had seen dragoons marching near the quays. The commanding officer had sounded the same. The thought of Rory turning into such a man dismayed her. However, she had seen only his reticence at first and mistaken it for a hard heart. She was wrong.

Her heart sank as she looked back toward the family. After they crossed the river, the *sceilp* was no longer visible. The family had vanished like sad, thin shadows to be blotted away by clouds. Something plucked at her arm; the wind perhaps. When she turned to look again upon the heath, a sad specter ran behind her, a leering harlequin with a skeletal face dressed in a jester's garb. He held a potato in both hands. As she watched, the potatoes melted into a mass of black, putrid liquid. She shook the vision from her head and then turned her attention to the road.

After four more hours of traveling, they stopped at Bangor, a village of stone buildings lining the Owenmore River. Briana, Rory, and Brian ate their food near the cold, blue waters as the horses drank and munched the spring grass. Brian, as a surprise, had procured meat and eggs from a rather dingy public house. Then they traveled another three hours before arriving at their stop for the night, the stone cottage of Frankie and Aideen Kilbane, who lived south of Ballycroy on the strip of heath bordering the western slopes of the Nephin Beg. The Kilbanes earned their living by hosting travelers traversing the boggy road between the southern inlets of Blacksod Bay and the mountains. They tethered their horses to a picket line near a small shed and fed them from their supply of oats. Plenty of fresh water was available for the animals.

That evening, they shared scones and potato bread in addition to a watery carrot soup provided by Aideen. The couple, Briana noticed, looked in good health, as if the blight had not affected them. Frankie played the flute and guitar after dinner while Aideen sang. Frankie told them of the skeletal travelers, the famished animals, they had seen on the road outside their door. They could not help everyone, he said, and often they had to shelter their own livestock in the house to protect them from being stolen.

Soon, Briana nodded off in the warmth of the log fire. The Kilbanes pulled rush mats into the main room for sleeping, while she and her father retired to straw beds in a separate area reserved for travelers. Rory slept near the door, not far from the stone fireplace, with the Kilbanes and their long-haired hound at his side. The dog barked once during the night at something that rustled outside. Rory checked on the horses, and nothing was amiss.

They left early the next morning after a good breakfast and payment to their hosts.

Warm sun and the pony's rocking motion nearly lulled Briana to sleep as they traversed the rolling hills to Westport. The land rose and fell across cultivated farms, until the road led them high over the wind-swept bay at Mulranny. After brief stops and more hours of hills, the cloudy peak of Croagh Patrick, where the Saint had fasted for forty days fourteen hundred years earlier, appeared as they rounded a curve. The base of the purple and green mountain, the Reek, shimmered in the late morning sun. Her father had told her the Saint's story years ago upon her first visit to Westport.

Westport, with its towering monument in the center of the village and its graceful stone, arched bridges, was only a few minutes away. They crossed the brown, iron-laced waters of the Carrowbeg River and ascended the top of a hill to the south of the village center. The harbor, shining and blue with white-capped waves, lay to the west. Near the horizon, far past the end of the quay, the spars of two tall ships pierced the air like black arrows. Another ship was harbored as well: a sleek steamer, a vessel Briana had never seen before, outfitted for sail or engine power.

"The steamer's in," her father said. "I hope we're not too late."

"Never too late," Rory said. "If they're not onboard they'll be in the public house."

As they watched, one of the tall ships set off in Clew Bay, veering toward the open Atlantic. Its lower sails caught the northwest wind, and soon it was cutting across the hard, blue waves and out to sea. Briana saw several sailors, as tiny as ants, climbing hand over hand up the masts. What must it be like to be on one of those ships or on the exciting new ship called a "steamer"? Lucinda had said little about her voyage from Liverpool to Belmullet except to complain about her cramped cabin and her bouts of seasickness.

Lucinda loved her travels; Briana was happy at home. The familiar cliffs at Carrowteige, the bracing freshness of the air, the feel of the boggy earth underneath her bare feet, were all she needed. The ever-shifting Atlantic provided the only change of scenery she required. Lear House, despite its troubles, was home — worth keeping and fighting for. She imagined herself as an old woman sitting by the cottage fire with Lear House standing solidly by. Would her life be different from what she pictured it to be?

After traveling west, past a large stone house — a mansion of greater size than Lear House — they arrived at the quay and its row of multistoried buildings. Men hustled through the port to the doors of various merchants while donkeys pulled wagons loaded with boxes and wooden chests. Several single-mast sailboats creaked against the stone quay. From the signs, she could tell most of the shops were related to the sea: a sail maker, a mast carver, merchants specializing in the shipment of goods. An apothecary business that claimed to sell food as well as medicine was shuttered. A chain hung heavy and morose across the door of a grain merchant.

Rory tethered the horses to iron spikes driven into the quay rock. Brian dismounted and fed the hungry animals from their dwindling supply of oats.

Rory placed his hand between the brim of his cap and his eyes. His gaze was soon directed at the steamer anchored in the bay. "It's the *Tristan*. I'll see if I can find the Captain."

Briana got off her horse and stood by it. Several English sailors dressed in white breeches, dark jackets, and blue caps stared as they walked by. They whispered what she suspected might be salacious words judging from their sneering looks. Would they have spoken such words in front of a lady in their home country? She focused on the Reek, while her face flushed from the unwanted attention.

Rory arrived a few minutes later with a satisfied look on his face. "A sailor from the *Tristan* told me the Captain and most of the crew are at a pub called The Black Ram. We can get water and food there for the horses."

They mounted the animals and retraced their route, past the mansion, to the village center.

"I'm sure it's not hard to find," Rory said as they descended the hill by the monument. Before crossing the bridge again, they found a lane that ran east along the Carrowbeg. The sign of The Black Ram, a devilish animal with curled horns painted over a white background, swayed in the wind.

A group of sailors congregated on the benches outside the pub's door. They talked, laughed, and smoked their pipes while tipping their cups.

Swells of laughter boomed from the establishment. The door stood open, and the intermingled smell of tobacco and stale ale struck her as they traveled past. Other unsavory odors filled the air. Several sailors emerged from the shadows at the back of the building, buttoning up their breeches as they walked. She held her breath for a moment, hoping that Rory would let her go with him.

"Wait here with the horses," Rory told her.

"No. I'm coming inside. Da can stay here if he wants."

"Not me," Brian said. "I could use a drink."

71

Rory secured the animals to a tree near the river. "All right, but stay close. We don't want any trouble with the English Navy."

Two windows were set into the pub walls on either side of the door. Through the wavy glass, Briana saw a room full of sailors conversing at tables and leaning on a long wooden bar against the back wall. She walked into The Black Ram between Rory and her father, Rory leading the way. The sailors hushed when she entered. The silence lingered for more time than she would have liked, as two dozen pairs of eyes ogled her; but soon the men resumed their chatter.

A hazy cloud of pipe smoke obscured the room. Rory craned his neck looking for the Captain. Briana supposed the officer might be dressed differently from the others, but no man stood out from the crowd. As they weaved around the tables, Rory headed toward a chair draped by a long jacket with split tails. A tall man with wavy black hair dressed in white breeches and a cuffed white shirt leaned against the bar. He was older than the other men, more seasoned, with a ruddy, weathered face. Briana believed he might be the Captain. Apparently, so did Rory. He approached the man, who gave him a wary look.

She moved behind Rory to hear the conversation. Her father hitched his thumb toward the bar. "I'll leave this to a younger man," he shouted at her.

"Are you the Captain of the *Tristan*?" Rory asked.

The man put down his cup, turned, and thrust his elbows back on the bar. "Aye, sir. Why do you ask?"

"I've come for a favor," Rory said.

The Captain studied Rory, sizing him up for what the request might be. Rory leaned close to the man.

The laughter and songs echoing through the pub blocked Briana from hearing more. A woman in a black dress and long, dark hair stood behind the counter and poured her father a mug of poteen. Brian paid the woman and leaned over, intent on talking to her. She smiled and casually drifted away from him, more concerned about serving her large contingent of sailors than chatting with an older man.

Briana caught her arm as she walked from behind the bar. "Do you have a pail for water?" She was eager to get out of the pub, away from the smoke and the raucous laughter.

The woman scoffed and pushed Briana's hand away. "Fool, do I look like I have time for that with all these Englishmen thrashing about?" She cocked her head. "Don't get me wrong. Business is business."

"We've come from Lear House at Carrowteige. Our horses need water."

The woman's eyes brightened, and she pulled a battered metal pail from under the counter. "Oh, I have a soft spot in my heart for animals. I can't keep track of all the stray dogs and cats. I feed them when I can. There's plenty of water in the Carrowbeg with the rain we've been having. Help yourself to the pail — just bring it back." After handing it to Briana, she went about her business of flirting with the sailors and taking orders.

Rory was involved in his conversation with the Captain, who seemed to have loosened up enough that he was laughing now. Briana threaded her way past the tables, out the door, and into the sunshine. It felt good to be out of the close, smoky bar and into the fresh air. She walked past the men and made her way to the river. Several women were washing clothes near stone steps that led down to the water. Briana slipped past them with a "hello" and dipped the pail into the brown water. The chilly current washed over her hands.

She gathered the pail and returned to the animals. They drank greedily, lapping at the cool liquid with their pink tongues. A shadow fell across her horse.

"A real Irish lass," a man said in English. The shadow weaved behind her. "I've been watching your horses so no bastard takes them."

Briana turned her head to see a red-faced sailor lolling behind her. His eyes had sunk into his head from too much liquor. She wanted to ignore him, but he staggered toward her, his face bloated from the drink. He locked his arms around her waist, squeezed, and fitted his pelvis against hers.

Still holding the pail, she said in English, "I appreciate you looking after our animals, but get away from me or you'll be lucky to have children."

"Ah," the sailor cooed in her ear. "I hear Irish country girls are the best."

Briana steeled her body, twisted, and threw the remaining water in the sailor's face. He yelped and sputtered backward. The shock seemed to temporarily sober him up. His cheeks flushed with rage. Before he had a chance to speak, Briana kicked him in the groin and sent him sprawling to the ground. She stared at him defiantly.

He rose on his elbows, recovered enough to spit out, "You little bitch! I'll have you in the mud!"

But before the sailor could rise up, the Captain's black boot came down upon his chest. "Enough, you idiot! Get back to the ship and clean yourself up, or you'll be in the brig." The sailor, his lips quivering, gawked at his Captain. The officer lifted his right leg and stamped it close to the sailor's face. Rory, bristling with his own rage, rushed to the officer's side. Briana knew he was aching to thrash the sailor.

Moaning, the man tried to lift himself from the ground but fell back. The Captain grabbed the sailor by the left arm, lifted him, and shoved him toward the ship. The other sailors, some whistling and catcalling at their mate, watched as he staggered down the lane.

The officer approached Briana and extended his hand. "I'm Captain James. I apologize for my man. I make no excuses for his behavior, except that he may have had too much of your fine Irish whiskey. How can I make up for his poor manners?"

She shook his hand and, without hesitation, said, "You can give us food."

Captain James nodded. "The least I can do, miss. If you give me an hour, I'll gather some. Let me get my coat." He turned and walked inside.

"Are you all right?" Rory asked after the

officer left. "The Captain and I were coming out the door when we saw the water fly. By God, you didn't need my help."

"I had to take matters into my own hands," Briana said. Her father had taught her to defend herself because he knew how much she loved to roam the countryside. Brian, a slight man who fought like a hellion, had given her the means to save herself from a sailor intent on doing harm. With no mother to guide his daughter, Brian had done his best.

Rory kissed her hand and held it to his chest. "I'd always like to be around to protect you." His words were sincere, and she realized that life outside Lear House had become perilous. Fortunately, fate had handed her a sailor who was an easy mark, drunk as he was. The thought of a sober man attempting the same chilled her.

The proprietress stood smiling in the doorway. Her father peered over her shoulder, his face cheerful with a tipsy smile. Briana returned the pail to the woman, thanked her, and grabbed her father by the arm. "Come on, Da. You've had enough."

"You've got a hell of a daughter, there," the woman said to her father.

Her father had consumed more than his share of poteen and seemed giddy with delight. "I haven't had such a grand time in ages." He kissed the woman on the cheek. "We should come to Westport more often." The proprietress scoffed and swiped her fingers against her cheek, dispersing the kiss. She disappeared into the smoky room.

The Captain returned with his coat. Its brass buttons shone against the blue wool, gleaming like golden spheres in the sun. "If you wouldn't mind me using one of your horses . . ."

"I'll accompany you," Rory said. They mounted the animals and rode off toward the *Tristan.*

Briana and her father sat near the river, enjoying the warm sun. None of the sailors bothered them, although their voices became increasingly loud as the drink flowed. After an hour, another sailor returned with Rory. He dismounted from the pony and said, "With the Captain's compliments . . . and his humble apology." He handed a large leather pouch to Briana and then walked back toward the ship.

Rory and Brian waited with eager smiles for a glimpse of the contents. Her father whistled when she opened the pouch. The Captain had given them dried meats, biscuits, several cakes — all neatly wrapped — and a bottle of French brandy.

"We've been handed the pot o'gold," her father said, eyeing the brandy.

Rory took a look as well, salivating over the biscuits and cakes. "Yes, but I'm not happy how it happened."

"Hands off." She slapped their fingers away and closed the pouch.

This time it was Rory's turn to whistle as he turned his gaze toward the road that led to the quay. "Would you look at that."

A squad of dragoons, attired in their red vests and long breeches, marched over the bridge alongside wagons loaded with bags of oats and other foodstuffs. They were headed toward the port. The soldiers, muskets slung against their shoulders, were positioned on either side of the cargo. The drivers appeared to be Irishmen who had been paid to haul the goods. They looked neither left nor right at the silent men and women who stared at them as they passed.

"I can't believe my eyes," Briana said. "The very food we grow is being taken to the port — leaving Ireland."

Rory turned, his eyes dimming. "I'm afraid so. That's why the *Tristan* is here — to make sure that this food gets out safely . . . to feed the English."

The dragoons couldn't be fought, nor could the laws regarding exports be changed. Tenants needed to make money to pay their rents. They could do that only by selling the food they grew.

"I've had enough of this spectacle," Rory said. "We'll eat before we get to the Kilbanes'. I don't want to deprive them of their food." He sneered at the wagons and the dragoons trudging away from them. They mounted their horses and trotted north on the road leading out of Westport.

The afternoon shadows had deepened, and Briana noticed something had changed since they had come into Westport that morning. People — fifty of them at least, men, women, and children — lined the road out of town. They looked like sad ghosts in their dirty clothes. Briana rode up next to Rory, unsettled by the sight.

"They're going to Westport, perhaps Castlebar, looking for food and work," Rory told her.

They were sad ghosts. Families clad in worn clothes huddled along the side of the road. Nearly everyone was barefoot, many clutching a satchel of belongings. The ghostly walk, the sunken faces and eyes, the pitiful lethargy, reminded Briana of the family she had seen living in the *sceilp*.

The starving people watched them from the road with eager eyes searching for food, seeking hope in a world of misery. Briana looked at the pouch of food given to them by the Captain and wondered how long a family could exist on the treasure they carried. A week? Perhaps longer if the food was properly rationed. As the town and Croagh Patrick faded in the distance, and the northern hills came into view, the stream of ragged people thinned. They had, like animals, disappeared in the brush.

As she rode, she saw only the vacant stares of the starving. Rory was right — she couldn't save them all, but perhaps she could help the man who had stopped them at the river. If she had her way, he and his family would enjoy some of the prized food they'd received from Captain James. But there were others to think of as well — the tenants, Rory's brother, and his family. Hard choices would have to be made with so little food available.

Briana took one last look back. Westport had disappeared under the swell of hills, but Croagh Patrick's peak still towered on the southern horizon.

How could the government let this happen? How many would die? She shivered, although the sun warmed her shoulders. Fear had spread its icy fingers over her. This wasn't a dream. The dragoons were escorting food out of Ireland. How long would it be before this disaster touched her and her family?

Her mind swirled with thoughts of how to save them, but there were no easy answers. How could she fight an enemy she couldn't see who robbed them of their strength? She straightened in the saddle and vowed to carry on, to protect her father and Lear House as best she could. Her father's horse trotted ahead. She fought back tears. Brian's stooped back already showed the physical and emotional toll the blight had taken, and this was only the beginning.

CHAPTER 4

They stopped near a stream that ran down from the burnished slopes of the Nephin Beg. "So, the *Tristan* carried no Indian corn?" Briana asked as she looked at the pouch the Captain had given them.

"Not a kernel," Rory answered. "No relief to be had for the people. My brother was right about the ship but wrong about the corn. The Captain said more corn would be delivered, but it would go directly to the storehouses to be distributed."

Brian shook his head. "We made a trip for meal the government is supposed to be supplying to the starving, yet there was none."

"No negotiation as the landlord's agent needed," Rory said. "Save it for another time."

The conversation didn't cheer Briana, but there was nothing she could do about a failed journey. At least they had returned with some food. She led her horse to the rushing current, clutching at her back, which was stiff from the long ride. The late afternoon sun sparkled on the dewy bank as cold drops of water splashed against her ankles.

Brian stretched on tiptoe, his hands high in the air, as fatigued from the trip as she.

Deep shadows cut across the grassy mounds, bringing back pleasant memories of a childhood spent playing on the Lear House lawn. She had always loved the spring and the nascent promise of summer. Summer. The most beautiful season in Ireland. Her mother had died in winter during the deep, dark days with no light. Winter was her least favorite time of year.

The horses munched on the oats Rory threw on the tussocks. Briana rested in the shade of a sycamore. Light shimmered in variegated patterns across her dress as the leaves shifted in the breeze.

The bleakness of the situation blunted their conversation. They said little as they ate the remainder of the provisions they had packed for the journey. Rory and her father sampled a few bites from Captain James's gift. Briana tried to stop them but failed.

"That's enough," she said, and took back the pouch. Part of the treasure, some of the cakes and the dried meat, should be saved for the starving family. The pouch was lighter, though, and she peered inside it. "Where's the brandy?" She looked at her father.

"When will the corn arrive?" Brian ignored her question and wiped his mouth with his sleeve.

"The Captain said later this month. We may have to make another trip to Westport. The journey would be faster if we traveled by ship by way of Belmullet." He rubbed his hands, a sign of his anxiety that Briana knew all too well. "Even the Captain admitted the situation is not good. The Indian corn is coming into Cork. It has to be processed before it can be sent out to distribution centers. At least, that's the way he explained it to me."

"Westport, every harbor, will be crawling with soldiers," Brian said. "They'll have to protect the corn from the starving when it comes, even as they take away what we grow."

"I'll ask one more time — where's the brandy?" Briana closed the pouch and drew it close to her. "At this rate, there'll be little left for anyone. Did the Captain say he would help us get the meal?"

Rory pulled the brandy from behind his back, lifted the bottle in a tease to Briana and popped the cork. "He was a nice-enough Englishman, but he didn't make promises." The sun painted his body with a gold light. "Sometimes promises can't be kept." He turned to Brian. "If she hadn't kicked that sailor in the privates, we wouldn't have this. Now we know how to get food."

"Take it easy on the brandy," Brian said, and took the bottle away from Rory. "That's expensive stuff." Her father took a swig, smacked his lips, and sighed. "Excellent. Let's keep this bottle. No more taking nips from Master Blakely's lot."

Briana snatched the bottle from her father. "We've other things to think on besides liquor." She knew that her father was trying to make the best of uncertain times, but it bothered her to see him enjoying expensive brandy a little too much.

"Let's savor life while we can, daughter." He reached for the bottle in a failed attempt to get it back.

Briana ran to her horse and strapped the pouch to the animal's side. She stood defiantly in front of it, blocking her father's way.

Irritated by his daughter's impudence, Brian recognized that he wouldn't get another sip. His smile faded and his face turned sullen. "Let's enjoy the present. There'll be enough time to mourn."

"There'll be no future if we don't save what we have now," Briana said.

Her father sighed and skulked off. "Stubborn . . . but sensible."

"We should be off," Rory said, ending the standoff. "The Kilbanes live an hour or so away. I'd like to turn in early so we can get on the road by dawn."

They traveled by the light of a half moon until they arrived at the home. Candles flickered through the cottage window. Rory sheltered the animals near the shed and fed and watered them as Briana unloaded the valuable pouch from her horse.

Frankie and the dog welcomed them at the door.

"Would you like something to eat?" Aideen asked as they entered the cottage warmed by the turf fire and the candlelight.

"Thank you, but we've already eaten," Briana said.

"How about a drink of poteen?" Frankie asked.

Brian chuckled as Briana answered, "These two men have had enough of that too."

"Sounds like I missed something," Frankie said. "Let's gather around the fire."

Rory and her father took a mug of poteen anyway as they talked about the disappointing journey to Westport.

"We're worried too," Frankie admitted after hearing their tale. "The travelers that pass by have nothing. We give what we can, but if no one can pay we'll soon be as poor as they are." He picked up his silver flute and played a few notes that disappeared on the air.

Aideen strummed on the guitar, but her melody also faded. No one seemed in the mood for a song.

"We should get some sleep," Rory said, and rose from the dirt floor. "I'm going out to check on the animals."

A sad air fell over the cottage, which was usually filled with song and laughter. Briana helped the Kilbanes prepare for the night, and when Rory returned they all headed to bed.

After almost a day's journey, they arrived at the river south of Carrowteige, about an hour from Lear House. Briana scanned the bank looking for the *sceilp* the family had constructed but saw only the rushing water and brush waving in the wind. The clouds darted across the sky as Rory pointed toward the river.

"We have to stop here," Briana said. "This is where they were."

"I made it a point to remember the spot, and I almost missed it," Rory said. "Early morning light is different from afternoon light. If you want to look, go ahead." They halted the horses and Briana jumped down, her heart pumping fast at the prospect of finding the starving man and his family.

She ran to the spot Rory had pointed to. The roof of sod and branches remained over the *sceilp,* but no one was inside. Only a silent muddy hole, smudged with the imprints of bodies and footprints, remained. A white handkerchief lay atop the muck. Briana bent to pick it up but stopped in mid-reach. A wave of black dots skittered across the fabric. She screamed and jumped back.

"What's wrong?" Rory called out, alarm in his voice.

"A handkerchief's been left behind. Something's on it."

Rory dismounted and walked to her. He grabbed a stick and lifted the cloth. It twisted in the air as the line of bugs skittered upon it. He studied it carefully. "Looks like lice."

Brian called out. "You touched that man two days ago."

Rory nodded. "I'll be sure to bathe when

we get home."

"In hot water," Brian added. "And boil your clothes. Briana and I should too."

Rory dropped the cloth back into the hole. She watched it flutter to the ground and then noticed something in the mud beside it.

"Look," she said to Rory. A fleck of metal glittered in the light. He took the stick and dug around the object. After a few seconds, he lifted it out on the tip of the branch — a silver band caked with mud.

Briana took the ring and studied it. "Maybe it's a wedding band. I hate to think . . ." She didn't want to finish her thought that the ring had slipped off the thin fingers of the man or the woman who had lived in the burrow. The thought saddened her. "This ring may have been all they had and now they don't even have it." She tossed it in the hole. "Maybe they'll miss it and come back."

Rory tossed the stick into the brush and smiled sadly. "They won't be back. The ring will do them no good."

They walked back to the horses.

"I wonder where they've gone?" Briana asked.

"Who knows," her father replied. "Maybe back to the hills . . . maybe to find relatives

— anyone who can help them."

Sorrow swelled within her for the starving family and the loss of the ring. Life was transitory, fleeting, but such symbols proved the family had been alive — they had existed. She also realized that except for the grace of God, her family might be suffering the same fate. Briana crossed herself. "I'm thankful we're safe."

"Amen," Rory said, and shook the reins of his horse.

The trail turned northwest, bringing them ever closer to Lear House. Briana watched Rory as he rode, his body swaying with the horse's as they bounced over the heath. The ring proved life was too short. She and Rory needed to be married soon. They had known each other since childhood, but there were good reasons they had never married. Her father needed her at Lear House; Rory was farming and taking care of his parents, a job that kept him busy from dawn to dusk; but, most of all, she didn't want to disappoint her father, who seemed to think she might find a better match than a poor tenant farmer. Brian had high hopes for Lucinda in that respect. But there was more to love than money, and the ring in the mud proved it.

■ ■ ■ ■

Despite a chill in the air, Rory thought heating water for a bath was too much trouble. He would have to make two trips to the well, carry heavy pails to his cabin, start a fire, boil the water, then let it cool enough to take a bath, strip, lather up, and pour it over himself. He had been upstairs at Lear House, including the Master's bathroom, several times while accompanying Brian on his duties. How luxurious it must be to sink into hot water in a mahogany tub, lined with lead. He imagined Briana kneeling next to him in Lear House, handing him a bar of scented soap. However, such thoughts were for the rich, not a tenant farmer. Perhaps in his next life he could afford a tub.

And he was tired from the journey. Caring for the animals, chatting with Jarlath about the trip, and cooking a small evening meal had consumed all his energy. He cautioned Jarlath to remain silent about the failure to bring back Indian corn, because he didn't want to panic the other tenants. Stocks were running low, but enough food, including the remaining seed potatoes, might carry them until the next harvest.

He stripped off his shirt and threw it in

the corner of his cabin. The wool sweater his mother had knitted for him years ago hung from a wooden peg in the wall. He still managed to fit into it — a benefit from work and youth. He dared not put it on until he had bathed.

Sleep would also have to wait until he had scrubbed himself. The scratchy straw that made up his bed was a perfect home for lice. Even his wool blanket would have to be boiled. He looked around his cabin for something to cover him. His cooking towels were too short to stretch around his waist. He would have to carry another pair of breeches and a clean shirt to the beach.

The cabin was slipping into darkness as he stepped out into the brisk wind. He looked west expecting to see a few people, but mostly the fields were empty. The tenants were inside, huddled around the turf fire, supping on what food they had. By daybreak, they would be up, tending to the potato crop they hoped would flourish.

A half moon hung in the eastern sky, and the stars lay sprinkled in glittering points across the dark expanse. He knew the path to the sandy bay by heart. There, he could swim in the chilly Atlantic waters. If the cold and salt didn't kill any lice he might have on his body, nothing would.

He sprinted down the road, his bare feet striking against the hard lumps of the pebbled path. Soon he was at the beach. The wind charged in from the sea and smelled of brine . . . and what? Something stirred in the air, or was it his imagination — the promise of a land far away? Adventure, perhaps? The smell of Canadian pine couldn't drift across the Atlantic. He'd heard of men traveling to Liverpool to sail to America to work the rails or to cut lumber in the forests of Quebec. But that was life in a new world — one he couldn't afford.

Maybe there was no smell at all except the salty air. Anxiety had fueled this brooding notion. The thought of leaving Ireland hit him like a punch to his stomach. He wanted to stay on the land he loved, to keep his small home and farm at Lear House. The woman he loved was also in his future, along with children and prosperity. He wanted to grow old and die on the land he was born on. Only two other people he knew had the same fervent wish — Briana and Brian. He loved them both for it.

Still he had to face reality. The crop had just begun to sprout. Hopes were high, but some of the tenants had turned the soil over early and the results were frightening. The seed potatoes showed the black signs of decay. He feared another failed harvest lay ahead. If all the remaining seed potatoes were eaten, there wouldn't be any for the following year.

The bay opened before him in a wide curve facing south and west. He couldn't go far into the water; the currents sweeping in from the Atlantic were cold and treacherous and could pull a strong man into the ocean to his death. The sea cast up a jagged reflection of the moon in shimmering white triangles that extended across the bay as far as he could see. He breathed in, savoring the salty air, its tangy odor invigorating him.

With thoughts of hunger and death lurking in his mind from the Westport trip, he again sensed the importance of his home and the land that meant so much to him. He had always known it, but this night every nerve in his body tingled with life and anticipation for a better future. Nothing could convince him to give up. He would fight any adversary, be it physical or mental, with Briana by his side.

He stripped off his dirty breeches and shoes and put them a safe distance away from his fresh clothes so there would be no contamination between them. He walked down the sand to the shoreline and stuck his right foot into the water. His toes cramped, numbed by the cold. The bracing wind cut into him. He had swum in these waters often in the early spring, mostly on childish dares. Many times he had joined his friends, after much poteen, for a swim in the bay on the turn of a new year.

He turned, ran up the eastern slope, and stopped. He let out a yell; then, running as hard as his legs would carry him, he thrashed into the bay until he splashed facedown in the brine. The cold shocked his body, paralyzing his limbs and taking his breath away. He struggled up through the waves, chest deep, and sputtered out water for air. He shook from the cold, stumbled closer to shore, and splashed the water over him, rubbing his chest, arms, and legs. He dove back into the ocean once more and swam as long as his body could stand it, then rose, spat out the salty taste, and waded to shore.

A figure in the moonlight, approaching from the southern end of the bay, strode across the sand. Rory shook like a dog and swiped the water from his torso. A man, dressed in dark breeches, white shirt, and jacket, continued his trek toward him.

He had no choice but to display his naked body to the stranger. The man would be by his side by the time he got to his clothes. As the figure came closer, Rory recognized him as Connor Donlon, a Lear House tenant who farmed a half acre farther up the hill from his cabin. Connor was a few years older, married and the father of four children, two boys and two girls. He and his family kept mainly to themselves, but Connor had a reputation as a hothead — a man easily provoked by words and liquor. He was a bit shorter than Rory but muscular of chest and arms.

Connor stopped a few feet away and stared at Rory. "Taking a swim, are we? I see the water's cold tonight."

He shook off the insult, grabbed his clean breeches, and stepped into them. "No woman's ever complained." He shivered in the chilly wind and reached for his shirt.

"Of course," Connor said. "How many have you bedded?"

Rory refused to be provoked, knowing that anything he said would get back to Briana. "What's your game tonight? Why are you walking the bay?" He put his arms into the sleeves.

Connor glanced at the moon. "I was coming home from a meeting with some of the lads — you might like to join us as well — if you have the nerve."

Rory buttoned his shirt, waiting for Connor's explanation.

"Are you headed home?" Connor asked.

"Let me get my clothes," Rory said.

"I've heard you wear the green ribbon."

Rory picked up his dirty breeches, holding them at arm's length from his body as they headed north along the bay. "Yes. I'm not ashamed. What's it to you?"

"They're not our kind," Connor said, following him. "They've done good deeds in the past, and blood has been spilt, but they don't have our interests at heart." The path widened near the top of the dune, and Connor strode up beside him. He pointed to the tracts of land surrounding Lear House. "The Ribbonmen couldn't care less about us. They're more concerned with the Church and ending Protestant order, driving out the Orange. For the most part, the Ribbonmen have their heads stuck in useless books. The Mollies on the —"

"The Molly Maguires. I should have known." Rory stopped on the road. "The Tithe Act came out of the Ribbonmen's struggles."

Connor stepped closer to him. "That was eight years ago. It doesn't help us now. Can't you see what's going on? How did you get involved with them, anyway?"

"A man from north Connacht." Rory pulled away from Connor. "An intelligent man who wants the Ribbonmen's influence to spread. That's all I can say. You figure it out — use your head." They walked up the road and stopped a few yards from Rory's door.

"We've had enough war against each other — the Ribbonmen against the Mollies," Connor said. "Join us and do something that can help the tenants of Lear House. Those northern men have their heads in the clouds."

Connor's demanding tone caused the hackles on his neck to rise. He had never considered joining the Mollies, because he questioned their actions. For all the reasoned struggles championed by the Ribbonmen, the Mollies seemed crude in comparison. They sometimes dressed in women's clothing, blackened their faces, stole farm animals, and threatened landlords and their agents. If nothing else, his relationship with Brian and Briana had quelled his enthusiasm for joining the group.

"I'll wear the green ribbon," Rory said.

The man put his hands on Rory's chest and gave him a slight shove.

His body tensed, but he remained calm. "That won't work."

Connor smiled. "I know the reason. There's a woman and her agent father at play here."

His adversary was getting too close to the truth. "Leave Briana out of this. She has nothing to do with the Mollies."

Connor slumped against the sod wall of Rory's home. "All right then, I'll beg. We need you because we want a man connected to Brian Walsh — a man who can help us win over the agent."

Rory shook his head.

"Why don't we settle this with sport? The winner chooses his allegiance, with any men to follow. The village is in need of entertainment, and there hasn't been a good fight in many a year." Connor raised his hands as if seeking approval for his suggestion.

Rory was in no mood for a fight, but he had been challenged. The decision was easy. He would never live it down if he spurned the dare. "Name your time."

"Two days from this day at twelve o'clock in the village center. Rain or shine. It's easy to settle a dispute with a gentleman's agreement."

Rory nodded. "I'll be there." He watched as Connor skirted a fence before disappearing behind a hut.

He took a towel, gathered his dirty clothing and blanket from the cabin, and threw them by the fence. No one would bother his clothes during the night.

Rory herded the pig inside and lit the candle that sat on the wooden stool near his bed. He lay on the straw and covered himself with it. The straw would itch and he would be scratchy in the morning, but at least he could sleep without the fear of lice. Shadows flickered on the mud walls. He tried to sleep, but an angry Briana filled his thoughts. She would be furious about the fight. He expected to get an earful when he told her tomorrow.

"You've agreed to *a fight*?" Briana scowled and remembered the time long ago her father had fought. The ugly event brought up childhood memories of her father stumbling about the cottage, his face red and puffy with wounds. Rory was more like her father than she had imagined. Brian had done the same for sport.

She stepped outside and closed the door to the cottage, keeping Rory out of earshot from her sister. She clasped the latch with her hands.

"I'm fighting Connor Donlon tomorrow at noon."

The fear from years ago, when her father

had dragged her and Lucinda to the village, came roaring back. She tried hard to keep from shaking. "I forbid it."

Rory's gaze never wavered. His voice was as calm as the sandy bay on a tranquil summer evening. "I have to fight when I've been challenged."

"Ridiculous," she countered. "Connor is like a ram. He'll tear you apart."

"Well, he'll do it only once, I suppose. Then we'll be best of friends." He reached for her, but she flattened her back against the door. "Besides, it's been a long time since there was a good fight in the village. Maybe the excitement will keep our neighbors' minds off bigger problems."

Briana shook her head. "What's so important about fighting Connor Donlon? You've known him for years."

He put his arms on either side of her so she couldn't escape from the door. "Yes, but he hasn't been my friend."

The door shook and Briana struggled to hold on to the latch.

"Let me out," Lucinda called out in English. "What kind of childish prank are you playing?"

"I refuse to speak that language," Rory said. "She can talk all she wants, but I'll answer in Irish."

Briana let go of the latch and stepped aside. Lucinda burst out of the cottage, her face red with frustration. "What is going on out here? Are you two conducting a tryst? If so, you're far from hiding it."

Briana laughed and made up her mind to follow Rory's lead in speaking Irish. She doubted that Rory knew what a "tryst" was.

Lucinda had powdered her face, painted her lips, and adorned herself with pearl-drop earrings and a simple gold necklace. Briana had never seen the jewelry before. They must have been articles purchased in England. The dress she wore, red, with pleats, was more common than the one she had arrived in. Still, her sister's appearance made her feel dowdy.

Lucinda smoothed her dress and stood waiting for an answer. When none came, she said, "We'll be late helping Father at Lear House. . . . If you'll excuse us, Mr. Caulfield, we have business to attend to."

"Mr. Caulfield is going to fight Mr. Donlon at noon tomorrow in the village center," Briana said.

Lucinda gazed at Rory with amazement. "A fight! It's barbaric how men use their fists to solve problems. They should be penned and castrated like common farm animals. We have enough troubles." She scowled.

Briana gaped at her sister, whose sour expression had turned to a self-satisfied smirk. She grasped Rory's hand but looked at Lucinda. "Sometimes, sister, you amaze me."

Lucinda pulled her away from Rory. "We'll be amazed by Father's curses if we don't get down to the manor. He needs our help. Good day, Mr. Caulfield."

Rory bowed to them both and then walked ahead.

Lucinda ushered Briana down the path and looked to the sky, her right hand covering her eyes. "The sun won't be out for long." She pointed to a line of gray clouds sliding in from the northwest. "The Stags of Broadhaven will get a lashing today."

The clouds covered the sun by mid-afternoon, turning the sky a mottled ash. The inside of Lear House was no better. Briana found the dim library as oppressive as the day. "Do you want me to open the shutters?" She stood near the windows, which were covered by the heavy wooden slats.

Brian bent over the desk but said nothing. Not wanting to be bothered, he waved her away in a gesture that she had seen many times before. Numerous ledger books lay opened before him. In one, he wrote his notes by the light from the lamp he had set out on the library desk.

Rebuffed by her father, her head swimming with numbers, she walked to the great room, where Lucinda sat reading on the settee. Briana, pressed against a pillow, took her seat at the opposite end. A morose light entered the expansive windows, allowing her sister enough illumination to see the printed page. Lucinda put down the novel.

Briana lifted the book and read its cover: *Sybil, or The Two Nations, by B. Disraeli, M.P.* "Is it good?" The question was innocuous but a needed diversion after going over the accounts with Brian.

Lucinda slumped against the silk back of the settee and sighed. "I'm sorry I carried it from England, but Sir Thomas insisted." She flicked her fingers at the book. "Dreary as a December day, if you ask me. It's about the lower classes in England. Sir Thomas gave it to me as a primer on how *not* to live."

Briana pushed the book between them and inched closer to her sister. "You've adopted a different attitude since you've become a governess. You've changed."

Lucinda looked at her with surprise. "How so? I certainly don't feel it — only a little older and wiser. Governing three boys has forced me to grow up in ways I never imagined, and it's given me an education in the higher social classes that I would never have received here."

"That's what I'm talking about, sister. You only speak English. You put on airs, as if *we* are the lower class. You've become *affected.*"

Lucinda stiffened on the settee. "I suppose that remark could be taken as an insult, but I prefer to think of it as a compliment. I have been *affected* by my experience as a governess, meeting people of a high standing in Manchester and London. It's shown me that there's a world beyond County Mayo."

"I'm sorry, I don't intend to be rude, sister," Briana said. "In fact, I want us to be closer, but I feel we've drifted apart as the distance between us has grown. That's natural, I suppose."

Lucinda leaned toward her and grasped Briana's hands. "Haven't you ever desired to get away from Lear House, to see beyond it, to experience more than the churn of the surf and the incessant screech of the wind? Sir Thomas has made that all possible for me because I studied hard when I was a child. When the time came, I was prepared to accept his offer."

Briana withdrew her hands. "Yes, you read while I worked — 'tis true. But I've no desire to spend my days with stuck-up or stuffed-up boys. I imagine Manchester and London to be wretched when it pours, even worse than our home . . . here I have the sea, the cliffs, and the fields. They're all the company I need."

Lucinda clasped her hands. "You have more than that. Everyone knows your desire for Rory Caulfield."

She blushed at her sister's reference. "Yes, we've been friends for years and our affection has grown, slowly, respectfully, but we've both held back from displays of emotion." She glanced sideways, avoiding her sister's stare. "There's been little time for that with you being away and Rory taking care of the farm. Besides, our relationship is more than desire."

Her sister didn't blink at the assertion. "Affection? Emotion? Desire? What about love? That's a word you've never used in respect to any man except our father."

"I know you and Father are opposed to any union between us." She uttered the words almost without thinking, exposing her deepest fear to her sister. She had to face the fact that she loved Rory without reservation and that she must counter whatever objections were raised. Did it really matter if Lucinda opposed her marriage? Briana was certain that her sister's resistance would thrive upon the fertile grounds of economics and worldly matters that only those living outside of Carrowteige, perhaps even Ireland, could embrace. Who was Lucinda to talk of love? The real demon in her head came from her father, whom she wanted to be happy. It was Brian's love that had buoyed her through the years, and in that devotion she found it hard to introduce Rory into a perceived emotional upheaval possibly filled with guilt or betrayal.

Surprisingly, Lucinda scoffed. "Far be it from me to sway your heart — I've never been able to do that. Father, I imagine, will have the last word on Rory Caulfield — as he should. He thinks you can do better, and if you would look beyond Lear House, you might find that's true."

Her sister's words jabbed her, and a wave of irritation skittered over her. "And what about you? Do you pine for Sir Thomas, the eligible owner?"

A blush colored Lucinda's face, and she shifted her gaze to the floor to avoid the question.

Briana noted her physical response and

said, "I have my answer."

Lucinda looked back at her with determination. "My relationship with Sir Thomas is strictly one of business. Any show of affection would violate the contract between employee and employer."

"All business? So, such thoughts have never crossed your mind?"

"Don't press me, Briana. I have as much a stake in Lear House as you do. If you took the time to look beyond shallow observations, you might find that I, in fact, am more concerned about keeping our fortunes together than you."

Briana rose from the settee and stood in front of the window looking out at the gray clouds scudding over the bay. She felt ashamed of her pointed attack on Lucinda, who had done nothing wrong but take on a paid profession and keep in the good graces of the manor's owner. Perhaps she was jealous of her travels, her knowledge of the world. She couldn't bring herself to say she was sorry, but she turned and said, "If you are concerned as I am about our future, then we'll see eye to eye. For that, I'm grateful."

Briana and Lucinda jumped when a loud bang echoed through the hall. They ran to the library to find their father standing over the desk, his hands planted firmly on the top, his face hidden from view. He slowly raised his head as they entered.

Briana had never seen him in such a state, face flushed, eyes wide, and wispy hair streaming like silver lightning bolts from his head. "What's wrong, Da?"

He drew in a breath. "Damnation. . . . Sir Thomas isn't going to be as understanding as I am. More money is going out than coming in. The tenants have been in arrears for months and I've been looking the other way, but this can't continue. I understand they have nothing to give. . . ." He gazed at the pile of books on the desk. "I beg and there's nothing to give. They sell the crops they can but have no food to eat thanks to the rot." He put his hand on one of the massive ledger books. "Slamming this book on the table probably didn't help the potatoes in the ground."

"If you wanted to startle us, you succeeded," Lucinda said.

Briana asked the one question she thought would make her father feel better. "Can I get you something to drink?"

He sank into his chair and called them to his side. "No, stand here. Keep me company. I have something to show you."

"I fear for his health and mind," Briana

whispered to Lucinda as they walked to the table. They parted and took their places on either side of him, Briana on his right and Lucinda on his left.

He opened the ledger to the most recent entries and pointed to the pages carefully inscribed in brown ink. "Look."

Briana looked at the left-hand top page and worked her way down the sheet. It was divided into five columns. The second in from the right was marked *Collections,* the final row, *Owed.* The *Collections* column had a few notations at the top, but none going forward from midpage. The *Owed* column was filled with notations. The sums were small but added up to greater debt. Knowing the current output of tenant farmers, she could see little relief for those who resided on Lear House lands. The right-hand page was mostly empty except for a few zeros that her father had already filled in.

Briana stepped away from the book to the darkened windows. The room, already gloomy, threatened to crush her in its sad reality. She had grown up with the tenants named in the book. She had played with the children born here, helped out when people needed a hand, sung and danced with them at fairs. To see them in such peril clawed at her heart. Even the man who had worked his way into her heart was falling behind. And there were others on the grounds whom she knew only by sight. Tenants were subdividing their own property to relatives as families swelled. The implication was clear. Briana turned to see her father sitting in the chair behind the desk, his face pale and drawn in the lamplight.

He closed the ledger. Lucinda said nothing.

"I can pay Sir Thomas an eighth of what he is owed this month of April — if that," he said. "Next month there will be nothing."

It frightened her to see her father so vulnerable to circumstances outside his control. The new potato crop might be failing after the wet winter and damp spring. The winter sea with its cresting swells had been so dangerous in the long, dark months that even the bravest men had forsaken the waves. The small *curraghs* weren't built for such bad weather.

"Let me put it plainly. *We* may face eviction if the estate cannot come up with the monies owed." Her father sank back in his chair.

"That's impossible," Lucinda said. "Sir Thomas would never turn us out."

Briana, hands clasped in front of her, strode to her sister. "Wouldn't he?" Her ears felt as if they were on fire from anger. "Why not? He has every right to. Do you know something about the owner's charitable attributes that we don't? Do you feel you can save us from these unfortunate circumstances through Sir Thomas's goodwill? Perhaps you can use your charms to soften the blow." She regretted her words, but the anger in her body had turned to panic.

Her father looked at her with disgust. "Hush, Briana. It will do no good to defame your sister or Sir Thomas." He pushed the ledger away, causing one of the other books on the desk to crash to the floor. This, in turn, caused his voice to rise. "I will not have my daughters at each other's throats during this crisis," he shouted. "Clear heads are needed in troubled times."

The thump of the book and her father's words drained the anger from her body. She faced her sister. "I'm sorry. I spoke in haste. . . ."

Her sister glared at her, surrendering not an inch of goodwill.

"I will tell you both something that I've kept to myself," Briana continued in a softer tone. "I'm not going to apologize for my action, because I felt it was necessary, but now

I see it was futile."

Her father shifted uneasily in his chair. Lucinda looked at her with unforgiving eyes.

"I wrote a letter to you, sister, that you never received."

Her sister's face softened a bit. "I'm touched, but your letter never reached me."

"I have no ready explanation for that, except a supposition," Briana said. "Perhaps Sir Thomas delivered only the letters he wanted you to receive." She paused to steel herself against a harsh reaction from her father. "October past, I wrote you to ask Sir Thomas to take pity on the tenants and our family."

Brian rose from his chair, his face etched with fury. "You what?"

She stood her ground, undaunted by her father's anger. "I did it for *us* and the tenants. I saw what was happening. Rory showed me the plague — you know that. It was no secret last fall. Now, it's worse —"

"You had no right to stick your nose in the affairs of Lear House."

Briana patted her hands in the air, attempting to calm her father. "What do you think I am — a chambermaid, a servant of this house? No, I'm much more than that. I love this house and want to remain here. It would kill me to lose it. Sir Thomas needs to know what is happening on his land. I asked him to forgive our debts for a time."

"Very biblically stated, sister," Lucinda replied. "I would argue that our landlord is a businessman who has obligations, but one of good heart. I'm no authority on the matter, but I surmise that the rents from Lear House contribute to Sir Thomas's ability to pay for his Manchester estate. Even the rich have responsibilities. This latest news would be most distressing to him. Still, I can't imagine that he would evict the tenants."

"Well, it makes no difference," Briana said. "The letter was lost, or not delivered to you. . . . Regardless, it made no impression on the owner."

"I hope to God it was lost," Brian said. "It's something an idiot would do. It's the Lord's miracle that Sir Thomas did not come down upon my head." He returned to his chair. "I've made excuses for the tenants in my letters to him. I've told him the dwindling payments would be made up with interest."

"Well, this *idiot* is not waiting to be thrown out upon the road," Briana said, feeling that she was justified in writing the letter. "If you would like to join me in coming up with a plan to save our home, we can discuss it at our evening meal. I'm headed to make soup from the seed potatoes we've saved."

Her father said nothing. She walked to the library door and then turned. Brian's face was partially covered by his hands, which formed a steeple of fingers around his head. "Go on," he said. "I'll be there in a few minutes. I need to think. I'll close up the house."

"Don't be long," Lucinda said, joining Briana.

As they walked to the cottage, Briana trailed her sister, who had little to say as they crossed the lawn, now damp and slick from a light rain.

"I find it disturbing that I never received your letter," Lucinda said when they reached the cottage. "You're right. These times aren't good for us — even worse for Father. We should plan for our future." Lucinda opened the door, and they stepped inside.

The turf fire warmed her, slaking the damp from her clothes. She marveled that her sister had come to a similar conclusion about the blight when she most likely would resume her duties abroad as a governess. "So you'll stay at Lear House?"

Lucinda rubbed her hands over the fire. "I didn't say that. I said we should plan for our future."

Her mind raced. What thoughts could she offer as they dined? What scheme could she come up with? How could they save Lear House? Try as she might, no plan came to mind. She feared that if they didn't think of something soon, her family would be no better off than the one they had encountered at the river.

CHAPTER 5

Rory stood in the doorway of his cabin and stuck his hand out in the rain. Cold drops gathered in his palm. He let them collect in a small pool and then shook them off, wiping his fingers on his breeches. The fog and low clouds swirled over the sandy bay, lifting, dropping, circling in a hazy mist. He imagined Connor Donlon, bare chested, muscles solid as granite, swooping, dropping, circling as well, as he thrust his fists at Rory in the village center. The fight was in less than an hour.

The turf fire had burned all night in his cabin. Each time sleep nearly found him, he woke startled by the blazing fists of his opponent haunting his dreams. Briana also chastised his fight while he slept.

Women don't understand these things. Men must take a stand. It's about pride; no, something more — survival — the right to call yourself a man, a protector. Briana would never understand that argument; Lucinda even less so. What was she teaching those pampered young Englishmen about manhood? To be men or fops?

The bitter taste of disgust stung his mouth even as he chuckled about Lucinda's comment about castrating Irishmen for fighting. Only he and Connor could be hurt by this challenge. The village might find it entertaining on a dreary day. He half expected Briana to show up, ordering him to call off the fight or pay the consequences. She had become a strong woman with a mind of her own since the rot had taken the crop. That was one of the many reasons he loved her. In his eyes, Briana, even more so than her sister, was able to think on her feet, to be independent of others. She was the one who cooked, cleaned, helped care for the animals, and sewed with the women while Brian managed the books.

He returned to the fire and rubbed his arms and chest to get the circulation going in his limbs. The embers hissed and sputtered as rain pattered through the smoke hole onto the flaming peat. Puffs of steam rose in the air. He bent over, stretched, threaded his fingers together, and thrust his arms above his head. His two shirts and blanket lay neatly folded on the straw. They, along with his breeches, had been boiled to kill any lice.

Perhaps Briana would show up at the fight and hold his shirt for good luck. If not her, then one of the other village women would be sure to oblige, pleased to be his good luck charm. Stripped to the waist, he was confident his muscular figure might capture flattery from the opposite sex — words that would stroke his pride. After the go-round with Connor, he could tease Briana about the lovely young woman whom he'd favored. A healthy dose of jealousy might make for interesting conversation later.

He found the half-empty bottle of whale oil that Brian had given him for helping with odd jobs at Lear House. It was too precious to waste outside of lamps, but on this occasion it might help protect him from Connor's blows. He removed the glass stopper from the narrow bottle and poured a few drops in his right hand. A strong fishy odor filled his nostrils. It was as if he was on the boat himself, grappling with the whale as it was pulled onboard from the sea. He smeared the brown liquid over his arms and chest, saving some of it for his face. The slick oil, along with the rain, would make it harder for Connor to land a punch. Of course, the rain worked both ways. He might have trouble getting a blow in as well.

The smell revolted him as he spread it on; the reek of it almost made him retch. He stuck his head out of the cabin for fresh air. After several deep breaths, the queasy knot in his stomach settled. The rain flowed off the potato ridges, running down the hill to the road, which had now turned into a muddy mixture of pebbles and muck.

He sat for a time on his straw bed, imagining how Connor would attack him. Would his adversary strike his chest, an uppercut to his chin, a jab, a hook? He would be prepared for any maneuver his rival would throw at him. Rory had fought three times before: once, at five, with his older brother, whom he had soundly thrashed; a second time, when he was eleven, with a boy, now a man, who still lived on Lear House land. That argument had begun over the question of who was the better fighter. The bout had been a draw as far as Rory was concerned. They had both returned home to their mothers with bloody noses. And the third, and most glorious occasion, occurred when he knocked out a young man who was vying for Briana's affection. They had staged the fight on Benwee Head on a brisk spring day on the cliff overlooking the Atlantic. No one else was in attendance. Briana had no knowledge of the fight, or the cause of it. Rory had promised not to mention it at the request of the defeated man. As such, they had accepted the outcome and were still friends. That was how a man behaved.

His deceased father's pocket watch sat on the stool next to his bed. It read eleven forty-five. Rory reached for his shirt knowing that it would soon be awash in whale oil. The rain would mix with it, turning the garment into a soiled mess. He slipped it on over his slickened arms and then reached for two white strips of cloth he had torn to wrap around his knuckles.

When he arrived at the village center, up the road from the farms, he was shocked at the number of people who had turned out. Connor had spread the news, although Rory doubted his adversary had trumpeted the real reason for the fight. The match was a friendly contest between two men who had decided to favor Carrowteige with an entertainment. Rumors might spread that the fight was over Briana, but how ridiculous that would seem to anyone who knew the man. Connor was happily married and adored his wife and children.

Rory had told only Briana, Lucinda, and Jarlath, but judging from the crowd, more than one person had spread the news. Men he recognized, mostly tenant farmers who were friendly with Connor, circled the village center, which often served as a gathering place. They pulled their collars tight around their necks as water dripped from their hats. A few puffed on their pipes, protecting the bowl from the rain with their free hand. Others, looking sallow and lean, were unknown to him. They must have been from the hills or other villages near Carrowteige. A man would come to a fight on an ugly day to be entertained, or perhaps he would be lucky enough to find a free cup of poteen.

The few merchants who were open stared from their doorways. Many businesses were closed and padlocked because of shortages. Most business owners, including the proprietor of the general store near the bay, had suffered some effects from the blight.

Rory searched the crowd for Briana but didn't see her. A few women, their heads and faces covered by scarves, huddled in doorways sheltered from the rain. He could barely see their eyes. His heart fell a bit knowing that Briana wouldn't be there to cheer him on, but what had he expected? *Come to your senses. She was against this fight from the beginning. She wouldn't show up with roses and a smile!*

Few smiled at him. Some men gave him a knowing nod, others a look of bored indifference, as if more pressing matters occupied their minds. He could understand why. Father O'Kirwin joined the crowd at the last minute, but Connor was nowhere in sight. His rival was sure to come. The man would never forfeit a fight.

No sooner had the thought crossed his mind than Connor pushed through the crowd, his two young sons following their father. He stopped and directed the boys to stand with a farmer Rory knew. Connor then slopped through the mud in his boots. He reminded Rory of a workhorse pulling a wagon. Connor stopped in front of him, looked up into the rain with blinking eyes, and said, "Bonnie day for a tumble."

Rory nodded but swallowed hard, taken aback by his rival's enthusiasm. The fight would be a tough go if he didn't muster an equal intensity. If his heart wasn't in it, he would be thrashed. He reminded himself that he was fighting for a political cause he believed in, but the thought had crossed his mind since his confrontation with Connor that perhaps the Mollies could do more for County Mayo than the Ribbonmen.

Connor stripped off his shirt and threw it to one of his boys. The man had already wrapped his hands. He stepped back and raised his fists.

His adversary's chest and arms were rippling muscle. Connor's biceps, now bulging, looked like mounds under his flesh.

For a second, Rory considered dropping the challenge. If he joined the Molly Maguires the whole affair would be over — but not forgotten. He would be the coward who had capitulated, and would forever be remembered that way. Better to fight than to be the butt of scorn and ridicule, to be called a coward.

He shed his shirt and threw it near the ring of men who stood in back of him. In his quest to find Briana, he had forgotten the idea of giving it to another woman. Now he was out of time. He took the cloth strips from his breeches and wrapped them tightly around his knuckles.

He raised his fists in front of his face.

Connor advanced.

Rory ducked the jab, his boots sliding in the mud. Out of the corner of his eye he caught sight of Father O'Kirwin mimicking their swings.

Briana stuck her head around the corner of the gray stone building that sat several yards from the village center. Water dripped from the roof onto her waxed cotton hat and then the shoulders of her coat. Her father had declined to accompany her because he was tired, and although a fight would have been a fine diversion on a sunny day, he was not in the mood to stand in the rain. Of course, Lucinda shuddered when Briana asked her — half as a joke — if she wanted to attend. "I'd rather die first" was her sister's curt reply.

She shook her head and watched the two men go after each other. She remembered her father's fight years ago and how her stomach had churned at the sight. Blows thumping against flesh, bodies thrown against each other in anguished cries, the crack of bone, blood pouring from mouths or noses — how could any sane man agree to such nonsense? Why was Rory so pig-headed about Connor's challenge? What difference did it make whether he was a Ribbonman or a Molly Maguire? At least, as Rory explained it, the Ribbonmen had rallied to help Catholic Ireland. Lives had been lost, but that was history. What had the Maguires done recently, except stir up trouble? She was unsure what they wished to achieve, and their tactics seemed underhanded, bordering on anarchy. She'd heard rumors of men dressing in women's clothes under cover of darkness to disguise their identities, of sheds and homes being torched, landlords and agents threatened with death, farm animals killed. She wanted none of that and, least of all, for Rory to be part of such a group.

Connor leapt at Rory and slammed him in the chest, then caught him in the stomach with a jab. Rory groaned and fell into the mud with a slosh. Connor stood above him, swinging his fists, taunting him, urging him to get to his feet. Rory lifted on his elbows and struggled up from the muck.

It was a mistake to come. She quickly banished the thought — her father had chided her for leaving the cottage. "You don't have the stomach for it," he warned. She might have believed him a year ago, but since October when the blight first appeared and life in Mayo sputtered like a flame in the breeze, she had begun to take stock of herself. It was increasingly hard to be the docile housekeeper, the woman who stood in the shadow of her older sister. People were dying. Lear House had been mostly spared, but the blight had arrived only six months before. The words flowed into her head: *We should call it what it is. A famine. A great famine.* Life could get much worse under this misfortune. The tenants had been able to struggle through the harsh winter through their own perseverance, but another crop failure would be disastrous.

Rory straightened and landed a hook on his rival's left cheek and then an uppercut to the chin. Connor, dazed, staggered under the onslaught. He shook his head to rid himself of the stunning force of the blows. He rushed at Rory, arms thrust out, but slipped in the mud. Both men fell in a heap in the brown slop, thrashing about, trading blows as the muck flew up around them. They both struggled, flinging the muddy water from their eyes.

Briana took her eyes off Rory and Connor for a moment. Most of the men in the crowd looked weaker, thinner, than she had ever seen them. They stood with blank faces, their clothes draped from their bony limbs. The women huddled in the doorway. One of her girlhood friends, Heather, held on to a woman too weak to stand by herself. Briana stepped closer to see if she could help.

Heather spied her and held out her hand. "Don't come any closer, miss. She's not well from hunger. She came with her husband looking for food. They expected there might be a fair at this fight."

"Heather, it's me. Briana." Her friend had

never addressed her as "miss." She inched forward, unnerved by Heather's tone yet astounded by her willingness to aid the sick woman. What if she had lice? If so, Heather was exposing herself as well as her family.

Her friend forced a smile. "Forgive me, Briana, but we've seen so little of each other lately. I'd begun to think the Walsh family didn't care what happens to their tenants."

"You know that's not true. My father is busy with the accounts — we're all trying to make ends meet. We just got back from Westport days ago, looking for food for the manor and the tenants."

The sick woman turned her head toward Briana. The gray skin on her face clung to her skull. Strands of hair extended from the rim of her cap. Briana observed the mottled flesh, dark and light, pearl colored; the sunken cheeks; the dull, blank eyes.

"What of your sister who sits in your warm cottage with her books?" Heather's mouth turned down in a smirk.

The question stung Briana. "My sister is employed by the owner and is trying her best to win concessions for us all." Her words were a partial lie — Lucinda had made no previous effort on the family's or tenants' behalf; she had, however, since agreed that steps must be taken to save Lear

House. She was not about to draw and quarter her sister in front of Heather.

"Let's hope she succeeds," Heather said, and turned back to the sick woman.

A roar went up from the men in the crowd. Rory and Connor were flat on the ground again.

Rory straddled Connor's stomach and pounded his rival's face, right and left, left and right, with punches from his wrapped hands. The hard blows reverberated across the center until the crowd quieted, enthralled by the attack. Connor's head lolled under the assault.

Blood coated Rory's knuckles; he bled from a cut below his left eye.

The older of Connor's sons, a boy of no more than eight, sprinted from the circle and jumped on Rory's back. The child pounded his fists on top of Rory's head until Rory thrust his arms backward and dislodged the boy, who fell sideways in the muck. The child rose, swiping at the mud and ready to resume his attack, but Connor stopped him with a stiff arm. A grumble rose from the crowd.

Connor lifted his head and said, loud enough for everyone to hear, "You've won. I didn't think you had it in you."

"Thank God," Briana muttered.

"Fool," Rory said, and then rubbed his jaw. He stuck his hands in the mud and slowly lifted himself off Connor. When he was on his feet, he extended his muddy arm and pulled the other man up. They shook hands and stood looking at each other until Connor broke out in a laugh. Rory followed. Soon they were slapping each other on the back and jabbing at each other. The two men gathered their shirts and slipped them on over their muddy bodies.

Idiots. Both of them. All of this, and for what? A slap on the back?

Briana was about to sneak away to Lear House when something caught her eye. Connor's boys clutched their father's knees. They both had tears in their eyes.

Connor knelt down and gripped them by the shoulders, whispering to each in turn. The boys left their father's side and walked to Rory. They extended their hands. Rory smiled broadly, lifted each, and hugged them. Holding the younger boy, Rory talked with Connor for several minutes as the crowd dispersed.

A smile broke out on Briana's face as Rory held Connor's sons. Her heart filled with pride at the friendship and integrity that Rory had shown to his adversary. These thoughts confirmed what she had felt for a long time: Rory Caulfield would make an excellent father. She turned, circled behind the stone buildings, and finally found herself on the muddy path back to the cottage.

The rain let up somewhat as she walked down the lane. Gulls skimmed over the slate-colored waters of Broadhaven Bay. The sky was getting lighter in the west, a sign that the daylong rain was coming to an end. She kicked a large pebble with her booted foot, and it landed with a muddy splash in a puddle a few feet away.

She stopped in front of Rory's soggy cabin. The sod looked as if it was about to melt in the damp. The few gray rocks embedded in the walls were dark and slick. There was no reason not to go inside. Neither her father nor Lucinda were expecting her to be home by an appointed hour. All would be well, as long as she was at the cottage in time to put the cooking pot over the fire. Maybe he would enjoy her company after the fight, and she could tell him that she had witnessed his victory.

The pig snuffled near the entrance, snorted at her, and then trotted away, happy to be outside in the mud. She stepped inside and shut the door to keep out the damp air. The turf fire warmed her face. She took off her coat and hat and tossed them at the foot of the straw that made up Rory's bed. His blanket lay folded neatly across it; a thin cotton rectangle stuffed with down served as his pillow. Everything was in its place: the candle on the stand; his other shirts, breeches, sweater, and coat hung from the wall; the fire pit, free of dirt and ash, burned with precision in the center of the room. Even his pots and pans gleamed from cleaning. When she was his wife, she would have nothing to teach him in the way of housekeeping.

"I can't believe a man can be —"

The door opened behind her.

Rory stood silhouetted against the leaden sky. A cut under his left eye bled, but the bruises on his face caused her more concern. They raged purple and ragged on his forehead and left cheek. He leaned against the door and tried to smile. His shirt was open and coated with oily splotches. His chest, face, and arms were spattered with mud.

"Every muscle in this poor body aches," he said, limping into the room. "The next time, I think my principles will be damned. Thank God that's over. I should have thrashed Connor with ease. He's older than I am, a father with children."

She resisted the urge to call him a fool to his face. Instead she watched as he walked outside, stripped off his shirt, and bathed his face, arms, and chest from a pot of cold water. He returned, threw the blanket aside, and sat on the bed.

"Would you like to come to the cottage for supper?" Briana asked.

"No, my stomach aches. Some warm water to wash my face would be nice." He touched the cut under his eye and winced. "What brings you here? I didn't expect to see you since you avoided the fight."

Briana swiveled the cooking stand over the hot coals, poured water into a pot, and positioned it over the fire. It would take some time for the water to warm enough to be useful.

Rory moaned, massaged his head with his fingers, and then lay back on the straw.

Her breath caught, and she looked away somewhat embarrassed by her thoughts. It would not be good for her da or, God forbid, Lucinda to catch her in Rory's cabin, especially in his current prone position. He was handsome; no woman in the village would deny it. Even with a swollen face, the bloody rags around his knuckles, he stirred her heart.

A slick coating of russet hair covered his

chest. His pectorals, swollen and crimson from the fight, heaved with each breath. His lean stomach curved in a concave depression leading downward to breeches pressed tight against muscular legs. He was still strong compared to others because he and Jarlath had worked to save oats, rye, and potatoes once the blight had begun.

She wanted him in that moment, and she hoped that he might feel the same. Pushing back her carnal thoughts, she turned again to the fire. She touched the gently swirling water in the pot with the tip of her finger. It was warm, not scalding.

"Do you have a cloth I can use to clean your face?" she asked.

"Under my shirts," he said.

She found it, poured the warm water into a pan, and placed it beside his head. She sat next to him, dipped the cloth into the liquid, and swabbed the bruises on his face.

A smile of gratitude shone on his face, an emotion as true as any she'd ever gotten from him. His hand brushed against hers, and the warm touch of his fingers jolted her.

"Not too hard," he said. "My face feels as if it's been beaten with a club."

"My sister was right about Irishmen." She rinsed out the cloth in a pan of cold water.

"Oh, the devil with her." He took her hand

and guided it over his face as she washed him.

"You won," she said. "I hope you got what you wanted." She added a touch of sarcasm to her voice. "Whatever that might have been."

"I did and I didn't."

"What do you mean?"

"I won, but I've agreed to join the Molly Maguires."

She sighed, and her head sank against her chest.

"What's wrong?" He lifted up on one elbow. "I pledged to fight Connor. I won. It was my decision to dictate the terms. Simple as that."

Briana rose from the bed and walked to the fire. She dropped the cloth into the water, now at the point of boiling. "You never told me what you were fighting for — only that it was a 'matter of principle.' Well, you've won, and now you're joining the Maguires? What for — more fighting and bloodshed?"

Rory swiped a lock of hair off his forehead. "Let me explain." His face soured, as downtrodden as a scolded puppy.

She loved him, but lately she had found his actions disagreeable. Fighting Connor was one thing, but the Maguires were another matter. Her mind would never be calm because of constant worry about him. What if he was arrested for treason or, worse yet, shot in some senseless battle against the government? An instinct to flee rushed through her, but his forlorn expression softened her heart. "Go ahead," she said.

"I've worn the green ribbon, but I've decided Connor is right. The Maguires will get more done here — in the village, in Mayo — we must resist the owners, the agents, and the ways of English tyrants who govern as if we deserve this plague." Anger filled his voice. "They, who take our food and eat, while our people starve —"

Briana held out her hand. "Stop. Don't you dare include my father as part of this tyranny." She took a dipping stick, fished the cloth from the water, and let her anger and the cloth cool before tossing it to Rory.

He rubbed his face, chest, and arms with it and dropped it into the pan by his bed. "It took Connor Donlon to change my mind. He was willing to fight for what he believes is right, and by God, he is right. People are dying and nothing's being done. I hope I've not come to this decision too late. Our voices must be heard."

Her hands shook and her body felt as if

her bones had turned to tallow. The anger underlining Rory's words meant that he was willing to fight, perhaps even die, for the Maguires. She swayed toward his bed. He caught her and guided her down beside him.

"Have you given no thought about us?" she asked, catching her breath.

"Of course," he said in a warm voice. "I love your father, as my own rests in his grave." His swollen and bruised fingers worked at the cloth strips around his knuckles. "I know your father and your sister think less of me than you do — and, I must admit, there is reason in their thinking." He flung the bloody cloths into the corner and turned her face toward his with his hands. "What have I to offer? A pig soon to be slaughtered because there is nothing left to eat? I have no money, little education. Your father has always scolded me because I cannot read. Your sister thinks of me as an uneducated farmer, and perhaps she's right. My chances to gain favor with your family are slim."

Briana nodded. "I'm not going to tell my sister of your association with the Maguires, but I can't keep this a secret from my father. He's sure to find out from someone in the village. You can't stop gossip." She softened her tone. "But it's not my family you need to win over. You know where my heart lies. It has been with you since I saw you when I was still a child and you were a young man and I had no idea what that joy in my heart meant. My brightest memories are those of us walking in the village, singing with friends, walking the cliffs, watching the waves crash against the Stags of Broadhaven. Remember the time my father told us the ancient story behind Lear House?"

"Yes," he said, "but we aren't bewitched swans destined to swim for nine hundred years until the curse falls away. The famine is real, and death walks through Ireland."

Sadness pricked her heart. Lear House was her home — all she had ever known — and she wanted it to remain so. The idea of losing her family and her home shook her to her core. "Then we must do what we can to survive."

"I realized that when I beat Connor today. Even in my victory, he was right and I was wrong. The time for debate has passed. The Maguires live for action, not words."

He grasped her hands with a rough and calloused grip. She stretched his fingers and caressed the sore knuckles. He flinched. Then she moved her hands to his face and stroked the side of his head. Rory moaned and lay back on the bed.

She hovered over him for a moment and then kissed him.

He placed his arms across her back and pulled her toward him.

She wanted to melt into him, cover his face with kisses, run her fingers across his chest and stomach until he was fiery with desire, but he was bruised and bloody from the fight. She kissed him again, drew away from his body, and nestled against his side.

He pulled her close, but she pushed herself away. "No, not now," she said. Her mind reeled from his decision to join the Mollies. A husband who condoned violence, who put himself in danger, was a different matter. He had chosen a path that she could accept only if he made some concessions to her terms. She didn't have the courage in this moment to ask him to change his mind or take a lesser role in the group. Yet she loved him and felt closer to him than she had ever been. That feeling brought up the disturbing thought that she might have to choose what was best for her.

She sat on the bed listening to Rory's breath. Her father, now that the afternoon was growing late, would expect her home soon. She rose, left him lying on the bed, gathered her things, and asked, "When will I see you?"

"Tomorrow," he said with a rueful smile. "I have no fear of showing my face, but I'm not sure how others will react to it."

She opened the door and was greeted by the still murky day. She took a deep breath, intentionally filling her lungs with air cleansed by the rain and the wind off the ocean. The force of it chilled her face and arms. Wrapping up in her coat, she headed for the cottage. Her father and sister would be expecting their supper of oats and bread. Her mind whirled with thoughts of Rory and the way life had always been at Lear House. She was fighting to preserve her family and history. Rory was fighting a different battle that seemed destined to touch them all.

Cooking would be a small distraction, but her mind would be elsewhere — on what mattered most — saving Lear House and their lives.

CHAPTER 6

May 1846

The rat skittered beneath the pantry door; its long tail slithered after it like a snake gliding into its den.

"Damnation." Brian held a candle before him, happy his daughters weren't around to hear him curse. Of all the rooms in the house, the kitchen was his least favorite. At the back of the main structure, it stood against the hill that rose to the Atlantic cliffs. Aside from a small glass inset in its door allowing an occasional peek in from the owners, Blakely's ancestors had no interest in stepping into the kitchen as long as the food and the service were up to their standards. The room was damp in the summer when the rain streamed down the slope and cold in the winter when the northwest winds howled down the hill from the ocean. On this rainy day in early May, the kitchen remained true to its nature: the stove and cabinets dull in the candlelight, the air murky.

He had come to the house to write letters and review the books once again. The accounts looked bad — every month they looked worse. With the crop failing, more men had turned away from the land looking for work in cities or in other countries. While farming, men would be lucky to earn a few pence a day from their crops. Brian had heard of income, with work scarce, of a tuppence half-penny a day, often less than what they earned from their lands. No family could live on such low wages.

Without a potato crop and little or no money, the family would be lost. The tenant farmers had come to rely on the potato. How many family suppers had he been invited to in better times? Every Irish woman knew how to serve them boiled, cubed, or mashed, fried in the form of cakes or in soups with buttermilk. He realized now that culinary history was part of the problem — women only knew how to cook potatoes.

He opened the cupboard and looked at the once-filled jars of oats and rye. He picked one up, and the light weight of it shocked him. Supplies had dwindled so much that Briana had to ration what they ate. Rat droppings lay on the shelves. Even the little beasts were fighting their way inside for food. There was nothing to eat outside, no human refuse to feed them, so instinct brought them into the house. He and Rory had talked about making a second trip to Westport to get Indian corn. Looking at the remaining food in the pantries, he realized the journey would soon be a necessity.

He sighed and thought of Lucinda and Briana still in the cottage. Sleep had ended early for him, long before dawn, cut short by the worrisome tasks that weighed on his mind. Lucinda, surrounded by her books, would be asleep in the largest bedroom. Briana was awake now, preparing breakfast from their ever-decreasing supplies. She slept in his room when Lucinda was home. Covered by a muslin sheet, he preferred to sleep on a bed of rushes and straw in front of the fire. His bedroom was too redolent of memory: his wife's wooden crucifix and rosary beads, her lace collars and stickpins, the family drawings she had collected over the years. All these reminded him too much of the past when life was tolerable — even good — as he remembered it. Yes, there had been times of famine and pestilence before, but they were balanced by times of plenty and pleasure.

Now times were frightful, and he had no answers even after long discussions with his daughters. Rory had told him matter-of-factly that a provision ship had been plundered in County Kerry in April when a mob of women and children stopped provision carts from going to the shops. They had taken only food, and no one was injured. He also told him with less enthusiasm that landlords, agents, even tenant farmers, had been threatened. The farmers were "encouraged" not to pay their rents. He suspected that Rory had found out such news through his affiliation with the Molly Maguires, but he didn't want to know for certain, because he shared Briana's aversion to the group.

She had told him on the sly about Rory's decision after fighting Connor Donlon. The young man's participation in the group didn't please him, but what could he do? As far as he was concerned, it was his business as long as no harm came of it. He scratched his chin. Sometimes it was better to "let sleeping dogs lie."

He stepped into the hall leading to the stately entrance of Lear House. The pale light of dawn filtered through the glass panels on either side of the door. How cruel for all these grand rooms to sit empty for nine months of the year, only to await the pleasure of Master Sir Thomas Blakely, who had strong attractions to liquor, gambling, and women, and who, with dwindling funds of his own, couldn't afford to save Lear House should finances undermine its foundation. The solid oak furniture, the ancestral paintings, the hand-painted china, the blue Delft vases on the mantel, might add artistic pleasures to Blakely and his guests during the short summer months, but what of the rest of the year? He had learned every chink in the tile, every chip in the floorboard paint, every crack on the staircase.

Could these rooms and the items in them be used to support those who needed aid the most? What was Lear House, and its furnishings, worth? As agent of the estate, he had a good idea — a tidy sum of a hundred thousand pounds or more that could support many Irish families for years.

He stepped into the dark library following a circle of light radiated by the candle. The worthless ledger books lay open on the desk, as useless as the house. They struck him as hollow, shallow, mere shadows of a former greatness, now diminished by debt and famine. He ran his fingers down the sheet studying the names, families he had known for years: the Baileys, with their two young daughters who always looked for sweets; the Canavans, farmers for generations on Lear House lands; the Donlons, with their love of dogs and cats; the Duffys; the Flynns; the list went on. Men and women he had seen marry, become parents, raise a family, and die. They were his own — fellow travelers on life's journey.

Despite what anyone thought in England, or in the Irish government, or in the press, a full-blown famine was ravaging Mayo. Something had to be done. But what? Perhaps he was too old, too sentimental, to think clearly about such things, and he worried about his daughters. Lucinda, the most educated, he saw as the intellect of the pair, and Briana the body and heart. Lucinda had shared her earnings with the family and kept some for herself, at his insistence, for her later years. He expected her to return to her governess duties after the summer, having been dismissed by the family in the late spring. If she was in England, he wouldn't have to worry. Briana was another matter. She was happiest at home roaming the cliffs no matter the weather, talking with the farmers, cooking and cleaning. He knew she wanted children, and someday he prayed that would happen. A grandchild would have made his wife happy. She now rested in her grave of sixteen years near Carrow-teige. The winter of her death from the grippe had been the worst of his life. Perhaps, if he could convince them, his two daughters could work together without rancor or jealousy and find a way to save Lear House.

He blew out the candle and walked through the hallway made dim by the rain. Briana would have breakfast waiting at the cottage.

The door was ajar. He looked into the great room — nothing stirred in the shadows.

"Briana?" he called out. "Lucinda?" No one answered. Apparently, he had not closed it properly when he came in.

Satisfied that no one was in the house, he stepped out on the stone terrace. He closed the door and then saw the paper thrust under the knocker. Dread filled him even before reading it, and his hand shook a bit as he opened it. The silvery dawn light allowed him to read the scrawled words that looked like a child's handwriting.

First, retribution, and then death, if nothing was done to alleviate the suffering of the Lear House tenants. It was signed *MM* at the bottom. The Molly Maguires? He would ask Rory about this threat; perhaps he would recognize the writing, forced as it was.

He clutched the paper to his heart and prayed that God's will be carried out, that the Maguires should understand he was not a bad man. He was only doing his job. Lear House had so far been relatively unscathed by the famine, but he and his daughters couldn't hold out much longer. Even they would be touched, and the Maguires surely knew that. Then a horrible thought struck him: What if Rory was involved in this? Could the young man be so callous, so unforgiving of a man who had often thought of him as the son he didn't have? It wasn't possible. Rory could barely read and didn't have the skill to write such a note. He stuck the paper in his pocket and surveyed the tenants' homes on each side, pearly smoke wheeling to the sky from the thatched roofs.

He was looking for an intruder on the grounds when he spotted the black specks on the hillsides. He strained to see them through the rain. They were huddled together near the stone and brush fences that separated the estate from the surrounding land and village. How many he couldn't say — a dozen, two dozen, maybe more, bunched in clumps like muddy pillars against the sweeping hills. The men stood apart, sheltering their women and children with their coats.

He gasped. What could he do for the silent figures who lined the hillside?

Brian locked the door, then scurried down the steps and across the lawn. He felt like the rat he had seen earlier, running from trouble. Their eyes bored into him, past him, pushing him, it seemed, into Broadhaven Bay.

He opened the cottage door. Briana stood near the fire, cooking. He struggled to catch his breath, to speak of what he'd seen as her welcome smile faded.

"Da, what's wrong? Are you well?"

He pointed out the door and sank into his chair.

Briana was in her brown skirt and beige apron, her hair held in place by a kerchief. Lucinda sat at the table, her hands and face freshly scrubbed, her dress smoothed down to the tops of her shoes with their tiny heels.

"Look for yourselves," Brian said.

His daughters dashed to the door and stepped out in the rain. They soon returned with questioning looks on their faces.

"Are those people?" Lucinda asked. He could tell she didn't want to believe her eyes.

"Of course," Briana said. "The famine has reached us."

"What are we to do?" Brian asked. A disquieting uneasiness rose in him, which until now he had been able to avoid. "I have no answer."

"Breakfast is ready," Briana said, returning to the fire. She scooped cooked oats out of the pot, covered them with honey, and placed them on the table.

The irony of her words wasn't wasted on him. "We don't have enough to feed them. I saw firsthand how the supplies are dwindling. Even the rats are searching for food."

"Certainly not," Lucinda said. "A few handfuls of oats won't feed dozens of squatters, let alone the tenants."

Briana ate a spoonful of oats and then placed her utensil on the table. "There must be something we can do."

Lucinda dug into her bowl, looking thoughtful as she ate. "I'll write a letter to Sir Thomas asking for his help — in the hope that he gets it before he departs Manchester for Lear House. He's the only one who can save us."

"Really!" Briana chided her. "Too little, too late. If Sir Thomas failed to deliver my letter to you, he already knows what's going on here. It's the mark of a callous man."

Lucinda shot her sister a disapproving

look and quietly excused herself from the table.

Brian gazed at the breakfast in front of him. He had lost his appetite and doubted that Sir Thomas would get the letter in time. He leaned back in his chair and studied his daughter. He could tell Briana was fuming by her reddened face and blazing eyes. Lucinda, however, had been the picture of clarity and poise as she walked to her bedroom to craft her message to the landlord.

Briana swirled the hot water in the tub with a washcloth.

"I have no time for such foolishness," Briana said. She looked at her father — his pasty face sagged in the candlelight flickering from the table. "A letter to the landlord will do no good, I'm convinced. We must save ourselves."

Her father picked up the note signed *MM*, read it again, and placed it on the table.

Briana read it as well, and her blood boiled. She didn't care if her father saw her anger as she gathered the breakfast dishes and put them in the tub.

I can't wait to give Rory Caulfield a piece of my mind. If this is the murderous group he's joining, I have no use for . . . She stopped the thought. *No use for . . .* She couldn't convince herself to think it without shuddering. *No use for Rory?* How could she live without him? A man might live without a woman, but no woman could live without a man! That was the way it had been since Adam and Eve. She didn't want to believe her own musing — she knew widows and a few spinsters, but no woman ever flourished without a man in the family. It didn't seem fair.

She grabbed a towel from the hook and dried the bowls and cups. They would be returned to the place where they always sat in the old oak cabinet her grandfather had made seventy years before. She studied each piece as she placed them on their shelves. A spiderweb of light played across their dull surfaces. There was no porcelain china in the cottage — those fine serving pieces were reserved for Lear House. The cottage dishes were cracked and chipped from age, scarred by use, but still serviceable. Their shine had diminished long ago, but history followed them — a story that couldn't be changed.

"May I take this letter to Rory?" Briana asked her father when she was done with her task. She spoke softly because she didn't want her sister to hear.

"Yes, but I'm sure he had nothing to do with this," he answered. "I'm more concerned about the families gathering outside the estate."

"Let me handle this." She wanted to get to the bottom of the note.

"I'm sure you will, but be kind. I know what you think of him."

His words soothed her somewhat. She put the note in her coat pocket and stepped out into the chilly morning. Shielding her face from the rain, she looked past the tenants' farms, toward the fences, and up the sloping hillside. The sky was ringed with clouds that dripped like watery fingers from the heavens. The black lumps she had seen still huddled near the top of the eastern hill. On any other rainy day, had she not known the landscape so well, she would have seen them as dark stones upon the landscape. But some of the "stones" had crossed into the tenants' acreage, while others remained rooted in place.

Rory was talking to Jarlath when she arrived. His brother cocked his head, alerting Rory, who turned, swiping the rain from his face. The pig snuffled around his feet.

"Jarlath and I were discussing what should be done with this fine specimen." He pointed to the animal. "Either I sell him for as much money as I can, or he gets butchered to feed us for a few months. Either way, I'm glad to have him."

Briana didn't want to talk about the pig. "I must see you. *Alone.*" She nodded to Rory's brother. "Sorry, Jarlath."

He bowed slightly, and the rain dripped from his cap. "It's no matter. The business can be decided at another time" — he pointed to the families gathered around the estate — "but soon, otherwise he may disappear." He tipped his cap and returned to his cabin.

"What's the hurry?" Rory asked. The skin around his eyes crinkled with irritation.

"Inside," Briana said, her anger simmering.

He held the door open as she entered his cabin. Everything was much like it had been the last time she had visited, after the fight. She took off her coat, shook it outside, and then took the page from her pocket. "Look at this," she ordered.

Rory held the letter to his face and said, "A thousand pounds for my pig? How generous." He lowered the note and scowled. "Don't be cruel, Briana. You know I can read but a few words."

She took the letter back and shook it in front of him. "Of course I know you can't read, but I thought you might have some knowledge of its content. It's signed, I believe, by the Molly Maguires."

"I know nothing of it." He sat on the three-legged stool near his bed.

"Well, let me educate you, Rory Caulfield. My father found it tacked to the door of Lear House this morning. He was so upset he could barely talk." She read it to him, in a heavy, concerned voice, emphasizing the threats to the Walsh family and the estate. "Do you know who wrote this . . . tripe?"

Rory shook his head and leaned back against the earthen wall. "They will never hang you or set a torch to Lear House. Can't you see they're using the only method they think will get results?"

"Through intimidation and threat?" Briana threw the note on the bed. "This is the group you have so willingly joined?"

"It won't happen."

"Why not? You've told my father of threats being made against other owners and agents, of livestock being stolen and killed."

"Do you think the only reason I joined the Maguires was to cut up cows and threaten good people, who for the most part are managing as best they can? I can't speak for all, but I'm willing to give anyone a fair go."

He rose and walked to her. She wanted to step away, to ignore the flames that rose in her heart anytime he approached. It would be easy to sink into his arms and let him mollify her, but the situation was much too serious to be blindsided by romantic notions. She stood her ground and asked, "So, why did you join?"

"I want to help my neighbors and friends across Mayo. Nothing that's written in that note will happen at Lear House. I won't let it. With Connor and me on the estate you'll be protected. We'll know what's being planned." He reached for her.

"That's small comfort." She turned before he could embrace her. "Then who wrote this? It had to be penned by someone who knows us. How could this get by you?"

"I'm new to the Maguires. Maybe it was someone in the barony. Maybe a lad from Belmullet or Erris? Who knows? Tempers are short and passions are long these days."

She pushed the note aside and sat on the bed. "That's why I'm worried. The world's been turned upside down. We're in the midst of blight, spread by wind, rain, or the hand of God. No one knows how it got here, and no one can stop it." She pointed to the east wall, picturing in her mind the people camped outside the estate. "Have you seen what is waiting for us?"

He sat beside her and took her hand. She looked at the strong fingers caressing hers, his flesh hardened, knuckles calloused, from work in the fields. His touch gave her added strength, the feeling that he would protect her family . . . but at what cost?

"Jarlath and I discussed more than the pig," he admitted. "We walked among the people this morning. None have the fever that we could see, but they have come from those who are dying from it. They had no choice but to leave."

Briana remembered the lice swarming over the handkerchief of the starving family. "You've taken a great risk."

"I bathed, and so did Jarlath. None of those looking for food had the dark color of the fever or ravings like a drunken man." He paused. "My brother and I have decided to take in the families we can. We will ask them to bathe and boil their clothes just as we have — and then we will feed them from what we have. Others will do the same."

"But what if some grow sick? What if the disease spreads to you, then to the other tenants, and then to Lear House? What if you too die?" Her body constricted with a sudden fear.

And what about food? Some stores remained in the manor's kitchen, but rationing was the only solution until the next potato crop came in — if it came in at all.

"I can't think about it for long, or I'll go mad," she said, and leaned against him. Suddenly, she felt like a selfish, insolent child longing for more than she could have. It seemed the only answer was to make do with less, until . . .

"Believe it or not, I feel the same way." He moved his hands to her shoulders and gently maneuvered her back on the bed. She wondered if he would try to kiss her, but he lay nestled against her, the heat from his body warming hers.

She looked into his pale blue eyes and touched a lock of his red hair. "I want to do more. . . ."

Rory fixed his gaze upon her. "What can you do?"

She rose on one elbow. "We have a little food at Lear House — not enough for a feast for all — but perhaps I can gather enough supplies to make soup for the hungry. We will share what we can."

He kissed her, but the picture of those huddling against the rain tempered her thoughts. "If I could let them into Lear House, I would," she told him. "They would be safe, warmed by the fire, and fed."

"Your father, as good a man as he is, would never allow it," he countered. "If word got out to Sir Thomas that the Walsh family was sheltering the homeless, you'd be evicted from the estate before you could offer an excuse."

She rubbed her hand against his arm, feeling the powerful hardness of his muscles. If opening Lear House wasn't possible, the idea of feeding those who came to the estate was probable. She *had* to make it happen.

"I can use the two large stewing pots behind Lear House to feed them. They're used when the summer guests are in residence," she said. "There's only one person I need to convince — my father." Perhaps, if she got him to talk to the people, her task might be easier.

A few minutes after Briana departed, Rory grabbed the note, put on his hat and coat, and sprinted to Connor's home. The heath squished under his boots. He glanced at the wet and starving people as he sloshed up the hill. Soggy figures snaked through the blackthorn hedges and the scrub trees that lined the road to Carrowteige. Hands reached into the branches, snapping them. Near the edge of the lane, piles of earth had appeared. The nameless faces were making *sceilps,* burrows they would line with sod and cover with branches to serve as shelters. The men worked while they had the strength to do so. Maybe there were too many people to take in as he and Jarlath had discussed. Their scheme was a plan born out of pity and kindness but upon further consideration it may have lacked practicality.

His anger rising, Rory jumped the low fence that delineated Connor's land, leapt across the potato ridges, and stopped at his neighbor's door. Connor's home was larger than most, constructed to accommodate his wife, four children, and previously the grandparents who had died a few years earlier. Sturdy lintels crossed the two windows on the front of the house. Those beams along with a tidy thatched roof lent a solid appearance to the structure, more so than many of the mud huts. Through one of the windows, he saw Connor's wife, Sheila, bent over the fire. Connor, clad only in his breeches, was talking to his children.

He hammered his fist against the door while peering through the window.

Sheila looked up in surprise and disappeared for a moment before opening the door. She smiled at Rory. "Come out of the rain. You look as mad as a wet cat."

"I need to speak to your husband," Rory said stoically.

"My husband? I'm not sure I like that

after the fight." She clasped Rory's jaw with her hand. "You seem to be on the mend." She hitched her thumb over her shoulder. "My poor husband can barely keep his shirt on with all his bruises."

Connor scooted his wife to one side. "Shoo," he said. "Get back to the fire." Sheila patted his stomach and went back inside. Connor stuck out his hand in greeting.

Rory shook it. "Close the door."

He shut it. "Why so serious?"

Sheila was right. Connor's chest and stomach were still bruised from the blows Rory had landed. He had never expected to inflict such damage on so stout a man. Connor noticed Rory giving him the eye. "You did me in," the man said. "A father of four should think twice before he takes on a bachelor."

Rory handed him the letter. "Do you know what this is about and who placed it on the Lear House door?"

Connor scoffed. "I read as well as you do." He studied the note. "Makes no sense to me. I can make out a few words I don't like. What does it say?"

Rory's jaw clenched, but he forced himself to relax. "It says the Mollies are going to burn Lear House to the ground and hang

Brian and the entire family."

"Jesus and the Holy Ghost." Connor whistled and crossed his arms. "Who would say that?"

"I've been to one meeting with you," Rory said, "and nothing of the sort was ever discussed. If this is the way the Mollies operate, I want nothing to do with it. Brian was rattled, and so was Briana." He squeezed closer to Connor to get out of the rain. "The Maguires have standards, you know — 'assist to the utmost the good landlord in gathering rents; cherish and respect the good landlord and agent; take no arms' — so whoever wrote this note didn't give a hang about the rules."

The Molly gathering that Connor had taken him to after the fight seemed more like a social than a rally of angry tenants. The men had congratulated them on a good fight. During the meeting, one of the more educated men from Carrowteige had read the rules. The rest of the time, everyone exchanged gossip and drank poteen. In fact, nothing was accomplished other than to set the next meeting. Rory overheard uttered threats to agents and landlords, but they seemed more like boasts than plans. Only the men's sullen looks underscored the severity of their talk.

"We'll get to the bottom of it when we meet next," Connor suggested.

"I suppose," Rory said. "I hate to wait another three weeks. Have you seen what's going on?" He pointed to the black dots lining the hillside.

Connor shook his head and raised a hand to cover his brow. "What is that?"

"Starving people." Rory was amazed how easily the words slipped off his tongue.

"You're full of good news, aren't you?"

"Yes, bloody full of it." He watched as a few men emerged from the *sceilps* that now lined the road into the village. "I'm going to talk to them. Jarlath and I are going to do what we can."

"What?"

"Feed them — take them in?"

Connor backed against the door and shook his head. "I applaud your Christian charity, but I can't . . . you understand . . . what if they're sick? I've a wife and four children in this house. If they've got the fever, I want no part of it. I won't expose my family to that."

Rory understood. A man needed to protect his wife and children. If he were in Connor's position he might do the same. Both he and his brother, despite his family, were willing to take the risk if the men and women agreed to bathe and boil their clothes. He pulled his coat tight and stepped back into the rain. "None of us should have to deal with the fever or the famine, but I'm afraid that's what the Good Lord has given us — our Cross to bear. We must make the best of it."

"I wish you a good day and blessings upon you." Connor opened the door and stepped inside. "I'll find out who wrote that letter."

Before Connor closed the door, Rory caught sight of Sheila and the children gathered around the fire. They were eating and drinking from their cups and bowls and looked as happy as a sunny spring day. Someday, he and Briana would have children of their own. His desire had never faded over the years, and only his respect for her and Brian had tempered his sexual appetite. On long summer nights when he could see Briana, his hormones had nearly gotten the better of him.

But how long could the peaceful picture before him last? It reminded him of stories he had heard about medieval castles under siege from warring clans. The castle was protected for a time, but under continuous attack it fell. He had a horrible feeling, as he made his way toward the starving people, that the castle was about to fall.

Briana was surprised to find Daniel Quinn, the poet, and Father O'Kirwin at the cottage when she returned from her visit to Rory. She greeted them, placed her wet coat near the turf fire, and then warmed her hands in the heat. She had last seen the poet in the fall before the blight hit. He looked older, thinner, with strands of gray threading through his black hair. The priest looked the same as when she had seen him at Mass the previous Sunday, perhaps his face a little more sour from ferrying over from Belmullet in the rain.

The conversation had died with her entrance, and she debated whether to go into her bedroom. She looked past the fire into Lucinda's room where a candle burned on the desk near the window. She could see only her sister's hand as it moved pen across paper.

No. There's nothing they can't say in front of me. She sat on the piecework rug near the fire because all the chairs were taken.

Her father harrumphed. "As I was saying . . . they have no legal right to be on this property or to demand anything from Lear House."

Briana bristled at her father's words, although they were true. Even though Sir Thomas wasn't on the property, her father was bound to carry out the owner's wishes. Those legalities made it highly unlikely that he would agree to feed those who had gathered, therefore holding the lives of the starving families in his hand. She lowered her head and gazed at the red, blue, and green patterns in the rug; her spirits sagged as she listened to him.

Father O'Kirwin lit his pipe and blew a few puffs of smoke toward the roof. "I understand your objections, Brian, but think of the people. They deserve our help. We must 'do unto others.' "

"If I could help I would, but the food and the house aren't mine to give. Why did they come to us anyway — because we've so far escaped the famine?"

The poet shook his pipe at Brian. "I know you're a better man than that. You've helped me on many a desperate day in my life." His eyes clouded to the point that Briana thought he might cry. "Why, I might not have lived through my lonely times if it hadn't been for your kindness." He sucked on the pipe stem, and his mercurial mood shifted. "By the way, have you a drink?"

Brian glared at him. "I've some expensive

French brandy that was given to me by a sea captain, but you'll touch none of it." He leaned forward in his chair and thrust his hands toward the glowing turf. "Besides, saving your poor body is a far cry from saving who knows how many others. If I feed them all, I'll have nothing left for my family."

Briana raised her head and spoke. "Sir Thomas isn't here. How would he know if we fed the people?"

Her father's eyes narrowed, looking at her as if she were a petulant child. "That's not the point and you know it."

"We can make do," Briana answered quickly. "I have a plan."

Father O'Kirwin's face lit up. "Please tell us. We are beyond prayers."

Briana told them of her idea to make soup in the two large cast-iron cauldrons. "We'll put them on the grounds — in back near the kitchen — and serve those we can. We have bowls. As people eat, we'll wash them and reuse them." She studied her father, who looked on stoically. When she was a child, she'd been able to melt his heart with a shy grin or a pouty smile and get him to do most anything she desired. But in these times, the realities of the famine had lessened her powers of persuasion. "It's the least we can do — help our countrymen."

"Agreed," Father O'Kirwin added. The poet nodded.

Brian leaned back in his chair. "I'm not convinced. We barely have enough to eat ourselves."

"We'll use what we have," Briana said. "If we run out, we'll find more food." She flinched at her words because finding food would not be easy.

Quinn stood. "You must see what you're dealing with, Brian. Come look at those you're turning away."

"I must see to their needs," Father O'Kirwin said. "Who will join me?"

"Yes, Da," Briana said. "Some tenants plan to feed the starving from what they have stored, and offer them shelter."

Briana and the priest stood next to Quinn, and the three looked down upon Brian.

Her father squeezed the armrests of his chair until his knuckles blanched. Finally, he rose. "All right . . . all right, I'll at least take a look, but I warn you, when the food is gone — it's gone."

They donned coats and hats and walked into the rain, leaving Lucinda behind to finish her letter. Despite the damp weather, a hint of spring hung in the air as if the sun longed to break through the low clouds. Briana could feel it in her bones, the yearning for warmth, a happy thought that disappeared as suddenly as it had appeared in a flurry of cold drops that set her shivering.

The poet led the way up the lane as Briana, her father, and the priest followed.

My God, the earth is full of life. The vastness of the land from the hills to the sea never failed to thrill her. The sloping land surrounding the manor with its sod homes and potato ridges was green, verdant in spring splendor, a yellow dandelion in bloom here and there, the hawthorn resplendent with white flowers standing thorny guard along the lane. It was bad luck to cut the bush, for fairies lived among its branches. She would never tempt fate no matter how pretty the blooms. And above her, in the headlands, the yellow tormentil dotted the earth like a small rose as it climbed the slope to the sea cliffs.

At the first of the *sceilps,* a man, woman, and child sheltered inside the hole, shivering in the rain. The man shielded his family from the elements with his body. The damp molded around them like a watery coffin. The scrub branches protected them somewhat from the dripping rain, but it wasn't enough to keep them dry. Briana's heart ached for them because they had nowhere to go. The people had dug into the heath with their bare hands — or with a crude spade if they were lucky enough to have one — taking the branches from the few bushes. There were no trees to sit under for shelter.

The priest stopped before them — three pairs of sad eyes gazed at him like those of animals trapped in a cage. They could have been the family she had seen on the way to Westport — drained of life, devoid of spirit — but these weren't the same people. All around her, the faces peering from the hovels had the same downtrodden look.

They were dressed in dirty rags spotted with holes, caked with mud, leggings and dresses shredded along the ankles. A few wore shoes cracked or split at the seams. The staring faces were thin as parchment, skin stretched so tight across the bone that their flesh looked as if it might split. She wondered if they felt the horrifying sense of death that she suffered from looking at them.

Father O'Kirwin knelt before the first *sceilp* and prayed in a low murmur as the rain pelted his coat. Briana had rarely seen him without vestments, and never ministering to unfortunate outsiders. Most village Masses were held at the "Mass Rock," a gathering place by the cliffs at Benwee

Head. The priest extended his arm to bless the man.

"Wait," Brian said. "What if they have the fever?"

The priest stopped in mid-reach after the warning. Brian's face flushed red from the admonishment. The man in the hole stared pathetically at those peering down at him.

"Forgive me, Father," Brian said. "I shouldn't interrupt your business."

The priest looked up at her father and nodded. "It's my duty to give the blessings of God when I can." He turned back to the man, making the sign of the Cross over his skeletal frame. "How long has it been since you've eaten?" Father O'Kirwin asked.

The man attempted to speak, but only a dry hiss came from his dark, parched lips. The child, a small boy, moaned next to his mother.

Brian whispered an oath and turned to Briana. "Are they all like this?"

Quinn answered. "Nearly all. I grab a beggar's bite when I can by offering a song, but these people don't even have a poet's luck."

"If only we'd been able to get the Indian corn," Briana said.

"I wish it was that easy," the poet said. "I've seen what the imported meal does to them. Our women don't know how to cook it, our children can't digest it. It takes days to make it fit to eat and tastes nothing like a potato. I've seen people devouring berries, twigs, and leaves in the bog. They're lucky if they can catch a fish, or have a bit of meat from a dead farm animal. If they can find nothing else, they eat putrid potatoes. Many are sick to their stomachs and bowels — so sick they can't walk. Then the fever attacks; people turn black and die. It's a hideous sight, and sickening smell when death takes them —"

"Enough!" Brian wheeled and turned his back to the family.

"Da!" Briana rushed to her father. "This is why we have to try . . . even Rory says so. He wants to feed those he can."

Brian shook at her words.

She lifted his chin with a gentle touch of her fingers. His eyes brimmed red with tears. He swiped them from his cheeks, pulled his daughter close, and said, "The hell of my dreams seems like heaven compared to this. I've prayed to God, to all the Saints, that this famine wouldn't touch my family. I can't understand how a loving God would visit this upon his people. We've prayed, we've been obedient, and now we're dying." He squeezed Briana. "I love you and your sister so much — I'm trying the best I can to hold the family together."

The priest rose and put his hand on Brian's shoulder. "I have no answer for your questions. The Lord doesn't speak to me, other than through his works. Often I don't understand His ways. I try to look at the good in life, to have faith in God."

"God will do no good unless we act," Briana said. She looked down the lane and saw two naked children standing near a fire beside Rory's cabin. He dropped their clothes in a steaming vat and then stirred the water with a stick. Their parents were nowhere in sight. They were probably in his cabin drying off and getting dressed.

"I'm going back to Lear House," Brian said, stiffening in the rain. "I'll take stock of our supplies and see how much we can give to these people." He grasped Briana's hands and said to Father O'Kirwin and Daniel Quinn, "I'll need help building the fires around the pots."

"Thank you, Da," Briana said, and kissed him on the cheek. "I'd like to go on with Father O'Kirwin, I won't be long."

Brian left them and walked down the muddy lane toward the manor. Lear House stood solemn in the drab daylight, blankly staring back at her with its silvery gray windows and weathered slate, somber and soulless, nestled between the cliffs and the bay.

As she watched her father, her skin prickled, on edge from the task in front of her. She had never thought much about her future, because it had never been threatened, with never a consideration that it might end. Now, everything she had known was crumbling.

The priest left the first family and moved on to the next. There were many *sceilps* to visit down the road. Those who could walk could come later to eat. Perhaps Father O'Kirwin and Daniel Quinn could carry food to those who couldn't come to the house.

She counted her blessings, many that she had and many that she had taken for granted, as they visited each of the starving families. No more would she look complacently upon life. She waved to Rory as she, along with the priest and the poet, walked on the lane above his home. He was so consumed with the family that he didn't see her. Rory was a good man, one not afraid of work or giving his best in any situation. Lucinda might be enamored of Sir Thomas, but in no way could a gentrified Englishman compare to the man she loved. She chastised herself. How could she think of love when death had spread its dark arms around Lear House?

She made up her mind. After she fed the people, she would ask Rory the most important question of her life.

CHAPTER 7

Lear House sat at the end of the lane. The cliffs and the turbulent Atlantic lay to the west, beyond the slope on which the house stood. The starving had come to the manor, driven from villages to the east or the mountains to the south by rumors of food.

The people in front of her were as real as she, yet they could have been foxes burrowing in a den. She blinked away tears as she stared at the man, woman, and children huddled together for warmth. This kind of pain and suffering was unknown to her — in fact, unknown to anyone living on the grounds of Lear House. Everyone had witnessed death before, but it had been quiet, as silent and stealthy as a cat stalking a bird. And those deaths had been followed by holy ritual and, eventually, rejoicing that the departed had taken their place in the arms of the Lord. But now it seemed God had deserted the families in front of her as well as the whole of Ireland.

Even Daniel Quinn, who had remained with her, stood back from the *sceilp* shaking his head, and now and then averting his gaze from the family. He turned, clutched his head, and folded his arms against his chest. Even he, as a poor man, was affected by their plight.

She wondered why she had come, why she had followed the priest and not turned back with her father. It would have been easy to return to Lear House and leave the starving behind. But fear had made her a stronger woman. She decided to stare death in its face, to look past its hideous image, and focus instead on the future — to comfort who she might save.

Briana stepped forward to offer what solace she could.

The man and woman, their bones poking through their ragged clothes, sat shivering in the mud. An older boy and girl sat stupefied on either side of them, but sometimes they shook, as if someone had wound them up like a clockwork toy, before they returned to their catatonic state. The woman held a small boy in her lap. His face reminded Briana of a dead sheep she had seen once, teeth and blackened gums drawing down past shriveled lips. His skull showed under the taut skin; his eyes were sunken and hollow. His little chest heaved, struggling for contorted breaths that escaped in shallow gasps.

The skies opened as the priest knelt in front of the family. Briana came closer, but Father O'Kirwin waved her back. "There's nothing you can do here. I fear it's too late for the little one." The priest returned to his duties, asking the name of the child. The man mumbled a name Briana couldn't hear.

Despite the downpour, Father O'Kirwin's words rose like a song rushing with the deluge. The sky turned from gray to black, and the rain rushed from burrow to burrow down the side of the lane, inundating the families who had found the slightest of shelters. The priest placed his hand on the child's forehead as Briana braced her feet in the mud.

Daniel Quinn leaned toward her, his long hair curling in damp strands on his neck. "Such terrible times for our people. God has cursed us."

"If you believe that, we have nothing to live for," Briana said.

The poet's voice bordered on a song. "Bring back the features that joy used to wear. Long, long be my heart . . ."

Briana had never heard the verse and studied him quizzically.

"The words of our own Thomas Moore, Ireland's most celebrated poet. I, too, long for better days." He looked at the priest and shivered in the rain. "Father is saying the Last Rites."

Briana knelt next to the priest, listening to the Latin he muttered.

Daniel cocked an ear in the priest's direction and repeated the rite. ". . . may the Lord in his love and mercy help you with the grace of the Holy Spirit. May the Lord who frees you from sin save you and raise you up . . ."

Father O'Kirwin, rain dripping from his cap, squinted at them. "I have no oil for anointing, no Body of Christ to give. This child shall go to God as he is, an innocent lamb." He turned back to the family.

Briana lowered her head and recited the Lord's Prayer. When she had finished, the woman's eyes caught hers. Life flickered in them, but a tear mixed with the raindrops on her cheeks. The woman uttered words as soft as an invocation, and Briana heard "Help us" through the parched lips. Briana nodded, her eyes tearing as well.

She wished the nightmare in front of her would evaporate like waking from a bad dream, but the cold drops on her shoulders reminded her that what was happening was real. She was awake, fully aware of Death's hand upon the child.

The priest crossed himself, and then the boy. The child gasped several times, a grating, raspy breath, his eyes open. He rattled against his mother's stomach and then lay still in her lap.

"Is there wood for a coffin?" the priest asked her.

A numbing pain filled her. The priest's mouth moved, but she heard no words. She stared at the mother and the dead child, thinking of the terrible loss.

The poet touched her shoulder with shaking fingers. "Briana, Father asked you if there's wood for a coffin."

The child was so young, so innocent; his life ended because there wasn't a scrap to eat. Her tears broke in a torrent like the rain.

The mother thrust her head back with outstretched neck, and the low wail that Briana had recognized from deaths long ago poured from her throat. The keening rose to a shriek that she could never have imagined coming from a starving, sick woman — like the death throes of a mortally wounded beast. Soon the other women picked up the keening until the cry filled her ears and spread across the land. She wondered if Lucinda heard it, if the terrible sound penetrated the cottage, cut through the walls of Lear House and echoed across the vast bay. Would it reach Sir Thomas Blakely ensconced safely in his Manchester home?

The keening continued until it reverberated into a gentle thrum with the faltering rain.

She rose without answering the priest and lurched down the lane to Rory's cabin. He was inside with the family. They stood, most half naked, their clothes drying around the turf fire. Briana called him outside, leaving the others to their privacy.

"I heard the keen," Rory said as he closed the door.

Briana nodded, unable to speak about the child's death. Her lips opened but no words came out.

"It's all right," Rory said, and pulled her to his chest. "You don't have to talk. Cry if you want."

Sobbing, she melted against him. If only she had the courage to ask the question, to talk about what she desired more than anything in the world. The dead child, the starving families surrounding Lear House, reinforced her conviction. If not now, when? If she waited, life might make her desire impossible.

Don't be selfish, fool. He's helping a family and all you can think about is what you want. She pulled away and wiped her eyes on her coat sleeve. Everything was somber, a picture of black and white: Rory's cabin, Lear House, the starving people. There was no color in the world. How she longed for a sunny day, for the bright colors of the spotted orchid upon the somber heath, or a walk on the beach, her feet warmed by the sand.

"Do we have wood for a coffin?" she finally asked.

Rory's brow lifted.

She lifted herself from his chest. "For a child."

His eyes dimmed. "So that's what it was about. A child. . . ." He scuffed his boot in the muddy earth. "Everything was quiet and then the wailing started." He shook his head as if to fling the thought from his mind. "Jarlath may have some bog-oak planks. That may be the best we can do. If more die, we'll have precious little."

"Please, no more deaths," she said as if she were invoking a prayer. "There are birch logs behind the cottage Sir Thomas imported for the fireplaces, but I need those to heat the cauldrons."

Again, he looked for an explanation.

She hadn't had time to tell him of her plan

183

to feed the starving. "We're feeding the people tonight, as many as we can. I plan on making soup. Father is checking on the stores now."

"You are a wonder." Pulling her close, he kissed her.

Cherishing the press of his lips upon hers, she deepened the kiss, not caring who saw them — be it her father, Lucinda, the poet, or the priest. It didn't matter. She settled against his strong chest, smelling the Irish earth upon his body. In that moment, she loved his strength, his determination to do right, his unwavering loyalty and love for his family and her — all the characteristics that had bound her to him from the beginning — though it had taken her years to define those feelings. His love would guarantee a home no matter where they lived. She sensed that more than ever now that danger loomed over them.

The famine was not far behind, riding a pale horse that galloped toward her. The imminent danger strengthened her dreams and desire. After everyone had been fed tonight, she would ask Rory to marry her. She had never been so sure of anything in her life.

Her father tapped pen against the paper

while tallying up the list. Briana and Lucinda sat on the edge of their seats awaiting the results.

"I've made the count," he began. "We have enough to feed the people here for three days if we use supplies sparingly. I'll send Rory to Belmullet tomorrow in the hope that he can secure enough meal to hold us for a few more weeks. After that, we'll have to think of something else."

Lucinda frowned and breathed deeply before her words spewed out in English. "Am I the only one in this house who isn't mad?" She thrust out her hands in frustration. "Have either of you thought of the consequences of this ridiculous action? What happens when Sir Thomas finds out that none of our tenants can pay the rent, yet *we* are feeding *strangers* from our supplies? How do you think *he* will react when he arrives at Lear House next month and finds there is no food to eat? Shall we have him eat cake?" She placed her hand on her chin in a thoughtful pose. "What will happen when the word spreads and hundreds more starving people flock to Lear House to be fed? Have you considered the consequences of such an action? We will be overrun with no food to give, and Lear House *will* be burned to the ground and the nearest tree will be our gallows . . . as the note says."

"I hardly think it will come to that, sister," Briana said. "If you had seen the people for yourself — if you had seen that child die in his mother's arms. Where's your heart?"

"My heart is here with my family, but I also seem to be the only one with a practical head. I've dispatched the letter to Sir Thomas, and we need to wait for his reply." She shot a defiant look at her father. "Frankly, I'm disappointed in you."

"No need to sharpen your tongue on me," Brian responded.

Stung by her father's words, Lucinda recoiled in her chair. "I shan't listen to such nonsense, and I'll take no part in the 'serving' this evening."

"Lucinda, see reason," Briana begged, thinking a show of kindness might sway her sister. "We need your help."

"It would be wise to aid your sister," Brian scolded.

"And if I don't?"

"Remember that you, despite your age, still live under my roof."

"Under the kindness and the employ of Sir Thomas, we all live here," Lucinda countered. "So far, I've only asked that he take pity on the tenants and us. He might like to know what liberties are being taken at Lear House."

"You wouldn't," Briana said, shocked at her sister's effrontery.

"It doesn't matter." Her father closed the ledger and tapped it with his forefinger. "By the time your letter gets to the landlord, the deed will have been done — long over — and, despite your protests, I really don't think you want us to be driven from the estate."

Lucinda stood, ready to walk out the door.

"Do you, daughter?" Brian prodded.

A small breath escaped from her mouth before she answered. "Of course not."

"Good." He pointed toward the kitchen. "We have a lot to do before we feed our people. Let's get started?"

Lucinda stopped at the library door. She looked uncertain whether to go with them or return to the cottage and bury herself in a book. Briana grabbed her sister's hand and pulled her down the hall.

Three hours had passed before the two steaming cauldrons of frothy oat soup were ready to eat. Rory, Jarlath, and some of the other tenants added carrots and dandelion leaves. Briana tasted the hot liquid, which reminded her of thin oatmeal mixed with vegetables — the brown broth wasn't pleasant to look at, but it was nutritious and hot.

Grateful that the rain had stopped, Briana eyed the sky, which churned with clouds as dark as raven's wings. Her father had set two torches at the back of the house for light, adding to that from the fires under the pots. The moaning wind and the flickering shadows cast an eerie pall over the evening. Many who ambled down the lane to Lear House resembled skeletons, with brittle bones showing under desiccated skin.

Lucinda handed bowls to the people. Brian ladled the soup, and Briana handed them a thin slice of bread. Sitting or standing, the starving ate on the wet heath behind the house. When the bowls came back, Briana washed them and returned them to Lucinda to give to the next in line.

Most said little while they ate, but some spoke in raspy whispers and told her father of others not strong enough to walk. Briana sent Daniel Quinn to deliver soup and bread to those suffering on the side of the road. Father O'Kirwin had priestly duties to administer and went about his business after eating.

Rory returned with the family whom he had given shelter. They had traveled on foot from Belderrig to the east. "We heard that

Lear House might have food," the man told Briana as he leaned against his wife for support. Briana welcomed them, amazed that word had traveled so far.

Connor Donlon and his oldest son showed up near eight-thirty. Most people had been fed and the cauldrons were nearly empty. She took pride in knowing she and her family had helped as best they could. As she dipped a bowl in lukewarm water and wiped it with a cloth, Connor approached the table. His son, the one who had hammered Rory at the end of the fight and inherited the broad shoulders of his father, walked alongside.

"I want to thank you, Lucinda, and Brian for what you've done tonight," Connor said in a low voice. "The Mollies will not forget your kindness."

Rather than soothe her, the words bristled the hair on her neck. "Did you see the note that was tacked to the manor door?"

Connor's shoulders tensed. "Rory showed me."

"Let's hope they consider us friends at the very least." She dunked another bowl into the water and then dried it. Her father stood nearby casting a suspicious eye upon their quiet conversation. She turned to Connor and whispered, "My family would be most grateful if we weren't hung by our necks or killed by some other torturous method the Maguires might come up with."

"Rory and I will make sure that doesn't happen." He shuffled his feet in an awkward manner, clearly uncomfortable with her troubling imagery.

She faced him, her voice low but sharp. "Can you guarantee that, Mr. Donlon? Over the years, my father has shown nothing but kindness to the tenants of Lear House. He has seen your children born, cried with you at your grandparents' wakes, assisted in the fields when you were sick and needed help bringing in the crops." She dropped another bowl into the water. "I will tell you to your face, Mr. Donlon, that I don't like the Mollies or their methods. I hope that Rory, and you, will have none of it."

He tugged his son in front of him. "What I do, I do for him and my other children. I have no cause to hurt anyone." He placed his strong hands on the boy's shoulders. "We shouldn't be turned off our land like sheep to the slaughter. If need be, we will take action." The boy nodded — although Briana wasn't sure he understood what his father was implying.

"My father has never mentioned eject-ment; neither has Sir Thomas." Briana turned her gaze back to the cleaning pot. "By all the Saints, I hope it never comes to that."

"No one can predict the future," Connor said. "All we can do is pray that this curse is lifted. If not, I don't know what will become of Ireland." He pulled at his son. "Come, let's go home and let Miss Walsh do her work. Thank you for your time and your good deeds." He walked off with the boy, saying nothing to Lucinda or her father.

She thought back, trying to remember if Connor had ever called her "Miss Walsh." Perhaps, a few times he had called her by that name — at a fair or a dance — and then in congenial familiarity. Tonight, the salutation sounded forced and brittle, much like her friend Heather sounded the day of the fight.

Her father sidled over, ladle in hand. "You gave him an earful, and you were right to do so. We're doing all we can."

"Are we?" She meant the question sincerely. She cursed under her breath and wondered if two more nights of serving food was all that Lear House could do as Sir Thomas sat in his country home eating meat and potatoes and sipping brandy. The thought made her insides churn.

"Have you had anything to eat?" her

father asked.

"I've no stomach for it tonight," she said. Her father probably thought it was because of her concern and sadness for the starving, but the question she wanted to ask Rory, and the answer he might give, weighed more heavily on her mind.

The odor from wood smoke wafted over the dark lawn of Lear House as Brian extinguished the last torch. The fires under the cauldrons had collapsed to a pile of simmering red coals.

Briana and Lucinda finished putting away the bowls after receiving the last one from Daniel Quinn. The poet, exhausted after carrying soup to the *sceilps,* had accepted her father's offer of the cottage floor for the night.

Briana walked from the kitchen and watched the last of the people file up the lane in the chilly wind until they disappeared in the shadows. A few families stepped into tenant homes near the manor. She could only see the top of Rory's cabin from the ridge behind the house, but she knew the family he had taken in had already made their way back.

Her heart quickened as she thought of asking him the question. Perhaps she should wait and let him ask. But why? It had been on his lips many times before. She believed his reticence came from the subtle indifference of her family and his lack of confidence about his worthiness to take her as a bride. The day's events had convinced her that now was the time. If they waited too long, the famine might make it impossible for them to marry.

Lucinda emerged from the kitchen and drew a bucket of water from the cistern. The lines in her face and the circles under her puffy eyes were a plum color in the embers' light. Her sister wasn't used to such menial tasks; her work concerned the intellect, not the physical. Lucinda dipped a cloth into the bucket, wrung it out over the ground, and then dabbed it across her face.

"I'm exhausted." Her sister wiped her hand across her forehead. "Two more nights of this and I'll be ruined."

"The other choice is to do nothing." Briana understood her sister's complaint but was in no mood to sympathize.

Lucinda's mouth puckered. "Sir Thomas would never let us starve like common folk. I will be happy when he arrives to set things straight. This can't go on." She let the bucket fall back into the tank with a plop. "I long for the past when we had a cook and a servant and we didn't have to worry about food."

"Those days are gone," Briana said. "Each day seems likely to bring more tragedy. We must hope for the best despite our trials."

"What hope?" Lucinda turned to the kitchen door. "The only hope we have lies in England. We should look there for our salvation." She looked over her shoulder. "Father's inside. We'll lock up the house and go on to the cottage." She clasped two fingers over her nose. "I hope Father makes Daniel Quinn take a bath." Her nasal voice retained an aristocratic air despite its sarcastic tone. "I don't believe he's bathed in ages. And I hope he doesn't snore."

Despite the affectation, Briana laughed. "Good night, sister. I'll be to bed shortly."

Lucinda disappeared into the kitchen. Then two shadows glided across the windowpane as candles bobbed in unison with Lucinda's and Brian's footsteps until the glow dimmed to darkness.

She walked to the ridge above Lear House and watched the turf fires' smoke fly from the tenants' homes. She wished she had brought her shawl, but she hadn't needed it while working in the heat from the cauldron fires. A shiver raced over her. The time had come to act.

Walking up the lane, she skirted the east side of Lear House. To the south, she could barely make out the sandy beach and the white curl of waves cresting against the shore. If only the night had been filled with stars and the heavens swept clean of clouds, she might feel more confident. But the thick overcast threatened to crush her under its sullen weight. She leapt over the puddles still in the road. Would he accept her? What if he didn't? She had never considered that he might turn her proposal down.

Rory's cabin lay dark. The smoke coming from the roof trailed into the air only to be scattered by the wind. If they were all asleep, she could turn back and no one would know the difference, but that would only serve to delay her anxiety.

She steeled her nerves and knocked softly on the door. After a few moments, it opened with a low creak. Rory stood in front of her, a blanket wrapped around him. He stared at her, his eyes fixed on hers, as if she was a harbinger of bad news. Before he could close the door, she observed the family lying on scattered clumps of straw, sleeping in a line, the man being nearest the entrance. The mother and two children slept closest to the fire.

They stood face-to-face, Rory looking

drowsy and gray in the somber light.

"Is everything all right?" he asked, and took her hands in his.

"Yes," she said, but then faltered. *This isn't my duty, my place as a woman.* Any confidence she carried drained from her apprehension. She felt as weak as a dollop of cream. *I've made a giant mistake.*

"Something is wrong," he countered. "Otherwise, you'd talk to me. . . . Did the day upset you?"

"Let's walk to the beach. I have something to ask you."

"You're shivering. Let me get my coat."

She was so absorbed with her proposal, she hadn't noticed that her arms and legs were trembling.

Rory ducked inside to get his garments. Once outside, he positioned his coat across their shoulders so they could walk side by side to the sandy bay.

The waves crashed against the windy shore as they descended the slope to the beach. Despite the dull sky, the water glimmered with a muted phosphorescence, which Briana had seen many times in her life, particularly when the ocean churned with fury. The sea had comforted her when she was lonely, cheered her when she was sad, but most of all, it remained a constant in her life. She cherished its power and beauty.

They settled at the base of a tall dune capped by grass, sheltered from the wind but damp from the day's rain. Rory spread his coat beneath them so they could sit on the wet sand. He positioned himself by her side to protect her from the wind slashing through the flailing grass.

Rory cradled her close to his body. "What you have to tell me must be very important to drag a man out of bed." He brought his voice almost to a scream to be heard over the wind.

Her romantic notion was deflated by the howling wind and the damp sand. Dragging Rory to the bay was foolish, not a passionate moment at all. "I'm sorry, I guess this wasn't a good idea." She found herself talking as loudly as he did. "We can go back."

"Oh, no," he said, positioning her closer to him. "You're not getting away so easily. Come on, out with it."

There was no avoiding the question now. She could make something up, some easy excuse, but that would only make her feel weak. Rory was the man she had wanted and hoped for, for many years. She swallowed hard and looked up to the stars and uttered a silent prayer. Her words flowed quietly up to God. Their release, the power of the thoughts, sent a gentle thrill through her. Her eyes filled with tears at the depth of her love. A few times, during Mass at the rock, she had felt a similar way, but those days had been scarce and stemmed from a communion with nature rather than a union with the man she loved.

He looked at her with questioning eyes and gently pinched her arm. His irritation showed in an even louder voice. "Go on! Out with it!"

"I want to marry you." A blast of wind shredded her words.

"What?"

She leaned close to him, her mouth next to his ear. "I want to be your wife!"

His body rocked away from hers, as if the tide had pulled him toward the ocean, as his face turned darker, veiled by the scudding clouds. She imagined that he might not be able to speak, that his lips were quivering, his eyes wide with astonishment, his brain unable to make sense of what she said.

Their separation lasted only a few moments. He said nothing but folded his arms around her back and drew her close. He kissed her once, a short burst of forceful passion that was withdrawn almost as quickly as it was given. Then he kissed her again, longer, with a gentle strength that lingered upon her lips even after they drew apart. He placed his forehead against hers, slipped off the cocoon of his coat, and knelt before her. "I'm doing what any man should do in this situation. I'm asking for your hand in marriage. It won't be easy, but I think we've both considered that. Your father and your sister won't champion our union — I guarantee it. I don't have much to give — only the love that I've held for you for so many years."

Her heart thudded as she savored Rory's words. "That's all I want . . . to share your life and love."

"You shall have it, then. Will you marry me, Briana Walsh?"

"Yes!" Her voice rose as high as her excitement.

He rose, kissed her once again, placed his coat over them, and nestled beside her. They sat for a time in the joy of the moment, gazing at the stars, listening to the wind and the crash of the surf.

Rory broke their silence. "We do have some serious matters to discuss."

"I know," she replied. "I'd prefer not to think about any of it, but we don't have the luxury of time. That's why I stated my intention."

"I have no excuse for not proposing, other than I've been afraid of what your father would say. Lucinda's another matter." He patted her hand. "Hard to believe I could fight Connor Donlon but be scared of your father's wishes for you. I didn't want you to be ashamed of me because I wasn't . . . good enough."

"Never." She kissed his cheek. "My father respects — I think even loves you, and I believe he will give us his blessing. My sister, as you said, is another matter."

"When should we tell them?"

"Tomorrow, if the time is right. I'll send a message to Father O'Kirwin as well."

"If Father O'Kirwin agrees with your father —"

Briana released her hold on his waist and cupped a hand over his mouth. "Then we'll get married in secret."

The wind roared past them, ruffling Rory's shirt. "A secret?" He laughed. "How will you hide the fact that you're living with me — and what if we have a child?"

The memory of the mother holding her dead son flashed into her mind, and the thought caused her to sway against him. *What about children? Dare we bring a child into this world when there is no food?* They were not easy questions to answer considering they were both Catholics and bound by God to propagate.

She decided to defer the question to another time. "We'll talk about that later. Let me worry about my father and Lucinda." She wanted to kiss him. Not another minute was to be wasted with disaster raging around them. Briana cupped his face with her hands and kissed him the way he had kissed her. When their lips parted, she knew, for the first time in her life, how lovers truly felt when passion, devotion, and loyalty met.

She rose and faced the northwest wind head on. It blew fiercely against her, nearly knocking her off her feet. She reached down for Rory. "Let's go. I must get back to the cottage. I don't want my father to worry."

Rory stood and shook the sand from his coat. "Not nearly as worried when he finds out his favorite daughter is getting married to a tenant farmer."

"Let Lucinda marry for money," Briana said. "That's why she has her sights set on Sir Thomas."

They walked, hand in hand, huddled under his coat. As they neared the crest of the path that led up from the bay, Rory said,

"I've never had the pleasure of meeting this Englishman. I've only laid eyes on him from a distance."

Briana shuddered, but her reaction wasn't from the chilly wind. She hated the thought of Rory meeting the owner, but there would be no way of keeping them apart. Their conversation, if anything more than pleasantries, might be strained by Rory's political beliefs. She hoped her future husband would keep his association with the Molly Maguires a secret from the landlord. But that concern would be minor compared to what Sir Thomas would find out on his return to Lear House.

Her head swam for a moment with so much to consider: the famine, the starving people looking to Lear House for food, her marriage, the negative reaction she expected from her family, the possibility of being thrown out by the landlord. It was too much to bear; she had hoped to be happy and carefree on the day she became engaged.

Those dark thoughts hung over her when she left Rory at his door and slowed her walk to the cottage. She looked up the slope for any sign of the people who lived in the earthen burrows. Nothing moved. Only the wind rattled the scrub brush rows. It seemed as though all of Ireland were disappearing.

She nearly tripped over Daniel Quinn, who was stretched out on the floor near the door. Her father lay closer to the fire. Lucinda was asleep in her bedroom.

She undressed in the shadows of her room, crawled into bed, and pulled the blanket over her.

Sleep was slow to come as her mind filled with terrible thoughts of famine and death — jitters she believed no woman should have to face on such a happy night. When she finally fell asleep, she dreamed of starving people with faces that had no mouths. Even if someone wanted to eat, there was no way to ingest food. Children clawed at her with their scrawny fingers. Under the flesh, she could make out the outlines of the white bones that held their bodies together. The vision of mouthless children, fur growing in tufts from their faces, blackish-green spots on their arms and legs, their clothes soiled with their own waste, jolted her awake in a sweat.

She threw off the blanket, sat up, and wiped the perspiration from her forehead. Several minutes later, her labored breathing had subsided enough that she could lie down again. No mother should see her children die. She vowed, as she covered herself, that her children would never suffer like those she had seen.

CHAPTER 8

Briana cursed the pot as the hot metal singed her thumb and forefinger. Her father and sister walked into the kitchen just in time to see her grab a towel and pull the scorched utensil from the woodstove. After a difficult night, when her only solace was securing her marriage bond with Rory, she had burned the oatmeal for breakfast.

"Damnation, daughter," Brian said, "what's gotten into you?" He waved the smoke away from his nose. Lucinda sniffed the air with disdain.

"It's bad enough that we have little to eat without you ruining it," Brian said, and lifted the few remaining jars. "Yes, only a few more days. Rory will have to go to Belmullet."

Briana's heart sank. Not only was it difficult to deal with shortages, but now her fiancé was being sent away as well. She scraped the salvageable oatmeal into bowls, poured more hot water into them, and placed them on the table. "Sorry. Add a dash of salt and you won't notice."

"We have salt?" Lucinda asked. Her skirt rustled against the table as she sat down.

"A pinch or two."

Brian retrieved the salt tin and opened it. The crystals had turned brown and brackish over the winter.

Lucinda scraped the burned oatmeal bits aside with her spoon and gave her father a concerned look, which Briana couldn't help but notice.

"Sleep well, my daughter?" Brian asked.

Lucinda interjected, "I slept like a log after yesterday's chores." Briana took a few bites from her bowl, her stomach gurgling as she considered the best way to break the news about her proposal. She pushed her bowl to Lucinda. "You can finish mine if you like." Her sister accepted the extra porridge, digging about in the crispy oats.

"I have something to tell you," Briana said. Suddenly, she was aware of everything in the kitchen: the cabinets, the dishes, the pie tin resting on the counter, the pots, the pans, all the items she had known since she was a child. It was as if she were sitting in a painting, frozen in time, the room drawn into sharp focus. Her nerves tightened, causing the hairs on her arms to bristle. "Rory has proposed to me, and I've accepted." The words escaped from her clenched lips, and the breath fled from her lungs. She had considered saying she had initiated the proposal but decided better of it.

As she expected, no congratulations were forthcoming. Her father lowered his head and placed his spoon on the table. Lucinda stared at the opposite wall, where the cabinet rested, her eyes unmoving. Briana was certain that her sister would oppose the marriage.

After a long silence, her father spoke. "Well, I can't say this news is unexpected, but I do have . . . reservations."

"Yes?" She had assumed he would object, and she pushed back her rising anger because tears would spoil the day.

He rose from the table and walked to the small east window from which shafts of hazy sun filtered into the room. He circled in the sunny patches before he finally spoke. "Rory Caulfield is a good man, and I believe he would be a good father, but have you considered that there may be other men who can bring you more security?"

"I have, but I'm not in love with them," Briana countered.

"All these years, I've seen your affection for Rory, and I thought your young love might fade — but it hasn't. I've seen how he cares for you, but are there not other men in the world who would do the same?"

"Men with money . . . like Sir Thomas?"

Lucinda winced but said nothing.

"I wasn't thinking of our landlord, but your sister has seen much more of the world than you and knows that life — can be better . . . different from what we know." He stood behind Lucinda, his body bathed in the morning light.

"I love Rory with all my heart," Briana said. "I've known it since we were children, and he has as well. You've known it too."

"What about children in this time of famine?" her father asked, putting his hands on the crest of Lucinda's chair.

She blushed. Last night, they had broached the subject of bringing children into the world only to put it off for later discussion. Prior to that, they had spoken casually about babies and raising a family, but in the way that any young, optimistic couple in love would have talked. "We haven't discussed it, but we will."

"You shouldn't wait," Brian said. He tapped Lucinda's shoulder. "Daughter, don't you have anything to say?"

Lucinda shifted uncomfortably in her chair. "I've made my feelings known — only to be ignored. Briana has a mind of her own, and one not easily swayed."

"True words," Brian said, and returned to his chair. He sat and folded his hands. "So, it appears the deed has been done and I have no say in the matter."

Briana nodded. "I'm calling for Father O'Kirwin. If we don't have your support, Rory and I will get married without your blessing."

"During our most precarious time, you've made a decision to be married."

She grasped her father's hands. "For exactly that reason. Time is short."

Her father was about to speak when a knock on the back door reverberated through the kitchen.

"Who is it?" Brian asked.

"Rory," the voice replied.

Could he have come at a worse moment? We'll see how he handles my father.

"Come in," Brian said. The door opened, and Rory stepped inside.

Briana could tell from the scowl on her father's face that Rory had come at an awkward moment.

"I didn't mean to disturb you," Rory said, "but I wanted to know if I'm to travel to

Belmullet."

"Sit down," Brian said. "I'd offer you some tea, but I'm not sure we have any." He nodded at Lucinda, who took the hint, excused herself from the table, and walked down the hall toward the library. Rory slid into a seat and gave Briana a knowing look.

"I'm glad that you came to offer support," Briana said.

Rory's face flushed. "I didn't know. . . ."

"I understand that you are to be my son-in-law," Brian said, rising from the table to once again pace near the window. "Much of my life after taking my position as agent has been one of 'damned with faint praise.' " He stopped, put his hands on the window-sill, and stared out at the lawn and the farms beyond. He began again as if speaking to the air. "Sir Thomas has been a difficult boss, but he has blessed my family with food and shelter through good times and bad. I think I have treated you much the same, and I may come to regret it. I have always wanted the best for my daughter, but it appears our days are destined to become worse. I will accept your marriage on two conditions — that you treat my daughter with love and respect and that you let no harm come to her that you can stave off. Considering our situation, it will not be as easy as you think."

Rory rose and extended his hand. "Your conditions are fair. I understand how much you love Briana and want the best for her. I will provide it."

Brian shook Rory's hand. "Then there's nothing more to say. We'll await a wedding day."

Her heart swelled with joy, and she leapt from her chair to kiss Rory.

Brian coughed as they caressed each other. "Back to business . . . yes, go to Belmullet tomorrow. We need food."

"Send Jarlath's son to find Father O'Kirwin," she whispered in his ear. "Tell him to meet me at three this afternoon at Benwee Head."

Brian and Rory departed, leaving her alone with a joyful spirit and a washtub of dirty bowls.

A hazy afternoon sun topped the heath, leaving a sky dappled with high white clouds and checkered light.

The hillside was dotted with tenants spading their land and, above them, the starving who had come to Lear House. There was little the farmers could do other than tend the potato crop and wonder what lay next. It was too early to judge the next harvest.

A man washed his children's faces in the puddles that had collected in the road. Those who recognized her from the night before stood by their burrows, like admirers before royalty, the men taking off their hats, the women nodding in appreciation, for the generosity she and her family had displayed. The gestures gratified her but at the same time made her feel uneasy because other than her father's position as agent and her sister's good graces with Sir Thomas, little separated her family from them. She wanted a bright future as much as they did, but how could you fight an enemy like the blight? Despite feeding these people, she could feel their silent fear, their despair, as she walked barefoot up the lane.

An abandoned sod home that Father O'Kirwin sometimes used for Mass when the weather was bad at Mass Rock stood like a dark lump a short distance from the village. Its rickety door of two oak planks was ajar. It was open most days when he was in Carrowteige.

She looked inside it on the chance that he might be there before their meeting. The hut was empty except for a small table, which held a drawing of a man and woman, most likely the priest's parents.

As she continued on the trail to Benwee

Head, the sun beamed through the thin clouds and fell in warm patches on her face. She let her shawl fall from her shoulders, draping it against her back and arms, and wondered if the priest might already be at Mass Rock near the cliffs.

The path from Carrowteige led up the heath to the Rock. She knew it by heart, having descended from it to the village after many Masses. Sheep and goats used the path on their way to grazing grounds near the cliffs. The sun scattered her shadow across the brownish-green ground. She chose her steps carefully to avoid slipping, but enjoyed the feeling of the cool damp earth squishing between her toes. The yellow of tormentil and dandelions glowed around her in the afternoon light.

She never tired of the views from the cliffs or watching the waves swell and crash upon the Stags of Broadhaven, which rose like a row of sharks' fins from the sea. But if you half closed your eyes, the gray rocks, tinged with green, looked like the graceful humped backs of swans swimming to shore. She only had to imagine the long necks of the waterbirds, the transformed children of Lear, whose stepmother had cursed them to swim the oceans for nine hundred years.

The plateau opened before her, and the

Stags jutted from the steely blue Atlantic. How odd that Lear, who had loved his children so much that his jealous wife had magically transformed them into swans in her desperate attempt to regain his undivided love, would be the namesake of the house she had known since birth. When the curse finally lifted, Lear's children had died from old age and were buried at a nearby island.

Mass Rock stood nearly ten yards back from a spot dotted with tarns on Benwee Head. Windswept, it thrust up from the ground, a lonely sentinel for thousands of years scarred by sea brine, wind, and rain. Many times during Mass a tern or gull sailed over the top of the rock and silently eyed the congregants. Father O'Kirwin would laugh and say the bird was a sign of good fortune to fall upon Carrowteige and the surrounding villages. The birds had proved him wrong.

Shadows had begun to grow long. Briana looked across the barren plateau, disappointed that the priest wasn't there. She could think of no other place he could be unless he had been called to the east for a pastoral need.

She looked back at the path and then heard her name. The priest was striding along the cliff edge in his black cassock.

Briana rushed to him.

He smiled and grasped her hands. "I got your message, but the boy had no idea why you wanted to see me."

"I hoped you'd come."

"A sure bet," he said. "I love the cliffs at Mass Rock." He turned and looked at the sea, hitching the cloth satchel that held his priestly goods over his shoulder. Beyond them lay a vast horizon where the ocean and sky met, divided by a thin, gray line of clouds.

They found a rock ledge a few yards back from the cliff. Briana sat beside him and tightened her shawl around her shoulders. The wind buffeted them with its brisk force.

"Why are you wearing your robe?" she asked. "It's not Sunday."

A wistful smile formed on his lips. "Because God and I needed to talk." He clasped his hands and shook them at the sea. "I'm in a state, Briana. I've never seen such human suffering in all my time as a priest. It's shaken me to my core."

She studied him. His expressions, which she had known since the early days of her religious upbringing, were familiar to her. He was in his early fifties, a man who would have had no trouble wooing a wife had he not been a priest. His temples had grayed, but the rest of his full head of black hair remained mostly untouched by age. He possessed a strong chin, and his eyes, full and round under strong, dark brows, were the color of the sea. In all her interactions with him, she had never seen his face so drawn and his mood so melancholy.

"I thought the answers to my prayers would be delivered at the Rock," he said. "After more invocations than I can count, I have only doubts. Why has this tragedy struck us?" He lowered his head into his hands.

She was shocked at his brutal honesty, his lack of faith. The priest had never talked this way to her before. She didn't believe God would punish Ireland out of spite. What had she or her countrymen done to deserve starvation and death? Were there too many people for the amount of food the country could produce? Was the government doing too little to aid them? To blame God was too easy. "I don't have your religious training," she replied, "but why would God be so cruel?"

He lifted his head. "That's a question we should all strive to answer." He slapped his palms on his thighs. "Maybe I'd feel better with a drink in my belly and a good smoke.

Not a drop of liquor or a plug of tobacco graces my bag."

The sea air coursed over them as they looked out upon the ceaseless waves. Hardly ever did the briny scent of the ocean rise over the cliffs — only on the calmest days when the fog rolled in. Briana's hair lifted in the rushing wind. "All we can do is pray, and hope — and live our lives." She leaned closer to him. "I have a favor to ask — that's why I've sought you out this afternoon."

His shoulders slumped with her request. "I'll try. All of Carrowteige owes *you* a favor after last night."

"I'd like you to marry Rory Caulfield and me."

His dour mood shattered with the joy of her announcement, and a wide grin broke out on his face. "A wedding? A celebration of union! Oh, Briana, it's just what we need during this sad time. When is the date?"

"Tomorrow?"

"Tomorrow?" His eyes darkened. "So soon."

"Yes, I want to get married as soon as possible."

"You aren't —"

She cut him off with a gentle laugh and then blushed at the thought. "No, not at all. Rory and I would never . . ."

He averted his face for a moment, concealing a blush of his own. "I certainly didn't think so. Then why the rush?"

She pulled a blade of grass and studied its damp, green form. "When I saw that boy die in his mother's arms, I realized that we must make the most of our time on earth, for heaven is never far away."

The priest nodded. "Especially in these times. . . . Of course, your father knows of your plans?"

She threw the grass into the wind and looked out over the sea. "Yes, he's given us his blessing," she replied without mentioning her father's reluctance.

"But so soon," the priest said in a pained voice. "What about the banns? Witnesses? The Mass would be a sham."

"You can dispense with the banns. My father and sister will witness the wedding."

He rose and strode toward the cliff, the wind rocking him on his feet.

She walked to his side. They stopped a few steps away from the steep drop to the ocean-washed rocks below. Briana clutched his arm. "Father, Rory and I have been in love for years — since we were children. We aren't rushing into this decision. If anything, the famine has shown us that time is not to be wasted. We seek only God's blessing. My sister absolutely thinks that I shouldn't marry him — that I should seek someone of a higher station." She let go of the priest's arm, clasped her hands, and stared out to sea. "Those are her thoughts; she stated no objection."

The priest nodded with a thoughtful look in his eyes. "I see."

A sudden gust lashed them, knocking Briana back on her heels. Father O'Kirwin led her away from the cliff to the Mass Rock. He guided her to its eastern side, out of the wind. She leaned against the rock, its quartz flecks sparkling in the sun. The rock stood strong and sturdy against her back.

"I've had to dispense with much in my priesthood of late." His lips curved down, and his eyes grew soft with nascent tears. "I have always followed the Church's precepts and teachings. I have always looked to Rome for guidance, but not even Rome can help Ireland during this time."

"If Rome is to help, when will it arrive?" she asked with bitterness.

He reached into his cassock pocket and pulled out his rosary. The blue and black beads gleamed in the light as he handed it to her. "I have prayed more in the past six months than I've prayed in my thirty years as a priest. I've come to a conclusion —

and it is not one I've shared with anyone. But after our talk today, I feel you should know. Let it be a lesson for your marriage."

She nodded, awaiting the priest's pronouncement.

"God is ignoring our prayers." He paused. "Death is coming for us, and there's nothing we can do to stop it."

His words drained the joy from her body. She cringed at the thought of losing herself to eternity before she'd even had a chance to live a full life. From birth, each day was one day closer to death, but did it have to be so immediate, so quick to come calling, when so much was left to live? Perhaps she understood the "lesson" that the priest offered. What good were banns, witnesses, and objections when a specter looked over your shoulder? It was the best time of her life to be married, but also the worst. She and Rory would have to deal with realities she had never imagined — among them the birth of a child into a world stricken by famine.

"I've seen so many die, and more will die every day," the priest said with a shiver. "My prayers have not been answered, and Death has not been kind. The starvation, the fevers, are beyond my worst nightmares of hell. You've not held a man or woman in your arms, yet, who is nothing but bones surrounded by desiccated flesh — or seen them, as I have to the east, thrown into unmarked graves because there are no coffins, or time for consecration."

"I don't wish to see it," she said.

He shook his head. "I hope you don't have to witness more than what you already have. I hold little hope for Ireland. My faith is dying with the futility of my prayers."

Her heart ached for the priest as well as herself. "I'm sorry, Father."

"Don't be," he responded. "You've already demonstrated your will to live . . . to grasp what joy you have left." He pointed to the rosary that she held. "Touch the Cross, the Body of Christ. Pray with me for a moment — my faith is not entirely gone."

She did as he asked. Throughout her prayer, she heard nothing but the whistle of the wind around the Rock and the low rumble of the waves thrashing against the shore. She prayed that the famine would end; that the horrible deaths from disease and starvation could be alleviated through His power into a miraculous recovery; that she and Rory would be married, someday have children, and would be able to live out their lives together. Eventually, she opened her eyes and lifted her head to find the priest staring at her. He took back his rosary and concealed it in his cassock.

"Time and death are working against us," he said. "Perhaps God has brought us together so I would understand that we aren't *all* destined to die, and that we must take hold of our lives as best we can, with His blessings."

Briana hugged the priest. "Thank you, Father."

"What time tomorrow?"

"Three? Here at Mass Rock?"

"Yes." He stepped away from her. "I should get back to the *sceilps* and attend to my duties. My heart breaks with every death. I can only pray that these families are reunited in heaven. Will you be serving food again?"

"For at least two more nights."

They walked down the footpath to the village. Out of the wind, she was warmed again by the afternoon sun. If she hadn't known about the famine, the starving people surrounding Lear House, she would have thought it the most brilliant, the most glorious of days because the land glowed green in the sparkling light and she was going to marry Rory.

Briana thanked the priest and headed back to the cottage. The people by the lane, with their bony faces and spidery arms, stared at her. The image of the famished dead lying in a ditch, buried in a hastily dug pit, filled her mind. She struggled not to see it: the emaciated bodies thrown unceremoniously in a swampy hole near a bog or hollow. How did these people even have the strength to bury their dead?

A woman shrieked far away, and the sound faded as quickly as it had come. She looked back but saw nothing on the hill. Those who lined the road must have heard it too, but they only continued their vacant stares. Everyone was growing used to such horrors. She thanked God that He had taken care of her family but wondered how long His blessings would last. She thought of Father O'Kirwin's failing faith and wondered if hers would fade as well.

She passed Rory's cottage, the potato ridges and earth around them still swampy from the previous rains. He was not at home or at his brother's; she had hoped to tell him the time of the wedding and that he wouldn't be going to Belmullet as her father had asked.

When she arrived at the cottage she found everything quiet and orderly: The dishes had been stacked neatly in the cupboard, and the turf pit, dwindling to a few red coals, had been swept clean of ash.

In her father's room, where she stayed now that Lucinda was home, she opened the small oak chest that sat in front of the bed. She lifted the scarred lid gently, for the chest was already a hundred years old, and rummaged through the scarves and sweaters that lay on top. Near the bottom, she found the black dress her mother had worn on her wedding day. She pulled it out and felt the cloth, which seemed coarse and dry after thirty years. If only her mother could be here today! She would have loved Rory and welcomed him into the family. But sixteen years earlier, she had died in the bout of sweating sickness that had struck Carrowteige. She, her sister, and her father had been sick as well during that hard winter, but they had recovered. Her mother's body was thin and ashen when it was taken away by Father O'Kirwin and the manservant. Her father had told her not to cry, because her mother had gone to a better place. She cried anyway.

As she ran her fingers over the black cloth, she wanted to cry again, this time from an unsettling mixture of joy and pain. She replaced her mother's dress in the chest because it was too fragile to wear and considered what she would don for her own wedding. The simple brown dress she had on would have to do, festooned with a few handpicked flowers.

After expressing some irritation about Briana's afternoon absence, Lucinda lifted bowls from the cupboard, preparing them for supper. Brian was tending the kettle fires on the lawn in back of the kitchen.

The sun was far to the west, throwing the room into darkness. Lucinda lit a small candelabrum and placed it on the table. The four yellow flames flickered, the smoke curling into the air, their circular penumbras vibrating against the ceiling.

After some small talk about the soup and bread, Briana came to the point. Lucinda was facing the cupboard, taking more bowls from their places.

"Rory and I are to be married at three tomorrow at Mass Rock," Briana said. "I hope you will come." She had found Rory late in the day and confirmed the date.

Her sister stumbled but then caught her footing without dropping the crockery. After a merry laugh, Lucinda said, "Thank you, sister, for the invitation. I wondered whether I would get one. It's been a dismal afternoon, Father's been in a foul mood — he wouldn't tell me why, other than to say there was something he needed to discuss with both of us." Lucinda lowered the bowls gently to the table and stared at her. "So this was not a morning jest as I hoped it would be. My God, why are you doing this?"

"I'm marrying the man I love," Briana said, controlling her irritation. "It's as simple as that."

"Simple?" her sister shouted. "What are *we* to do?" Lucinda held up her hand, quelling any objection. "No, no, no. That's selfish of me, isn't it? I have the employ and good graces of Sir Thomas and a career as a governess in England. Father is Sir Thomas's agent, and thus will be kept on here or be thrown out on the road if Lear House fails. Who will take care of him?"

"Rory and I will, if no one else will."

"In a mud hut with barely enough room for the two of you? It's preposterous!" She slammed her fists on the table. "You'd condemn our father to life as a peasant?"

"Enough," Briana snapped. "You don't understand. You'll never understand true love." Her temper had gotten the better of her.

Lucinda's body sagged as she reached for the table.

Her words had cut deeply into her sister's heart, and Briana regretted her remark — it was a cruel thing to say. "I'm sorry," she muttered. "I didn't mean that."

Lucinda stiffened. "You *did* mean it. I know the level of your sincerity when it comes to me. I've tried my best to counsel you, to lift you above your petty dreams, but I can see that my words, and my example, have been held in small regard. What you're doing is impetuous and foolhardy at best. A marriage to Rory Caulfield will be disastrous." She spread her fingers on the table and leaned forward. "You've always been the pretty one — I've accepted that. But I'm the one who understands how the world works, what it takes to improve yourself and to be held in higher esteem. You'll never take that away from me. My life *won't* be taken away with insults." She withdrew a handkerchief from her sleeve and dabbed at her eyes.

Briana stood rigid on the other side of the table. Her sister's assertions held a stinging ring of truth. "I'm sorry, Lucinda. Rory and I suspected that you and Father might object — but I've asked for consent, and it's been given. Our time is too precious to waste in argument. I know you want to keep the house together as well, but my heart lies with Rory. I feel yours is far away in a place where our father will never go. I'm needed here — with Rory."

"But what can you do? What *really* can you do to save us and Lear House?" With the last question, tears slipped down Lucinda's cheeks. She was sobbing as Brian entered the kitchen from the back door.

"What's going on," he said. "Are you two at it again?"

Lucinda turned away from them and dabbed her nose. "We were discussing the marriage — it's tomorrow."

She feared what her father might say, but she didn't want to prolong his displeasure with her decision. Brian shuffled toward her, his hands wrenched in front of him from working with the heavy cauldrons. He winced as he walked, his face etched with deep lines.

Briana took a deep breath and then said, "We're being married tomorrow at three."

Her father stopped and then leaned against the table piled high with bowls. He remained calm, his face expressionless. His lack of emotion frightened her. She gazed at him — perhaps there was slight resignation in his face, certainly not anger or disappointment. Whatever his mood, she judged it more satisfactory than what she was expecting. After what seemed an eternity, he finally spoke. "Long ago, I gave up turning you over my knee. It seems that both of you are in a hurry, but I've given my consent. Rory Caulfield is a good man." He turned back to the door. "Bring the bread out. The soup kettles are warm."

Lucinda wheeled on her father. "That's all you have to say?" she asked indignantly, and lifted her hands in exasperation. "Rory Caulfield is a good man? I should bite my own tongue rather than speak ill of my sister, but this has gone —"

Brian put a finger to his lips. "Shush . . . Then don't speak, daughter. We are a family and should be forgiving of our mistakes and grateful for our victories. Briana and Rory will sort this out. They will make their own way." He stretched his arms over his head and then ambled toward the door. "We have more pressing matters to worry about than a marriage. When will Rory go to Belmullet?"

Briana was relieved her father had not scolded her. He was right, heavier matters weighed on all their minds, which probably accounted for Lucinda's irritation as well. As he reached the door, Briana said, "Thank you, Father, for your understanding. Rory and I won't disappoint you."

The next afternoon, thick, gray clouds

rolled in from the Atlantic, spreading a chill over the manor. Briana watched them advance in misty waves over the bay. Spring had retreated under a gloomy attack that seemed a final blow from winter's hand. She stood quietly in front of the hall looking glass, primping her hair, plucking at one strand and then another before tightening them back with a bow. Even the heath flowers would be damp now and not an asset to her brown dress.

The tall clock near the staircase rang out at the half hour. Her father checked it every day to make sure it never stopped in its steady task.

Shortly thereafter, just past two-thirty, Lucinda, attired in a blue dress, and her father, wearing his best breeches and jacket, met her in the great room at Lear House. The foul weather had left her feeling as if she had made a mistake to plan the wedding at Benwee Head. But she loved the cliffs so much she could envision no other place for the marriage except at Mass Rock.

She greeted them with few words and nervous looks.

"I'd expected more smiles on your wedding day," her father said, and withdrew his pipe from his pocket. "This is a day for a smoke and a nip from the bottle."

Briana hugged him and then her sister. "Marriage day jitters, but I'm happy you're both here." Lucinda smiled but said nothing.

However, Briana knew what was bothering her was more than nerves. Earlier, from her vantage point on the lawn, she had seen tenants take to their fields. Only the young and old among the men mostly remained. Many husbands had taken what little provisions they had in hopes of finding relief work in Belmullet or Bangor. The women, attired in their scarlet mantles and yellow kerchiefs, stood among the potato ridges with their spades and with foot irons to protect the soles of their feet. They looked like cresting waves, each rising and dipping, back muscles straining, as they dug silently into the earth.

But the sadness she felt upon seeing the women was punctuated by her own soon-to-be role as a wife. How would she and Rory survive in a land ravaged by famine? How could they bring a child into this world knowing the hardships that lay in front of them? Despite the joyous day, these questions gnawed at her. She wanted to ignore the alarming feelings twisting inside her, but try as she might they bubbled in her mind.

"We should be going, or we might miss the wedding," Lucinda said. There was a hint of sarcasm in her voice.

Often she found that, of late, she was happiest when Lucinda was away in England; but then she would remember brighter days, fond times of old, when they were almost friends rather than the social adversaries they had become. There were moments, sometimes weeks, such as when their mother died, that they were childhood companions, weeping and consoling each other, determined to make sure that the family remained together. Was it only irritation with her sister's "airs" that increasingly soured her return to Lear House? Possibly, but she also wished Lucinda would accept Rory, if not into her heart, then as a member of the family.

They took the shorter western path that bordered several precipitous cliffs before ending near Benwee Head. They had all climbed it many times before. The wind buffeted them as they ascended, the cold cutting through her shawl and dress to her bones. The village path may have been more comfortable, but there was little time to spare.

The trail tightened to a narrow goat path above the foamy billows. Briana clutched the tussocks as she climbed, much like the ponies who used the tufted grass to their advantage. Lucinda groused under her breath about "using a more civilized route" but followed Briana. Her father brought up the rear.

By the time she reached the plateau her heart was beating wildly from excitement and exertion. She smoothed her dress and looked for Rory and Father O'Kirwin and spotted them, heading toward Mass Rock, topping the path that came up from the village. The priest was attired in his cassock; Rory wore green breeches and a dark jacket over his white shirt. Many Masses were held at the rock since Catholic persecution had begun years ago. The law of 1829 had given Catholics the legal right to assemble, but the tradition of worshipping in a secret natural setting or in a secluded home had continued.

Smiling with a face ruddy from the climb, Rory approached her with open arms. He drew her close and kissed her as the priest watched them from his stance near the rock. The stubble on his chin raked her cheek.

"You might have shaved," she teased him.

He gave a sly smile. "By now, you should be used to the way I look."

"Children and witnesses," Father

O'Kirwin called out. "I have people to serve, and I'm sure, Briana, you have another night of cooking to attend to."

As she stood before the priest, she didn't want to think about cooking and serving, or even the hungry. Her marriage, the happiest day of her life, should be the only thing on her mind. What awaited her after the wedding would jolt her back to reality: the starving families, the dwindling stores of food at Lear House, the bankruptcy of the tenants — those problems awaited after the Mass was through.

Her father and sister took their places on either side of them while the priest began, "I know in my heart you are a husband and wife who will work together for the good of the Church, Ireland, and its people," he said. He read the vows and then asked them to take each other as man and wife.

"I do," they repeated to each other.

At times, Briana looked over her shoulder expecting her father and Lucinda to charge toward the priest with scowling faces, shouting their objections to the marriage, but in the end there were none.

Rory slipped a simple gold band over her finger, his mother's wedding ring. Jarlath and his wife had given it to him several years ago because he was the remaining unmarried son. The ring was scratched and worn in places from his mother's hard work. Briana didn't mind; in fact, she cherished it all the more for having belonged to Mrs. Caulfield, a strong, devout woman who always protected and loved her family. She hoped to be the same kind of woman to her new husband.

Father O'Kirwin blessed them, and the wedding ended.

"I wish you well and a life filled with happiness," Brian told his new son-in-law. Lucinda offered her congratulations and shook Rory's hand. Briana appreciated her sister's gesture. The three departed on the path back to the village, leaving them alone.

They walked toward the edge of the cliff, but chilly blasts from the northwest stopped them from venturing too close. Under the gray eddy of clouds, white gulls and black-tipped terns soared near Kid Island like a whirlwind of flying dots, catching the updrafts from the sheer rock. As they stood, arm in arm, looking out at the iron-colored waves tipped with foam, the impetuosity of her marriage suddenly struck her. In a sudden panic, she asked Rory, "Did we make a mistake?"

He shrugged. "I don't think so," he said, and then laughed heartily. "Of course not.

I'm happy that it's done. We have each other." He turned her so they stood with their sides to the wind and then kissed her.

She pressed against him and felt safe and warm against his chest. The rushing air forced them together, and the heat from his body surrounded her like a cocoon. Her body arched in the ecstatic joy of his touch. For a moment, she swooned, closed her eyes, and saw only blackness. The ocean dropped away, the faint cries of the sea birds receded; her body melded with his as their souls fused together.

"How do we consummate this marriage?" Rory asked as they broke apart.

"It's simple," she said, and laughed.

"I'm not joking." His face darkened. "I've a family staying with me, and tonight I plan on helping you feed the people."

"We'll make it happen," she said.

They descended the trail to the village center. As they walked, Briana savored this moment together as man and wife. Even as Mrs. Caulfield, she wondered whether she and Rory would have any chance at happiness. They arrived at his cabin, and Briana felt the shift in his mood. His body tensed, and any happiness, any smile, that was left over from the wedding vanished.

The family he had housed sat outside staring at the pig that Rory and his brother had protected day and night. Her heart melted as she looked at the emaciated parents and especially the two young children with protruding eyes and drawn faces. Yet, observing them and feeling Rory's anger, Briana began to understand why he had joined the Mollies. His sympathy and love for the people, his desire to set wrong to right, drove him to take action. Perhaps, his way — direct, radical — was better than her attempt to save the starving by feeding them. That could only last so long.

She kissed his cheek and clenched his hand. The message was given — she would see him tonight when the people were fed. The four poor masses of skin and bones that gathered outside Rory's door occupied her mind as she walked to Lear House. They mattered more at the moment than did her marriage bed.

More people gathered for supper than could be adequately served. Near the end, Briana rationed the oats and bread so at least everyone got a small helping. No one was happy about the situation, and other than a few offers of congratulations on their marriage there was no celebration.

The mood was dismal when the four of

them gathered in the kitchen to finish cleaning up.

"I'm afraid you'll have to make the trip to Belmullet tomorrow," Brian told Rory as he wiped down the table.

Briana looked over her shoulder at her husband, who gave her a downcast look. She knew what the journey meant — rising early, no lounging about to enjoy their first night as man and wife.

"I'll be happy to go, sir," Rory said with a half smile.

"There'll be none of that now," her father said. "It's Brian or Da . . . not sir."

"Thank you . . . Brian."

There was an awkward silence before her father spoke. "Speaking of sir, this came by post today." He withdrew a letter from his jacket pocket and tossed it on the table.

Lucinda dropped her dish towel on the counter and darted to the letter. "It's from Sir Thomas," she said breathlessly.

"I've already read it," Brian said. "He's expected here in two weeks' time." His shoulders drooped and he sat at the table. "I'll have plenty of explaining to do when he arrives."

Lucinda looked askance at her father. "What do you mean 'explaining'?"

"I'm too tired to talk about it tonight,

daughter," Brian said. "Everything will be out in the open soon — Sir Thomas will realize how difficult the situation has become at Lear House."

Lucinda tapped the letter against her heart and then handed it back to her father. "I will be happier when Sir Thomas arrives. Life will be much better."

Briana hoped her sister's prediction would come true, but she doubted that the Englishman would offer much help to the starving, or to the tenants who, through their lagging payments, contributed to the estate's financial ills. As their lives crumbled, so would Lear House's fortunes.

Brian tossed the letter on the table and managed a smile. "But we do have some happiness in our family." He rose and put his arm around Rory's shoulder. "Maybe a small drink of French brandy and then off to bed. A couple should have privacy on their wedding night." He directed those words with a wink to Rory. "Bedrooms aplenty upstairs. Sir Thomas will never know."

Briana's heart jumped at the thought of spending her wedding night in a Lear House bedroom, because such an extraordinary thought had never entered her mind. She ran to her father, hugged him, and kissed him on the cheek. "Da, you're too kind."

"Yes, too generous indeed," Lucinda said.

"Hush, daughter," her father said. "On your wedding night, you'll wish for something special."

"I will, and I'll have it." She turned back to drying the bowls.

"Let's have a drink and a chat outside before the embers die," Brian told Rory.

Before they left the kitchen in search of the brandy, Rory whispered to her, "I'll say good night to the family and make sure Jarlath takes in the pig. I'll meet you upstairs."

"I need to gather a few things from the cottage," she whispered back.

After the men had gone, Lucinda said, "Congratulations, sister, you're the first of the Walsh daughters to be married. I look forward to my own vows . . . someday." Her words were spoken in a dour tone that indicated she was still melancholy about the union.

Briana shrugged off the slight. Nothing could ruin her mood. Her mind was filled with thoughts of Rory and the happiness they would share before his morning trip to Belmullet.

Her feet barely touched the ground as she ran to the cottage to gather her things for the night. All her years of padding over the heath hadn't prepared her for the feeling of the earth flying beneath her shoes; each dewed blade of grass propelled her forward until she collapsed, giddy with joy, against the oak door. She caught her breath and stepped into a room she had known all her life but that now looked different. How many nights had she gathered around the fire pit with her father and sister? How many nights had she and Lucinda sat at her father's feet listening to him read Shake-speare or tell Irish folk tales of fairies, sprites, hobgoblins, and ghosts, scaring the life out of them, only for all of them to end up in gales of laughter.

Strange, she didn't feel older, but a building sense inside her forced her to consider her life as a married woman — a woman who would have children with all the re-sponsibilities of motherhood. For an instant, the image of the dying child in his mother's arms entered her head again, but she quickly brushed it away, revealing a blank darkness she had thrust upon herself. That was quickly replaced by the tingling, raw-nerved emotions of a wedding night. She wanted to dance through the cottage but allowed herself only a quick jig around the fire pit. Rory would be waiting, and she set about her tasks.

She gathered her brush and a clasp for her hair and changed into her yellow dress, a color that would brighten both the night and the bedroom. She sneaked into Lucinda's room and looked at herself in the small looking glass that her sister carried in her travels. Perhaps it was the dim light from the oil lamp, but her skin appeared too white, too washed out, so she pinched her cheeks and, to redden them, nipped at her upper and lower lips with her teeth. While at the mirror, she brushed and clasped the strands of her long, dark brown hair at the base of her neck.

She sat in her father's chair, took off her shoes, and examined her nails. Her feet were dirt free. Holding her hands away from her face, she saw that her fingernails were clean from doing the dishes. She took a cloth from the wash bucket and dipped it into the cool, fresh water, scrubbing her face and exposed skin. With that done, she took one last look around the cottage, inhaled deeply, and set out for Lear House.

Lucinda was walking up the path to the cottage. They exchanged a nod and said good night to each other, both unwilling to open a more grievous wound between them.

The door to Lear House was unlocked.

Briana left her shoes in the hall, lit a candle, and climbed the stairs. Her father had not specified which bedroom to take, but she thought that among the rooms, the most grand would be Sir Thomas's. The thought of making love, even being close to Rory in the Master's bedroom, sent a shiver down her spine. It was as if she was, for the first time in her life, decadent — as if she were a naughty child again, getting away with an indecorous act. Her father had assured her that Blakely would never find out. She imagined that Rory might have a different feeling about being in the bedroom — one of comeuppance for the man he despised.

She pushed open the door, and the room unfolded before her. It smelled musty from being closed for the winter, and the white cloths that covered the armchairs and the dresser were still in place, but the bed, a four-poster in English mahogany, sat in its heavy glory against the east wall, its fine cotton spread and sheets reflecting the candlelight.

She carefully removed the dust cover from the night table, revealing an oil lamp and two books of maps. The dust spread through the light and settled on the floor as she lit the lamp from the candle's flame.

Past the window, the cresting waves on

Broadhaven Bay were barely visible against the pervasive dark. She opened the west window to let in the fresh breeze and to clear the must from the air. Having nothing else to do, she lay down on the bed, put her feet up, hardly noticing the heavy drowsiness that overtook her from the day's events. The cool ocean air brushed over her face. How wonderful the evening was! She had a bit of happiness — a wedding night filled with joy even as the famine raged across Ireland.

When she awoke, Rory was sitting next to her on the bed, cupping her head with his strong hands.

She rose up to meet him, but he stopped her with a gentle touch. She lay back and gazed into his face. He had shaved! She brushed her fingers across his smooth cheeks. The candlelight played across his face, and the flickering shadows only made him more handsome in her mind.

"I couldn't be kissing you with whiskers," he said, and intertwined the fingers of his right hand with hers.

"I'm glad you did," she said, and then sighed with contentment. His skin smelled of soap and fresh water. "I'm also glad we waited until our wedding night."

With his left hand, he slowly undid the

buttons on his white shirt, revealing his chest and stomach. "There's no need to wait now." He kissed her and then positioned his body over hers.

"We'll be careful," she said, touching a finger to his lips.

"Yes."

He pressed against her, and the white curtains across the west window flapped inward from a sudden gust. The candle sputtered out, sending the room into darkness.

But she didn't care. Her best friend, her lover, her husband, was over her now, and his strength had become part of her. At that moment, all she ever wanted and needed was in this room.

CHAPTER 9

May 1846

The day dawned bright and clear with a light breeze off the Atlantic. The weather was idyllic, but the mood of the Walsh household was anything but placid for the arrival of Sir Thomas Blakely. In the morning, Briana left Rory at their home to help her sister and father at Lear House. Lucinda primped as she and her father dusted and swept the manor.

Her sister rushed from looking glass to looking glass, making sure she appeared her best for her employer's arrival. She even put on the yellow dress patterned with white periwinkles that she had worn when she had arrived from England. She fashioned her hair in a tight bun, applied color to her cheeks and lips, and sought Briana's approval of her appearance, which she gave without reservation.

By mid-afternoon, everyone was looking

up the lane that led to Carrowteige as often as her sister. Lucinda paced, mopping her brow with a perfume-scented handkerchief. Briana wore her brown dress and plain shoes. She had no desire to preen before Sir Thomas and few clothes to wear anyway, all of which hung on wooden pegs on Rory's cabin walls. Now that she had moved in with him, life had taken an even more austere turn, but one that she didn't mind. Now Lear House seemed more like a foreign palace planted on Irish soil than a childhood second home.

Her father looked like a smart servant in his freshly laundered shirt, breeches, and vest. The kitchen, nearly depleted of food, had been washed and scrubbed until its table and chairs glowed from the polish. All the furniture had been dusted, the pillows fluffed, the windows thrown open to allow fresh air to circulate throughout the musty rooms. And, of most importance to the owner, a year's worth of ledgers were stacked in two columns on the library desk for Sir Thomas's perusal.

The starving people, and the families housed by the tenants, had moved on after the last feeding in April. Once Brian had announced that there was no more food, they had slowly disappeared, abandoning their burrows by the side of the lane. There was no uprising, no grumbling, only a great sadness that dispersed the people in silence after many thanks had been given. Rory had made the trip to Belmullet and secured supplies that they hoped would feed more, but there was only enough to nourish the family and a few others. The last few days of peace had allowed Briana to put the famine out of her mind and settle in at the cottage with Rory.

A few minutes after three, they heard the clack of hooves and the grinding of wheels in the rutted lane.

Lucinda, who had been fanning herself near one of the windows, started in her chair. "He's here!" The excitement in her voice rippled through the air.

Brian rushed from the library to the entrance. Lucinda led the way as they stepped into the afternoon sun. The carriage, a shiny black rig with dappled brown-and-white horses, gleamed in the light. The shades were lifted, allowing them to see into the compartment. When the rig came to a stop, Sir Thomas leaned forward in his seat. Even Briana admired his handsome figure. Nine months had passed since she had last seen him.

He was tall, of medium build, neither

corpulent nor thin, with ruddy cheeks despite the overall whiteness of his skin. His black sideburns spread out in a full brush near his chin. His lips were topped by a dark mustache; his hair, a rich obsidian, was thick and parted to the right in a full sweep. Upon seeing them, Sir Thomas's mouth parted in a thin smile that was more an acknowledgment of his arrival than an expression of cordiality.

The driver leapt from his seat and extended the steps under the carriage door. Sir Thomas alighted from the coach with a confident gait, hat and cane in hand. He gave a curt nod and then stood waiting their acknowledgment. Briana watched as her father bowed and Lucinda curtsied.

She returned the nod, a bit flustered by the exchange of protocol. She no longer wanted to simper before him, nor was she awed by his social standing. A quiet reserve had grown inside her regarding the owner. Her attitude toward him had changed since she had seen him last, partly from her marriage to Rory and his distaste for the English and partly because of her sighting in Westport of food heading to England that could be used to feed the starving Irish. Twenty sacks of Indian corn transported from Belmullet to the store at Broadhaven Bay was all Rory had been able to secure. Now they were learning to cook and prepare it for the tenants at Lear House.

Sir Thomas stepped forward. He wore gray-striped pants, a white shirt, a blue ascot, and vest, all embraced by a waistcoat that accented his slim figure.

"I'm always happy to be here," he said, and then breathed in deeply. "Insufferable journey, however. The voyage from Liverpool is trying, but spending the night in Belmullet can drive one to distraction." He handed his hat and cane to her father and walked to Lucinda. Her sister held out her hand, and the landlord kissed it lightly. He then turned to Briana, who made no move of her own. Sir Thomas sloughed off the slight with a shift of his eyes that caught her attention. The landlord, with his glance, had *taken her in* — if she had to describe the feeling she would have said that he *admired* her, perhaps even *desired* her, but the look was brief and could have been misunderstood. Surely Lucinda had noticed her employer's distraction and would bring up the matter later.

The driver and Brian unloaded two trunks from the back of the carriage and hauled them into the entry. With the driver's help, the trunks were hoisted up the stairs to the

Master's bedroom. Brian soon returned, and the driver was sent off after words from Sir Thomas. A few tenants watched as the carriage jangled toward the village.

Sir Thomas, having taken his cane from the hall, settled in a wing chair parallel to the window. He looked out across the green lawn to the thin line of waves cresting in the bay. After contemplating the view for a minute he turned to Lucinda, who had taken a seat opposite him. "You're looking well." He swiveled the cane between his palms. "In fact, you're all looking well, despite what I've been hearing about Ireland. I almost decided not to pay a visit this year . . . but Manchester can be quite inhospitable in the summer. Besides . . ." He looked at Briana, who sat next to her father on the sofa. "I cannot always be an absentee landlord. I have much business to discuss with your father."

Brian nodded but said nothing.

"So how goes Lear House?" Sir Thomas asked, lifting a brow. "How are my tenants?"

An awkward silence spread across the room. Lucinda looked past the owner to the bay. Brian stared ahead as if unsure how to answer.

Briana broke the stillness. "People are starving —"

The words had barely come out of her mouth before her sister held up her hand. "Let's not burden Sir Thomas with unfortunate details."

"Of course, but we must be honest," Briana replied.

"Boorishness can be confused with honesty, sister. There's time enough to discuss such issues later. Sir Thomas must be tired from his journey."

Blood rushed to her face. She wanted to slap the smug look off her sister but shrunk back in deference to her father, who looked at a loss for words. If Rory had been in the room he wouldn't have let Lucinda get away with her pompous attitude.

Her father sighed. "We all could be better, but Lucinda is correct — we can discuss it later, after you've had a chance to go over the accounts."

"Yes, I am tired," Sir Thomas admitted as his face brightened slightly. "I've asked the Andersons, the Rogerses, and the Wards to join me early next week. They will be staying for a month or so. I'd like you all to join me at tea tonight so we can discuss how best to make them feel comfortable."

"The Wards?" Lucinda asked.

"Yes, they'll be bringing their three sons — the ones for whom you are governess. I assured the Wards that you would have no problem continuing the boys' studies while they were here — with a stipend, of course."

Lucinda put on a brave face, but Briana could tell that her sister was seething under her forced smile because she wanted only to capture the landlord's attentions while he was in residence, not tutor three boys.

Her father's face turned white and sullen. "Certainly we could use the money, but I wonder if inviting guests is the wisest course of action. . . . Begging your pardon, Sir Thomas, but the times are . . ." His voice faded in the air.

"Are what?" Sir Thomas asked with the feigned innocence of a child who had never sensed peril.

"Dangerous," her father said.

"Really? It can't be as bad as some in the government make it out to be."

"It's worse," Briana said, "but we wouldn't want to ruin your evening meal." The acid in her voice burst through.

Sir Thomas paid no attention to the jibe. "Yes, tea is important. I'll head upstairs for a rest. What am I being served tonight?"

"A surprise," Briana said.

"Well, whatever it is, I've worked up an appetite. I look forward to it. See you at six o'clock." He rose from his chair and walked as far as the stairs. "Do we have any of that good port left?"

Brian turned to him. "Yes, but we have an even better bottle of French brandy," he said, referring to the remains of the bottle given to them by the Captain at Westport.

"Excellent." Sir Thomas climbed the stairs, his heels clicking on the stone.

"Welcome back, sir," Brian said to no one in particular as the Master's bedroom door shut. "Lear House is not what it used to be." He rested his chin on his intertwined fingers. "How am I going to tell him that we hardly have enough food for us let alone three other families?"

Lucinda, her eyes downcast after hearing Sir Thomas's summer plans, shook her head and settled back in her chair.

Briana knew what she would have to ask her husband, and she dreaded the question.

"You want me to slaughter my pig for an Englishman?" Rory pitched his soiled shirt upon the straw bedding. "I'd rather cut its throat and feed it to my starving brethren — and that's just what I'll do to keep him from enjoying a feast."

"Well," Briana replied, "be stubborn and bring his wrath down upon our heads. He'll find out soon enough how little food we have. We can roast the animal and make meals for days."

"He's going to be here for months," Rory snapped.

"Yes, and you can't avoid him all that time. Sooner or later, he'll find out that we're married and that you're part of the Walsh family." She wanted to tell him that more English families were coming for the summer but decided against it considering his present state.

Rory collapsed on the straw and covered his face with his hands, exhausted from helping his brother catch and preserve fish. In Jarlath's canoe, they had taken advantage of the tranquil day in the inlets north of the bay.

She sat beside him and put her arm around his shoulders. "You smell like fish," she said, hoping to bring a smile to his face. The salty tang of the catch and the rich ocean brine that saturated his body filled her nostrils.

He pulled away from her, in no mood for gentle jests. "*You* can tell him we're married. I'm in no need of his company — this evening or any other day."

"How about a fish?" she asked. "A large one that will serve four of us — just for this evening. Sir Thomas is in for much bad news tomorrow. A good meal might soften the blow he's about to take."

"Ask Jarlath if he can spare a fish," Rory said gruffly. "I'll eat some of the Indian corn you've prepared."

Her mouth puckered at the thought of eating the corn meal. What she, and for that matter all of Ireland, wouldn't give for a good crop of potatoes! The next crop, if it didn't fail, wouldn't be in until August, a month that couldn't arrive too soon as far as she was concerned. But aside from this day, and a few other splendid ones, when the sun shone clear and bright in a cloudless sky and the ocean reflected the blue serenity of the heavens, the spring had been a dull gray with uninterrupted bouts of rain. The relentless downpours and the muddy heath were enough to crush the brightest spirits.

The Indian corn gave the tenants no comfort, either. Rory and Brian had distributed the bags after hauling them from the store. They had been given freely, only for the recipients to find the meal unpalatable. The kernels took days to soften, hours to cook, and disintegrated to an unappetizing mush. Briana had asked many of the tenants' wives if they knew a good way to cook the corn, but no one did. Most of the women had only cooked the potato in various ways. The meal was as foreign to them as something they might find on the other side of the world.

Realizing she was getting nowhere with her husband, Briana kissed him on the forehead and said, "I'll take care of your clothes in the morning. Please don't be angry with me. I need to be there for my father . . . and sister."

Rory nodded and stretched out on the straw. She closed the door and walked along the back of the cabin. The pig was settled happily in the mud by the makeshift fence.

Jarlath was outside his home, adding fresh water and salt to an oak tray filled with fish.

"Your brother is in a bad mood," she said. "He said I might ask you for a fish to prepare for the landlord's supper."

Jarlath and Rory shared many of the same physical characteristics: broad shoulders, sturdy legs, and weathered hands that affirmed their years of hard work in the fields. Lifting the tray, he asked, "For the Englishman?"

Briana nodded. An unexpected wave of shame swept over her.

"Rory was sullen the whole day," Jarlath said. "It's a waste to be so sad on a rare day like this." He pointed west toward the sinking sun, which threaded the sky with translucent yellow beams.

"Please, Jarlath, I've no time to discuss our moods. I understand how you and Rory feel about Sir Thomas, but he has kept my family alive for many years. I need something to feed this man, or the devil will find a new home in Lear House tonight."

He held the tray in front of her. "Take your pick. Salt is scarce. I can't save the lot for long; we have to cook them within the day."

Briana had cooked fish a few times in her life — they were rarely the main meal. She didn't enjoy the gutting and cleaning, but she had no choice this evening.

Jarlath pointed to the catch. "Mackerel — we couldn't haul in cod and pollock."

She looked over the array of silver fish with the black stripes running vertically down their sides. One of them seemed as if it might feed four people. "I'll take this one." She lifted it and held it underneath the tail fin. The smaller fins leading up to the tail poked into her fingers. The fish wiggled in her hands.

"Be careful," Jarlath said. "Sometimes you think they're dead and they're not."

"Thank you." She ran to the road, then to the kitchen door, all the while trying to hold the slippery creature in her hands. She was glad the kitchen was empty. She didn't need her father or sister standing over her shoulder, souring her mood more than it was.

Lucinda declined to help Briana cook, wanting nothing to do with the chores that might stain her dress or cause her hands to smell like fish. However, her sister offered to serve, which Briana felt was a bit of a victory.

She scooped up the sizzling fillets with a wooden spatula and spooned them onto the delft plates. The preparation had been simple; they were coated with some of the remaining flour, pan fried in oil, and drizzled with buttermilk. They smelled strong and meaty, and Briana wondered if Sir Thomas would have an appetite for them. He would have to; otherwise, he would go hungry like the rest of County Mayo. Few supplies were left in the kitchen. Another week of the landlord in the house and the food would be gone.

"Is there nothing else to serve?" Lucinda asked.

Briana flinched at her sister's presumption. She and Rory had been reduced to eating the imported meal, while her father and sister survived on the remaining grains and seed potatoes left in the larders. Bugs and rats had reduced even those stores despite their best efforts to keep them at bay.

"I can put out some of the Indian corn mush, if that's what you'd like," she told Lucinda. A smile rose on her face. "What a grand idea. Sir Thomas should see what the rest of us eat."

"No," her sister responded with a look of dismay. "He'll be happy with the fish. Perhaps a nice breakfast tomorrow."

"With what? The flour is almost gone. *I* might be able to scrape together oatmeal. Remember I have a husband to feed as well."

Lucinda turned, her back quivering. From her position at the table, Briana heard the sobs coming from the other side of the room. She walked to her sister and put her hands on her shoulders. "Come now," she said, "the fish will get cold. We'll get by." Even as she said the words, she imagined that life might become more difficult.

"You needn't point out that *I* have no husband." Lucinda, her face puffy from tears, faced her. "What will we do? Lear House has no food, no money. We'll lose the only home we've ever known." She placed her hands over her face and moaned.

Briana dabbed her sister's eyes with her sleeve.

"I've tried so hard not to give in to fear, but ever since those *starving* people arrived . . ." Lucinda took out her handkerchief and wiped it across her face. "I must compose myself. . . . Sir Thomas can't see me this way. I must look a fright."

"You look fine, sister." Briana's eyes welled with tears because she understood her sister's sorrow was about more than a lack of companionship. Lucinda was deeply concerned about their welfare.

Briana shook her head and tried to think of the fine spring day outside, anything to take her mind off the famine, but the memory of the starving came back to her, particularly the boy who had died in his mother's arms. "I still see their faces. I even dream about them. But we can't let fear stop us. We must be strong."

Lucinda picked up two of the plates. Briana took the others, and they carried them to the dining room, where Sir Thomas and her father were already waiting. The landlord sat at one end of the table, Brian at the other. The bottle of French brandy the sea captain had given them sat in the center between two oil lamps. Judging from the smile on his face, Sir Thomas had already downed a few drinks.

"Much better than poteen — that rotgut you call liquor," the owner said as they walked in. Both men rose from their seats. Sir Thomas cut a striking figure in his black waistcoat, breeches, and boots. Again, as it had earlier in the day, his glance lingered over Briana as he sat down. She placed the fish in front of him and took her place on the north side of the table, while Lucinda served her father and then sat opposite Briana.

Sir Thomas stroked his mustache and asked, "This was the surprise?"

Briana nodded. "We're lucky to have it."

Her father bowed his head and muttered a quick prayer in English asking for a blessing on "the food we are about to receive."

Briana kept her left eye on the landlord, watching him as he fiddled with his fork. He didn't respond in any manner to the prayer but kept his eyes open and refrained from offering an "Amen."

Lucinda poured water for everyone at the table. A tepid evening light filtered in through the dining room window as the oil lamps stood ready.

Sir Thomas bit into the fish and then put his fork upside down on his plate as if he was finished with the meal. He looked across the table to Brian. "How has Lear House fared in all this business?"

Her father straightened in his chair, his mouth twitching as he searched for a response.

Lucinda answered before her father. "We need your help."

Briana shifted in her seat, shocked at her sister's words.

Brian raised his hand and spoke in a tone of gentle reproach. "I will speak for the family, daughter." He paused. "Sir Thomas, you haven't seen the suffering we have. I could describe the horrible times we've witnessed, but I fear you wouldn't believe me, not having seen it yourself."

"Go on," Sir Thomas said, and took a sip of brandy, "but get to the point."

"The failure of the potato crop last year has precipitated an unparalleled disaster in County Mayo," Brian continued. "You saw nothing of the suffering when you arrived in Ireland?"

The owner picked up his fork and scraped it over the mackerel, then placed the utensil on the edge of the plate. "One can rarely relax on the crossing from Liverpool to Westport. The ocean is often rough, the wind still chilly this time of year. I spent most of my time in my cabin. During my night in Westport, before departing for Belmullet, I was unaware of any trouble."

"You were escorted from the ship to your lodging and then back to the quay?" Brian asked.

"Of course." He looked askance at her father, as if the question was unnecessary. "After arriving in Belmullet, I got into the carriage. I fell asleep almost immediately until we were well away from the port. I looked out on the bog, which holds no particular beauty for an Englishman, and then the heath, which flows in a colorless, undulating line. Finding nothing to hold my interest, I turned my attention to a book."

"So you saw no people along the road, living in burrows, emaciated, starving? Or lines of folk in Westport, clamoring for food? Did you smell the stench of rotting corpses?"

"Father, really!" Horror spread across Lucinda's face.

"I do remember seeing a crowd of people hovering near the inn as I arrived in Westport," Sir Thomas replied casually and smiled. "But that's not unusual in Ireland, is it? You Irishmen are always looking for a drink." He put his thumb and forefinger under his nose and pinched his nostrils. "I also carry snuff to protect me from country smells. It's quite pleasant, really. You should try it."

Briana's neck bristled from a building rage. She fought to keep her anger in check knowing it would be best to do so for her father's sake.

"What *we* have seen is not *usual,*" Brian countered. "I realize now, after hearing you, Sir Thomas, that most Englishmen have no idea of what is taking place here."

The landlord leaned forward over his plate of cold fish. "The Prime Minister has said nothing, nor has, for that matter, our young queen, Victoria. We English have taken to the new way of modern life and industry. The mills and the rails are uniting the disparate regions of our nation. Prosperity seems assured. Yes, we read of rival factions within the government, but it's the usual stuff of politics. Nothing about Ireland has drawn our attention." He smiled with a self-assurance that bordered on a smirk, pushed back in his chair, and studied Brian with cautious eyes. "If you have bad news, get on with it."

Briana looked at the fish on her plate, also cold and untouched. Her appetite was fleeing along with her resolve to hold her tongue.

"When word of the famine arrives, it will

be the Irish who suffer, not the English," her father said. "The laws your government lords over mine are not equitable. They favor one over the other — you don't have to think hard to discern which nation earns the indulgence of the Queen." Her father quaffed his brandy and then started for another. He stopped mid-reach. "No, I want to be sober when I say these words." He put his glass on the table. "Lear House is bankrupt."

Sir Thomas stiffened, the ruddy cheeks drained to a pale ash, and the swaggering confidence he had carried in his demeanor softened.

Briana, buoyed by her father's words, could hold back no longer. "We have no money and only a few days of food left in this kitchen."

Her father raised his hand, signaling her not to speak. "What my daughter says is true. You are welcome to review the accounts tomorrow. All will be laid out before you. Every tenant on the estate is in arrears. The grain has been sold, the potatoes are gone. The tenants have little to eat. Lear House has been lucky — we have been among the last to see the effects of the famine, but soon we will be as desperate as the rest of Mayo."

"Why was I not . . . informed?" His austere expression transformed into one of disbelief.

"Perhaps you were . . . by two letters," Briana said.

"I don't know what you're talking about," Sir Thomas snapped.

From his angry expression, Briana surmised that either the landlord was unaware of the letters she and her sister had sent, or he had been caught in a lie.

"You weren't informed for precisely the reason I told you," Brian continued. "We were the last to know. Over the past few months the famine has gotten worse rather than better. We prayed that God would look upon us with fortune, but that has not happened. The spring has been wet. Some say the blight comes from the rain and wind. If the summer is rainy and cold, the August crop may fail as well. It will be a disaster for Ireland."

Sir Thomas rose from his chair and walked to the large window that looked east toward the sloping heath and the village. Briana followed his line of sight as well. Beyond the lawn, the tenant farms concealed most of the potato ridges, now cradling the young crop. In the distance, the surrounding hills turned greenish black in the fading light.

The color reminded her of turbulent summer storms that had lashed the estate with pitchforks of lightning, blasts of thunder, and torrents of rain. The owner stood silent for several minutes with his back to them before he turned.

"If Lear House has no money, I'm afraid *you* are in trouble." He directed his words at Brian, a hint of menace in his eyes. "There are not enough funds to support this estate and the house in Manchester. If you cannot find the money, you will lose your home — it's as simple as that. I will have to vacate Lear House and eject its inhabitants."

Lucinda's face turned a sickly gray as she reached for her water and gulped it down.

Briana looked at her meal, still untouched, and then at her hands. They were not as pretty or as supple as they were when she was younger. She tried to think of anything but the landlord's words: cleaning the cottage, feeding the pig, preparing corn meal, mending Rory's breeches and shirt, helping her father at Lear House. But her mind was ablaze with dire thoughts and few words.

Sir Thomas had issued an ultimatum — one she thought unfair after the years they had given him. Dirt had collected under her nails. She'd had no time to clean them after preparing the mackerel. Her fingers grew cold in her lap.

"I've had enough to digest for one night," Sir Thomas said. He moved to his chair, gripping its back with his hands. "I bid you a good night. I'll look at the books first thing in the morning — after breakfast." His thin sardonic smile brought some color back to his cheeks. "If we have enough food for breakfast."

Lucinda, who had kept her head bowed during the conversation, looked up and nodded. "I'm sorry, Sir Thomas. I hope this in no way affects our working relationship."

He breezed by the table, saying as he passed, "That's a subject for another day." He stopped at the door and turned back to them. "Oh, there is the matter of my guests. I suggest we find a way to feed them when they arrive. Until tomorrow." He turned into the hall.

Her father stroked his chin and then said to Briana, "Thank you, daughter, for preparing this meal. It shouldn't go to waste. We can divide Sir Thomas's portion."

They ate in silence as the finality of the owner's words sank in.

CHAPTER 10

From his vantage point in a hollow to the east of Lear House, Rory watched as the Englishman rose from his chair and moved to the dining room window. What was going through Sir Thomas's mind? Crouched in the shadows near a makeshift fence, Rory wasn't close enough to judge the owner's mental state, but the landlord's motionless figure revealed his displeasure.

Rory moved like an Irish fox, taking advantage of the deep shadows cast by the setting sun. He wished to steal closer to see a dinner he considered an exercise in forced opulence. Imagine a feast for the Englishman while his countrymen starved! But time was short — soon even Lear House would be in similar peril. He tried to rid his mind of that troubling thought, but the famine's inevitability came crushing down upon him.

Perhaps he had been too hard on his wife

and her wish to keep the landlord happy, but *damn it all,* why cater to the whims of the oppressor? He and many other Mollies believed that Irish silence and English law were conspiring to starve the country. But how close would disaster come? What if the tenants were evicted? Would revenge, even violence, be visited upon Sir Thomas and the Walsh family? He remembered the note tacked to the manor door and the horrifying heights that his imagination had taken him: the burning manor, the bodies of Brian and his daughters hung from the cornices. But Briana was his wife now, and things were different. He would protect her at the cost of his life — that was as certain as the tides in Broadhaven Bay.

He had sheltered his wife from something else as well. His trip to Belmullet to arrange for the last supply delivery had so nearly broken his spirit, he had confided in his father-in-law when he returned.

"Are you ill?" Brian had asked after Rory found him alone in the cottage.

Rory shook his head. "What I've seen . . . I've barely the words to talk about it." He lowered his head, rested in a chair, and sighed. The thought of telling Brian what he had seen exhausted him.

"Tell me," Brian said. "You made arrangements for the Indian corn. What else is troubling you?"

Rory lifted his head and looked at him, ashamed that he was on the verge of tears. Brian was a tough man — he had seen death and disease and many bouts of misfortune during his life — but Rory was certain the man had never seen anything like what he had witnessed.

"The money you gave me from your savings is gone," Rory said. "I had to use it all to get the twenty sacks. The Captain and the dragoons each took their cut." He gazed at Brian through damp eyes. "I nearly worked the pony to death to get past the starving along the road. They reached for me, clawed at me, begging for food.

"They're pouring out of the hills looking for anything to save them. At first I couldn't tell what was speckling the road among the ash and alder trees, but when I stopped my horse, I discovered the truth. Bodies lay in burrows, scattered in the bogs, dogs eating them. The stench . . . even the wind couldn't knock it away." He slumped in a chair, surrendering to despair. "Promise me that you'll never tell your daughters what I've told you. We must spare them from more sadness."

Brian winced but nodded in support of

the promise.

Good. Brian needed to know the truth, to know what he was implicitly, silently, supporting by earning his livelihood as the landlord's agent.

Brian crossed himself.

"You know what will happen next," Rory said. "The pig will go, then the farm animals, then all the food will be gone. If we can't fish, what will we eat? Seaweed? A frog? Birds' eggs? There'll be nothing left." He lowered his head again, averting his eyes from his father-in-law, certain that no man had answers to his questions.

Brian got up from his chair and put his hands on Rory's shoulders. He had never felt so helpless, and he welcomed his father-in-law's comforting touch. "Come to Lear House and see what I've done. I've shored up the larder so the rats can't get into it," he said. It was a small gesture designed to take his mind off his troubles.

He blinked away the memory of that awful trip as he watched Sir Thomas walk from the window to the dining room door, then vanish after turning the corner.

Rory rubbed his arms and trod down the lane toward the bay. From there, he could get a better view of the Lear House façade. The chilly air bit at his body as it quickened off the Atlantic. He watched as an oil lamp moved across the large window above the center of the house — the owner's bedroom.

As he watched the light, he was surprised at the angry, violent thoughts that popped into his head. How easy it would be to fire a shot into the window. Everything would be over. The Walsh family would be free of their controlling landlord and with his death their responsibility to Lear House. The notion frightened him, and he sprinted down the lane. He couldn't believe he was thinking like an assassin, a common murderer, capable of acts he'd never have imagined in more tranquil times.

"Murder can't be that easy," he said to the air. "It will only bring trouble down upon us all."

"Who wants more trouble?" The question came out of the gloom. Rory pivoted and found Connor Donlon standing a few yards away near the path that led to the beach.

Rory bit his tongue for thinking aloud.

Connor strode up beside him. "So, the *Master* has arrived."

"My only *master* is God," Rory said. "I don't want to give the landlord more power over us than he already has . . . and that he has in his capacity to evict."

Connor's face reflected the pink afterglow

of the setting sun, shadows darkening the circles beneath his eyes and his sunken cheekbones. The strain of feeding a family of six had taken its toll upon his friend. "Have you been eating?" Rory asked.

His friend didn't answer immediately but looked toward a potato ridge that extended down from a farm. Connor bent over, swiped his hand across the ridge, and muttered what sounded like a prayer. He looked up at Rory. "I pray that these tubers come up healthy and strong by August. They look as if they may." He pointed to the young leaves, green amongst the black sod.

"I hope you're right," he responded, trying to erase the skepticism from his voice.

Connor straightened. "My wife and children come first."

Rory had never known Connor to approach anything from a position of weakness. Now that the famine had seized the estate, all the tenants were struggling for their lives. He understood the man's willingness to make a sacrifice, but he also knew that Sheila and the children couldn't manage without the family provider. *More trouble, more death. When will it end?*

They watched from afar as the lamp crossed the window a second time. Even though the shades were drawn, they could make out the landlord's shadowy form.

"How easy it would be," Connor said to the air.

"Don't speak ill," Rory said, culpable of the same thought minutes earlier. He shivered, knowing their minds were following a similar murderous path.

"It won't be me, but it would be easy," Connor said. He put his hand on Rory's shoulder. "I saw you walking down the hill. I came to remind you of the meeting tomorrow night."

"I haven't forgotten." He wondered how the discussion might differ from previous meetings now that Sir Thomas had taken up summer residence at the manor. Would the threat to Lear House gather momentum? He looked toward the manor, where the stone was turning from gray to black in the gathering dusk, its windows dull and blank now that the lamps had been extinguished.

"Were you invited to dinner?" Connor asked.

Rory groaned. "I had no stomach for it." He shook hands with his friend. "I've got to get home before my wife. I craved a walk — that's all."

Connor left his side. "Whatever you say, my friend. I'll see you tomorrow at the meeting place."

They walked together in silence from the bay and headed east along the hillside until they parted.

Brian Walsh sat in the chair facing what was, on most days, his desk. He threaded his fingers together and absentmindedly rotated his thumbs. These were the worst hours he had ever experienced, with the possible exception of the day his wife died. Even that horrible time was tempered by the knowledge that she had been delivered from the pain and suffering of her illness. The outpouring of grief from the smallholders, from friends in Carrowteige, the soothing words from Father O'Kirwin, had also eased that day's sting. As far as he could tell, today held no such promise.

Even breakfast had been a disaster. The landlord had expressed his displeasure at the tiny oatcakes he had been served a few hours before. There was hardly enough sugar and butter to make them palatable, he told Lucinda, his reluctant server. Briana had returned to her husband after making the cakes.

Sir Thomas now sat behind the desk, leaning forward, his eyes moving over the neatly formed lines of figures entered by Brian under the categories of land, occupiers, annual value, rate, arrears, totals, and observations. He closed one ledger and opened another. After a brief time, he shut it as well.

The stale odor of aging paper wafted through the library. The books were already old when he had started working on them, passed down as they were from the previous agent.

"Most distressing." The landlord sighed and leaned back in his chair.

"The point is . . ." Brian felt it almost unnecessary to say more. The landlord had already told him what would happen if the rents weren't paid. Why fight the inevitable? He screwed up his courage and continued, "What can be done? We will take the necessary steps to save Lear House."

The owner pushed back his chair and studied the crammed oak bookcases that lined the room. Brian took in the profile of his employer and the erect posture of his authority. With a full head of black, curly hair; sideburns extending to muttonchops; and a sharp, aquiline nose, the landlord did indeed cut an aristocratic figure. He understood how Lucinda found him handsome and charming, but considering her lineage as the daughter of an Irish land agent, and the seemingly endless bounty of young, highborn ladies who filled Manchester and its countryside, her chances of marriage to Sir Thomas were slim. But who was to say where a heart could make its home? Witness the marriage of Briana to a tenant farmer. He was an organized man, and over the course of the year, life had become messier than he wished. As one grew older, living was supposed to be simpler, not studded with complications that led to matters of life and death.

Sir Thomas picked up the quill pen and tapped its feather against his cheek. He retained this position for several minutes, keeping Brian in suspense while awaiting an answer to his question.

Finally, the landlord turned slightly, his face framed in the window's half light, and spoke. "I'm afraid there's nothing to be done. The house will have to close at summer's end. Perhaps even before that. I pray that somehow I may extend courtesies to my guests, but what are we to eat when there is no food to be found? If I'm lucky, I can wrangle something from the local Constabulary or a ship at Belmullet. Of course, that will require money." He thrust the quill toward Brian in an accusing manner. "I hold you responsible for letting the accounts fall to such a disastrous level. If you had been doing your job, this would not have happened."

In dismay, Brian stared at the scarred oak floor.

The landlord came up with questions of his own. "How *do* we get food? How do we support the estate when there is no money to be had?"

Flushed from the accusation that he was responsible for the misfortune, he took some time to construct an answer before responding. "Surely I cannot be blamed for an act of God. I assume a plan for food applies only to you and your guests? Are there no extra funds from Manchester to support Lear House?" He thought of the landlord's guests savoring fine dishes while the tenants starved.

Sir Thomas dampened a bitter laugh. "Do you have any idea how much it costs to support my home in England? Lear House is a luxury. Manchester is my legacy and heritage, as well as the employer for a staff of seven. They are indispensable to me. I'd heard of other owners closing their homes in Ireland, but I'd hoped it wouldn't come to that. I had no reason to believe it would, but now I see the truth of the matter. There is no other choice."

Brian looked up, stone-faced, unable to

counter his employer's argument. The thought of losing the manor crushed him, as if an unseen weight had tumbled upon him. He had devoted his life to the manor — the estate and the surrounding lands were the only home he had ever known. From his birth in the village, to his employment by Sir Thomas's father, through his marriage, the birth of his daughters, and the death of his dear wife, Lear House had stood witness to it all. Now it was ending, and with it, the life he had always known.

He stared with damp eyes at his employer.

Sir Thomas rose from the desk. "If there is nothing to be done, you will continue to work until the time comes to close Lear House."

Briana could not stop thinking about how badly the conversation with the landlord had gone the night before. Her father was at his wits' end; her sister was crushed by the owner's ultimatum and the prospect of governing three children while the landlord entertained his guests. She was also concerned about her husband, who had greeted her coolly when she arrived at the cabin after helping clear and clean the dishes at Lear House the previous evening. He was no happier this morning when he found out that she had to cook the landlord's break-fast.

She desperately wanted to rid her mind of turmoil, and a walk after breakfast was the best medicine she could think of. However, her love of walking was tempered by the crumbling burrows of the starving who had crowded the lane less than a month before. There were no dying people now, but their suffering remained foremost in her mind.

The day was cool, the clouds the color of pale slate. Fortunately, it had not begun to rain, and she occupied her mind by picking light yellow primrose, brilliant yellow flag, and the white fragrant blossoms of haw-thorn. She gathered them in a reed basket and was on her way back to the cabin when she spotted Sir Thomas striding toward her on the path leading up from the sandy bay.

"I've been searching for you," he said, casting a lingering gaze over her body. But the carnal stare disappeared as quickly as she noticed it.

She had no desire to speak to the landlord and held her tongue. Her sister saw the obvious in Sir Thomas: his good looks, money, and property; all obliterated, in Bri-ana's opinion, by a grandiose proclivity for privilege. Sadly, Lucinda would be happy with him for a time — until he abandoned her for the arms of a mistress. She imagined him secretly sweeping his lover up a grand staircase in Manchester while Lucinda, blissfully unaware of his doings, sat alone in the dining room fretting about the perfect china service for her next tea party. She loved her sister, but she knew how vain and pompous she could be, faults that would tie her blindly to the landlord.

Briana waited for Sir Thomas to speak.

"The flowers are beautiful," he finally said. "Are they adornments for your father's cottage?"

He sounded almost civil. "No," she replied, a bit embarrassed by her timidity. She shook it off, realizing that the landlord knew nothing about her marriage to Rory. "They're going in a small vase in our cabin."

His eyes narrowed, and he gave her a questioning look. "*Your* cabin?" He put his hands in the pockets of his blue waistcoat. For a moment, he looked like a child who had lost a toy.

"Yes. I guess my father didn't tell you." She decided to walk on; he could either follow or remain behind.

He caught up and walked beside her. "Your father and I talked about many things — mostly unpleasant — but he never mentioned that you had moved out of the cottage."

Briana turned, and the wind caught her hair, blowing a strand over her eye. She tucked it behind her ear. "I married Rory Caulfield some weeks ago. We live in the cabin near the lane." She pointed up the path to her home, whose thatched roof was barely visible.

The landlord didn't miss a step. Briana had no idea whether she had shocked him or merely entertained him. He seemed unperturbed, judging from his gait and expression. They strolled a few yards along the lane.

"I don't believe I've met him."

She repressed an exasperated sigh. "I believe you've seen him — once or twice. You probably don't remember, of course."

He dismissed the rebuke with a smile. "Well, I offer my best wishes for a long and bountiful marriage." He extended his arm in a gallant gesture.

Briana hesitated, unsure whether to accept his courtesy, but then relented, thinking there was no reason to be rude; in fact, some civility on her part might benefit Lear House. She hooked her arm through his, but he withdrew it, kissing the crown of her hand. As his lips touched her skin, she longed for the gesture to be over. His fingers chilled her as much as his lips. She excused herself with a curt, "Thank you."

They stopped near the cabin, and she waved to Rory and Jarlath, who were kneeling next to a potato ridge. Beyond them, a farmer was mending a thatched roof while his wife handed him the rushes. Rory returned her wave, but with an obvious distaste she could discern even from her distance.

"I have a favor to ask of you," the landlord said. The wind ruffled his hair, and he shook his head as if savoring the breeze. "I do love it here. It's a shame that I may have to close Lear House until this nasty business is over."

She bristled at his threat to close the manor and his audacity to ask for a favor in the same breath. "You act as if you have no choice," she responded.

"I don't. I can't support two households, particularly one that is empty of funds — and food."

"Nothing can be done? Can't you sell off land in England, or take a loan against your home?"

He chuckled. "And throw good money after bad? Absolutely not. Consider my position, Briana." He gazed at Rory and Jarlath and the other tenants working the fields. "My grandfather, my father, and I have supported this land as our birthright, but times have changed. What was once a modest proposition has now become expensive to maintain. And with a crop failure, there seems to be no alternative." He brushed his hand through his hair. "I've been fair, but I can't be faulted for the negligence of tenants to keep their obligations. Sadly, I think Lear House's days may come to an end."

"I can think of nothing else." She looked down at the flowers in the basket, some already withering.

"I'm sorry," he said, and looked genuinely glum. "If I could think of something to save Lear House I would." His lips parted in a narrow smile. "But about my favor . . ."

Briana nodded.

"The Andersons, the Rogerses, and the Wards are coming at the end of the week. There's no telegraphy in this part of the world and no way of reaching them by post before they depart. They will arrive, and I will be entertaining guests in a house with limited food." His mouth crinkled in concern.

She understood his plight but felt little sympathy for him or his society friends. "You could deliver a message to Belmullet and tell your guests to take the next ship back to Liverpool."

His eyes widened with distress. "I would never be able to hold my head up in Manchester if I did that." He clasped his hands. "Your father and I have duties to attend to. Do you know someone who would make the trip to Westport for five pounds, meet with my connections, and bring back the food we'd need?"

Briana gulped, taking in Sir Thomas's words. Five pounds was a fortune for her and Rory. She'd be more than willing to make the trip if she couldn't talk her husband into it. "I can arrange it. Who should we talk to?"

"Either Captains James or Miller. One of them should be in port. Both owe me favors and, I think, would be most happy to fulfill my wishes. If not, there are others. . . . Money talks. Have the supplies shipped to Belmullet and then on to the store."

Briana remembered the lean sea officer Captain James, who had rescued her from the drunken sailor who made unwanted advances.

"Whom do you have in mind for the trip?" Sir Thomas asked.

"My husband and I."

"It's settled then. I suggest you start

tomorrow. Order as much as you can for the next month. Another trip may be required." He pulled twenty pounds from his pocket and handed it to her. "Spend it on supplies — five pounds is for you."

"Expect us back in four days." She pocketed the notes and thought of Lucinda saddled with the household chores. "My sister will not be happy."

Sir Thomas grinned. "I'm sure your father can find a woman to cook and clean for a few days in your absence." He bowed, kissed her hand, and struck off in long strides down the road to Lear House.

She returned home, threw open the door to let in the fresh air, and fussed with the flowers. After cutting the stems, she drew a cup of water from the bucket, poured it into the glass bottle, positioned the flowers, and placed them on the small table. The colors burst forth against the shaded walls, brightening the murky day and her mood. She fingered the note and marveled at her good fortune. Then a question struck her. Why didn't Sir Thomas make his request through her father? The answer seemed obvious — he was looking for her. He *wanted* to see her. That's why he was so kind.

She stepped out of the cabin and peered around the wall. Her husband and Jarlath were walking along the neighboring ridges, inspecting the crop. There was no time to waste; they might start today if she packed what food they could spare and readied the ponies. They could spend the night at the Kilbanes' cottage, as she and Rory had done on their first trip.

She walked up the hill, skirting the conacres, until she found Rory and Jarlath outside a neighbor's hut.

Smiling, they turned and greeted her heartily.

"It's nice to see you both in a good mood," she said.

"Take a look, my love," Rory said, and pointed to an adjacent potato ridge. "We have reason to be in a fine frame of mind."

Briana peered at the mound. Vibrant green leaves had burst forth from the vines — the first sign of a healthy crop. She threw her arms around her husband's shoulders, hugged him, and then blew a kiss to the earth. "This is wonderful, but I have even better news." She pulled the twenty pounds from her pocket and waved it in front of them.

Jarlath whistled. Rory stared at her with his mouth agape.

"Where did you get that?" Rory asked.

She suspected that he knew the answer

but paused to keep him in suspense. She relented after her husband's face soured. "Sir Thomas is entertaining guests and wants us to make a trip to Westport to secure food." She held the notes close to his face. "Five pounds is ours."

Jarlath whistled again.

"Just for going?" Rory asked.

Briana nodded. "How soon can you get the ponies ready?"

"In an hour or so."

"I'll gather supplies," she said, and left them at the ridge to take in the extra bit of good fortune she had added to their day.

Lucinda did not take the news of the journey well, complaining that she would be stuck cooking and cleaning while her sister enjoyed herself in Westport.

"Don't be ridiculous," Briana said to her sister. "You would never make the trip on a pony, let alone enjoy it."

Brian reminded his elder daughter that the road to Westport was lined with sadness and potential danger and that Briana and Rory would be doing the landlord and, thus, Lear House a great favor. After Lucinda continued her complaints, her father assured her that he could find a woman willing to do the cooking — at a cost. The thought of wasting money caused Lucinda to reconsider her position.

For her part, Briana poured corn meal mush into cups and covered them with cheesecloth, placed the few leftover fish fillets in a tin, and wrapped soda bread in napkins. All the food fit into a satchel that Rory could strap to his pony. Supplies were scarce: No cheese was left in the larder, the potato scones had been depleted months ago, and the oat jars were almost empty.

A few minutes after noon, she and Rory were on the horses, the animals' bodies thinner than she had remembered. Because oats and potato slops were scarce, the ponies now grazed on the heath like sheep. Their ribs protruded underneath their mottled coats. Still, the animals took to their natural rhythm through the tussocks, their hooves dodging the watery hazards of the bog. The ponies' muscular strength and the wind pushing at her back exhilarated her.

"Don't push them too hard," Rory yelled at her. "We'll be lucky to make it to Westport." He handled the reins lightly, saying, "The last thing we need is a dead horse." He took a swig from the leather flagon they carried for water.

Crossing the river at the shallows, after allowing the animals to graze and drink, they headed south toward Bangor and the rise of the Nephin Beg. Soon the land sparkled with mist as drizzle from a gray sky peppered their faces. They tightened their caps and stiffened their collars against the cutting wind as they traveled east of the iron-colored waters of Carrowmore Lake. In their favor, the chill from the Atlantic remained at their backs.

The joy of riding soon turned to monotony under the dull sky. The *sceilps* dotted the side of the road as if whole villages had burrowed into holes. Except for the cry of the wind, an eerie calm permeated the hills and bogs along their route. Under the somber clouds, no animals moved and no birds sang as far as they could see and hear. Even the peat-fire smoke that should have been swirling from the hillside huts had disappeared. The world had withdrawn into silence.

For several hours they traveled saying little to each other, more concerned in protecting themselves from the wind and damp than carrying on conversation. When the mist ended briefly and the sky brightened to a light gray, Briana shouted to Rory, "You've been quiet on this trip. In fact, you've been quiet ever since the Master arrived."

Rory slowed beside her and uttered an

audible *ugh.* "I wish you wouldn't bestow that title upon him."

"I understand your dislike of Sir Thomas," she responded, "but like him or not, *Rory Caulfield,* he's the owner and we have to make the best of it. You'd be better served to think of a way we can use him to our advantage rather than exacting revenge, as your Mollies seem hell-bent to do."

Rory's face tightened. "Well, *Briana Caulfield,* I detest what's happening in Ireland and I want to do something about it. Is that wrong?"

"Yes, when it leads to violence." Briana decided not to debate the issue as a chill settled over her.

A few miles down the road as the peaks rose on both sides of them, Rory's face relaxed a bit, his demeanor more open to suggestion as if a thought had struck him. "I'm missing a Molly meeting to do this for the *Master,* but food is more important than talk," he said. "What if you're right? Instead of working against the man, I might 'kill him with kindness,' as the proverb says."

Briana was happy to see this potential shift in her husband's thinking. As the day proceeded, they plotted ways to save the manor, but their talk of quick relief was quelled by the estate's lack of food and funds.

The afternoon had grown long when the Kilbanes' cottage came into view. From their first sighting they knew something was wrong. The dwelling had a deserted look about it — the feeling that one instantly recognizes from a house that's been abandoned.

They brought the horses to a stop on the edge of a boggy woodland. The sparse vegetation surrounding it would be enough to sustain the animals for the night in the absence of grain.

Rory dismounted and walked to the cottage door, which hung at a lopsided angle from the frame. Briana watched anxiously as he peered around it before stepping inside. He disappeared for several minutes before reappearing with a puzzled look.

"They're not here," he said. "It looks as if they haven't been here for some time. The traveler's room is empty too." He rubbed his chin. "Even the dog is gone."

Briana swung off her pony. "Gone?" Her skin crawled with dread.

"Yes. The fire pit is cold and dusty. The place has been ransacked. Empty pots and pans are scattered about, but there's no food."

Something horrible had happened — she was certain of it. Rory led the horses to a stream not far from the road.

Gooseflesh broke out on her arms as she stepped inside. The cottage was just as Rory had described: the table on its side, the cupboard drawers open, the straw beds a jumble of clothes and blankets. The Kilbanes' business of hosting travelers had thrived over the years, but their source of income, through the exchange of goods or money, had dried up with the famine.

The clouds and mist outside made the interior even murkier. She looked for an oil lamp but found none. *Why would the Kilbanes disappear?* She had just asked herself that question when she heard Rory swear behind the cottage. She ran out the door and rounded the corner to the back of the dwelling.

Rory stared at the ground and held up his hand. "Don't come any farther! Don't look!"

But the warning came too late.

The Kilbanes lay on the ground, their bodies decomposing on the damp earth. Frankie's legs had been chewed to the bone by animals. Aideen was stretched on her side, but Briana could see that her lovely face was partially gone — the skull and jaw bones, and teeth, showing through parts in her hair.

Her stomach churned and she fought to keep from retching as she turned away.

"They've been shot," Rory said.

He put his hands on her shoulders as she looked back toward the road on which they had come. Shaking, she longed to be on that road now, heading back to the safety of their cabin and the sanctuary of Lear House.

Rory's voice quivered. "God rest their souls. Probably murdered by robbers who took their food and money."

"Murder," Briana said, and the word ricocheted through her brain.

"Some crazed, starving soul killed them so he could feed himself or his family, I would guess."

"We can't stay here tonight," she said. "How can we sleep in a house where people were murdered?" She shook so violently, her arms fluttered by her sides.

"We can't sleep outside in the cold and damp," he said in a calm voice. "At least in the cottage we can light a fire and eat. We can bring the horses in too." He encircled her in his arms to stop her shivering. "I'll take the bodies into the bog and weigh them down so the animals won't get them."

"I can help," she said, although her heart

wasn't in it. How much of the gruesome work could she take?

"No," Rory said gently as he led her to the door. "Why don't you build a fire and settle us in for the night?"

Tears rose in her eyes. *How had it come to this?* The Kilbanes murdered. She wanted to run as far away as she could from this house, but they had no real choice but to stay.

He kissed her on the cheek and stepped inside the cottage while she waited outside. "If I can find a pair of gloves I'm going to use them."

She gazed at the ponies as she fought to rid the image of the Kilbanes' bodies from her mind. Life had slid into tragedy and nightmare. She'd never known anyone who had been murdered, let alone been near their bodies. Murder was something that happened in Dublin or London, not in County Mayo. Of course, there was plenty of fighting — men took to it like roosters in a yard — but never killing. It was unheard of. For the first time since Rory had shown her the blighted plants, she felt that Lear House might slip from her family's grasp. Everything she loved was coming to an end, and there was little she could do about it. She walked to her pony and stroked his flank. The earthy smell of horse flesh comforted her while the mist pattered down on her cap. At the moment, the animal was all the company she had.

His head bowed, Rory emerged from the cottage with gloves and then disappeared behind its walls.

Rory found the gloves next to the fire pit. He knew that Frankie had used them to dig in the bog, because they were spattered with peat. He put them on as he stared at the bodies, wondering who could have committed such a heinous act.

He placed his shoes on a tussock near the back wall, rolled up his breeches past his ankles, and prepared himself for the unpleasant task of removing the bodies. What if their arms came off in his hands or their legs detached from their sockets because they were in such a state of decay? What if they were swarming with lice or maggots? He forced those unpleasant thoughts from his mind as he grappled with the unpleasant undertaking. There would be no "proper burial." The bog would have to do.

He lifted Frankie's body underneath the arms and hoped for the best. The corpse rose from the ground. He looked away from the man's bloated and gray face, which bore no resemblance to the host who had shared his home and hospitality. Dragging the body across the swampy ground into the shallow waters, and nearly retching from the stench, he found a rivulet that spilled into a wider, deeper pool.

Leaving Frankie, he returned for Aideen. She was lighter, but the body had stiffened into a constricted position. He had to carry her in his arms to the swamp. He deposited the body near her husband's and then went in search of rocks heavy enough to secure the two under the water. Finding them, he placed the rocks on the corpses and watched them sink beneath the flowing water. By the time he was finished, he was sweating from the gruesome work. He took off the gloves, washed his hands in the rivulet, and splashed the water on his face, hoping to rid the stench from his nostrils.

The bodies undulated from the force of the swift shallow current. Aideen's hair waved like a mermaid's under the sea, exposing the white bone of her skull. The water was deep enough from spring rains to cover the bodies, and if the wet weather continued they would remain in their watery graves throughout the summer.

If I were a priest I could do this right. He bowed his head, said a prayer for the dead and for the living, and asked for the forgiveness of all sins. He crossed himself and then returned to his shoes.

Who would do this? Could it have been the Mollies? He knew that some tenants had been asked to pay "dues" to the group, in addition to the landlord's rent, an impossible task when food and money were scarce. Men like Brian Walsh had been threatened, but the Kilbanes weren't tenants and probably had no interaction with the Maguires. No, this was murder, plain and simple, for food and money.

He returned to the front of the cottage, his head filled with unpleasant thoughts. Briana was standing next to the horses. She looked small, somehow delicate, drenched by the persistent mist. His heart ached for her, but a silent strength emanated from her focused gaze. She had chosen him, and he would keep her safe through the night in a home tainted by death.

CHAPTER 11

Briana searched the house looking for the Kilbanes' guitar and flute. Frankie had played the flute and guitar while Aideen sang on the first evening Briana, Rory, and her father had stayed there on their trip together to Westport. The night had passed in a blur of food and song. The Kilbanes would never have given up their musical instruments willingly for anyone.

She and Rory talked briefly about the murders after they ate, but the topic gave her the chills despite a roaring turf fire. Rory was certain the instruments had been taken to be sold. He had inspected the shed and found the Kilbanes' livestock to be gone as well.

That night, Briana kept one eye focused on the door as she catnapped her way through the hours in a corner opposite the fire. Every creak and pop rattled her nerves and set her stomach tumbling.

Her husband had done everything to make their stay as comfortable as possible, including building a fire large enough to keep the cottage warm and lit throughout the night, propping a chair against the door to keep out unwanted animals and intruders, and sheltering the horses in the traveler's room.

When dawn's tepid light seeped around the door frame, she fell into a deep sleep and dreamed of leering, emaciated faces.

When Rory shook her awake, she felt hot from the fire, tired from not getting enough sleep, and irritable from the prospect of the impending journey. They heated the last of their mush and soda bread and ate it before saddling the horses. The sun was blocked by thick clouds, but the mist no longer fell.

Briana said a prayer for the peaceful rest of the Kilbanes' souls as the horses trotted away from the cottage. She hoped they wouldn't have to spend a second night in it on their return to Lear House.

Several hours later, they were within sight of the purple-hued peak of Croagh Patrick. The road had become clogged with a mass of people who flowed toward Westport like fall leaves fallen into the Carrowbeg. As they had done at Lear House, families burrowed into the earth, but here the shelter was less substantial. Sod and wood were scarce, having already been depleted. Thin men, women, and children in ragged clothes scattered about the road. If not in the burrows, the families trudged toward the village with eyes cast toward the ground.

From the mountains, from the hills, from the farms, they came to Westport looking for food and work. Those who could walk appeared to be half-dead, their emaciated legs barely able to support them. Their clothes were ragged and torn, the skin of legs, arms, and backs showing through ripped fabric. A few reached out for them as saviors on horseback — faces twisted by the excruciating pain of hunger. Those who were able rushed toward them, begging. They clawed at the ponies' sides and pulled at the animals' reins as if to devour the horses themselves.

"Get away!" Rory lashed out with the straps, slapping some people across their hands. They groaned and staggered away, unable to gather the strength to stop the animals.

Briana cringed at their destitution and her husband's violent action, which seemed like a whip in a slave owner's hands. "Must you be so rough?" she yelled.

Rory turned on her, his cheeks red with rage after they had passed the crowd. "Rough? If I don't fight them off, we'll be lucky to get to Westport. They'd eat the animals out from under us, if I didn't stop them." Fury flared from his eyes. "Do I need to remind you that we have twenty pounds in our pockets — a fortune by any man's measure. I'm sure the Kilbanes were murdered for less." He pointed down the road. "Do you want us to end up like that?"

Briana craned her neck to see what he had spotted. The village buildings were coming into view through the hills. In the distance, Croagh Patrick's peak stood obscured by drab striations of ash-colored clouds.

He thrust out his hand again, and this time she saw.

Bodies. Some blended in so well with the trees and earth that she had to look twice to spot them. Corpses. Scores of them strewn across the fields like bloated seeds.

The bodies lay in crumpled heaps, while around them black and tan specks whirred in the underbrush. She strained to see, unable to trust her eyes. The men, women, and children who walked in silence behind them, or stood complacently in the ditches, also seemed unaware of the dogs that were devouring the corpses, snapping at the tattered clothes, ripping flesh from the bone, eating the dead to keep themselves from starving.

She gasped and uttered a prayer, the horror too much to take in. "My God" was all she could say.

"Rough? *You* don't want me to be rough?" Rory's voice sliced through her with its bitter edge. "Look what our English governors, our protectors, are allowing to happen. It's good the wind is blowing off the sea or we wouldn't be able to stomach the smell."

"Please, Rory," she said as a nauseous despair filled her.

He lifted from his horse, and his chest heaved in a monstrous moan as tears rolled down his cheeks.

Briana sidled next to him. The immensity of the famine, the pressure of holding everything together, including fearing for the lives of his brother's family, had caught up with him. He needed to mourn the deaths of their countrymen, not bottle up his rage. The word struck her like a hammer blow as she rode beside him. *Rage* had hastened his entry into the Mollies. Now it was driving her husband, and she feared that its savage power might consume him.

The starving, standing in shadowed doorways, hunched by the side of the road, lying in ditches, quietly shuffling down the street, remained a constant presence as they entered the city.

Dishes clattered in The Black Ram, the public house where Briana had been accosted by the sailor. A cluster of starving Irishmen, beggars seeking scraps of food, huddled near the door but did not venture in. Inside, English sailors sat comfortably smoking their pipes and eating breakfast, less raucous than they would be later in the day when liquor flowed freely.

"Poor devils," Rory said as they passed their countrymen. "Begging for food, looking for work, or maybe transport to the Continent. No English sea captain is going to hire a starving Irishman unless it's for swabbing slops off the decks."

Traveling above the village, past the stately mansion that looked to the east, they made their way to the port seeking the Captains the landlord had mentioned.

The *Tristan,* Captain James's ship, was not in port, but another, the *Cutter,* a three-masted steamer with sails folded, rocked in the swells of Clew Bay. Briana remained on her horse as Rory dismounted and made his way down the dock. Two seamen attired in white pants and tunic shirts talked to him for a short time. When he returned, he smiled and patted her horse's flank.

"Our friend, the Master, seems to have everything worked out," he said with gentle sarcasm. The breeze off the bay swept through his hair. "Miller is the Captain of the *Cutter.* He's in his quarters, but I do expect he will see us. Even the crew knows who Sir Thomas Blakely is."

They sat for a time watching sailors offload sacks of meal from a smaller ship that had dropped anchor in the bay. Two dragoons, attired in their high boots and stiff capes, guarded the navy men. The job was routine, organized and leisurely, as if the famine didn't exist. For all their nonchalance, the crew might as well have been in a port half a world away. Sailors hefted sacks across their shoulders; some hauled the goods in wooden carts to awaiting wagons. A few emaciated Irishmen hovered at the corners of the stone port buildings like dogs looking for a handout. Rory stuck his hand in his pocket and fingered the money given to them by Sir Thomas. Briana noted his nervous gesture, which led to her own anxiety about who might be watching them. Uneasy, her eyes snapped around the quay.

After a half hour, a sailor invited them to board the *Cutter.* The ship was anchored far out from the shallows to avoid being grounded at low tide. They boarded a skiff manned by two men who rowed them, bouncing over the waves, to the *Cutter*. One of the sailors helped Briana climb the rope ladder before escorting her and Rory across the top deck to a small door that led to a flight of narrow stairs. "The Captain's quarters are up top," the man said. "He's expecting you."

As he left, Briana looked out across the deck. The view was magnificent. On the eastern horizon, the village sat in the hills beyond the imposing stone buildings of the port. To the south, Croagh Patrick thrust its peak into the clouds. To the west, the bay swells gave way to the infinite stretch of turbid Atlantic waters.

The staircase led to another dark, wooden door inset with a circular portal of wavy glass. It provided the only light in the enclosure. Rory knocked, and a gruff voice responded, "Enter."

Captain Miller sat behind a large mahogany desk, his back to a wide expanse of windows looking north across the bay. He was corpulent, much like a fighting dog, older and stouter than Captain James. He wore a buttoned-up waistcoat and breeches of white, his stern face lined with scars from a lifetime on the sea. However, his eyes twinkled with a hint of benevolence from under his white hair, as if he managed to hold two contrasting personalities. Briana had no doubt after meeting him that the Captain adhered to strict English discipline. He invited them to sit and then waited for them to speak. Rory looked to Briana to tell the story, apparently hoping that the officer would be more amenable to a woman's charms.

"Sir Thomas Blakely has asked us to come in the hopes —"

He stopped her with a wave of his hands. "I know what you've come for, and I'm sure Sir Thomas is prepared to pay for it."

Briana nodded. "The better part of fifteen pounds."

The captain's lip curled in a crafty smile. "I've known the man and his father before him. I've sailed with their textiles out of Liverpool for many years. Yes, I know how the family operates. They get their way."

"We've come to ask for —" Rory said in English.

The Captain's hand went up again. "You'll be getting ten sacks of oats, ten sacks of meal, three *generous* ham hocks, and if I feel unselfish, two large wheels of cheese. That's all fifteen pounds will buy these days."

Rory's face turned crimson, and he clutched his chair.

Briana feared that her husband might erupt in front of the Captain.

"That will barely feed Sir Thomas's guests for two weeks," Rory said. "We'll need twice that amount to get by for a month." He slid forward in his chair, barely hiding his contempt for the officer. "Where is all the other meal going?"

"It's really none of your business, but as Mr. Charles Edward Trevelyan, the assistant secretary, has pointed out, the English government has but one obligation to the Irish — the purchase and distribution of Indian corn to be placed at various depots by the commissariat." He paused, allowing his words to sink in. "Does that make sense to your provincial minds? Have I made myself clear?"

"Quite," Briana replied in a stuffy English accent. For once, she wished Lucinda were in her spot to spar with the Captain.

"You can thank Sir Robert Peel for the purchase of the meal. Most of it is going to the supply center for the Killeries in Connemara County where it will eventually be distributed."

Rory took the currency out of his pocket and tossed it on the Captain's desk. "I've heard enough. We'll be on our way as soon as we can be assured that the supplies will be shipped to Belmullet and then on to Carrowteige."

"You have my word," the Captain ordered, and deposited the money in his desk. "It's good you didn't come with a wagon. The less those poor Irish blighters see, the better. It would be best for you not to be seen with supplies. Something unfortunate might befall you." He tapped a pistol on his desk. "Good day to you." He dismissed them with a wave of his hand, looked down at an entry book, and began writing.

As they waited for the skiff to take them ashore, a sailor approached them carrying a satchel of oats and two hunks of cheese. Shortly, the ship's first mate, carrying an object wrapped in black satin, appeared at their side.

"With the compliments of the Captain," the mate said, and handed it to Rory. "He says you might need this." A note was pinned to the satin, which Briana read aloud: *With good wishes to Sir Thomas Blakely, friends by blood, Captain Cedric Miller, HMS Cutter.*

"They must be related," she said. "He's being generous."

Rory scoffed. "This food won't last

through the summer, depending on English appetites. What will the landlord do then?"

"I suppose he'll buy more."

"Yes, as Lear House goes down, he and his guests will dine in splendor while Irish food leaves our shores."

One sailor took the oats and cheese and descended the rope ladder like a trained monkey. Briana was second, her shoes slamming against the ship's hull as it rocked with the waves. The sailor clutched her legs as she neared the skiff and guided her to its bottom. Clutching the satin parcel, Rory was next, followed by the second sailor.

The saltwater leapt in silvery bursts over the bow as they skimmed across the bay. Sitting on a plank seat, Rory opened the satiny folds of the object given to him by the first mate. "Hello, what's this?" He whistled in amazement. "It's a . . . pistol."

Briana peered at the burnished metal and the flame-patterned wood resting on the satin.

"He's given us the complete package," Rory said in amazement while poking at the cleaning rods, flints, balls, and powder flask that had been concealed by the satin. He lifted each item and inspected them separately. He returned them to the cloth and said, "I've no idea how to use this." He picked up the pistol and held it by its barrel. "I suppose I could hit someone over the head with it."

The sight of the weapon chilled her, and she wished the Captain had left it on his desk. She preferred not to imagine a scene conjured by the Captain: the starving grabbing at the horses or throwing themselves in front of them in an attempt to steal anything they had. Rory would have to load and fire and reload while people swarmed over them. She was familiar with the long guns passed down through inheritance to a few lucky tenants, but her father had never kept a hunting rifle, because there was no need. Lear House had provided all the food the family needed without having to hunt, and Sir Thomas was not a particular fan of the sport. "Please put that down," she said. "What if it's loaded? You could shoot yourself in the leg. Besides, the note says the pistol is for Sir Thomas."

"I might forget to give it to the owner. After all, it's for our protection." He maneuvered the pistol until it was aimed toward a port building on the horizon. "I think this has to be pulled back in order to fire." He pointed to the hammer, but then flinched, apparently unnerved by the thought of suffering an injurious blast. He rewrapped the firearm and held it carefully in his lap.

Soon they were ashore and the skiff was headed back to the *Cutter.* Rory fed a portion of the oats to the horses. Briana stashed the remaining grain and cheese in her saddlebag. The cheese was heavy and thick, and the aromatic scent of cultured milk made her mouth water.

They shook the reins, and the horses trotted through the wooded lane until they arrived at The Black Ram. While they were stopped, Rory filled their leather flagons with water from the public house as the animals drank from a pail and munched on grass.

The men who had crowded outside the establishment earlier had disappeared. Briana had no idea where they had gone. After a closer look, she spotted them in other doorways along the road, but shrunken, hidden like insects avoiding the heat of the day. In the short time she and her husband had been in Westport, the poor souls had withered to nothing, as if the additional hours with no nourishment had sapped their strength. These people had no fortitude left to stop ponies, let alone fight for food.

Heading north, they left Westport behind. The animals picked up their pace, refreshed by the oats and water. The overcast lifted and the lighter skies cheered her, for she had no desire to spend another night in the Kilbanes' cabin.

"We can spend the night outside," she suggested gently, hoping he would take the hint. She was more than willing to curl up with him and the animals under the stars. It would be uncomfortable but preferable to spending the evening in the cottage befouled by death. The pistol added little comfort, although it would be nearby if they needed it. Neither one of them knew how to fire it.

Rory found a brook running southward through a level field a short distance from the Kilbanes' home. He tethered the animals to the scrub brush that lined the water. The horses grazed while she and Rory ate cheese. Exhausted by the day's ordeal, they curled up in the shelter of a grassy hillock. Now that night was falling, Briana couldn't wait to get home. Still, the famine was foremost on her mind. How long could these trips to Belmullet and Westport continue before their luck ran out? Would they even have the strength to make more journeys?

As night fell, she marveled at the luminous hooves of the horses, made that way by the bog insects crushed in their path. Sleep found her as she snuggled against Rory under the cover of their saddles, the horses close by.

In the middle of the night, Rory's hand gripped hers. By the tightness of his fingers, Briana could tell the gesture wasn't one of romance but rather one of alarm. Another finger crossed her lips, indicating that she should remain silent. As the cold night breeze swept over them, one of the horses snuffled. Rory stiffened as someone stepped coolly around the horses.

A hand touched the tip of her toes, and she screamed.

Rory lunged toward the intruder.

Briana could see little in the dark, moonless night except the nebulous form of a man who staggered backward from her husband, apparently as shocked about the situation as they were.

"Get away!" Rory said as he collared the man. Briana feared the intruder might be armed — the pistol the Captain had given them was lying between them. "Why are you sneaking around at this hour?" Rory berated the stranger as he cornered him.

"I meant no harm," the man said in a strangled voice.

From his accent, Briana could tell he was from Mayo, not from Carrowteige but probably from the surrounding mountains. Briana jumped up, ready to defend her husband and to harangue the man for being a thief. She swiveled, suddenly aware of her surroundings. The land spread out in a flat, gray line to the black mountains. The only light came from the glow of the stars. *What if he's not alone? If only I knew how to use the pistol.* She shuddered at a newly formed thought of using a weapon to protect herself and her family.

"Who are you?" Rory demanded, and flung the man down on the sod, his dark form flailing like a leaf in the fall wind.

The man steadied himself on his elbows and said, "Clan O'Keevane. Malachy O'Keevane. I've been wandering for days trying to get to Westport or Cork to board a ship to Liverpool. They say there's railroad work in England. I had to leave my wife and children behind." A coughing spasm ended his speech, and he rolled on his side, head to the ground.

"Have you got the fever?" Rory asked, his tone gruff with suspicion.

The man raised his head. "Not that I know of. I've felt cold of late." He groaned and then straightened his body.

"No food?" Rory asked.

"I thought someone might be dead by

these animals," Malachy said. "One never knows these days. I was hoping to find food. If not, I thought I might kill me a horse."

"I'm glad you didn't, Mr. O'Keevane. My wife and I need these horses to get back to Lear House."

"Lear House?" Malachy asked, astonished. "My traveling companion told me about Lear House."

The hairs on the back of Briana's neck stood on end. She moved closer to the man.

"This is my wife, Briana Walsh Caulfield," Rory said. "We just came from Westport."

"Who is your companion?" Briana asked the man, trying to shake the flutter in her stomach.

"He joined me yesterday on the road. At first I thought he was mad, but I think he's only suffering like I am. He says he's a poet living off what others have to offer, but no one has anything to offer these days. . . ."

"Daniel Quinn," Briana said, and Rory nodded. "There can be only one poet who knows Lear House. Where is he now?"

"He's not told me his name. He only calls himself the 'poet.' We've camped out in a deserted cabin up the road." He pointed toward the Kilbanes' cottage. "Nothing much is left there — a few old pots and pans that aren't worth much if you have nothing to eat. A place to rest the head. That's all. I couldn't sleep, so I thought I'd take a walk to keep my mind off me stomach."

"Go back to the cabin," Rory said. "We know where it is. I promise, we'll give you a bite of what we have in the morning."

The man rose and staggered toward them. "You do have food! Oh, praise the Saints. It would be wondrous to eat a meal again, something to tide me over until I can get to Westport."

Rory shook his head. "We have little. Get some sleep. We'll stop by at daybreak."

The man left them, and Briana walked back to the hillock; Rory joined her after checking on the horses.

She looked up at the white haze of stars arching overhead and thought of those sleeping in burrows with no food for their stomachs. How long did they have before they collapsed from starvation? That question led her to wonder what it would be like to die. Would she be standing at the gates of heaven or hell? So much death surrounded them, but perhaps they could help this man and Daniel Quinn.

She grasped Rory's hand after he had settled beside her and said, "There's one thing I want to do when we get home."

Her husband cuddled close and whispered, "Yes?"

"Learn to shoot that pistol," she said, half thinking it might be necessary.

After daybreak, they freshened up and then mounted the horses. Briana wasn't looking forward to stopping at the Kilbanes' cabin, but she wanted to help the man who had found them in the night.

Malachy was sitting by the door when they arrived, puffing on an empty pipe. The sun cut across his face, and Briana was able to see his features clearly for the first time. His cropped, black hair fell forward on his head. He might have been in his thirties, but he looked older due to his sallow complexion, shrunken cheeks, and watery blue eyes set in their dark hollows.

The man nodded and sucked in one last breath as Rory alighted from his horse. "No tobacco," he said. "At least I can smell the old plug." He took the pipe from his mouth and tapped it against his knee.

"Is Quinn here?" Rory bent over Malachy, who answered with a nod and hitched his thumb toward the cottage.

Briana wondered why he was so close to the man, but her husband soon turned and whispered, "No lice, no fever." Rory ducked inside, leaving the door partially open. Briana was left with Malachy, who told her that his family came from the mountains east of Ballycroy. "Not a lovelier spot on this earth," he was telling Briana when Rory reappeared.

The early morning rays struck her husband, and she realized how much Rory had aged in the weeks they had been married. Flecks of gray dotted his red beard, his face had grown thinner, and his eyes were bleary and red from distress.

"It's Quinn, all right," Rory said. "What's left of him. He doesn't have the fever, but he's all skin and bones."

"He needs food and water," Briana said, and reached for her satchel.

"We all do," Malachy said. "We *hope* God will provide."

She thought of the crucifix in her father's room and her conversation with Father O'Kirwin before she and Rory were married. How much did God care about Ireland? The priest had expressed similar misgivings. Had the Creator deserted them? She supposed she would never understand why the famine had stricken them, any more than she could understand why the stars kept their places in the heavens.

The morning light filtered through the door, partially erasing the gloom inside.

Quinn, wrapped in a blanket near the fire pit, moaned and raised his hands to shield his eyes.

Briana grasped four handfuls of oats from the satchel while Rory stoked the fire and collected water for boiling. Soon the cabin was filled with the smell of burning peat and the warm, toasty odor of simmering oatmeal. They had no buttermilk to pour on the oats, so they settled for hot water. Rory cut a thin slice of cheese for each of them, adding a little more sustenance to the meager meal.

After a prayer, Malachy propped Quinn against the mud wall and fed him. The poet could hardly open his mouth to eat and several times he choked on the oats. Briana held his lips open as best she could as the man placed the spoon on Quinn's tongue. Briana managed to get cool water down his throat. Finally, the poet could take no more, and he slumped to the floor despite Malachy's continued urgings to eat.

"He's had enough," Briana said. They finished their oats and cheese as she thought about the times at Lear House when Quinn had entertained the family with song and verse. How far he had fallen — this time further than all the previous bad times put together. He was a kind man who had been thrown out of his family at a young age for being "useless." Briana's father had been fascinated by the poet's knowledge of Irish music and history; thus the two had struck up an intermittent friendship after meeting in a public house in Bangor.

Soon, Malachy rose, thanked them, and strapped his small kit to his rope belt. "I've no idea what lies ahead, but it's time to go."

Rory shook his hand. "Look for the *Cutter* and Captain Miller. Talk to the sailors and mention Sir Thomas Blakely. The name might not get you onboard, but it can't hurt."

Malachy repeated the Captain's and Blakely's names. Briana noted a genuine note of happiness in his face, something her husband had lacked of late. "I thank you for your kindness," he said, and ambled toward the door. He turned and looked back at Quinn, who had fallen into a fitful sleep on the blanket. "You will take care of him? He's not a bad man, I think, just a bit mad from hunger."

Briana nodded. "We won't desert him."

They watched from the door as Malachy headed south toward Westport. The man's shadow flickered over the bog as he disappeared down the road. Briana pushed the hair back from her temples, poured warm water into a pot, and rubbed it over her hands; the dusty smell of burning peat covered her clothes and skin. A bath would be wonderful, but that would have to wait.

She washed the pots while Rory tended the horses, making sure they were fed and watered. There was no reason to put out the turf fire; it would burn itself out in the pit. She placed the utensils on their hooks and straightened the few things left in the cabin, knowing that Aideen's spirit, like any Irish woman, would be pleased by her tidiness. The chore was minor but left her feeling satisfied.

Despite the poet's presence, a shiver raced over her from the ghostly memory of the murdered family. She ran from the cabin and stopped near the road to catch her breath. Rory was nowhere to be seen. In a panic, she called out his name.

He appeared, a few moments later, shoes in hand, from behind the cabin.

"The bodies are still there — undisturbed." Rory squinted in the sunlight. "Who would do such a thing? I'm sure they didn't have much."

"Someone desperate," Briana replied. "Get the poet. My father would never forgive me if we left him here to die."

Rory stepped into the cabin and returned

with Quinn in his arms. "He's light as a feather," he said while positioning him over the horse's back.

Briana took another look at the cabin as she mounted her horse, flushed with the strange feeling that she would never again see the cabin as it stood now. If squatters didn't make short work of it, the elements would, because without repair the sod walls would eventually crumble.

The Kilbanes' home dropped from sight as they rounded a curve in the road. Rory held on to Quinn's back with his left hand and guided the pony with his right.

Soon the sun and the rhythmic stride of her horse lulled her into a pleasant sense of security she wished would never end. Lear House was only a day's journey ahead. Then the thought of Sir Thomas Blakely entertaining his English guests while others starved demolished her pleasure.

CHAPTER 12

June 1846

Most days the rain poured off the manor's slate roof, turning the rock walls a damp gray as bleak as the hours that dragged by. The weather was miserable for much of the late spring and early summer, keeping Sir Thomas's guests housebound with little to do and much to complain about. The Andersons, the Rogerses, and the Wards, with their three sons, had arrived a few days after Briana and Rory had completed their trip to Westport. Nine guests now filled Lear House with an additional four to come — a quartet from Dublin hired to provide music for the planned ball in mid-June.

In the ensuing weeks since their arrival, the Ward boys had kept Lucinda busy with tutoring duties, which she described to Briana as "mostly child's play because they can't keep their minds on anything except roaming the countryside."

Daniel Quinn had taken up residence in her father's cottage, much to Lucinda's chagrin. Her sister was put out not only by the children but by the fact that the "odd poet" had invaded her home. Quinn was gaining strength now that he could at least be fed the scraps the Master and his guests didn't want. But Briana had noted a big change in the poet's personality. Formerly, he had been somewhat happy, despite being subject to creative melancholy. Now he was morose and kept to himself while wandering the cliffs or staring silently into the flames of the turf fire.

Even though the famine raged around them, Briana was shocked by the amount of food Sir Thomas and his guests wasted, but it surprised her less when she considered English tastes and sensibilities. The guests were unaccustomed to being needy. Only her begging and Lucinda's contriteness convinced Rory to sacrifice his pig to the cause of the landlord's stomach. Rory, perturbed by the request, stated he knew the day would come, as he gutted the beast, and wished the animal had not been sacrificed upon the altar of Sir Thomas Blakely.

Jarlath offered what fish he could catch for evening meals, but the foul weather and corresponding unfavorable seas kept his canoe onshore most days. Of all their food, the Indian corn was the least palatable and the most despised not only by Briana and her family but by the guests as well. No amount of preparation or fancying up the meal made it edible. Most of it was deemed unpalatable, returned uneaten, and served to the poet or the horses. The animals displayed their dislike as well, preferring to munch on the heather grasses and gorse seeds when they could.

Even through judicious use, the supplies dwindled by the end of two weeks. Rory would soon have to make another trip to Westport if the landlord wished to feed his guests.

"The next trip I'll charge him ten pounds," Rory said one night after they trudged to bed, exhausted by the day's labors. The candle threw wavering circles of light on the ceiling.

"Have you thought of a plan to save Lear House?" Briana asked, hoping to lift their conversation above despair.

Rory pulled up the blanket and shook his head. "Nothing — and believe me, I think about it all the time. If there's an easy way, I can't find it." He turned on his side toward her. "I don't know what good ten pounds would do us. Even his money is useless here

— there's nothing to buy."

"I haven't been able to think of anything either. Da told me only a few old coins have been collected this month. With nothing to sell, there's no money coming in."

Rory raised on his elbow and looked at her with an intensity that unnerved her. He studied her for a moment before asking, "Have you ever thought about going to America?"

She stared back, the blood draining from her face. She had never, in all her days, considered leaving Lear House. Born and reared here, she had only known this life and she was committed to keeping the family together even though the Walsh family had no claim to the property. The blight had not changed her mind about her ancestral home. Now, after months of dealing with shortages and the ever-present hunger, she still had no desire to leave County Mayo. She shook under the blanket, although the cabin wasn't cold.

What would the family do in America? Her father and sister would certainly object to leaving — for different reasons. Lucinda would not forsake the Continent for the United States. She had one goal in life, and that was to capture the heart of the landlord. Her father would laugh at such a suggestion, saying that he was too old to make the trip and that he would never want to be more than a walk away from his wife's grave. Ancestry, land, and sentiment were too important to him. Her mouth puckered, but no words came out.

Rory interlocked his fingers, lay back, and put his hands under his head. "I see more anger than you do, Briana."

She knew he was serious; he hardly ever used her first name.

"I was able to shake some sense into most of them at the last meeting, but they're on the verge of erupting," he continued. "They know the landlord and his guests are cavorting about with food on their plates while Irish families starve. If the Englishman sends me away to Westport again yet offers nothing to the tenants, there'll be hell to pay. I promised to do what I could."

She placed her hand on his chest, feeling the rise and fall of his breath.

He clutched her fingers and ran his thumb across her knuckles. "Men are leaving Ireland to find work. One of the Mollies who went to England stayed two months and then came back. He told us how it works. Most leave their wives and children behind, walk to Dublin, and take a cattle ship to Liverpool to work rail construction near Manchester. They send a little money home to the family, but it's hard, backbreaking work. The men are crammed in flimsy shacks hardly better than living in a ditch here. Others head to America for the same business."

"So their families won't starve," Briana said, offering the only optimistic thought she could.

Rory nodded. "But at what cost? They keep them happy with poorhouse wages, cheap liquor, and women who spread disease. Living there is worse than hell. And to tell you the truth, I don't think I'm cut out for the rails — in England or America. I wouldn't be happy clearing tunnels, moving rocks and dirt, bowing and scraping to some English boss or, worse yet, some hired Irish manager with a chip on his shoulder. If I had to make a choice, I'd say our chances would be better in America." He grasped her arm gently. "All I'm asking is for you to consider the possibility before you reject it completely. Do we want a child born into this hardship — with only suffering for a future?"

His gaze had shifted from quiet intensity to thoughtful appeal. She thought of the times they had made love, sometimes with guilt carried in their bodies because they knew the Church wanted them to procreate despite the famine. Still, they had prayed for God to forgive their sin and tried every way they knew how not to conceive.

"We want a child, but we don't want . . ." Rory's eyes grew wet with tears.

She knew what he wanted to say: *We don't want to bring a child into a world where death is as likely as life.*

"By all rights, I should be the one to go," he said. "But if for some reason I can't, you must be the one." He nodded, kissed her, then rolled over and blew out the candle on the small table, plunging the cabin into darkness.

A thousand questions jumped into her head, but she was too exhausted to answer them. The dark and the immensity of the problems that faced them left her body drained and her mind bewildered. She snuggled next to Rory, knowing that this night there would be no lovemaking.

Several days later, on a relatively mild Monday afternoon, Rory met Connor Donlon and Noel Neary in a secluded area of Broadhaven Bay far from Lear House. Rory had replaced the satin wrapping the pistol and its firing apparatus with a muslin bag and carried it to a small inlet surrounded by sand dunes.

He spotted Connor and Noel, both Mollies, walking down the beach a few minutes after he arrived.

When the men reached him, Rory shook their hands. He felt awkward, knowing what was in the bag. Pistols were rare. He had told only Connor and Noel about the weapon given by the Captain and sworn the two men to secrecy.

"How's Heather?" Rory asked Noel. He was a slight man of considerable intelligence with a narrow face, wire-rimmed spectacles, thinning black hair, and eyes like a fox. Rory felt that, given the opportunity, Noel would have made a fine teacher.

Looking down at the sand, Noel answered, "We take it day by day."

Briana had told him about Noel's wife, Heather, the thin and sallow woman who stood next to her the day he had fought Connor. Rory had rarely seen her since.

"She's given everything to our children. To be honest, I'm not sure she'll live much longer if we can't manage a decent meal," Noel said. "Our neighbors have been kind, but now everyone is hungry."

"That's why we're here," Rory said, and opened the bag. "The Englishman is sending me to Westport tomorrow to get supplies for his grand social event on Saturday. He wants everything by Thursday." He paused as Connor removed the pistol from the bag and examined it. "I need it for my protection."

"I thought you hated the Englishman," Noel said.

"He's no friend of mine, but when he pays me, *and* I can secure food for him as well as my neighbors . . . I'll go." He patted Noel on the shoulder.

"It's a beauty." Connor's eyes sparkled with a jealous gleam as he turned the weapon over in his sturdy hands. "I've never fired a pistol like this, but it looks similar to one I've seen."

"This is what you do." Noel took the weapon and showed Rory and Connor how to clean it, place the primer and powder, and tamp down the ball. "Stand aside," he ordered, and pointed the pistol toward a dune. As Rory watched, Noel cocked the hammer with his thumb, aimed, and fired. The ball spewed streams of sand into the air. The percussion shook the air with a thunderous clap as the pistol belched smoke from the discharge.

"That should wake them up all the way to Carrowteige," Connor said, rubbing his ears.

"You try it," Noel said, handing the pistol to Rory.

He took the weapon and, following Noel's instructions, fired twice and then stopped, not willing to waste more ammunition. "So now we know how it's done," he said to the men. As he cleaned the pistol and then returned it to the bag, he talked about the Kilbanes and his experience at the cottage with Malachy. Everyone at Lear House and in the village had come to know about the murders. The poet had a darker side to his chosen profession — a bearer of news, often bad these days.

As they walked along the beach, Rory spotted a man paralleling them, ducking in and out behind the dunes to the east.

"Who is that?" Noel asked, squinting through his glasses.

"I know," Rory answered, taken aback by the man's proximity.

Connor stopped and stared into the dunes. "It's that daft poet, Quinn."

The poet stopped as well, stared back at them, and then trekked farther into the dunes.

"What's he doing — following us?" Noel asked.

"Who can tell?" Rory was annoyed with the poet for spreading the story about the

Kilbanes. After the poet had somewhat recovered, Rory had told him about the murders. Quinn replied that he had suspected something was wrong because the house was deserted, but he was too sick to care.

Rory looked down at the bag and considered the valuable contents inside. He would make sure the pistol was in a safe place overnight before leaving on his trip to Westport. Sir Thomas had offered Briana another five pounds for the journey. This time, Rory planned to stop at The Black Ram and buy as much food as he could carry for the Walshes and his brother's family — in addition to the supplies to be shipped to Belmullet for Lear House.

They arrived at the lane leading to the farms. Quinn had disappeared in the dunes. "One thing," Rory told them before they separated. "Promise me you won't let things get out of hand. I'll secure as much as I can to be divided between the families. What the Englishman doesn't know won't hurt him."

Noel nodded, but Connor looked less than enthusiastic about his request. He trusted the slight man to prevail when it came to calming tempers, but Connor's bullish impulsiveness often turned into a call for force.

The cabin was empty when he returned, for Briana was cooking the evening meal at Lear House. She had also agreed to help her sister with preparations for the ball while Rory was gone.

He took the pistol out of the bag, placed it in the corner, and covered it with dirty clothes. Briana wouldn't be doing any wash before morning. He lay down on the bed and thought about a question he had pondered for weeks. How could he get the family out of County Mayo by September before the Atlantic became too perilous to cross?

The ball was slated to occur on the Saturday after Rory returned from Westport. The supplies arrived at Belmullet on Friday and were shipped to the store the same day — causing some consternation with Sir Thomas for their late arrival.

Rory talked little about the trip because he claimed that nothing unusual had happened. He had met with Captain James, who was in port with the *Tristan.* They had exchanged money and goods with little fuss. Rory had slept two nights outside with little shelter and the pistol by his side. He told Briana he never had cause to use it, but she believed there was more to the story than he was telling.

On the day of the ball, the manor was filled with activity. The floors in the great room were broom swept and buffed with cloth, the furniture was moved against the walls to make room for dancing, the great table was hauled from the kitchen to the back wall for food presentation, and the alcove before the front window was cleared for the Dublin musicians. They had arrived on Friday also and made themselves at home overnight in the library and kitchen.

Briana and her father spent most of the day preparing what food they could. Oatcakes, ham, and a fish were prepared for the guests. Brian also tried his hand at the Indian corn and managed to prepare a dish that even Briana found somewhat palatable because of the judicious use of brandy.

Lucinda had begged Sir Thomas to give her the afternoon off from schooling the Wards' boys, and the landlord agreed. Briana knew her sister wasn't interested in helping out around the house at that late hour; her only concern was in making herself beautiful for the ball.

After most of the preparations had been completed, Briana rushed back to the cabin to wash up and change into her best dress.

Rory, sulking, sat on the bed looking toward the bag that held the pistol.

"I can't convince you to come tonight?" She dipped a washcloth in the water basin.

"No," he said. "I'm in no mood for frivolity and wasteful displays of consumption."

"There's barely enough there for the musicians and guests," she replied. "There'll be yet another trip to Westport before long." She patted her face with the rag and awaited his response.

After a long time he said, "There won't be another trip."

She looked at him, astounded by his words. "What?" Perhaps this was the reason, now coming out, that he had been so out of sorts and quiet after his return from Westport. "Why not?"

"Because the Captain told me so." He rose from the bed and stood across from her. "Sir Thomas has been playing a dangerous game — one that could lead to arrests all around if he isn't careful. But it's of no matter now. The game has come to an end."

Briana slipped out of her work dress, ran the cloth over her arms and legs, and then reached for her red one, which hung on a peg near the door. A shiver skittered over her. She dreaded his response but needed to hear more. "Why is it coming to an end?"

"Because Captain James and Miller are taking a cut by selling meal and other goods to landlords and agents that should be going to the community stores. The English, the commissariat, even the Irish government have looked the other way for a while, but now every bag counts. The accounting is strict, and the payoffs have stopped. Lives are in the balance."

She stepped into her dress and let Rory's words sink in. She felt selfish and ungrateful while fussing with her hair: *What of our lives? What will become of us now that the food has stopped?*

A sudden sadness washed over his face. "It's worse now than the last time we went. Starving people are everywhere. Those men who can stand are wandering like phantoms looking for work that can't be found, families wrenched apart by hunger." He lowered his head. "At the crossing south of Carrowteige, families are weeping, holding on to each other to say a last good-bye — men traveling to God knows where. It's a river of sorrows, the saddest place I've ever seen only a few miles from here." He clasped his hands and brought them to his chest as if he was praying. "They clutch each other, exchange a handkerchief as a token of their love. They cry as if it's the end of the world.

Who knows whether these men will ever be reunited with their wives and children again?"

Briana knew the crossing well; it was where they had encountered the starving family. However, she could imagine the horror now: somber, gray days; the clouds shedding rain on the bleak, stony riverbank. Families split in two, wrenched apart by the famine. She was torn between her duties as a wife and the daughter of the owner's agent. There was nothing she could do this evening despite their shared sadness.

He took her into his arms and cradled her close. "You look beautiful."

She pulled away, embarrassed by the compliment given after such bad news. "I'm sure I look as common as I feel."

"Go ahead," Rory said, settling back on the bed. "I'll be asleep when you get home."

She nodded and left him alone in the cabin, feeling as if her body was collapsing upon itself. The sinking sensation in her stomach made her grasp the fences for support as she walked back to Lear House. At one point, she stopped, clutched a rocky wall, and looked up at the manor. Its windows were filled with candles and oil lamps. How she had treasured such scenes when she was a child — the beauty and history of Lear House had sustained her. Now, in the fading light, the loveliness she had so revered seemed hollow and threatening. She wrested her hands from the stones, stood erect, and smoothed her dress. There was no time for forays into the past. She had to stand tall, allay her fear, not only for herself but for her family.

Rory found himself annoyed by the string music that drifted into the cabin as he lay on the straw. He pictured the fine men and women: the Andersons, the Rogerses, and the Wards, twirling around the floor of the great room. The three boys would be dressed in their breeches and waistcoats, sitting in chairs, swinging their feet to the music. Perhaps they would even dance with their mother in some old-fashioned step like the gavotte or the minuet — before the Irish musicians broke into a jig. He laughed at the thought of the Englishmen indulging in a country dance before his mind turned dark again.

The windows must be open because of the heat inside. The bastard knows it's torture to the rest of us, a slap across the face with this heartless display. Oh, stop fooling yourself, get dressed, and see what's going on! What can it hurt? You can't sleep anyway.

He pulled on a shirt and snuffed out the candle. Fog had moved in from the Atlantic, smothering Lear House with damp, low clouds that shifted in the wind like droplets blown from a fountain. Every now and then, light jumped from the manor windows to the gray clouds, revealing a misty haze that arched from the ground to the sky.

The music and laughter grew louder with each step he took toward the manor. He stopped south of it and found himself fascinated by the bodies moving past the windows. Judging by the merriment, clapping, and exuberant playing, everyone was having a good time.

All that was going on inside had nothing to do with what was going on outside. Just a few months ago, the road to Lear House had been lined with the starving. Now even Indian corn had been cut off from the manor. The next potato crop might fail, and the estate was collapsing into bankruptcy, so all the wine, song, and cheer in the world couldn't lessen the disaster threatening them.

Someone moved in the shadows outside the great room's large window. Rory fled to the path leading to the bay and crouched behind the slope of a sand dune. The figure slid next to the open window, keeping out of sight from those inside. As it moved closer to the light, he recognized Lucinda attired in the traveling dress she had worn from England. She positioned herself against the wall with her head cocked in the direction of the glass.

Almost immediately, Rory was also able to discern the objects of her attention. Illuminated by the light inside, Briana and Sir Thomas strolled to the window, a short distance from the musicians. The two moved close to each other and then separated as if in a dance themselves.

Lucinda cupped her hand, hoping to hear any conversation that might come from her sister and the landlord.

Rory fought back jealousy as the talk between the two continued for several minutes. Suddenly, Briana broke away, leaving Sir Thomas standing alone. Lucinda, witnessing the same, slipped into the darkness between the cottage and the house and turned toward the only available entrance at the rear — the kitchen door.

Rory rose from his hiding place and wondered what Lucinda had heard, why she felt it necessary to spy on them in the first place. Judging from the movements of his wife and Sir Thomas, the discussion had been an earnest one.

■ ■ ■ ■

The landlord's guests had drifted downstairs, toasted the occasion with wine from
reserved bottles, and scooped up plates of
food. The musicians, sporting black jackets
with satin lapels, played Mozart string
quartets while the ladies and gentlemen
dined. After dinner the quartet broke into
music more suited for dancing.

Everything had been going well until Sir
Thomas had drawn her aside. And he had
done it in full view of everyone, including
her father and Lucinda, a clever trick, she
supposed, to allay suspicion from his true
intention. But even after their conversation,
Briana was uncertain what his motive was.
Perhaps she had misunderstood his meaning.

A few minutes after she left the landowner,
Lucinda pounced on her in the great room
like a Fury. "What a disgusting display!"
Her sister's face seethed as she spat out the
words. If they had been darts, Briana would
have been mortally wounded.

Taken aback by Lucinda's hostility, Briana ushered her down the hall into the
kitchen. She closed the door and prepared
herself for a fight. "I did not initiate the

conversation with Sir Thomas, if that's what's bothering you."

"What did he say to you?" Lucinda asked in an accusatory tone as she stood with fists clenched by her sides. The green god of jealousy had consumed her.

"It's really none of your business, but since you've asked" — Briana leaned against the kitchen door to block anyone from entering — "I'm not sure what he wanted."

"Really." Lucinda huffed. "Don't lie to me. I know —"

"Know what?" A hot anger flushed her face. "You weren't eavesdropping, were you?"

Her sister's head drooped, and Briana knew she had heard their short exchange. Beneath her indignation she pitied Lucinda's obsession over a conversation. However, her sympathy, at the moment, did not extend to forgiveness. She felt like opening the door, leaving Lucinda alone with the lingering odor of cooked fish and the dirty pots and pans.

"I was standing by the window," her sister said in a calmer tone. "I couldn't help myself."

"Why would you do such a thing?"

"Because . . ." Her sister broke into sobs and walked in anguished circles around the spot where the table usually sat. "He looks through me," she said, pain filling her voice. "I try and try and try and he never gives me the time of day. I work for his friends, I school their children, I make myself presentable from morning 'til night . . . and nothing I do will turn his head."

"Is that what you want?"

"Of course it's what I want!" Lucinda shook her fists. "He is everything I've ever dreamed of!" She leaned against the oak cupboard as if she was too frail to continue, muttering words Briana couldn't hear. Her misery showed in the tight creases that lined her face.

Briana took a few tentative steps toward her sister. "Maybe he's not the right man for you. Maybe you've read too many books, set your sights too high."

"You've already made your bed," Lucinda said bitterly. "You've made your choice. I want more out of life than living in a cabin, but Thomas can't see my affection for him. He said that you look beautiful, that you are the most ravishing sight in Carrowteige."

"A compliment. Nothing more. I don't need flattery."

"He told you that life was easier in Manchester. He hinted that *you* would be happy there under a life of privilege. Did he invite your husband as well?"

Briana shook her head. "No, and you know that I would never leave him. That's when I ended the conversation. Privilege can be held over one's head until it becomes oppression. I wanted no more talk."

Lucinda covered her face with her hands in exasperation.

Briana touched her sister's shoulder. "I can understand your need —"

Glass shattered at the front of the house.

That sound was followed by the somewhat muted percussion of exploding gunpowder. Women screamed as shouts and curses echoed from those gathered in the great room. Briana ran to the kitchen door, threw it open, and raced down the hall. Lucinda followed with equal speed.

The sight before her was chaotic. Sir Thomas lay sprawled on the floor, blood streaming from a shoulder wound, soaking his white shirt and waistcoat. Mrs. Anderson and Mrs. Rogers, both stuffy and plump, cowered in the corner nearest the door clutching their sachets and fans. Mrs. Ward, however, used to the bloody adventures of three boys, bent over the owner, using her handkerchief to cover the wound while her husband cradled the owner's head in his hands. The other two husbands crouched nearby while Brian hurried for a glass of brandy. Briana rushed to the wounded man. Lucinda landed beside her, hands aflutter, horrified by the sight of her employer gasping on the floor.

"A glancing blow," her father said after he returned with the brandy. "A hand's width lower and the bullet would have pierced his heart." He pointed to the shattered looking glass at the back of the room, where the ball had lodged in the wall.

"I'm fine," Sir Thomas said, and tried to rise up, but fell back, wincing in pain. He clutched at his shoulder and shouted, "Someone get the devil who did this."

"I don't think that's wise," Brian said. "It's dark out. We'd be easy targets."

"Well, by damn, I'll go," Sir Thomas said. "I'm not dead." He attempted to get up again, but Mr. Ward restrained him with a firm grip on his host's arms.

"Get away from the window," Mrs. Ward yelled at her three sons as they crept toward it, attempting to look over the casement. "Sit on the floor and be quiet."

The boys frowned, showing disappointment at their thwarted curiosity, but complied with their mother's wishes.

"I'll get Rory," Briana said. "He can help

staunch the wound."

"It's not safe," her father objected while positioning the brandy glass on the owner's lips.

"Would you rather he bled to death?" Briana asked.

"Get your husband," Sir Thomas ordered.

"I'll go out through the kitchen," Briana said. A horrifying thought chilled her as she watched the landlord writhe on the floor. *Rory's pistol.* What if *he* had shot Sir Thomas? No, he would never have had a hand in such madness despite his hatred of the Englishman.

She felt as if stones had weighed her down as she pushed herself up and headed for the hall.

Rory burst in the front door and, seeing her, captured her in his arms.

"Sir Thomas has been shot." Briana pointed to the great room and then whispered, "Where have you been?"

"Talking a walk. I heard the shot from the beach."

Briana looked down at his feet, which were coated with sand. Relief flooded her. How could she have thought that Rory would shoot Sir Thomas? And what of the others at the ball — three boys, the guests, and the musicians. What insane person would take the chance of killing a child?

"Hurry!" She led Rory into the room.

Sir Thomas was sitting up now, and though he seemed relieved to see a man who could help him, his eyes couldn't hide the flicker of suspicion that streaked across them.

"Are there clean bandages?" Rory asked Brian.

"A few in the cottage," her father replied.

Rory shook his head. "I don't want anyone else to get shot." He looked to Briana. "Get me clean cloths from the kitchen."

Briana complied with his order and disappeared down the hall. She rummaged through a drawer where dish things were kept and returned with several.

Rory and Brian stripped the waistcoat from Sir Thomas and ripped his bloody shirt apart at the shoulder. "Give me the brandy," Rory said to his father-in-law. Brian handed the glass over with some dismay because he had guessed its use.

Rory took the cloths from Briana and then doused them with liquor. "This is going to sting," Rory said. He pressed a cloth over the gash that ran across the landlord's left shoulder and held it there.

"Damn!" Sir Thomas's face contorted in pain, and he howled at the ceiling, causing

Mrs. Anderson and Mrs. Rogers to wince as well. His outburst was short, however, and soon he was sitting with his left hand planted firmly on the floor while tending to the wound with his right. "That, ladies and gentlemen, was the signal for the evening to end," Sir Thomas said.

The musicians disbanded and the guests retreated to their rooms after saying a hurried good night. Briana was left in the room with Sir Thomas and her family.

Rory and Brian cautiously pulled the curtains across the shattered window and lifted the landlord to a chair. Sweat broke out on Sir Thomas's forehead.

Lucinda swabbed a handkerchief across his face. "Do you feel sick?" Her attention never wavered from her employer as he sagged in the chair.

"Sick?" he said contemptuously. "I've been shot. It burns like hellfire."

Lucinda backed away, rebuked by his gruff response.

"I'll wrap bandages on you before I take you upstairs," Rory said.

"Thank you," the owner replied, "but Mr. Walsh will give me a hand."

Brian lowered his head in a deferential nod.

"My concern now," Sir Thomas continued, "is in finding the bastard who shot me. I'm sure he wanted me dead, but he missed the mark." He stared at Rory. "Would you have any idea who did this?"

Briana again thought of the pistol.

Shaking his head, Rory said, "I was walking on the beach when I heard the shot, I ran from the bay to the house, but I saw nothing."

"Are there any witnesses to your actions?" Sir Thomas asked as Lucinda again wiped his face. He waved her away.

"I beg your pardon, sir. You'll have to take my word for it." He pointed to the sand on his feet.

As Briana was about to jump in to defend her husband, Sir Thomas lowered his head. "Brian, help me up the stairs — I feel a little faint."

The owner's face sagged under the pain. His black muttonchops glistened with perspiration, and his hair fell in damp curls across his forehead. Her father eased the Englishman out of his chair and placed his shoulder underneath the owner's right arm. The owner hobbled out of the room using her father as a crutch, but he turned at the stairs.

"I have one final thing to say . . . as we end the evening." His barely contained smirk irritated Briana. "At the end of the month, Lear House will be closed."

The announcement had been made — and they had known it was coming. Still, the news was shocking enough to take their breath away. Lear House would be shuttered and locked, and every tenant upon its lands would be subject to eviction.

Sir Thomas and her father climbed the stairs, never looking back, as she grappled with the calamity she had feared for months.

They said little as they stored the excess food, cleared the table, and cleaned the blood from the great room floor. The musicians, stunned as they were by the night's events, offered to move the furniture and kitchen table back to their original positions. Lucinda sobbed quietly as she worked next to them, and once their work was through she declined an escort back to the cottage. Briana had never seen her sister so despondent and feared for her safety despite her wish to be left alone. Her father had left Lear House for a few minutes and then returned with bandages and strips of cloth. Rory instructed him on the best way to treat the wound.

She and Rory closed up the kitchen and walked back to the cabin. Rory's step quickened as they neared their door. Inside, he lit the candle, placed the flame on the small table, and went immediately to the bag that held the pistol.

"It's here," he said with relief. He took the weapon out, held it in his hand, and then muttered, "By all the Saints."

"What's wrong?" Briana asked.

"It's been fired. Smell it."

She took the pistol and smelled the sulphuric odor of burned gunpowder. She handed it back to him and sat on the bed feeling heavy and tired, her mind filled with questions.

Rory had pronounced his dislike for the Englishman many times. How many other tenants, villagers, or Mollies had heard as well? Certainly he wouldn't lie to her, but would she be caught in a lie as well to cover his hostility toward the owner? Someone had taken the pistol and shot Sir Thomas — that was the only explanation. But who?

The shooting was bad enough, but closing Lear House crushed any vestige of hope she had been able to muster the past months.

She, her family, and the tenants were about to lose everything they had known — their history, their homes, and possibly their lives.

■ ■ ■ ■

PART TWO:
AMERICA AND
BEYOND

■ ■ ■ ■

CHAPTER 13

Late July 1846

Briana and Lucinda stood at the end of the lane leading to Lear House. Rain pelted Lucinda's umbrella, sheltering them both from the rivulets of water that poured down its curved top. Briana could hardly look at the manor, which would soon be a shell of its former self, the doors bolted and locked, the windows closed and shuttered.

Lucinda, more stoic, took in the events with the analytic mind of a governess. Briana wondered what her sister was thinking under her thick veneer of inscrutability.

The manor would be surrendered to the insects and rats that, as of late, had made it a nesting ground in their search for food. Briana remembered the once grand splendor of Lear House, now perched on the hill like a gray tomb. Even the few clear, beautiful days could not dispel the gloom that had drenched the house in a summer filled with rain.

Sir Thomas had made good on his threat to close the manor by the end of June, but the process took longer than expected because the books had to be audited, a census taken, and certain valuables secured for shipment to Manchester. The owner's wound, though superficial, had suppressed his enthusiasm for Lear House and Ireland. Although he told Briana and her father that he wanted to be back on English soil as soon as he could book passage, he was often hampered by fits of depression, which slowed his work. Briana noted he would take to his bed and remain sequestered until the evening meal was called. She supposed these bouts were related to his injury and the loss of Lear House, but she wondered whether other mental forces were at play.

As they stood, sister to sister, Briana imagined what was going on in Lear House with her father, Rory, and Sir Thomas enclosed inside. Rory was probably stone faced, seething, as he muttered about the worsening disaster of the famine. He could do nothing to fight Sir Thomas's orders, or the weather, or the political forces that had conspired against them. He was also holding a secret that she shared — the almost overwhelming proof that Rory's pistol had wounded the landowner. In much the same manner as her husband, Brian would cast a melancholy gaze as he went over the books, seeing his life's work and the fortunes of his tenants wiped out on the page.

Lucinda gripped Briana's fingers. The rare displays of warmth between them had become more frequent as Sir Thomas's behavior had turned reclusive. Her sister needed someone to lean on now that the heated fantasy of a romance with the land-lord had cooled.

Briana dodged the pelting rain from a sudden gust of wind. "We should probably see what we can prepare for dinner." Food consumption had slowed after the shooting because the invited guests had vacated Lear House; still, supplies were nearly gone. Only a half bag of oats and one bag of meal remained — fish were hard to come by because of the continuing torrents, wild winds, and perilous currents. The pig was, of course, gone and no other meat had graced their table since the day of the ball. Daniel Quinn, who had subsisted on table scraps, had disappeared without a good-bye a few days after the guests.

"I hardly care to go inside anymore," Lucinda said. They paused before the door, and Briana studied the gray eyes and pale skin of her sister's face. Sir Thomas rarely spoke to either of them now, preferring to deal with others. Lucinda had taken the landlord's remote attitude especially hard; Briana learned from her father that her sister strayed from her room only when required and often cried herself to sleep.

"You understand that he isn't in love with me — if anything, I'm a conquest," Briana said, hoping to assure her sister. She had never expressed this feeling so strongly before, but her sister's melancholia forced her to speak. "And I'm not in love with him. There's nothing he could say or do to sway me in my love for Rory."

Lucinda gripped the umbrella handle, her knuckles turning white. "Yes. I don't think he's in love with anyone but himself." The dark door of Lear House stared back at them.

"Have you given up on him?" Briana asked.

Lucinda pointed the umbrella at Sir Thomas's bedroom. "At one time, I would have done anything he asked, but when I found out the night of the ball that he cared nothing for me, and that he only desired my services as a governess to keep his friends happy, my feelings changed. The shot intended for him hit my heart instead."

Briana put her arm around her sister's shoulder. "I'm sorry you were hurt, but I'm glad you can finally see through him. I'm sure it's been painful."

Her sister drew in a deep breath. "More painful than anything I've ever experienced — a hundred times more painful than leaving Father and you to teach in England." She shook her head. "Yet I truly wonder if I'm over him. Being around him, seeing him, still hurts."

"Speak of the devil," Briana whispered, upon hearing footsteps. Her attention was drawn to the man in a great coat and hunting cap who opened the manor door. His left arm was drawn up in a white cloth sling that kept it crossed over his chest. Lucinda drew closer to her sister as they backed up on the wet terrace.

He stopped in front of them and tipped his cap. The rain wicked down the brim onto the slate. "I've informed your father that I'll be leaving on the morrow. The things I've selected will be picked up and transported to Belmullet for the trip to England. The house will be locked, and no one will be permitted to enter. The heavier objects — the furniture — and some of my clothes will remain here, in case . . ."

"In case?" Briana asked.

He tilted his head, and his blue eyes shifted uneasily as if he didn't want to respond. The rain ran down his cap onto his muttonchops. "Hardly proper to think about now, but in case the situation in Ireland should change. As of now, it's impractical for me to keep two households." He shifted his focus to Lucinda. "I'm sorry to say that the Wards have procured the services of another governess — one who is English."

Lucinda drew her hand to her mouth, stifling her shock.

"I think their minds were quite made up after the ball," the owner continued. "I'm sure you'll find a post here. I'll be happy to give you a reference." His mouth arched in a harsh smile.

"There are no jobs here," Lucinda snapped. "People have neither the money nor the proclivity for education —"

He cut her off with a wave of his right hand. "I'm sure there are jobs in Dublin or other *Irish* communities. Unfortunately, the matter is no longer my concern."

"That doesn't surprise me," Briana said with equal vitriol.

"Don't say something you'll regret, Mrs. Caulfield." His mouth narrowed. "I do owe your father and husband a debt of gratitude for aiding in my recovery, but the plight of the Irish people is beyond my control. You should be pleased that I've seen fit to give your father one hundred pounds to keep *him* from starving. If you're lucky, he'll share it with you. But remember, Lear House is bankrupt. Those notes will have to last for . . . who knows how many years. Let's pray it's not long." He tipped his hat again. "Good day, ladies. Until we meet again. I'm taking tea elsewhere this evening."

He walked away, disappearing in the rain along the western path to the cliffs.

"Pompous twit," Lucinda said, her words lost on the wind.

Briana laughed at her sister's observation but winced at the single tear that rolled down her pale cheek. She opened the door. "Let's warm up. I have something to tell you."

"At least we'll have a quiet evening — without him." Lucinda shook the umbrella, closed it, and left it leaning against the frame.

Their voices were muffled by the draped furniture; an eerie quiet had fallen upon the house. The gloom was broken only by the blaze that crackled in the library fireplace, chasing the damp chill from the room. Her father compiled papers behind the desk, while Rory, his back to the door, sat across from him. The two talked quietly as Briana and Lucinda passed by.

In the kitchen, they shed their wet coats and then looked for something to prepare for the evening meal.

"What shall we have tonight?" Lucinda asked in an airy manner. "Lamb chops with mint jelly, pottage with fish, potato stew, bread? And what for dessert? Bread pudding? Elderflower fool?"

Briana's stomach ached at the mention of such delicacies. She opened the larder door and pointed to the remaining bag of oats and meal. "How about oatmeal and water with a helping of mush?"

"I'll draw the water," Lucinda offered, picking up a pan.

Briana rubbed her belly as a wave of nausea roiled over her abdomen.

Lucinda dropped the pan on the table, rushed to her side, and guided her to a chair. "What's wrong? You look positively washed out." Her sister kneeled beside her.

Briana fanned herself with her hands as sweat broke out on her forehead. She relaxed in the chair and took her sister's hands in hers. "I do have something to tell you. I don't know whether to be happy or sad."

"What?" Her sister looked at her with curious eyes.

"I'm going to have a child."

Lucinda looked like Briana felt. Her sister also didn't know whether to be glad or horrified. Her eyes widened and she leaned back, rocking on her feet, stunned by the news. "I don't know what to say." Her mouth drooped in a frown. "How did this happen?"

Briana couldn't help but laugh. "How did it happen? Oh, sister, I'm afraid we need to have a long talk. Father has been remiss in his duties."

Lucinda blushed and shook her head. "Don't be ridiculous. I don't mean that. I mean — why did you decide to bear a child at this awful . . . time? How does Rory feel about this?"

"We didn't decide," Briana said. "An accident happened, although I'm not going to think of my child that way." She ran her hands over her stomach, feeling her belly, which was still lean despite her pregnancy. "We prayed about it, protected ourselves, even practiced abstinence . . . when we had the strength . . . but a child is coming, no doubt about it. We tried — we really did." She lowered her gaze. "I'd say Rory was happy when I told him. He wants to make life good for all of us now that a baby is on the way, but we both have doubts about the future."

"What will the baby eat after your milk runs dry?" her sister asked. "Will you have enough nourishment? Where will you live with this child if we're ejected?"

"Draw up a chair and sit beside me," Briana said. "I feel like I'm a queen and you're my subject. All these questions are making me dizzy."

Lucinda got a chair, sat, and awaited the answers with glazed eyes, the seriousness of her questions etched into the lines of her face.

"We've talked about it." She found herself reluctant to tell her sister of Rory's idea of leaving for America. Now that her sister had no job with the Wards, would she think that she and Rory were deserting the family? Could they all leave together? She still doubted her father would desert Ireland no matter what came their way. What if her father needed help after they had gone? She and Rory would not be around to look after him. Lucinda would be happy on the Continent, but she would need to find a job. The prospect of leaving Ireland brought up many more questions than she could answer. Shaken by the possibilities, she pressed her fingers to her temples.

Lucinda looked on, concern filling her eyes.

"We pray that the potato crop is bountiful in August," Briana said. "If not, we shall all have to make a decision."

"Perhaps the lout will let the tenants live on the farms and Father and I in the cottage until that time." Lucinda clutched her forehead. "I hate to think it, but he might evict us soon after Lear House is closed."

The lout? Her sister had changed her tune about the landlord. But Briana was convinced that if the Englishman showed any compassion, or offered any token of affection, her sister's revulsion would fly out the window like a loose canary.

"Perhaps," Briana replied. "Father has money for food, but we've lost our connections and there's nothing to buy."

Lucinda nodded. "That's why I'm worried about your baby. Maybe we can all go to Dublin, or England . . . or America."

Briana rose from the chair and walked to the stove. "Rory heard of men who went to Dublin and England looking for work. He says the conditions there are as bad as Mayo . . . worse in some ways for Irishmen. America seems a better choice, but it would mean leaving everything —" She choked, wiped the tears forming in her eyes with the sleeve of her dress, and pointed to the peat stacked near the stove. "We might as well get started. None of these questions will get answered if we go hungry tonight."

Lucinda got up and opened the kitchen door. "I'll look for some dandelion greens. Soon we'll have to send the men out for birds' eggs. If rabbits weren't so scarce . . . the horses . . ." Her words trailed off, but Briana knew what she was thinking.

Briana placed the peat in the stove and lit it. She yelled to her sister before she started out, "Don't say anything yet to Father. He's under enough strain."

Lucinda nodded and shut the door.

Sir Thomas put his booted feet on the scratched wooden table, sipped poteen from a scarred pewter cup, and marveled at his adaptability. He had walked in the rain, leaving the aging grandeur of Lear House to come to the welcoming arms of a woman who lived on the eastern edge of the village.

The liquor warmed his gullet and numbed the lingering pain in his left shoulder. He had drunk one healthy draft already and was now on his second. Despite the alcohol's hazy heat, and the comfort provided by his companion, he was eager to be on the next morning's carriage. How happy he would be to settle into the leather seat and be rid of Ireland — perhaps forever. Lear House would stand as it had for centuries before. That's what he wanted to believe. But times did seem different from the past: tenuous and fraught with peril.

He sipped his drink and his father came to mind — a stern man from West Yorkshire whose face reminded him of the marble busts of long-dead priests ensconced in moldy cathedrals — a man who would have whipped him within a lash of his life had he caught him in this situation. His father was a rock in the foundation of the Anglican Church and had little tolerance for humor and merry-making of any sort.

She called herself Julia, but he wasn't even sure it was her real name. In truth, he didn't care. She used to be pretty when he first started visiting her several years earlier in her small cabin on the edge of Carrowteige, but that was before the famine struck. Tonight, she looked haggard, old, and worn like the starving people Brian had described. He had come for sex, but because of the sling supporting his aching shoulder, and his miserable attitude, the evening had turned to companionship. Previously, in Julia's cabin, he hadn't worried about pretense, privilege, or the financial dealings of Lear House. Tonight was different. Oddly enough, he found himself asking the same question that the Walsh family had voiced on many occasions since his return to Ireland: *How could this terrible disaster have happened?*

"You haven't been by much this year." Julia sidled up to his chair, her back to the turf fire. "You're the only man I entertain," she said wistfully, as if she longed *only* for him.

"I hardly believe that I'm a solitary customer," he replied. "I've been busy with business matters."

"And entertaining English guests." She threw her head back and laughed as her long, black curls fell about her shoulders. "I should slap you. Isn't that what a lady of breeding does when she's been insulted?"

"Slap me and you won't get your coin." He studied her face and tried to look past the hardships that had aged her. A faded beauty shimmered on the tired skin. The rain dripped into the cabin at one end of the roof, but despite the nasty weather, the alcohol and conversation assuaged his troubles.

"I'm no whore," she said. "They would

run me out of the village. Your money helps me get through the year."

"Well, supper certainly wasn't worth it." He downed another swig of poteen. His head felt pleasantly empty now; even his teeth felt numb.

Julia glowered at him, taking offense to his statement. "Supper was fine. Food is hard to come by. I have to scramble for the bare essentials, and I'm doing better than most, I can tell you. There's no seed potatoes left and the meat —"

He cupped his hand over her mouth. "Stop. I don't want to know." He imagined that the stringy gray meat she had served him was horse, or worse yet, donkey.

She pushed his hand away. "Goat, and I was lucky to get it." She touched the sling covering his left arm and then gently massaged his forearm. "Not *up* for it tonight, heh?" Her brows rose as she thought of a question. "Who would shoot the likes of you?"

"I don't know, and I may never find out."

She leaned back, twirling a long strand of curls between her fingers, before giving him a broad smile. "I heard tell of a man at Lear House who got a pistol from a sea captain."

He started in his seat, and then leaned forward. "Who's the bastard? Tell me who

— as if I don't know. Who told you this?"

"Why does it matter? The truth is the truth."

"Get my coat," he ordered. "Only one man's been to see a captain that I know of."

She rose and retrieved his coat and hat from the peg near the cabin door. "No need to rush off. It gets lonely here being a single woman with the husband long dead."

He stood, swaying on his feet, and then reached into his pocket and pulled out a coin. "Here. More than enough for services rendered. I doubt I'll see you next year."

She threw her arms around his shoulders and attempted to kiss him.

He winced and pushed her aside. "Watch out. The shoulder is still raw." He put on his hat and coat and stumbled out in the rain. He staggered a few steps and then looked back. Julia stood in the doorway, her dark form silhouetted by the light of the peat fire. She was a sad figure, he thought, and most likely to die within the year unless she left County Mayo. *But where will she go?* The idea pained him, yet he shrugged it off. Where Julia went was of no concern. He stumbled forward, on his way to find Rory Caulfield.

They sat down to a meager supper in the

kitchen at Lear House. Little was said, and even the prayers over the meal were tinged with sadness. The thought on everyone's mind was not if, but when, the Constabulary would start evictions. Briana and Rory had looked at each other and then broached the plan of moving to America, but her father would have none of it. "I can't think about it on my last night in Lear House," he said.

"We do have one good bit of news to share," Briana said, hoping to lift the mood. Lucinda shifted in her chair, deducing what was coming.

"What's that?" Brian asked in a gruff voice.

"You're going to be a grandfather." Briana smiled, but only Rory returned her attempt at happiness. The announcement of a child was almost always a reason for rejoicing, but there was none of that in her father's eyes or demeanor.

"Congratulations," he said tepidly, and then went back to eating his mush. Under his breath, he muttered, "Another mouth to feed."

She let her spoon and the subject drop.

After the meal, Brian and Lucinda trudged back to the cottage, leaving her with Rory in the kitchen. The need to be alone, to take in her sadness, overcame Rory's insistence that she should return home with him. Protesting her obstinacy, he stopped at the cabin as she continued up the lane toward Carrowteige.

"I won't be long," she told him.

Tomorrow it will all be over. Briana couldn't bear the thought of losing the home she had known all her life as she walked toward the village to be alone with her grief. Her sister's umbrella protected her from the showery gusts. The rain pelted the back of her coat as she topped the slope and the village came into view. The buildings she had known all her life looked small and insignificant under the thick, drab clouds. Here and there a sliver of light burst forth from a grimy window or between the cracks of battered doors. The sadness that had plagued her in recent days struck again. Holding on to the umbrella, she doubled over near a burrow that had served as a shelter for the starving. Briana rubbed her abdomen and hoped that what she was experiencing was related to the food she had eaten, not something serious regarding her pregnancy.

She straightened, feeling slightly queasy, and started down the road.

A man strode through the rain. As he drew closer, she recognized the figure of Sir Thomas, but his usually confident swagger was disrupted by an off-balance sway. She was tempted to hide behind a scrub brush but instead decided to face him. He appeared to be drunk and, in that state, would probably have little recollection of their conversation in the morning.

He ambled through the darkness, his face as dull as his black clothing, and stopped a yard away, wobbling on his feet. "Who's this?" he asked in a drowsy slur.

His eyes were hidden by the tilt of his hat; all she could see was the occasional flash of white teeth between the lips. The acidic odor of poteen wafted from his mouth. She tilted the umbrella backward.

"Ah, is it the fair Briana?" He took off his hat and teetered through a bow.

"You sound like a drunken Shakespearean actor," she said, repelled by his condition.

"An astute observation. That may be, fair lady, but the disposition induced by your local drink has affected my temperament radically . . . altered my course by the minute . . . as I tramped through the village of Carrowteige." A giggle burst from his mouth. "I was ready to find the bastard and kill him — give him a dose of his own medicine. But now I have something else in mind."

His rambling speech puzzled her. "What

are you talking about?"

"Simply put, the man who shot me." He stepped even closer to her — so close she could see the hate in his eyes. The mirthful talk that had bordered on flirtation disappeared.

"I have no idea —"

"Of course you do."

She waited, the rain pelting her from all sides.

"It appears a tenant received a pistol from a sea captain. I know of only one man who has made such a journey since I've been at Lear House."

Briana knew it was useless to lie, and the disturbing image of her husband firing the pistol jumped into her head thanks to the owner's accusation. More than the truth was at risk. They would all pay dearly if Rory was arrested.

She kept quiet, protecting her husband from a landlord who wasn't as drunk as she thought.

"When I get to Belmullet, I'll give word to the Royal Irish Constabulary," Sir Thomas said. "They'll get to the bottom of it. I'd like to see the villain spend time in prison or maybe get sent away — far, far, away from Ireland. What do they call it? 'Transported,' I believe."

In her mind, she recounted the specifics of the evening Sir Thomas was shot — details the landlord already knew. Rory had gone for a walk on the beach, he had heard the shot, and then rushed to the house. The sand was still on his feet. That much was true. But the pistol had been fired.

"Should we visit your husband and see what he has to say?" He lumbered ahead, one boot slipping in the mud. He threw his right hand up, keeping his balance. "Damn this country! I've had enough."

She could hold her tongue no longer. "My husband didn't shoot you. He saved your life."

Sir Thomas pointed to Lear House, dull and vacant on the slope. "He *didn't* save my life. The wound wasn't fatal. He came to my aid after the shot had been fired. His eagerness would lead one to believe that he was close by. Perhaps he's a poor shot."

"*You* are being unfair," Briana protested. "He had nothing to do with it."

"Then who?"

Her mind went to the Molly Maguires. Perhaps one of them, maybe Connor Donlon, had sneaked into their cabin, taken the pistol, and fired it. But casting suspicion on someone else and bringing up the Mollies' hatred might only incite his passions. She didn't want to spar with him anymore.

"See, you have no answer because you can't defend your husband." He turned and cupped his right hand around her cheek.

Briana twisted out of his grip, ready to strike him with the umbrella.

Sir Thomas lowered his hand and clutched his injured shoulder. His mouth turned down in a forlorn smile, as if he longed to be close to her yet knew it was impossible. "You're quite beautiful." He reached for her cheek again, but then withdrew. "Why would you want to live . . . in this squalor? Your sister wants more out of life, but you're different. You're satisfied with what you have as a lowly farmer's wife."

He dragged himself toward Lear House as she followed behind.

"I love Lear House and want the estate to live on forever," Briana replied. "I'm happy being the *lowly* farmer's wife. Mayo is my home."

Sir Thomas chuckled. "An admirable dream for Lear House, but hardly practical. . . . Continue to say your prayers." He swung his right arm out in a punch. "I was ready to thrash your husband, but I can't fight one-handed . . . against a man who has proven to be a ruffian."

"That's the first sensible thing you've said

this evening."

He stopped within sight of her cabin. "I *am* going to notify the Constabulary — fair warning. I'll let them take care of the matter. I'll give a deposition before I depart for England. If your husband is innocent, he'll not be arrested."

"He is innocent," she replied as fear prickled over her.

He pushed back her umbrella and studied her face. "Beautiful."

A cold rain pattered against her. She backed away as he continued to stare.

"You'd *both* be happy in England, away from this." He sauntered down the road, swaying slightly, turned onto the path leading to the manor, and entered the somber dwelling. The door shut, perhaps for its penultimate time. She stood by her cabin wondering what Sir Thomas meant by *both be happy in England.* Who was the other person he was referring to — her husband or Lucinda?

Rory was asleep on his stomach, the lower half of his body covered by the blanket. She rubbed his back, and he stirred underneath her fingers. She undressed and slid into bed next to him. Her husband slept so peacefully that she didn't want to wake him with the news that the Constabulary would be questioning him for shooting Sir Thomas Blakely. It was bad enough that she would have a sleepless night.

When she awoke, her husband was gone.

After dressing, she found him talking with his brother. The sun shone in broad, yellow streaks through intermittent clouds. The rain had let up, but the houses, the fences, the heath, dripped from the damp. Patches of fog hovered over the lane leading to the village.

"You just missed his highness," Jarlath said, and then spat on the ground. He leaned against his cabin wall, his long legs stretched toward the road. "He didn't even wave to his loyal subjects as he passed."

"Not even a nod," Rory said. "The carriage shades were pulled, so I didn't even see him. A shiny, black one pulled by four horses the color of peat that looked better fed than the rest of Ireland. A sorry sight indeed."

The men waved to her father, who had rounded the corner of Lear House. His head was bowed while he tromped up the lane. Briana shuddered at his unkempt appearance, hardly ever having seen him in such condition. He looked as if he had drunk the night away and then fallen asleep in his clothes. Soot from the turf fire smudged his face, and gray tufts of hair erupted from the side of his head. He had forgotten to belt his trousers, and they hung loosely around his belly. His shirttails fell in a white swirl around his thighs.

"He didn't even leave me a key for the padlocks," her father said, his voice quivering. "I asked him what we should do if there was a fire or some other disaster that required us to get into the house. Do you know what he answered?"

Not expecting a cordial response, Briana shook her head as did everyone else.

Brian frowned. "He said, 'Let it burn.' "

"My God," Jarlath said, straightening against the wall. "The man is a demon."

"We can take an axe to the doors if we have to," Rory said.

"There'll be no need," Brian said. "Lear House will sit deserted, as alone as it's ever been, while we bide our time."

The house already seemed cadaverous to Briana, as if it had been killed by its owner, as lifeless as a dead animal with clouded, milky eyes.

"We're next," Rory said. "The evictions will come — mark my words."

Rory turned, balled his fists, and squinted into the morning sun toward the road that would take the carriage to Belmullet.

The waves of hate that emanated from her husband washed over her. She had known Rory since they were children, but for the first time she recoiled at his temper. His eyes flickered with murderous rage from the pernicious thoughts that billowed in his body. At that moment, she knew he could kill. The landlord was far down the road by now, so she gathered the courage to tell Rory what Sir Thomas had said.

"Please excuse us, but I must talk to my husband," she said, and led Rory away from Jarlath and her father. They walked past Lear House and the tenant farms, toward the cliffs. Soon, after numerous "good days" to the other tenants, they stood watching the crashing waves and the blue, turbulent waters. Everything seemed in its place, as it had for centuries, as black-tipped gannets dove into the sea and gulls sailed on out-stretched wings on the buoyant air.

They stood facing the wind, the sun at their backs. To their right, the rocky spires of the Stags jutted out of the water. To their left, the ocean swirled past the cliffs into the bay.

"You're right about America," she said, broaching the subject. "We must plan now with all haste." She picked up a rock and threw it, watching it fall over the cliff. "Father won't go, I'm sure. Lucinda might if we can sway her from England. . . . That leaves you and me."

Rory stared out to sea.

"Perhaps *you* should go to America," she said.

"And leave you here? What about our family, our child?" He planted his feet apart in a defiant stance. "That's not our plan."

"Sir Thomas is reporting the shooting to the Constabulary. They will be here in a few days to question you."

His eyes pinched in a narrow gaze. "Why would he suspect me?"

A gull cried out, shot upward from the cliff face and spiraled overhead. She savored the fleeting moment. To fly with such abandon as the gull, to live unfettered in the air and on the ocean. What would it be like to be such a bird, free from the cares of human life?

"He knows you have a pistol. I don't know who told him."

"I told you Noel showed Connor and me how to fire it long before the ball, but they would never shoot — Connor's a loose cannon, but neither he nor Noel are murderers."

"It doesn't matter," she said. "Sir Thomas

suspects you and will swear to that in a deposition. If they find you, you may be arrested."

He grasped her hands. "I've heard some men are so eager for transport they commit crimes so they'll be sent away from Ireland, but I'm not leaving you or Jarlath to hide in America. I'm innocent and I'll swear to it."

They walked away from the cliff as Briana's mind raced; she knew her husband's head was filled with similar dismal thoughts. She wanted him to leave, but Rory was right; to run away would be an admission of guilt.

They stopped in front of Lear House, where Lucinda, her head bowed, stood crying at the front door. Not wanting to leave her in such a despondent state, they turned up the lane. Lucinda blew her nose into a handkerchief, magnifying the dark circles around her red and puffy eyes. Her hair fell in limp strands around her face.

"Not a word from him," Lucinda sputtered as they drew close. "Not a good-bye or a good luck." She lifted the heavy padlock attached to the door and let it fall against the wood with a clank. "And now I can't even get to the library to read the books I love. What *are* we to do? I might as well starve, because I have no appetite." Lucinda collapsed in tears in Briana's arms.

Briana grasped her sister's thinning frame and stroked her hair, struggling to hold back tears herself. Lucinda's emotional breakdown weighed on her as much as the threat against her husband.

"We have to be strong for a number of reasons," Briana said. They were hollow words with little meaning other than an offering of support — useless words in the face of starvation and loss. But as she held her sister, an idea crossed her mind. Rory wouldn't be able to book passage out of Belmullet or Westport after Sir Thomas notified the Constabulary; they would be on watch for him, making it almost impossible for him to flee Ireland. If he managed to escape, it would all but seal his guilt, but perhaps he could find someone who would hide him until the real shooter could be found. But who would take him in? Everyone was suffering. No Lear House tenant had anything to spare, and Rory wouldn't leave the Walshes and Jarlath's family to eviction and starvation while he ran from the Constabulary. There seemed to be no way out for her husband.

"Sir Thomas thinks Rory shot him," Briana told her sister.

"I'll face the constable if he comes for

me," Rory said. "I'm not leaving anyone behind."

Lucinda looked at her sister, then at Rory, and a look of horror filled her face. "Sir Thomas thinks *you* shot him?"

"Yes," Briana said. "Rory's innocent . . . but the law is always on the landowner's side."

"He has influence with sea captains who are more than willing to take his money, but not the Constabulary, I think," Lucinda said, and looked at Rory. "I'll tell them I was talking to you when the shot was fired. After all, I was outside for a time. We both heard it and ran inside to see what happened." She looked away as if she didn't believe the alibi she had constructed.

"You *were* outside," Briana said, knowing her sister had never talked to Rory before the shooting. "Let's see if they dare come this far to question him." She grasped her sister's shoulder gently. "But there's something else I want to ask of you. . . ."

Lucinda dabbed her eyes with the handkerchief. "What?"

"Would you go to America if we had to?"

Lucinda gasped.

Briana took in her sister's astounded look, not knowing what her answer would be.

What a fool she is.

The carriage shuddered down the road, tossing Sir Thomas left and right in his seat. He had pulled the shades because he had no stomach for what Briana and the others had told him about the starving, the rats, the dogs, and the presence of death hanging over County Mayo.

The damn fool has no idea how beautiful she is. There's something about her that fascinates me — her strength, her spirit! Yes, she's pretty, but I've never met a woman like her. And what a poor excuse she has for a husband. What can he give her when I could provide everything a woman could want? She doesn't understand that love will buy little. Affection flies away when there's nothing to eat. Cold, hunger, and hardship will drive them to their breaking point. I pity her. . . .

His hand drifted toward the shade. He wanted to lift the black fabric. After all, it was childish to think that he couldn't deal with the sights along the road to Belmullet: the godforsaken heath, ugly mountains, or interminable bog. He had seen death many times: His mother and father had died at home; his aunt and uncle had died of old age at the Manchester estate; even workers under his employ had succumbed at the mills. Why should the poor Irish lying dead in the ditches affect him? It was God's will. They were meant to die. They had neither the power nor the privilege intended for the English.

He drew his hand away from the silk cord and settled back into the seat. Flashes of light blinded him when the shade rattled. Restless, he reached into his bag for a small book he had taken from the Lear House library. The dim interior wasn't conducive to reading; in fact, the carriage wasn't comfortable for much, although many Irishmen would have considered it a luxurious ride. He threw the book on the seat.

Sleep. Try to sleep. That will do it. God, get me out of this forsaken country!

He rested his head against the soft leather and closed his eyes. His stomach rumbled.

"My kingdom for a decent meal," he said to the air, and thought of the limited food choices he faced in Belmullet before boarding the ship that would take him to Westport and then on to Liverpool. Everything would be better once he got aboard. Hunger gnawed at his stomach, for he'd had nothing to eat in the morning — he could take no more mush or oatmeal. The bumpy ride hadn't helped. His left shoulder throbbed with every bounce. There was no getting around it. Something more than hunger was bothering him. *Anger?* Yes, anger and something else he hadn't expected to feel. He had experienced it few times in his life, mostly when he had disappointed his parents. His father called it "remorse" and deemed it a "useless emotion." If one does correctly the job of living, there should never be cause for remorse, his father had told him.

Remorse. For what? He thought on this awhile and then decided that perhaps he hadn't been living correctly, as prescribed by his father. *Am I to save Lear House and the people in it? It's too much to ask! Times are harder now than when my parents were alive. They would understand the difficulty of my predicament.* His musing switched from his mother and father to Briana. *I would gladly save her, but she's chosen another. What a fool she is when she could have had someone . . .*

The driver clucked at the horses, and the carriage slowed as water splashed against its sides. Then a sound he had never heard rang in his ears, like the cry of the damned in hell. He lifted the left window shade, looking out upon the flat bog, and saw that the carriage was crossing a river wide from the summer rains, somewhat shallow in this part but flowing briskly in white ripples over the rocks.

Ragged men, women, and children stood like black statues in front of the brush that lined the shallow bank, the women screeching in agony, clutching at their husbands. They seemed to be parting, for there was a group of men already on the south bank. They looked piteously back at the women they'd left across the river. The women's cries were hideous, nightmarish, and he wanted to block the noise from his ears.

The horses splashed through the rapids as the driver lashed the animals forward. Sir Thomas closed the shade again as the carriage sped past the starving men. He'd seen enough.

CHAPTER 14

August 1846

They stood on the highest potato ridge at Jarlath's quarter acre. The plot was above Rory's, so they had been optimistic that the potatoes might better survive the cold and damp summer on the elevated drainage.

"Will you look at this," Jarlath said to Rory, who stood with Connor and Noel.

Rory touched a sickly, gray leaf and it melted into a black slime in his hands. No need to put his fingers to his nose; the putrid odor of the rotted plants, already in the air, sprang up to his nostrils.

Connor pointed at the rows of plants on terraced land that led to the bay. "We're dead," he said bluntly. He crossed himself and then folded his thick arms against his chest. "My family will be moving on."

"The lumpers died overnight," Rory said, stunned by the dead plants around him. Yesterday, the plants were green and healthy.

Now, nothing could be done to save them. "Where will you go?" he asked Connor.

"I'm not sure," the man said. "Blakely may not be back, but the constable and soldiers will be. Brian told us to expect eviction if the crop failed. It'll be another Ballinlass — where they turned three hundred off their land, sentenced them to their deaths as far as I'm concerned. At least the owner let them keep the cabin timbers. I doubt if our landlord will be so kind. He'll grind us into the ground, and there's nothing we or the Mollies can do about it."

"We'll keep what we can," Noel said. "Let the landlord be damned. Who's going to tally the takings — Brian?"

Rory knew they were right. With this crop failure, the strength, the will to fight, would be sapped from the people, destroyed by starvation. He feared that even the Mollies would be splintered into "every man for himself" by this latest disaster. Their plans were disorganized enough as they were. How could you stand against Dublin Castle and the Palace of Westminster when you had no food?

"We'll walk to Dublin rather than have them take everything from us," Connor said. "Sheila and the children can stay with her sister while I look for work in England.

The rails are hiring, always looking for men."

"That's because they end up dead in a pauper's graveyard," Rory said. "It's no good there either."

Connor scoffed. "Better than here. If I work near Manchester, maybe I'll run into the big man himself — Sir Thomas Blakely. We might share a pint or two."

Rory appreciated Connor's attempt at humor, but when he looked back again at the plants he saw only dismal sadness, failure, and death. With a baby on the way, he had no idea how to escape these fates other than to face the Constabulary and get Briana and the Walshes out of Ireland as soon as he could.

The next day, Briana was dressed and involved in the day's chores. She had lit the fire outside under the water kettle for washing; now back inside, she was pondering how to make the morning breakfast more palatable. Adding a few greens to cooked oats was growing tiresome.

When a knock sounded at the door, Rory put down the tack hammer he was using to mend the sole of his boot and pulled on a shirt.

Briana opened the door. A small man with

a full head of black hair and equally dark whiskers speckled with gray stood outside, his breeches and boots spattered with mud. He wore a greatcoat over a faded and rumpled blue uniform. The collar came to a V below his throat, while brass buttons dotted the center from neck to waist. The circular cap he held displayed the Royal Irish Constabulary insignia. Briana had seen the cap on her trip to Westport. His soft brown eyes studied Briana and then shifted to the interior of their cabin. "May I come in?" he asked after completing his visual inspection.

Briana peered around him. He appeared to be alone. His chestnut mare was tethered to a post near the cabin.

"We'd be more comfortable outside," Rory said, and stood up from the bed.

"I'd prefer to talk in private, if you don't mind." The man stepped into the cabin. He offered his hand to Rory. "Edmond Davitt, Constable at Belmullet."

Rory had heard the name before but never met the man. He shook his hand. "Rory Caulfield."

Briana's stomach turned over because she was certain that the constable had come to arrest her husband.

Davitt took off his coat and surveyed the

room. "Please sit down, Mrs. Caulfield . . . that's right, isn't it?"

Briana nodded. She and Rory sat on the dried stalks that made up their bed while Davitt took his place on the wooden stool.

He reached into his pocket for his pipe, lit the tobacco, and focused his weary eyes upon them. "I won't take much of your time, because I was up early this morning and I have plenty to keep me busy in Belmullet." He turned his gaze to Rory. "But I want to hear your story."

"So Blakely turned me in to the Constabulary," Rory said with a scornful smile. He'd rushed to the aid of the ungrateful landlord!

Davitt nodded. "He cried all the way to the Commissioner at Westport. Frankly, the Commissioner has more important things on his mind — like protecting food from looters and making sure that the port runs smoothly." He clasped his hands together and leaned toward them. "He sent me to investigate rather than bother sending his men on a trip to Carrowteige. We're stretched thin as it is." His lips pursed. "The Commissioner was put off — Blakely's wound hardly looked more than one rough boy would give another with a switch."

"My husband rushed to assist him," Briana blurted out. "Without his help, Sir

Thomas might have died."

Rory held up his hand. "Please excuse my wife, Mr. Davitt." He shot a "be quiet" look to her. "I think the constable can make up his own mind about what happened."

"Can I see the pistol that was given to you by the Captain?"

Briana had no choice but to remain silent. Sir Thomas had given a thorough report to the officer.

"Captain Miller gave it to me in case we might have to protect ourselves while transporting supplies to Lear House," Rory said. He retrieved the pistol from the bag and handed it to the constable.

The man examined it for several minutes, carefully turning it over and upside down and smelling the remains of the spent powder before handing it back to Rory. "I imagine this was the weapon," he said.

"It was fired the night Sir Thomas was shot," Rory explained, "but I had nothing to do with it. Someone came into our cabin, took the pistol, and fired it." He then recounted the night of the shooting, leaving out any mention of Lucinda or her eavesdropping.

"Do you have anything to offer regarding your husband's story?" the constable asked Briana.

"He had sand on his feet," she said.

"From his walk on the beach," the officer replied.

"Yes, he's telling the truth."

"Do you have any idea who would want to shoot Sir Thomas?" Davitt asked Rory.

Briana suppressed her desire to interrupt. Why didn't Rory go along with Lucinda's alibi that she was with him when Sir Thomas was shot?

"No," Rory responded. Briana knew that answer was a half truth at best. Noel had showed Connor and Rory how to shoot the weapon, and any disgruntled Mollie might have taken a shot at the landlord the night of the ball. His eyes shifted to Briana and then back to the officer. "Several months ago, a note was tacked to the Lear House door. It threatened Brian Walsh, the landlord's agent, and the rest of the family, including my wife. I suspected that it might have been the work of a Molly Maguire, but we never found out who did it."

"We?" the officer asked with renewed interest.

"Yes, I'm a Maguire, but I've helped keep the peace at Lear House. My father-in-law is the agent here. I wish him and the family no harm."

"I see," the constable said, rising from the

stool. "I've a long ride back to Belmullet." He lifted his arms and then stretched them behind his back. "I've no fondness for the Englishman in this matter, but I do have a duty to the law that transcends my love for my countrymen. Unfortunate as it may be, Mr. Caulfield, you are under suspicion for the attempted murder of Sir Thomas Blakely and you are not to leave County Mayo under any circumstances without notifying me. I will make sure the Constabulary has your name and description at every office and every port. If you impede this investigation in any manner, or attempt to flee, you will be arrested. Do you understand?"

Rory nodded. "Yes, sir."

The officer reached for his coat and hat. "The owner's ego appears to have been scarred more than his body, but the law prescribes its own remedies no matter how slight the wound." He pointed to the weapon. "If I were you, I'd keep that pistol out of sight and end your relationship with the Maguires."

"Thank you, constable, for that advice," Rory said, rising to shake the man's hand.

Briana relaxed a bit as Davitt headed toward the door. She and Rory watched as he slipped the reins from the post, mounted the horse, and turned it east.

Before goading the animal, he said, "By the way, the bodies of a young couple, the Kilbanes, were found a few days ago. What was left of them was found in the bog behind their cottage. They'd been shot with a pistol owned by Frankie Kilbane. We found it buried behind the house. That find, Mr. Caulfield, saved you from being more of a suspect than you are. Be careful what you do." He tipped his hat, buttoned his coat, and spurred the horse with his heels. It trotted off down the road under the thick overcast.

Her heart racing, Briana stood rooted in the door thinking of her husband's temporary escape from imprisonment.

After Davitt disappeared, Rory collapsed against her. "I've never been so scared," he said.

She fought her own paralyzing fear and wrapped her arms around her husband. "You were so calm. I'm shaking now."

Rory breathed a subdued sigh of relief. "I have nothing to hide from Davitt, but I'm terrified of not being able to protect you and our baby." He kissed her cheek and then hugged her trembling body. "We were going to America — but that's changed. *Damn* him!"

She sank against him, thanking God that

her husband was still with her.

The wash pot popped and hissed as a few raindrops splattered on the red-hot metal. Washing clothes. Mending shirts and breeches. Making meals. They were such mundane acts, but ones she performed with love knowing that her days with Rory might be growing short.

"You'll go?" Briana leaned forward with her elbows on the table, astonished by the possibility.

Lucinda lifted the spoon, tasted the mush, and then spat it back in the bowl. Her sister threw the utensil on the table, her lips quivering as she struggled to express her feelings. "Yes, I'll go. I can't abide this any longer. America is surely better. If I don't leave Ireland, I'll die."

Brian cupped his hands around his bowl and lamented, "America is a beautiful country, I hear, but what else do we know of it? You may be exchanging one ill for another." His tone indicated that he was far from convinced.

Briana lit the candles dotting the room as the light faded in her father's cottage. She opened the door so the smoke and heat would escape into the evening air. The breeze swirled around her face, and it soothed and saddened her at the same time, for how much longer would Ireland's air caress her?

On Sunday next week, the *SS Warton,* a six-masted steamer, would be sailing from Westport for the United States with ports of call in Boston and New York. She and her sister intended to be on it. The news of the ship had come from Connor Donlon on his way to Dublin with his family. Connor had met a man returning to Carrowteige who promised to give Rory the news.

"I can't go to America, but I'm happy you've agreed to accompany my wife," Rory said to Lucinda. "I'll feel better knowing you are with Briana."

"I wish we could all go, but I must remain with the remaining tenants," Brian said. "I want no bloodshed when the dragoons and Constabulary arrive for the . . ." Her father's voice faded as she returned to the table, but Briana knew what he was going to say — *eviction.* But there was something else he didn't express — his love of Ireland and his desire not to leave his home.

Since Constable Davitt had visited the week before, scores of tenants had left their farms looking for work and food. "There's hardly anyone about now," Briana said. She looked at her sister, who bowed her head glumly over the table. "We're doing the right thing — the only thing we can do. Soon there'll be no one here but Rory, Father, and Jarlath and his family."

"We're lucky that Jarlath can fish and that your father has the blood money from an Englishman to tide us over," Rory said.

Brian put his hand over Rory's. "Hush about that! I, for one, am grateful for the generosity the man has seen fit to give us." He then lowered his gaze as well, as if it was humiliating to speak of charity after so many years of service to the owner. "At least my daughters will be on their way to America aboard a ship that has some comfort thanks to him."

Her father spoke the truth. Rory had told her of commercial ships that hauled lumber across the Atlantic from Canada and then returned to North America from England and Ireland. Those going back were crammed with Irish emigrants who had no choice but to book a cheap fare that often they could barely afford. Disease and death ran rampant on the filthy decks up top and in the sweltering, cramped, quarters below. Some had called them "coffin ships." The dead, overcome by starvation and dysentery, were stripped of their clothes and tossed overboard, their bodies delivered to an unsympathetic ocean.

Rory had made it clear that Briana and Lucinda would not be traveling aboard those terrible ships. There was too much at stake for his wife and the unborn child who grew in her belly.

Briana placed her hand on the mound below her stomach, giving it a gentle pat. *God be with us.*

Her father observed the sweep of her hand over her abdomen. "So it's settled. Rory and I and Jarlath will remain on the estate until we can stay no longer. God knows where we'll end up, but if He is kind we might find work in Castlebar or Westport. When the time comes, God willing, we will join you in America."

Despite his halfhearted attempt to smile, she doubted her father had any intention of leaving the estate. They would bury him in the small cemetery between Lear House and Carrowteige, where her mother lay at peace. A deep sadness stabbed her soul, causing her to wince in pain. She put her hands on the table and attempted to get up, but the tears flowed fast and her arms buckled underneath her.

Rory rushed to her side and lifted her up. She nestled against him, her eyes blinded by grief.

Lucinda dashed to her side as well and put her hand on Briana's shoulder. "Don't worry, sister. We'll be strong together. That's what you've always told me — to be strong. We'll make our journey an adventure."

Her insides shook, thinking of all that could go wrong. What if she never saw her father again? Once the ship left Westport, there would be no returning to Ireland before spring because of winter weather in the North Atlantic. What if they didn't have enough money to return? What if something went wrong with her pregnancy? Rory would be an ocean away, unable to help her. She would be a prisoner in Boston, in a foreign land with only what they could carry in a suitcase. It would never work.

Memories of spring at Lear House, when the desperate and dying came in search of food, filled her head. The sound of the keening woman whose son had died in her arms would never leave her ears. But those days had passed. She was blessed to have what she did. Those now living, destined to die as the famine raged on, would never see the opportunity she had been given. Despite her fears, the hope of gratitude filled her.

As Rory led her from the table, she stopped to clutch her sister's hand. "You're right," she said. "We will be strong to-gether."

The candles illuminated the dampness in her sister's eyes.

There was no turning back.

On Friday, the seventh of August, Briana said good-bye to Lear House.

Rory loaded their bags into a cart they'd rented from a neighbor, to be pulled by the two workhorses left on the estate. Briana was concerned that the animals might not make it to Westport. With oats and other grains gone, the skinny beasts had been munching on the sparse heath grass. The horses also weren't as agile as the bog trotters they had ridden previously to Westport, so the going would be slower.

Covered by a blanket and tarp, Briana, Rory, and Lucinda planned to sleep over-night in the cart or on the ground.

Briana had urged Lucinda to pack lightly, but her sister was irritated by what she had to leave behind. Lucinda had packed two dresses, in addition to the one she was wear-ing, leaving many others at the cottage. "So much that I worked for. . . . I don't know if I will ever see my books or good dresses again," she said.

They had hugged each other, and Briana

said, "Nothing can be done about that."

Her father, and Jarlath, along with his wife and son, stood at the end of the path leading to Lear House. Briana, from her seat in the cart next to Rory, looked down upon the four figures standing between her and the manor. They seemed small, helpless, diminished by the famine's life-changing power. In less than a year, her own life had shifted dramatically: She and her family had gone from relative plenty to nothing. And, as she looked at Lucinda, squirming uncomfortably next to the bags, she acknowledged how much her sister's life had changed as well. Lucinda had fallen in status from a governess for a wealthy English family to an unemployed woman with no job or marriage prospects in sight. Her sister had never owned the wealth she enjoyed in England, but being around it had enlivened her. All that was gone.

Briana had made her mind up not to cry when she said good-bye, because too many tears had already been shed. She had kissed and hugged her father and her in-laws before she climbed onto the cart, wanting to cut short her sad departure.

"You have the money I gave you?" Brian yelled to Rory as her husband took his place at the reins. "And the testimonial letter for

American customs. They'll need it for —"

Rory cut him off. "Yes, Father, for their passage, a room at The Black Ram, and some food for my return — if I can get it." He nodded and patted his coat pocket. "Letter and fifty pounds here. Protected." He pulled at the straps. "We should be going. The weather may hold tonight if we're lucky. I'll be back by next Wednesday, God willing."

Rory had told her that the trip would be rough going in the cart. The pistol, which she now hated because of its history, was concealed in Rory's travel bag. Her husband had insisted on bringing it along for protection, and she had disagreed.

Briana stared at the lane that would lead them through the village and then on the road to Westport. The few tenants who remained stood near their homes, offering feeble waves of good-bye. She shifted her gaze to the bay. Golden shafts of light punched through the overcast sky, streaking the blue-gray waters with glittering silver facets. Then, as quickly as they had appeared, the sparkling diamonds vanished as the sun disappeared behind the clouds. She wanted one last look at Lear House but didn't dare for fear she would run back to it and never leave, regardless of whether she could enter its rooms. She clutched her husband's arm. "Let's be off before I change my mind." She stole a quick look at Lucinda, who huddled in the cart bed with her head against her knees.

Rory shook the reins, and the horses wobbled forward. The animals' tails flipped in time with the sway of their bony flanks.

Her father and Jarlath's family called after them. She avoided looking back, at the manor, at the cottage, or even at their cabin as they rumbled up the hill.

I will come home to Ireland. I will see Lear House again. She repeated these words in her head as she held on to the flimsy hand rail bolted to the plank seat. With each bump and sway, she clutched her belly to keep the baby from rocking in her womb.

After a few hours' travel, they encountered a young man embracing his tearful wife at the river crossing. Briana recognized them as residents of Carrowteige. Their frayed, dirty clothes hung like rags upon their bodies as they clung to each other. Compared to the dress the young woman wore, Briana and her sister were clothed in splendor. The young man, his thin legs showing through the holes in his grimy pants, soon was left behind. His bony toes had punched holes in his shoes.

Seeing the young couple at the river of sorrows, Briana grew dispirited as well. She did, however, count her blessings. She and her sister were able to ride in a cart rather than walk to Westport, and the clothes they wore were in good repair. She wondered if the woman who stood on the bank carried a child as well.

"I wish we could offer him a ride, but the horses couldn't handle another body," Rory told her as they moved on.

As the wagon traveled south past the stony waters of Carrowmore Lake, the ochre hues of the Nephin Beg and the green bog lands came into view. Briana was amazed by the silence that surrounded them. No smoke arose from the hillsides; now deserted cabins had fused with the earth. The *sceilps* that had sheltered the starving had long been abandoned. A disturbing quiet came after the people vanished, the land empty. Apart from the occasional chirp of a bird, she heard nothing but the creaking cart as it rolled toward Bangor and Ballycroy.

That afternoon, in a secluded spot, they ate the dried fish Jarlath had given them. The wind stung less sharply here but was potent enough to send shivers racing over their arms and legs. Lucinda, sullen while she ate, said little. Rory, nearly as glum, made small talk about the rest of their journey.

After a few more hours of bumpy travel past the boggy hills, they stopped the cart south of the Kilbanes' deserted cottage, which Briana only dared glance at. That night she stared at the starry veil above as she struggled to sleep in the cart bed next to Lucinda. Rory slept on the ground guarding the bags stored underneath the cart.

The next morning, after a journey where the alder, sycamore, and chestnut thrust their leafy branches toward them like embracing arms, they stopped to eat near Mulranny. Like Carrowteige, silence pervaded the village. Briana marveled at the beautiful bay below the cliffs. To the south, the distant profile of Croagh Patrick stood like a slumbering god clothed in purple.

As they neared Westport, the starving plodded down from the hills as if a line dividing tranquility and despair had been crossed. Many had already died by the side of the road, their skeletal arms stretching into the air as if seeking the good graces of heaven. Others, pallid and half-dead, clutched each other in throes of agony, their emaciated bodies fused together as if corpses had risen from the grave to embrace. Briana covered her mouth with her handkerchief, repelled by the fact that she could do nothing about the suffering. Lucinda, who had never seen the ravages of the famine so clearly, gasped and closed her eyes.

Rory stopped the wagon at the river across from The Black Ram. He tethered the animals to a front wheel so they could graze and drink from a pail of cold water. "Wait here. I'll get a room for the night." He strode off to the public house.

The establishment seemed oddly quiet for a late Saturday afternoon. Perhaps no ships were in harbor; however, the *SS Warton* was scheduled to leave at ten the next morning, a Sunday.

"Only a year ago, I wouldn't have been caught dead staying in such a place," Lucinda said in a wistful tone and shook her head. "I've seen this public house when traveling from Westport to England and barely given it a look."

Lucinda was learning a lesson — one Briana had recognized for years: Nothing should be taken for granted, because loss came too easily from the hand of God. He was best served by doing good and being grateful for every blessing that came one's way.

"Times have changed for both of us," Briana said. "We're lucky to have each other." Her mind flashed to the journey ahead, and she drew her shawl tight around her body to stave off her apprehension about Boston.

Her father had told them that the Irish lived in particular sections of the city, and those enclaves were often segregated by the county. Emigrants from County Mayo might live on one street, while former residents of Roscommon might live a street away. He'd learned this from one of the tenant farmers who had received a letter from a relative already in America who had moved on to work the rails in Pennsylvania. The Walshes knew no one in Boston and would be making their own way.

Scowling, Rory returned from The Black Ram. He stopped short of the wagon and said, "They have no rooms, but there's a barn out back where we can spend the night. It cost only a few pence."

"What?" Lucinda broke into high-pitched English. "Spend the night with animals? In the hay? Jesus, Mary, and Joseph!"

"Exactly," Rory replied in Irish. "Before you get too upset, there are no animals, only a few stray dogs and cats."

"Charming." Lucinda shivered. "What will we do in the meantime? I was hoping to freshen up."

He hitched his thumb toward the door. "Have something to eat and drink. The proprietress says the *Warton* comes in at four. That's why they have no rooms. The English crew already paid for them. I imagine the pub will be a ruckus after that. We may be glad we're not spending the night above the pub. And the horses can spend the night in the barn with us. I won't have to worry about them being stolen."

Briana laughed out loud. She couldn't help it. The thought of her sister sleeping in a barn with two horses drove her into uncontrollable laughter.

Lucinda scowled at her, her eyes smoky with anger. "*What* is so funny? I find nothing amusing about this situation."

"Wait until tonight," Briana said, controlling her mirth. "The sailors will be drinking and rowdy. Rory is right, we will be better off in the barn." If the men relieved themselves on the barn, as she recalled from her first unfortunate visit to The Black Ram, the sound and smell alone would keep them awake.

Rory studied the barn, noting a few small gaps in the roof, and hoped it didn't rain. In the worst case, they would sleep under the cart, which fit comfortably inside. A small hay rick was attached to the back wall. The oak planking had a few holes that could use patching, but nothing so bad that drafts might disturb their sleep.

"Are you still hungry?" He offered Briana a last piece of corn bread because he hated how thin she'd gotten. Lucinda, too, but she wasn't pregnant.

"No, you eat it," Briana said. "I'm fine." She cocked her head toward her sister. Rory offered it to Lucinda, who gladly took it, broke it apart, and popped the pieces into her mouth.

Rory considered what he'd do for the rest of the evening before they all went to bed. The horses were safe after pulling the cart inside. They munched on the few remaining mounds of hay left in the rick.

He sat in the corner and watched his wife fussing with the blanket and tarp. Lucinda pulled a book from her bag, but it was too dark to read in the dim light. There were no candles or oil lamps here.

The thought of Briana's leaving filled him with a sudden fury. They were going to be separated because he was forbidden to leave Ireland. The landlord's face popped into his head, and he wanted to thrust his fist into his handsome smile. Another insidious notion forced its way in. What if Sir Thomas Blakely would do anything to sabotage his marriage to Briana, including asserting to the Constabulary that he had shot him? After all, the owner did seem to force his attention upon Briana, preferring to interact with her rather than Brian, his agent. It suddenly all made sense. He struck the thought from his mind, because his wife was leaving for America and nothing could be done about that. Besides, Blakely couldn't get his hands on her in Boston. His mood soured as the light faded in the barn.

Rory lifted his bag from the back of the cart and slid it under the seat. As the women talked, he took out the pistol and positioned it between his stomach and the waistband of his breeches. His shirt concealed the weapon's grip.

"I'm going over for a quick pint," he told Briana. "I need some air." The real reason, of course, was that he wanted to lift his spirits.

She looked at him with dismay, distressed that he would leave them alone in the barn. "You'll be all right," he said to soothe her. "I promise I won't be long." He boosted himself on the front wheel, leaned over the sideboard, and kissed her on the cheek.

He secured the door and stood in the

muddy lane that led to the pub. Near the side wall, the pungent smell of urine filled his nose, and he breathed out forcefully to rid himself of the odor. The sun was setting over the Atlantic and, as he had predicted, the drunken revelry in The Black Ram had begun.

Laughter and the roar of men's voices grew louder as he approached the pub's door. Inside, the sailors smoked pipes, drank, and played cards. Most, he presumed, were from the *Warton,* although a few were in service uniform. They looked as if they had stepped out of the English countryside: Their bodies were long and sturdy from good food and drink, their faces ruddy with the warmth of hearty eating. Their jocularity bounced off the walls and ceiling, dozens of conversations being carried on at once. But it wasn't these men he was interested in.

His eyes focused on a man he spotted seated at a table in the far corner. Trying not to draw attention, Rory sauntered toward the oak bar and ordered an ale. He peered right and knew the face. Daniel Quinn. He was drunk, but the Englishmen were paying him to sing and be the fool as they scooted ale and scraps of fried fish to him across the table.

Rory leaned against the bar, glancing sideways at Quinn when he could, not wanting to start a conversation with the poet. Quinn's clothes were rumpled and worn, and his black hair was longer, wilder than usual, but he seemed in much better spirits than when he'd disappeared from Lear House a few days after the shooting. The poet even cracked a smile under the concealing feature of a beard, swaying in his chair to the ribbing of his English comrades.

"Sing us an Irish tune, Paddy," one of the men shouted over the others.

Rory crept closer to the table, keeping his ears open.

"No, a poem and a song," another man shouted.

"Throw me a coin," Quinn yelled to the amusement of those at the table. "I'll honor the one who throws the most money."

The man who had asked for a poem and song reached into his pocket, withdrew a coin, and tossed it across the plates of fish. Quinn grabbed it greedily and thrust it into his jacket pocket. "What I wouldn't do for a smoke for my pipe," the poet lamented while the others roared with laughter.

"You'll get nothing more from me but a fist if you don't give us a poem and song," the coin thrower said.

"All right, all right," Quinn conceded. He cleared his throat as the men at the table quieted, and after placing his palms on the table he started a lengthy poem about the life of a wandering poet, thrown into madness by a famine. Quinn contorted his face, threw his hands in the air, and grimaced at the crowd. Rory was impressed with the poet's talent, but the words that caught his ears came near the end of his verse.

A man from nowhere came
And fired the pistol, but who's to blame
For no one but God on his throne
Would curse the man who killed an
    Englishman

A chorus of boos and jeers greeted the poet when he finished. Several of the men spat ale at his feet.

"It's my best work," Quinn protested, reaching underneath his chair and drawing out a silver flute. The instrument glinted silver in the candlelight as the poet brought it to his lips. Quinn broke into a slightly drunken version of an Irish jig while the men clapped their hands in time to the music.

Where did Quinn get the flute? He remembered that the last time he had seen one, silver like the one the poet was playing, was at the Kilbanes' before they were murdered. Frankie had played while Aideen strummed the guitar. The thought unsettled him, but perhaps it was another flute, or even if it wasn't, maybe the Kilbanes had given it to him. No, it made no sense. Frankie would never have given up the flute he so loved to play for his guests. Was it engraved? He didn't remember. He tried to slip closer to see the instrument as he finished his ale and then stopped, wondering whether he should drink another.

The room had grown hot while he sipped the warm drink, and he wiped the sweat from his brow. The ale, the smoke, and Quinn's poem disturbed him. He'd had enough of The Black Ram.

"Want another?" the proprietress said when she noticed his glass was empty.

"That's it for the evening," Rory said.

The proprietress answered with a wink. "Enjoy your stay in the barn, love," she said. "I'll try to keep them from pissing on you." Her laugh echoed over the men in the crowded pub.

He looked again at the corner table, but Quinn had disappeared. So like him to vanish in the blink of an eye. As he snaked his way to the door, Rory wondered if Quinn knew more about the Kilbanes' deaths than he had told when they nursed him back to health at Lear House. Perhaps it was worth mentioning to Davitt — if the man could ever get his hands on the poet.

He made his way back to the barn. A man was urinating on a bush, but not on the side of the barn. Rory grunted at him as he passed. He opened the door as quietly as he could, took off his jacket, and slipped under his blanket on the dirt floor. Behind him, the horses rested on their folded legs. The air was warm and filled with musky scents of the animals.

Briana stirred in the cart and Lucinda uttered a slight groan, but both seemed to be in the throes of sleep.

He tossed and turned during the night, sometimes from the noise but mostly from the stark reality he would have to face in the morning. He counted the hours and stared through the holes in the roof at the clouds scudding overhead. All he could think about was seeing his wife and sister-in-law off at the wharf as the *Warton* sailed for America. Although he tried to push the horrible thought from his mind, he wondered whether he would ever see Briana again and come to know their child.

His hands were clutched at his sides like claws as dawn broke.

CHAPTER 15

For a few pence more, the wan-faced proprietress provided them with a proper breakfast of oats and bacon. The woman, with her stringy hair and disheveled brown dress, looked as if she had never been to bed. The pub smelled of stale smoke and an ale-soaked floor, but when the food arrived it was flavorful and well prepared. The woman worked hard, Briana thought, but she was surviving the famine. There would always be men who could find money for a drink.

After breakfast, they fed and watered the horses, and they bathed from pails drawn from the Carrowbeg. They boarded the cart, and Rory prodded the team west toward the harbor. Briana sat on the bench by her husband, while Lucinda took her place next to the bags in the cart bed.

As they passed the imposing stone mansion, Rory said, "I saw the poet last night in the pub."

"Ungrateful wretch, disappearing like he did after you saved him," Lucinda chimed in over the rattle.

"He disappeared last night as well, after some disparaging verse about an Englishman."

"Really?" Briana clutched the railing as the cart jiggled through a shallow puddle. "What did he say?"

"Something about killing an Englishman." Lucinda shoved her head between them. "An Englishman!"

"I already thought of it as I lay awake last night," Rory said. "I'll notify the Constabulary here in Westport, and I'm sure they'll pass my suspicion on to Belmullet. At this point I have no proof. It's my word against his — it could have been anyone, and, despite that, it *was* my pistol. But it's important for me to clear my name." The bag containing the weapon sat at his feet.

Briana slid closer to Rory after Lucinda regained her seat. Tears creeping into her eyes, she clutched his arm. "I don't want to cry — if only you could come with us."

Rory loosened his grip on the reins and patted her hand. "I thought about that as well last night. Would it be easy to get onboard?" He lifted his chin and stared at the wharf buildings coming into view. "I'm sure every ship steward has my name, but there's a better reason for not leaving. Family. I don't want to leave your father and my brother alone. You and Lucinda should make the voyage. It's best for everyone . . . including our child."

She nodded, knowing that he was right, but that didn't allay her sadness. Someone had to look after their stubborn father. No amount of arguing could convince Brian to leave Ireland, and Rory had always been protective of his brother.

They rolled up to the massive stone buildings that lined the harbor. Black smoke poured from some of the stacks, but the strong west wind pushed the swirling lines of sooty vapor east toward town. A few smaller sailing ships were anchored next to the quay, but a steamship lay farther out, rocking upon the waves of Clew Bay.

A pair of uniformed dragoons leaned on the closed doors of a warehouse, watching the comings and goings of harbor workmen. No starving people loitered at the port — most remained clustered near the edge of the city. Briana wondered if they had been driven from the bay because supplies were heavily guarded and could be obtained only by theft. The dragoons, if necessary, would shoot to kill.

Near a wooden booth large enough to hold one person, they found the ship's steward. In a few minutes, Briana had purchased two one-way passages with money provided by her father.

Briana gazed at the Atlantic, which ended in a thin, gray line on the horizon. The immensity of the journey hit her with a sudden force, rocking her on her feet. The book of her life was opening up before her and, while frightened, she clung to the hope that this voyage might lead to a better life for her child and, later, her husband and father.

The skiff that would take her and Lucinda to the ship was rocking in swells at the quay. When the steward announced the boarding call, she clutched Rory for as long as she dared without bursting into tears. She wanted to be strong, not only for herself but for her husband. The wind rushed over her, filling her senses with the smell of the sea and the sound of the waves.

"I will miss you as if all my days were without you." Rory embraced her in a hug that nearly took her breath away. Behind her, Lucinda sniffed and blew her nose in her handkerchief.

Briana touched his face and then caressed his arms, committing his features, the scent of him, to her memory. "You and Father will write us when we find an address?" she asked, knowing that any letters exchanged wouldn't arrive until spring because there were no winter crossings.

"Yes. I promise." He stepped back as Briana and Lucinda boarded the skiff with other passengers. "Go. Be safe — and send word when the baby is born." His face sagged under the sad truth of his words.

The two crewmen pushed off from the wharf, and soon they were cutting across the choppy waves toward the *Warton.* Rory faded until he was a speck standing with the misty peak of Croagh Patrick behind him. A lump rose in her throat as she turned toward the ship, unable to bear the loss of her husband. Lucinda held on to her hand.

They boarded from a lowered gangplank that was tethered to the skiff and soon found their quarters — a small but comfortable sleeping cabin with twin berths. Briana placed her bag on the floor and patted the stuffed mattress, which seemed like heaven to her compared to the straw pallet at home. However, the close walls and the low ceiling crisscrossed by pipes soon had her craving the open air.

They made their way back to the upper deck. The ship's bell tolled, and the chain grated against the pulley as the anchor lifted from the sea.

"Look, it's Rory," she said with joy to Lucinda. Briana waved as she grasped the railing with one hand. He was there, a small figure among those on the wharf. Could he see her? The ship, with its massive wooden deck and towering stack, dwarfed her, adding to the insignificance she felt, particularly when she looked at the foamy Atlantic waves.

A light rain had begun to fall, and Briana pulled the hood of her cloak over her head while Lucinda wrapped up in her English coat.

"We're leaving everything behind," her sister said. "I can't say more, for if I do I might throw myself overboard." Her body quivered next to Briana.

"Don't be silly. Who will help me deliver the baby?" she answered, hoping to inject some slight humor into the conversation.

Lucinda didn't laugh, but tucked her arm through Briana's as they stared toward land.

The steam whistle blared, and the ship pivoted west in the harbor, the six masts still furled. Rory, the dock, the line of buildings that lined the wharf, the people who had gathered to see their loved ones off, soon dwindled to specks.

Briana leaned against the railing. *I hope*

he survives and that he takes care of Da. I'll find a job and send money and food. Will I see him again? Will my baby ever know its father?

A swirl of rain chased them below deck, where they found a window that looked toward Westport. As the ship churned away, Rory and the others disappeared as the sullen sky melded with the somber sea.

Lucinda was cheered by the grand ambiance of the *Warton* and the English pedigrees of the other passengers, so much so that she had little time for Briana.

Reading a dreary English novel or staring at the horizon through a portal to stave off sea sickness, Briana often sat alone rather than interact with others. Their berth, near the forward saloon, was close to the engine room. The low rumble of the steam engines, which sometimes lulled her to sleep, was never far from her ears.

Weather permitting, she found herself on the upper deck watching the billowing North Atlantic waves, chilly even in August. The brisk air helped her motion sickness, while the endless surging ridges fascinated her. They appeared in every color of the rainbow: foam green, steel blue, iridescent red and pink at sunrise and sunset.

Thoughts about her unborn child often came to mind in those times.

Briana envied her sister, who treated the voyage like an extended garden party, flitting here and there to invitations of luncheon and supper, cards, or gossip while she sat sequestered in the private ladies' sitting room. Guilt often engulfed her. Why should she dine in opulent luxury when those at home were starving? Her dismal mood, combined with her developing pregnancy, made her too tired and cranky to make conversation with people who didn't understand how desperate circumstances were in Ireland. She ate many suppers alone in the cabin. Besides, she had few dresses she felt comfortable wearing to the dining room.

"You must climb out of your shell and join me in socializing," Lucinda scolded her one evening seven days into the voyage. "Two sets of ears are better than one. I expect your help in finding the best place for us to live, since we know so little about Boston." According to the crew, the ship was nearing the western edge of the North Atlantic, south of Greenland, with at least another six days to go before arriving in America.

That night they dined with two English ladies from Liverpool who seemed to look down upon both of them despite Lucinda's previous experience as a governess to a wealthy Manchester family. They reminded Briana of the English guests who had visited Lear House, but on the whole not as cordial or sincere. The ladies were destined for a winter stay with "a sister" in Salem, Massachusetts.

"What will *you* do when you arrive?" one of the women sniffed as she absentmindedly flicked at the white egret feather in her hat.

Before Briana could answer, Lucinda piped up, "Oh, we have people waiting for us."

"Yes, scads," Briana replied, giving her sister a sly look.

Lucinda puffed up in her chair. "I shall teach and my sister shall . . ."

"Shall what, dear one?" Briana asked.

After another pause, Lucinda said, "Why, do what you do best."

The ladies wiggled uncomfortably in their seats, one of them giving Briana a snobbish look. Then they hurried off, their starched gowns rustling against the floor.

"Why didn't you play along," Lucinda whispered crossly after the women had gone.

Briana scoffed. "They have no interest in

us. They couldn't care less what we do." She gazed around the opulent room with its white and gold columns, pilasters of painted oriental flowers and birds, and walls of blue and gold. A few diners still remained in their seats finishing small desserts or sipping tea. "Look at them!" The passengers were mostly well-to-do English men and their wives, along with a few Irish who had enough money for or had managed to scrape together passage. "They have no idea what we've gone through. I feel positively embarrassed to be sitting here at a table loaded with food when Rory, Father, and Jarlath have no idea where their next meal is coming from."

Lucinda pursed her lips, controlling her ire. She fumed underneath the best silk dress she could haul to America while her eyes spat darts. "That attitude won't get us far in Boston. Those ladies have a point. We've discussed what we might do, but we must develop relationships. I can teach, and I suppose you can clean houses until you deliver the baby, but we'll have better luck if we get recommendations."

"We'll do what every Irish immigrant has done before, I suppose," Briana replied, but she had no idea what that might be. Everything was new, even the experience of traveling by steamship. Nothing in her life had prepared her for what might happen once they set foot on foreign soil.

Lucinda pushed back her chair and closed her eyes in frustration. When she opened them she said with a sharp tongue, "This ship is carrying mail from England. Perhaps we can work for the post when we get there."

Briana ignored her sister's jab as the ship lurched over the waves and her stomach rose and dropped. A cold sweat broke out on her forehead, and she excused herself from the table. Seeking a breath of fresh air before bed, she climbed the two flights of iron stairs from the dining saloon to the deck. She teetered across the slick wood, grabbing at whatever she could to steady herself. A crewman cautioned her not to go to the railing, but she insisted and he accompanied her.

Billows of clouds, which seemed to touch the ship's masts, concealed the stars. No rain fell, but the rushing wind brought a pleasant odor she had experienced only a few times in her life, always in late summer or early fall along the coast she knew so well. The warm, moist air brought to mind tales she had heard of the tropics and its exotic blooms, of strange plants and animals that lived in a world ruled by rain and heat.

The smell permeated the ocean air like floral perfume.

Below, the ebony breakers crashed against the iron hull. She could just make out the white roil against the ship as it crested with each oncoming wave. The vessel lurched wildly a few times, and the sailor pointed to the stairs leading below deck. It was time to go back to her berth; no one else had foolishly ventured into the evening air.

The *Warton* creaked and moaned through the night, rocking and sometimes shuddering sideways as if it might be wrenched in half. Briana sat up clutching the berth's railing with one hand and her stomach with the other. She fought off waves of nausea as her sister slept above her. Lucinda's voyages to England had apparently prepared her for the ship's violent motions.

By noon the next day, the seas had calmed to a gentle roll. Briana was shocked to see the rain-slickened upper deck covered in seaweed and even the stinking bodies of a few fish when she ventured up after luncheon. She stepped around the detritus, sat upon the doors of an elevated cargo hold, and wrapped the neckline of her cloak around her throat.

"May I help you, miss?"

The man's deep voice startled her. Briana turned to find a tall officer in uniform. His dress-blue cap was positioned on his head, as if it was unassailable in the stiff wind.

"I'm sorry," the older man said. "I didn't mean to alarm you, but few passengers venture out in weather like this." A smile beamed across his weathered face. His lean body and sturdy sea legs attested to a man who loved his job and the open ocean.

He extended his hand. "Captain William Hawthorne," he said in a formal but pleasant English accent.

She shook his hand and answered in English. "Briana Caulfield. Thank you for your concern, but I'm fine. I find that the ocean air and views of the horizon help my sea sickness. It reminds me of the cliffs at home."

"Ahh," he said as if he realized she was someone who appreciated the ocean swells. He gripped his hands behind his back, planted his feet firmly on deck, and rocked with the mild motion of the ship, his knees flexing with each wave. "A true lover of the sea. It's rare to find one in the fairer sex. I admire your fondness for its beauty." He pointed to the vast, unbroken ocean past the bow. "Last night was rough going, but we should be beyond the effects of the gale in a few hours. After that the winds will shift, and with sails up, we should make excellent time. Where are you headed — Boston or New York?"

"Boston."

"I see. I detect from your accent that you're Irish."

"County Mayo," she replied. "I don't suppose you know Carrowteige?"

"No, but I'm familiar with the northwest Irish coast and the hazards it presents to any mariner." He unclasped his hands and put a finger on his lips. "A legend exists there about children turned into swans — am I correct?"

Briana was amazed that the Captain would know anything about the Children of Lear. "I come from Lear House. It's owned by Sir Thomas Blakely of Manchester."

"Blakely . . . Blakely . . . the family name sounds familiar. Perhaps he's sailed aboard this ship."

She wanted to go no further in a discussion about the landlord or what the topic might lead to. "How soon until we dock in Boston?"

He cocked his head. "Five days if we're lucky, more likely six." His features tightened, and any hint of delight on his face was erased. "We have nothing to worry about, but I've received recent reports that Boston has turned away ships."

Briana pivoted toward him. "What?"

"The Customs House at Long Wharf has turned away ships with Irish passengers who carry disease. Fortunately, the *Warton* is not in that category — at least no one that we know of is sick — but passengers and immigrants may be held for processing. You can never tell what the Americans might do, but I can't say that I blame them. Would you let typhus carriers into your country?"

"If the ship was turned away, what would we do?" she asked, cringing inwardly at the thought.

"We'd find another place to dock — Salem has always been a friendly port. I know the harbormaster there." He stiffened with determination. "Never fear. We'll get through." He looked toward the bow. "You must excuse me. Duty calls. If we don't meet again, enjoy the rest of the voyage." He glanced at her with a stern, fatherly smile. "Be careful on the deck. We don't like accidents."

Briana nodded and gazed at the Captain's tall, elegant figure as he strode toward the bow. Her mind shifted uneasily to the new life that she and Lucinda would have to make for themselves. What if they couldn't dock in Boston? Briana had no idea where Salem was or how they would manage there.

Captain Hawthorne was right in his prediction. The *Warton* had passed the storm in the Mid-Atlantic and was now sailing in a southerly direction on favorable seas. Briana welcomed the spits of land, the strips of rocky, wooded coastline that slipped by on the northern horizon.

On their last day at sea, Briana returned to the cabin to find Lucinda tossing clothing out of her bag. "What in God's name are you doing?" she asked her.

Lucinda turned and then tumbled onto Briana's berth with a horrified gaze. "The letter and the forty-five pounds Rory gave me — I can't find them!"

Briana's heart fluttered. Rory had given them to Lucinda for safekeeping. It was all they had to pay for rent, food, and clothing. She jumped in to help her sister, rummaging through Lucinda's bag and searching every dark corner of the cabin.

"Think," Briana said, fearing they would have nothing after the search failed. "Where could it be?"

"Oh, God, I don't know," her sister replied. "I thought it was in my bag."

"We need that money!"

"You don't need to remind me!" Sighing, Lucinda sank down on the lower berth and cradled her head in her hands.

On the upper berth, Briana spotted the novel Lucinda was reading. She lifted the book by its cover and shook it. The pages spread out from the spine like a fan. The money and the folded letter dropped from their hiding place in the center of the book.

Lucinda clutched them to her breast. "Thank God," she said with a sigh of relief. "I don't remember using my book as a hiding place."

"A good idea," Briana said, examining the book's cover. "Hardly anyone, except you, would want to read this."

"Hush. Be grateful we have it."

They hoped they had enough money to get past the Customs Service, if necessary, but the letter was another matter. Her father had written it explaining his daughters' need to leave County Mayo because of the famine and the effect it had on the family. Both were to act as companions and aides to each other, according to the testament. If the letter had been lost, a strict Customs official might deny them entry into the country. Her father made no mention of the baby, thinking it might cause Customs to believe that Briana was coming to America only to have a child — to increase the Irish population.

That evening at dinner, they sat by themselves contemplating what their new lives would be like. Lucinda was exceptionally quiet through their meal as if something was troubling her. Briana found herself picking at her food, although she knew she should eat well this last night aboard ship.

"They didn't welcome us, did they?" Lucinda asked as they neared the end of the meal.

"Who?"

"These English prigs."

Briana couldn't believe her ears. "What did you say?"

Lucinda smirked and swept her fork around the dining room. "These fine ladies and gentlemen from England. It was Sir Thomas who invited me into his inner circle . . . but only for the good it did him as one who could deliver an Irish governess to his friends' children. He never thought of me.

"What will happen to us?" Lucinda continued, her face tightening as if it might crack open from vulnerability. Briana had seen her sister lose her steely resolve more than once since she had returned to Ireland. Before the famine, such emotional displays were rare.

Briana reached across the table and grasped her sister's hand. "We'll live in a boarding house until we find a home. I wish Father and Rory — even Father O'Kirwin — had known someone in Boston. Perhaps that would have made things easier for us."

Lucinda stuck her fork into a piece of chocolate cake. "Many times I dreamed of earning enough money, getting out of Ireland, taking the whole family with me. Wouldn't it be grand not to worry about money? Like —" She lifted a piece of cake, then put it down, and gazed at the white tablecloth.

"*He* was a fantasy, dear sister. One you need to forget. Sir Thomas wouldn't save us if he could." The repugnant thought crossed her mind that she might have saved her family if she had been willing to abandon Rory and sacrifice herself to the landlord. The idea made her skin crawl.

Lucinda lifted her head and cocked an eyebrow. "We'll see."

Briana did not share her sister's ill-founded optimism and gave up trying to convince her to forget Sir Thomas. They finished dessert and then left the dining saloon. Lucinda retired to the cabin, while Briana took one last look on deck.

The sky was clear and filled with brilliant stars that added to the warmth washing over her in soothing waves. The south wind caressed her as she looked west toward the horizon. Far away, isolated points of light twinkled amid the forests, and campfires burned orange where the land met the sea.

Taking her gaze away from the distant shore and looking at the calm sea ahead, she imagined Boston's harbor opening to the *Warton.* Thousands of people who lived in a city bigger than she had ever seen were only a night's sail away. She clutched the railing as feelings of excitement and apprehension raced through her.

She and Lucinda hurried to the deck after breakfast to watch the ship sail into port. Land as far as they could see ran in both directions from the harbor banks. Hazy, wooded hills loomed beyond a city lanced with church spires and with smokestacks that spewed pearly ash.

Under a luminous blue sky, she stood by her sister as the ship glided past the harbor islands. The sun warmed her so much that she had to fan herself with her hand. America was already different, and she hadn't even set foot on it. The harbor air smelled of sewage and dead fish, unlike the pure

Atlantic breezes that buffeted the Irish coast. Past the harbor, rows of brick buildings, many taller than she had ever seen, cut into the air. She got the sense that traffic coursed through the city's vibrant streets, alive with people and horses, goods and money exchanged as businesses began a new day.

The *Warton* headed for a central wharf that extended far into the harbor. People the size of insects crowded the docks in ever-shifting patterns, like ants scavenging for food. She spotted a crewman waiting near the rail. "Is this Boston?"

He nodded. "Yes, ma'am . . . we're docking at Long Wharf."

She smiled and clutched her sister's arm. The ship had not been turned away. They would be docking after all!

Her excitement grew as she and Lucinda took one last look at their cabin, gathered their bags, and offered a few quick goodbyes to the crew. They joined the hundreds of travelers eager to leave the ship as they congregated near the gangplank exit. The *Warton* sailed past the eastern end of the wharf, where wagons, crates, bundles, and baskets crowded the stone landing. The ship edged to the left. A group of sailors uncoiled thick ropes at the wooden pilings that rose up from the harbor perpendicular to the wharf.

The ship's whistle sliced through the air, and the engines throttled back from the power that had propelled them across the Atlantic. The vessel hugged the dock and soon crept to a stop with a soft thump against the pilings. From her point on deck, Briana saw two groups of uniformed men standing next to the lowered gangplank.

"Do you have the money and Father's letter?" Briana asked her sister.

Lucinda patted her bag. "Are you scared?"

"I'm excited, but nervous too," Briana said.

They inched down the steps and toward the gangplank, jostling elbows and bumping against bodies in the crowd. Some passengers had already descended.

Uniformed men were questioning those on the wharf — the few Americans aboard, presumably Bostonians, had little trouble passing by with only a brief conversation and a nod. One of the men detained an Irish family with two children. Frowning, the wife sat atop their bags and listened while the man questioned her husband. Their pale, young girl held her hands over her stomach while attempting to hide in the folds of her mother's dress. Briana suspected that the child, presumably sick, had forced their detention.

Before they reached the bottom of the plank, Briana took off her wedding ring and placed it in her pocket. She didn't want the Customs officers to know she was waiting for a husband to arrive as well.

When they reached the wharf, another man guided them to a desk where an officious young officer began his questions without a welcome. The dark-haired youth with eager eyes held a pen, which he periodically dipped into an inkwell. "Your names?"

"Briana Caulfield and Lucinda Walsh." Briana answered for them.

He wrote their names in his log book. "Reason for coming?"

Lucinda presented the letter to the young man.

He read it, passed it back to her, and looked them both over from head to toe.

"Are you ill, or have you been, at any time within the past month?"

They both shook their heads. Briana didn't mention her sea sickness.

"Do you have money to support yourself?"

Lucinda withdrew the pounds from her bag and showed it to him.

He seemed unimpressed. "You'll have to change that to bank notes before it'll do you any good. Go on." He waved them away from the table, concerned about dealing with the travelers who stood behind them.

They walked a few feet, put their bags down, and then took stock of their surroundings. Gulls soared over the ship in a journey to the outer harbor; others cried from the top of pilings and looked for scraps of food from a passerby. Even the birds looked different here — they were fatter and unafraid of humans.

"Now what do we do?" Lucinda asked with a frown.

"Find a place to —"

"You ladies look lost." The words, in English, were overly sweet but tinged with a gruff edge.

Briana swiveled to face two portly men with red, cherubic faces stained by the sweat dripping from underneath their caps. They were dressed in heavy work shirts, long pants, and black boots, and they looked as if they might be brothers.

"We're the Carsons," the larger of the two confirmed and bent down to grab Lucinda's bag. She kicked his hand away with a deft blow from her foot.

The man's hands flew back, shocked by her moxie. Briana was impressed with the physicality Lucinda had developed from working as a governess to three boys. "Here, miss, I was only trying to help. We're here to take young women like you to the finest lodgings you can afford in Boston."

"No, thank you," Briana said. "We can make our own way."

Lucinda stepped in front of her bag. "Keep your hands off my property," she ordered in her best English accent.

"Oh, cheeky." The man mopped the sweat from his forehead. "You won't find better accommodations than the Coatesworth Arms. That's what I get for trying to help you young ladies out."

"I'll give you cheeky," Briana said, and then swore at them with Irish curses that would have made her mother blush.

A young man strode up to Briana's side and asked in Irish, "Are these two giving you trouble?" He was tall like her husband, but instead of Rory's fairer looks, this man's hair was thick and shone black like the shell of an Irish mussel. His bright blue eyes took in the two men, who backed away after sensing trouble.

She could tell that the man who had rushed to their aid was from Mayo, but not from Carrowteige. The two large men disappeared into the crowd, and Briana studied her savior. He wore scuffed boots, Irish breeches, a white shirt, and a dark waistcoat. Despite his young age, his hands were chapped and scratched. His thick arms and shoulders swelled under his coat. There was something about him she immediately liked, but she cautioned herself that a handsome man could be dangerous. Still, his kind eyes and gentle smile gave her the confidence that he wouldn't take advantage of them.

He took off his round cap, held it in his hands, and continued in Irish. "My name is Declan Coleman. I'm from Mulranny. Did you see another pair of young Irish ladies onboard the *Warton*?"

Briana thought for a moment. She couldn't recall any other Irish ladies of young age on the ship. She looked to her sister, who had made more acquaintances, but Lucinda shook her head.

Declan shielded his eyes from the sun and looked up the gangplank. "I don't think they're here. I was hoping . . ."

His voice trailed off, and his face displayed a sadness that echoed in her soul.

"They might not have been able to travel on such a fancy ship. I'll wait until everyone's off."

"Who were those men?" Lucinda asked in English. "One of them reached for my bag."

"You speak English?" he asked, somewhat

449

surprised.

Lucinda nodded. "Of course. There's no need to speak Irish here — in America."

He smiled, and Briana could tell that he was teetering on the verge of laughter. "Where I live, Irish is all I hear," he replied in English. "Unless you're planning to go straight to Beacon Hill, you'll hear it too." He paused as if somewhat embarrassed by what he had to say. "Those men are runners — crooks — for boarding houses. Well, that's putting it politely. They're houses of prostitution. They steal your money, and then the women are forced to work there to get it back. Of course, the women pay for food and board. An awful scheme that I've seen too many women fall prey to. That's why I check every ship coming in from Ireland — so my sisters don't end up in a place like that."

"Thank you for looking out for us," Briana said. "We're in need of a boarding house ourselves."

"Are you here for good?" he asked, still keeping an eye on the travelers who trickled down the gangplank.

Briana shrugged. "I don't know how long — at least until things get better in Ireland so we can return to Mayo."

Lucinda pursed her lips. "We're seeking

security and a life outside Ireland — at least I am."

The sad look crossed his face again. "The stories I've heard are terrible. You're lucky you were able to travel in such luxury. The lumber ships coming to Canada and America from Ireland are floating death traps. Do you have money?"

"What business is it of yours?" Lucinda asked. She exchanged an artful look with Briana that wordlessly suggested caution in their dealings.

"My sisters are coming to live with me and my wife in an extra room we have. But if they don't come . . . we could use the rent." He studied the last of the passengers departing the ship. "We live in South Cove. I do woodworking for the new homes on Beacon Hill."

Lucinda was quick to reply. "If your sisters do come, your offer is a moot point. Thank you, but we should look for a place of our own before accepting. We should like to get to know you better before we partake of your hospitality."

His face softened. "In that case, I offer some unsolicited advice. Room and board are expensive. The Boston neighborhoods where our countrymen live are places an Irish pig wouldn't live — but most Irishmen have little money and no choice." His jaw tightened. "I know because I worked my way out. I hope you don't end up there. My offer stands if the room is available, which looks likely. Fewer ships will be sailing as fall approaches."

His description of living conditions alarmed Briana, but Lucinda was right — for the moment they should make their own way. They talked for a few minutes about Ireland and the sea voyage before her sister tugged at her, making clear her desire to leave the wharf.

"Can you recommend a boarding house for us?" Briana asked.

"The Newton on Beacon is decent and takes in young women. It's near Beacon Hill where I work." He gave them directions.

They both thanked him after he had finished.

"Remember my name — Declan Coleman — if you need help. Ten Loyal Street in South Cove." He tipped his hat. "I hope we'll meet again."

"I'm sure we will," Briana said.

They left him at the wharf, still wondering if his sisters might be aboard. Rows of brick buildings as far as they could see stood in front of them. Horse-drawn cabs trotted by as they neared King Street, a busy thoroughfare that merged with the wharf. Street vendors, selling vegetables and flowers, shouted "Ladies" at them and urged them to buy their wares.

Lucinda took a deep breath. "Well, sister, we are here. Shall we visit the Newton on Beacon?"

Briana nodded and thought of the men who had tried to take them to a house of prostitution. "Yes," she replied, for they had no other recommendation to consider.

CHAPTER 16

September 1846

A few days into September, Rory awakened at daybreak to the crunch of marching feet. He threw on his breeches and shirt and ran to the door.

Under an overcast sky, a detachment of dragoons and Constabulary officers tramped down the road toward the farms. With a glance, he judged that twenty-five to thirty men were headed toward the manor. The Constable of Belmullet, Edmond Davitt, who had questioned him about Sir Thomas's shooting, led the way on his horse. The dreaded time had come.

Rory pounded on Jarlath's door. His brother, swiping the sleep from his eyes, answered. "What's going on?" Jarlath's wife and son huddled, arms around one another, near the turf pit.

"They're here!" Rory pointed up the road, and Jarlath gazed past his outstretched arm.

"By all the Saints," Jarlath said as he eyed the men. "Hell has finally broken loose."

"Try to slow them down — as we planned," Rory said.

"I'll do my best," his brother replied, and then shouted to his wife and son to gather their belongings.

"I'll get Brian." He left his brother and sprinted down the lane past Lear House to the cottage, a faster path than jumping fences and potato ridges. His heart thumping, he looked back at the marching column of men and, trailing behind them, a large wagon pulled by two horses. That sight sent shivers racing over him because it meant the officers had come prepared to evict. He stumbled to the cottage door and threw it open to find Brian stooped in front of the turf fire.

"They've come!"

His father-in-law jerked his head toward him. "Blakely's made good on his pledge."

The waiting, the long discussions about eviction, had taken a toll on Brian. Rory could see the despair in the older man's sunken eyes. His father-in-law had shriveled under the weight of losing his daughters and the manor. His sagging shoulders reflected his dejection.

Rory, Jarlath, and Brian had tried to

formulate a plan for the remaining tenants, but no one knew exactly what to do. It wasn't a question of surrender but of insufficient choices. Many had already fled looking for work. From letters coming back to Mayo, the tenants had learned that working conditions were as terrible in Dublin and in England as those in the county. The public works projects had been suspended because of government costs. Jobs were scarce everywhere.

With nowhere to turn, nowhere to go, his father-in-law had decided to stay at Lear House until he was forced to leave. At least he would be at home where he belonged. Only a few families were left now: Connor and his wife and children and many others had deserted the estate for what they hoped would be a better life in England. Rory had tried to convince Jarlath to leave, but his brother refused to desert him, saying they'd "be stronger together." Only four other families remained, despairing of their situation but clinging to the small hope they could survive.

Brian remained seated, apparently in no hurry to confront the men. "We knew this day would come, but that doesn't make it any easier."

"Come on," Rory urged him. "Maybe

they'll listen to you — the landlord's agent."

Brian shrugged. "What can I do? Neither you nor I can fight an army. We must obey the law."

His father-in-law slowly rose and clasped his hands behind his back. He seemed a faded remnant of his former self, as if he had already been defeated by the men who were coming to Lear House. The respect that Rory had always felt for Brian turned to pity. He was a man impoverished by age, lack of money and food, and most important the will to fight. Rory could see the specter of defeat in Brian's eyes as he shuffled away from the fire.

"We can at least try to stop them," Rory said.

Brian cornered him at the door. "Don't be a damn fool. You'll die. My grandchild needs a father." His voice dropped to a whisper. "I didn't think he would do it. I hoped it would be different."

His words pricked Rory like a needle, and he considered them wise, but what of the obligation to protect one's home? Where did that responsibility end and forced subservience begin?

Brian put a hand on his shoulder. "I'll talk to them," he said. "Perhaps they'll listen."

Even as his father-in-law spoke, Rory

knew there was nothing either of them could do other than save what they could from their homes, like the pistol still hidden in his bag; he couldn't let the soldiers get the weapon.

They trudged to a stop in front of Lear House. Jarlath, his shirt hanging over his breeches, walked beside Davitt's horse. The officer ignored his pleas to stop their march. The constable held up his hand, pulled the chestnut mare to a halt, and dismounted.

"Good morning," Davitt said in a cordial tone and looked at Rory. "Mr. Caulfield, as I recall. . . ." He cocked his head and continued, "I'm sorry I couldn't personally receive the information you provided about the incident at Lear House, but I was away on business. The *possible* suspect has not been found. The investigation remains in force." He directed his gaze at Brian. "And, sir, you are?"

"Mr. Brian Walsh, the landlord's agent." He extended his hand, and Davitt shook it.

The constable lifted a rolled paper from a brown saddlebag strapped to his horse and handed the document to Brian. "You are named in this legal order."

Brian barely glanced at it before handing it back.

"Don't you want to read it?" Davitt asked.

"No," Brian said. "I know what it says."

Davitt looked back at his men and the wagon, coughed, and then said, "I should inform you . . . all tenants are to be evicted from manor property, including the agent, Mr. Brian Walsh, and that all dwellings on the estate, except Lear House and the shed housing the horses, are to be demolished in order for the land to be made suitable for farming and grazing."

"Farming!" Rory's anger nearly choked him. "That's what we do now!"

"I understand, Mr. Caulfield," the constable said, remaining calm, "but Sir Thomas Blakely's order calls for *all* the land, not just the current cropland, to be put to better use — moneymaking use — through farming and grazing to support the estate." He turned to Brian. "This pains me as well, Mr. Walsh, being an Irishman myself, and I hope you understand that I have no choice in this proceeding. The men are here to carry out Sir Thomas Blakely's legal rights." He held up his hand as a signal to his men. "We'll give you an hour to gather what you need before we begin." Most of the paid soldiers seemed complacent about their task; other officers, Irish who had friends or family members in the same position, glowered at the thought of what they had to do.

I want to kill him. Rory thought of squeezing his hands around Davitt's neck, then striking out in a blind rage against all the men who stood in the road. His fists were of no use against dragoons, and one traveling pistol couldn't take on thirty men. *I want to kill them all, but it's . . . hopeless.* The farmers who remained stood no chance against armed soldiers. And standing among the soldiers stood Irishmen who were being paid to do their duty. They surely had wives and children too — the likely reason they were willing to go to blows with their countrymen.

His fury faded and common sense took over. He pulled Jarlath aside so that he could confer with him and his father-in-law. "There's nothing we can do." His voice faded as the resignation sank in. "Let's save what we can and gather in front of Lear House."

Realizing he had little time to lose, Rory sprinted to his cabin. He collapsed in a heap on the straw that made up his bed. Not only had he been lonely — at wits' end — since Briana left for America, but now he was losing his home, *their* home, to that English bastard. He slammed his fists on the small table near the bed. It shuddered and tipped over, the candle holder tumbling to the floor. *What good is any of it? What the hell good is it?* Where was Father O'Kirwin? Where was anyone who could save them?

He swiped a tear from his eye. Briana had taken the few clothes she wanted to Boston — the rest would remain in the cabin. He opened the bag containing the pistol and began shoving his clothes inside. What else was there to take? A pot, a pan? No, he could find others if he had to. There was little to remind him of his family — no drawings, no mementoes other than his mother's rosary. He spied it on the peg where his clothes normally hung. Rory lifted it gently and fingered the small beads that made up the holy object. His spirit broke and the tears flowed. *Why did God allow this curse to happen? No food . . . families destroyed by a plague we can't control. We must have been horrible sinners.* He flung the rosary into his bag.

A scream shattered his thoughts and he rushed out of the cabin. Midway up the slope toward Lear House, he spotted Brian and Aidan Golden clutching Mrs. Golden as she extended her thin arms between the lintels surrounding the door to her home. The woman clamped her fingers onto the wood and refused to budge. Their two children cowered behind her dress.

Her anguished howls fractured Rory's heart. "It's my home — I'm not leaving!" She continued to cry out until her husband finally clawed her away. She collapsed against him and then fell, sobbing, to the ground. The children rushed to their mother and threw their arms around her. Aidan and Brian leaned over her as she wailed into the ground.

Rory shot an angry look toward the constable and the armed men. Most stood in a row, leaning against their weapons. Six of the dragoons had positioned themselves at the wagon. The men off-loaded a wooden apparatus that stood like an inverted V. Soon thick chains and a heavy log, the full length of a man, were strapped to the crude machine. He knew what it was — a battering ram to destroy the cabins. Their homes would be smashed to pieces until there was nothing left. Then the land would be cleared.

Aidan disappeared into the cabin as Brian comforted the distraught woman.

The few who remained walked down the slope. Jarlath and his family, Noel and his wife and children, the others, all were walking away from the land that had been their home for generations. They gathered near the constable's horse, which was tied to a bush loaded with a late summer profusion of leaves on the cusp of turning from green to gold. The children clambered about it, engrossed by the animal. They didn't realize they would have no home in a matter of hours. Soon they would have no food, no place of shelter from the late summer weather.

He couldn't stand to see his father-in-law so preoccupied with another home when his own was about to be destroyed. He hurdled the fences and potato ridges to reach him and then put his hand on Brian's shoulder.

Brian looked up as he held the woman. "There's nothing I want. If it all has to go, it goes."

Why was his father-in-law giving up so easily? Didn't he want to save any of the memories that lived within the cottage? What about his wife's crucifix that Briana had admired so often? The man who comforted the grieving woman was giving up not only on his claim to land but his life.

He only had a few minutes before the men would start — enough time to go to the cottage and then return to get his bag. The men were setting up the ram in front of his door.

His home would be the first to go.

Rory, propelled by a mixture of fury, horror, and sorrow, ran to the cottage. The books in Lucinda's bedroom, the simple furniture that had lasted for centuries, would be gone. Nothing could be done about that. He went into Brian's bedroom and gathered the crucifix and a small chalk drawing of his deceased mother-in-law. At least he could save those things for Brian. He ran out the door knowing it would be the last time he would set foot inside its walls.

Davitt was giving the order to begin when he arrived at his cabin. He glared at the man. "Give me a minute to gather my bag." The officer nodded and held up his hand to stop the order.

Rory took a deep breath as he stepped inside. The cabin smelled of the smoky odor of burned peat, the scratchiness of the straw. He muttered a quick prayer, said good-bye to his home, and, after placing the drawing and crucifix in his bag, clutched it to his chest.

He stepped out of his cabin and closed the door.

The men pulled the ram into position near the entrance.

Rory stepped away, watching his father-in-law walk down the hill with the Goldens and their children.

Out of the corner of his eye, he saw Davitt give the signal.

He didn't want to watch, but he couldn't stop from hearing the sound as he walked away. The chains creaked, the air rushed as the log hurtled toward the door; but even more distressing was the awful crash, the splintering shock, as the wood smashed to pieces. After that, the heavy thunks continued as the ram battered his earthen cabin into bits of sod.

Sir Thomas Blakely stretched his legs on the brocade ottoman in the grand salon of his Manchester home and sipped brandy from a crystal snifter. The Andersons and the Rogerses had departed a half hour earlier, so he no longer had to play the host. Only the housekeeper and the valet scurried about the dining room, removing the porcelain dinner plates from the mahogany table before carrying them to the kitchen. He observed that "his man" was acting more as a superior to the housekeeper than as a helper by ordering her about. That was the way it was supposed to be in all grand English homes, particularly in one run by a gentleman.

He took another sip of the pale French brandy, placed the snifter on a side table, and gazed at the blazing fireplace set into the far wall. The birch logs hissed and popped, sending an occasional shower of sparks arcing toward the fire screen. The sun was setting, and he took pleasure in watching the light fade across the lawn, throwing the linden and ash trees into deep shadows. His mood was as dark as the nascent evening.

Since the shooting at Lear House, entertaining had not been foremost on his mind. He found himself wandering the house during tedious days, finding little comfort in his business dealings, and thus, alone and miserable, forced into early retreat to his bedchamber. His shoulder still ached, and he found it uncomfortable to sleep without the aid of laudanum. The combination of liquor and opium usually served its narcotic purpose, but often he found himself startled awake at night, his bedclothes soaked in sweat.

As far as visitors were concerned, the Wards and their three sons were seldom seen because he couldn't stand the noisy commotion created by the boys. If their parents stifled them, the children turned sullen and silent, which was often worse than the exuberance they naturally exhibited. He had restricted the Wards' invitations and often refused those he had received, developing a newly found appreciation of Lucinda's skills as a governess.

He was also tired of the constant badgering by the Wards — the Andersons and Rogerses were included in this scheme — for him to find a suitable wife. Yes, there were a handful of potential companions to choose from, but he found them vapid and vacant of the charms he wished from a woman. None of them exhibited the slightest room for maneuvering, no willingness to take a chance, no joie de vivre, except for beaming faces if he mentioned ledger books or plans to attend a horse race or gala ball. He was bored by those amusements and sought other pleasures than those trifles from a suitable wife — pleasures he sometimes found himself ill-equipped to define.

The valet appeared at his side and asked if he required further service. He declined, adding that he would take to his bed shortly, but asked his man to fill the washbasin and make sure his nightclothes were laid out. The servant bowed and left the room.

Sir Thomas returned to his brandy and thought about the prospect of marriage his friends' badgering had produced. One woman, handsome with a zest for life, fired his imagination, but she was already married to a poor farmer. In his dissolute way, he had admired her for many years, and his feelings had been brought to the forefront by his last visit. How strange that the famine and his brush with death could focus his attentions on a woman. Previously, his business and social obligations and his parents had stood in the way of anything he desired. Those restrictions were gone now that his mother and father had died within weeks of each other in the past year. Fortunately, his father's will made no mention of marriage or whom he was to marry, and thus was incontestable. So the door had been opened to a vault that had been sealed by his parents.

By the time he'd had any chance to act on his imaginative fancy, the marriage had been carried out in Ireland. He'd kept his eye on Briana skillfully through her sister, only to have the prize wed another, a man beneath even her station. He understood that Briana was *below* his standing, but obsessive thoughts of love were hard to scour from the mind amid the chance that somehow all could be rearranged.

The fire deepened from orange to crimson, and the melancholy atmosphere of summer shifting to fall overtook him. He sank back in his chair, mentally fretting about the lackluster days to come, the short-lived beauty of golden leaves, the falling temperatures that would turn the moist, pliable earth to frozen hardness.

The woman he dreamed of was independent, her own thinker, headstrong but not obstinate, a woman who *participated* in life rather than eschewed it for societal convenience. That was the woman he wanted to marry. He hadn't yet found such a prize in England, so Briana dominated his fevered thoughts. He slapped his head sometimes hoping to get her voice, her features, out of his head, knowing that his life would be easier and more rational if he was rid of her.

Lucinda was nothing like Briana — he had known that from the time he had met them both years ago. She was stern, lacking in the kind of vitality he wanted — intelligent, yes; comely, no, but not hideous by any means. He had kept the governess around as a charm, a route to Briana, but the good-luck piece hadn't paid off, and the years had drifted by as his parents kept tight control of his ways and means.

Now that he was free, why didn't she realize how much he could do for her? Was she unable to comprehend how he could release her from the trouble and worry of a life that kept her one step away from falling into a pit of poverty and despair? He had even hoped to impress her with the ball he had thrown at Lear House, only to get shot for his trouble.

The question that kept him awake at night was, *How can I change her mind?* That question was easier to ask than to solve. The family was complex: Briana would have nothing to do with him now that she was married; his relationship with Brian was strained. He had observed Lucinda's fawning ways toward him and disregarded her attention except when it came to news of Briana. Considering the Walsh family, there was little chance that Briana could *grow* to love him even if he offered to bring the entire family to England.

The shooting had changed him. Now he realized how life could shift in an instant, and, as surely as one day follows another, desires could be fulfilled only if you worked toward them. Money, parties, all the licentious trappings of life were useless when it came to true love.

He drained the remaining brandy and set the glass on the table. The housekeeper would pick it up and tend the fire before she went to bed.

He yawned and rose on legs stiffened by the tension of his thoughts. He climbed the stairs, entered his bedchamber, and closed the door. Illuminated by candlelight, the milky liquid of laudanum sat on the night table next to his bed. He drank a draft before turning in and hoped that his sleep would not be interrupted yet again by strange dreams. It was a wish in which he had small confidence.

The Newton on Beacon had been their home for several weeks, but Briana, instead of finding it comfortable and homey, found it gloomy and depressing. She had taken a mild dislike to the building when she and Lucinda had first arrived on its steps. It was brick, flat and plain, but taller at three stories than she had imagined. They paid a month's worth of room and board, about fifteen dollars, for a top-floor room near the back of the building with a window that looked out upon a similar structure.

The woman who registered them flaunted her long, glorious Boston history and English heritage, and eyed them with a suspicious squint. Nevertheless, money won out and the last available room became a temporary home.

She wrote to Rory as soon as they arrived and posted the letter at the front desk. She had no idea whether it would make it to Lear House or whether he and her father would still be there.

As September drifted on, the weather changed: The wind sharpened to a pronounced chill, the clouds thickened, the leaves fell in profusion from the few trees on the open greens, the days grew dark by late afternoon. Fall added to Briana's dull mood. There was no getting around it — she missed Rory, her father, and Ireland — and the thought of having a baby in a foreign country depressed her because she likened it to not having a permanent home for her child. She often found herself staring out the window into the neighboring building, a warehouse as far as she could tell. Men hauled large crates into the empty spaces and arranged them until nothing showed in the window except wooden slats.

Both of them found it hard to make friends — even Lucinda who, on the whole, could be more gregarious than Briana because of her teaching experience. The women who dined with them at the house were mostly American or English rather than Irish. The Americans came from strange places Briana had never heard of like Vincennes, Indiana; Schenectady, New York; or coal-mining cities in northern Pennsylvania. A woman from one of the latter settlements told them that the Irish were "infiltrating" her hometown and that she wanted nothing to do with them. In fact, that was one of the reasons she'd left — because the Irish were taking away jobs meant for Americans. After that pronouncement, the woman turned on her heel and stalked away.

Failing to make congenial friends, they took it upon themselves to look for work on their own but found jobs scarce. Briana soon realized that the NO IRISH NEED APPLY signs in the windows were meant for them despite whatever hope she might hold out for even a menial job.

One mid-September Sunday morning, after a night of cold rain, the gray clouds pushed off to the southeast and the early morning sun blazed against the bricks. When they returned to their room after breakfast, Briana pulled the small chair in the room to the window and stared out across the rooftops. A hard blue sky to the north beckoned.

"Well, I'm certainly not going to sit in this room all day and wait for something to happen," Lucinda said while pulling on her sweater. "I'm going to search for any new Help Wanted signs."

Briana ran her hands over the bump on her stomach, her child now entering its fifth month, and wondered what excuse she could come up with to get out of looking for a job. The task had frustrated her beyond all measure and taken an emotional toll that had begun to border on physical resistance. "Can we take a walk by the river or at least do something fun today? We've looked for work for three weeks." Briana pictured herself barefoot walking along the cliffs at Carrowteige, enjoying the sun and the crash of the waves.

The baby kicked in the womb, and Briana patted her abdomen, acknowledging the strange sensation. She longed to see something besides the insides of shops and manufacturing concerns, to have conversations other than those with arrogant, surly men and rude women.

Lucinda fidgeted with the buttons on her sweater. "You can stay if you wish, but I'm worried about money — we've gone through it faster than I'd hoped." Her sister's eyes flashed. "Don't fool yourself. We can't carry on like this for long. Not only are we outcasts, but employers can see you're pregnant. I'd do my best to hide it."

"I'll do no such thing." She turned and stared out the window, although she realized that there was a great deal of truth in her sister's words. "I've applied for positions as laundress and housekeeper and gotten nowhere," Briana countered. "I'm afraid I have too little to offer Boston. I don't have the teaching skills that you do."

"We have to try harder," Lucinda said, wiping her handkerchief over her scuffed shoes. "Do you remember the name of the man who saved us from those horrible brothers when we arrived in Boston?" She stuffed the handkerchief back in her sleeve. "I believe it was Declan . . . Coleman?"

"Yes, why?" Briana had committed the man's name and address to memory because she instinctively felt she could trust him. In the back of her mind she thought one day they might have to call on him despite their initial urge to strike out on their own.

"Mr. Coleman said we could call on him for help. Considering our luck so far, I'm willing to try anything. I'm going to pay him a visit in —"

"South Cove."

"Yes, that was it." Lucinda started for the door. "What was the address?"

"Ten Royal Street," Briana said, and rose

from the chair. "I may go for a short walk while you're out."

Her sister shot her a withering look. "Don't exhaust yourself." She took a room key hooked to the wall and walked out.

The other key glinted in the light. Briana sat again for a few more minutes before freshening up in the bathroom at the end of the hall. Most of the women had already left the house. As she dried herself with a towel, she decided to journey past Long Wharf to an area near the waterfront where many Irish immigrants lived. She longed to reconnect with her people even though she was in Boston. Her face flushed as she fought back tears. She was homesick.

Briana made her way to the waterfront and then north until she was in the shadow of the white spire of Christ Church steeple. The walk cheered her, and she found herself stepping with more energy than she'd had in days. The sun warmed the clean, crisp air until she ventured into the heart of the Irish district. She had heard from the less-than-kind proprietress of the house that there were "swarms of bog burners" scattered throughout Boston; in fact, too many for her taste. She added, however, that if not for the Irish, Boston's swamps wouldn't get filled in, nor fancy houses built.

A strange odor filled the air around her as she walked through the lane that divided the flat, wooden buildings. Its greasy hardness drifted from the windows of the densely packed homes. The sizzling smell of fried potatoes carried on the air, a way of cooking little known in Ireland. And there were other odors as well: the bile-inducing odor of human waste after the slop jars were emptied on the muddy street, the potent stench of urine pooled in doorways, the dregs of stale liquor and beer drained against the sides of buildings.

Church bells pealed; muffled snores arose from open windows. Children laughed, or cried in pain, from the depths of clapboard houses. Dim Irish voices sounded in her ears, but many of the accents were strange and unintelligible. She gazed at the houses, some tilting at an angle from dereliction. Some doors couldn't be shut, yellowed newspaper covered cracked windows, and piles of stinking garbage clogged the lane.

Anxiety prickled up her arms and into her chest. Was this the promised land of America? Neither she nor her sister nor anyone in her family really knew what Boston would be like. Everyone assumed — like those heading to England to find work —

that life *must* be better outside of County Mayo. Perhaps living like this was preferable to starving by the side of a road, but if this was what America promised, the outcome she imagined was no better than living in a slum in Dublin or Manchester.

She walked carefully, dodging the slop and garbage, preoccupied with the squalor around her. What kind of life was she offering her newborn? She banished the question from her head, hoping that when Rory and her father arrived, the family situation would improve. Rory and Lucinda would find enough work to provide a reasonable accommodation for the family, and when the baby was old enough that her father could take care of it, she would also find work. Then their troubles would be over, and America would be a welcome home. Perhaps they could buy a small farm outside the city and grow their own potatoes, breed their own goats and pigs. The thought of having her husband and father close again brought her hope. But what of Ireland?

She passed a small square that held a plot of pale green grass. The color wasn't the rich, deep emerald of the land she loved. The sight saddened her and made her more homesick than ever. The houses closed around her again.

Briana heard the woman's County Mayo accent before her head poked from the doorway. Eager to contact anyone who might be considered a neighbor, she picked up her step. The woman wore a white blouse, a plain gray dress, and black shoes stitched along the sides. Nestled in the folds of her dress was a child — a small boy of five or six — whose eyes were as red as the top of his head.

Briana slowed and gave the woman a look but decided to get no closer in case the child was sick. She couldn't tell if he was ill or showing the results of a good cry.

The woman looked at Briana with a face filled with pride and courage rather than contempt or fear as she brushed back a wisp of red hair that had curled against her forehead.

Briana admired her courageous stance and asked in Irish, "Are you from Mayo?"

The woman scoffed, as if she couldn't believe Briana would have the gall to ask such a foolish question. "You must be new to Boston," she answered.

Briana felt like a fool and clasped her hands together.

The boy scrunched up his mouth and looked at her suspiciously.

"Yes," Briana answered.

"How new?"

Briana stepped closer to the stairwell that concealed the pair.

The woman shook a finger, bent over, and wrapped her arms around the boy's shoulders. "I wouldn't come closer — I don't know what's ailing him — a cold or something worse, but from the looks of you, you have no business approaching sick strangers with a baby in your belly."

She stopped. "A few weeks in the city. We're staying at a boarding house on Beacon Street."

The woman eyed her up and down. "Oh, the Newton. That costs enough to feed us for six months."

The sarcasm in her voice stung Briana. She had hoped to find something different in Boston — a friendly Irish community that stuck together despite the hardships thrown at them. She had no desire to spar with the woman. "I'll be on my way." Briana shifted, her hands resting on her waist.

The woman hesitated for a moment before asking, "What's your name?" Her tone was kinder now.

"Briana Caulfield from Lear House, near Carrowteige."

"Lear House? Never heard of it." She smiled. "I'm sorry. I didn't mean to be rude, but everyone on this block is from Mayo. We all ended up here and you've wandered square into it. Roscommon's a block away." She sat on the step above her son and stroked his curly red hair. "Addy Gallagher, and this is my son, Quinlin. He's named after my father, who came from even farther north in our country than we did."

Briana looked at her expectantly.

"Ballycroy. My husband and I used to farm east of the town . . . until the . . ." Her eyes clouded over and she grimaced.

Briana nodded. "I understand."

"I'd ask you to come in, but there's no place to sit with twenty-five of us in the house and some children in worse shape than my Quinlin."

Twenty-five? The house had two stories, but she couldn't imagine that many people in such a small dwelling. "Where are they from?"

"All over Mayo, but most not as far north as you."

She fidgeted, her fingers unintentionally forming closed fists, which she opened and closed to release the tension. "I'm sorry to bother you. I have to get back or my sister will be worried."

The woman looked at her with longing eyes, as if she wished she could leave her cramped home behind.

A callous veneer enveloped Briana's heart, and the unsympathetic feeling distressed her. She had witnessed horrible scenes in Ireland, but she'd never expected similar conditions in America. It saddened her to see Addy and her son in such deplorable conditions, yet she could do little to help them. Clearly Addy had no money and, most likely, little to eat, but charity had to begin at home. She and her sister had to be prudent. The woman was right — room and board was expensive at the Newton on Beacon. Their money wouldn't last forever. The only way to keep her spirits up was to recognize that life here might be as hard as in Ireland and then go on her way, leaving them behind — a cold thought that pierced her soul.

She had turned away when Quinlin coughed and cried out in pain. The boy doubled over on the step and clutched his stomach.

Instinctively, she ran toward him. Addy thrust out her hands, entreating her to come no closer.

"What's wrong, Quinlin?" Briana asked. Sweat broke out on the boy's forehead.

"Don't know," the child answered. "My stomach hurts."

Addy wiped away his tears. "I know what's wrong, and I can do nothing about it," she told Briana.

"What is it, Addy, tell me? Maybe I can do something."

"Maybe it's the same as killed my husband and forty-one others on the *Elizabeth and Sarah*. We left Killala in July and didn't get to Quebec until this month. We threw my husband, naked as the day he was born, into the sea. My son and I had nothing, and if it hadn't been for the kindness of a few others who were coming, we wouldn't have made it to Boston." She clasped her hands together as if in prayer. "I regret the day we boarded that ship. If only we'd known, we'd never have sailed. We'd have taken our chances in Mayo. My husband told me the night before he died he'd rather have given his body back to Ireland than be delivered to the Atlantic."

She wanted to reach for Addy, and the woman read the gesture from her eyes.

"Don't touch me," she said, unwilling to accept a sympathetic hand. "Who knows if I have it too." She peered at her son. "He's been on the pot for a couple of days now. He can't hold anything down. I didn't know he had slipped out of bed until I woke up. He was sitting on the step, shivering like he's half crazed, when I found him."

Briana studied the boy. His face and fingers had a withered look about them. She had been told about the fever, but Father O'Kirwin had described an even worse disease called cholera. Quinlin's feverish eyes had no bluish ring around them, and they weren't sunken in their sockets. His skin was still warm and red, not the translucent blue of the cholera victim.

"I think he ate something he shouldn't," Addy said. "He was fine until a few days ago. He even escaped the plague on the boat — but if — he . . ." She turned her head away and cried.

"I'll find a doctor," Briana said as Addy sobbed.

"We're all so close, living on top of each other." She wiped her nose on her arm. "I try to keep up, but I'll be indebted to you for anything you can do for my son."

"I'll do my best. I'll remember your name — Addy Gallagher." Briana looked up and positioned the house by the sight of the Christ Church steeple.

"It's famous," Addy said, drying her eyes and attempting to smile. "A man hung lanterns there during the American Revolution. Everyone in the house says we're lucky to live by such an important church, but I don't think an Irishman is allowed to step inside."

Briana forced a smile. Maybe the church was important, but living in its shadow didn't do any good for the thousands of Irish who were struggling to make this land their home. She waved good-bye to Addy and Quinlin and struck off toward the boarding house. In the forty minutes it took to get home, all she could think about was the sad woman and her sick son.

Lucinda arrived at the boarding house about an hour after Briana. Her sister wore an unseemly frown, a sober look equaling her own disquiet, and appeared to be in no mood to talk. Briana hesitated to bring up the visit to Declan Coleman in case something unpleasant had happened. Lucinda removed her sweater, rearranged a few things on their small desk, and then disappeared down the hall. Briana lay on her small bed and watched the afternoon sun inch across the windowsill.

When Lucinda returned, she burst forth with the angry words, "How dare they!"

"Who?" Briana asked, wanting to know but not wishing to incite her sister's rage.

"Bostonians — the English — all the puritans who live here." Lucinda plopped on her bed and gripped the spread with both hands. "We may have to move in with the Colemans because" — she paused, allowing her anger to steep — "because it seems there are few jobs for us unless we are willing to shovel dirt or haul lumber. Who knows? Perhaps we can lay railroad ties." Lucinda's unexpected laugh brimmed with sarcasm.

"I've seen it. It's worse than I expected." She understood why her sister would be frustrated. It only made sense, now that they had experienced what Boston had to offer the Irish.

Lucinda continued, ignoring Briana's words. "*You'll* be lucky to get a job as a laundress, while *I,* because of my teaching abilities, might have the privilege of serving some high-minded society lady her tea." She shook her head in amazement. "Can you imagine? We've traveled three thousand miles to be cooped up in this infernal house with no prospect for a decent job. Mr. Coleman told me how hard it is for Irish women to get along here. I was indulging in a fairy tale hoping that those "no Irish" signs didn't apply to us. Even our men are little more than cattle, driven to haul dirt, dig ditches, fill in swamps. He and his wife live somewhat comfortably because he's a skilled woodworker. Otherwise, they'd be as unfortunate as we."

"It's hell, Lucinda. I've seen it."

Turning a deaf ear again, Lucinda continued to stoke her fury. "The Colemans have a room about the size of this on the third floor they now use for storage. It would be too hard for you in the last months of your pregnancy to deal with the steps even if they cleaned it out. The kitchen is in the basement. We can't have the second story yet because Declan believes his sisters may yet come."

Briana sat up and glared at her sister. "I understand. Can I tell you about my day?"

"I'm thinking about both of us," Lucinda fumed. "What's so important?"

"We're not only dying in Ireland, we're dying here, too. A boy . . ."

"God in heaven, preserve us from my sister who thinks she can save the world."

Briana gazed at her hands. What could she do with them? Perhaps she could wash or sew, for she had experience at both. But what of the boy? She couldn't get Quinlin's face out of her mind. "He needs a doctor."

"You have no business being around sick children," Lucinda said. "For God's sake, Briana, you're going to have a baby in four months. Don't be a fool."

"I won't be near him if I can help it, but I'm sending a message to Mr. Coleman. Maybe he knows a doctor who can help."

"If you must, but I hope his services are free." Lucinda moved to the desk, where she wrote in the small expense book she kept there.

"Yes, sister." Briana shifted to the edge of her bed so she could look out the window. The sun had dropped below the buildings that sloped to the west. The distant trees had begun to turn from leafy green to orange and red.

After a few minutes, she left her sister and walked downstairs to the front desk. A young woman on duty dispatched a boy to the Coleman residence with Briana's message. The delivery cost only a few cents, but she knew her sister would be upset with her "frivolous" spending. Lucinda didn't need to know. Thinking of Rory and her father and Quinlin, Briana made up her mind that she must find work soon, whatever the cost, or they might end up like Addy.

CHAPTER 17

The proprietress knocked on the door early the next morning to say a man named Declan Coleman wanted to speak to Briana. Lucinda had already left the room for her morning bath. Briana dressed quickly and dashed downstairs, not wanting to keep Declan waiting.

He stood near the desk, dressed in a scruffy pair of workpants and a loose-fitting shirt. Declan's blue eyes flashed and he broke into a broad smile when he saw her descending the staircase. He extended his hand, which Briana shook.

"It was a pleasure to see your sister," he said in Irish. "I'm glad she was able to meet my wife. I'm fortunate that I don't have to work on Sunday." His warm hand released hers, and he ushered her toward two chairs near the front window looking out on Beacon Street. "Please." He gestured to one of the chairs.

She sat and clasped her hands in her lap.

"From your note, I see that you ventured north of the waterfront to Christ Church?"

She nodded. "I wanted to take a walk while my sister visited you." Her memory of the overcrowded homes and the sick boy brought a lump to her throat. "I had no idea of the terrible conditions here."

Declan sighed. "Many don't." He gazed out the window at the men who sauntered by wearing suits and hats on their way to work. "My job is not far from here, and I can't be late, but you wanted to know about a doctor."

Briana scooted forward in her chair. "Can you help?"

"I'll do what I can, but I can't guarantee anything. There are so many sick children and adults, all poor, who must fend for themselves. That's why so many of them die. Most Boston doctors won't give them a look without payment, and I don't know any Irish men of medicine."

Briana sank in her chair, thinking of Quinlin's pale face and red-rimmed eyes. "I can't get him out of my head. He may be dying while we're sitting here."

"Unfortunately, it's all too common and probably going to get worse if more Irish come to Boston." He cocked his head and put a finger to his lips. "I do know a man by the name of Furey, who comes from Roscommon. My supervisor knows him and introduced me to him. He gave a family on our block some medicine when their children were sick. I'll see if I can get something from him that will help the boy."

Briana's spirits brightened not only at the news that Quinlin might get help but at the kindness of Declan, who seemed to be one of the most generous men she had ever met. She had been right in her assessment of him as a good, decent man. "That would be wonderful. I can deliver it if I have to."

Declan rose from his chair. "Your sister wouldn't approve considering your condition, and I'm not sure that I do either, but I'll get in touch with Mr. Furey. If he can do something, I'll come by with the medicine."

Briana pushed herself up from the chair. The baby was beginning to weigh her down. "That would be so kind."

He took her hand again. "My pleasure. Now I must get to work."

A soft light filled his eyes as he waved from the door and smiled. The look was a knowing one that she had only experienced with Rory. It spoke of mutual respect and admiration and possibly even love given the right circumstances. Her breath caught for a moment as she caught his glance and suddenly felt ashamed of admiring another man besides her husband. Did Declan think the same of her? A blush warmed her cheeks as she trudged upstairs to her room. If Rory wasn't an ocean away he could see her swelling stomach, touch her belly, and feel the child inside. If he were here, he would tell her how much he loved her and how beautiful she was. Rory would protect her and keep the family safe from harm. She knew that as surely as the sun would rise.

Instead of conjuring up Rory, Briana had to deal with Lucinda, who sat on her bed brushing her wet hair. Scowling, she vented her impatience with Briana by asking, "Where did you sneak off to?"

"Declan Coleman was here," Briana answered.

Lucinda was silent, but judging from her dour expression, she was hurt by her exclusion from their meeting. "You were in the bath. Declan hopes to get medicine for the boy I saw yesterday."

Lucinda grimaced. "You should leave these people alone. Involving yourself may bring trouble down upon us."

Briana gathered bath soap and started for the door. "I don't feel that way . . . at all."

Lucinda brushed her hair in fevered strokes. "Once again, I will be looking out for both of us as I go out seeking work." She threw the brush on her bed. "You may sit here and dream of saving the world."

"We'll be going together if you'll wait a few minutes," Briana said tersely. She would find a job before her sister could even think of finding one! She composed herself and knocked on the bathroom door. No one was inside. She locked the door and filled the tub with hot water that had been hauled up by the scrub women.

As she sank into the warm water, she tallied up the losses her sister had experienced as well. Her hopes of a courtship with Sir Thomas and employment on the Continent had been dashed upon the bad fortune of Irish fields. And there was Lear House. She and her sister had been apart so much in the past two years, Briana had begun to think of Lucinda as an acquaintance rather than a blood relative. Their separation had marked their differences rather than brought them closer. And in Briana's rush to marry, and the horrors of the famine, she and Lucinda had little time to grow closer.

Why *did* she care so much what happened to Addy and Quinlin? Lucinda certainly didn't approve of her meddling in others' lives. She pictured the boy's face and thought of her own baby, hoping her child would not have to face such illness and want. But there were other images as well: the starving family at the river crossing, the child who had died in his mother's arms, the corpses along the road. She wanted to help. She cared about people even if she was an ocean away from her homeland.

She closed her eyes and immersed her head under the water. For a moment, she was at peace, hearing and smelling nothing, feeling only the comforting warm liquid washing over her skin. When she came up for air, she wondered whether Declan Coleman would be successful in his task.

Declan dropped off the medicine at the boarding house two days later as Briana was getting ready to look for work.

In her room, she opened the drawstring and peered inside. A clear glass vial marked in red with a skull and crossbones and the word *Laudanum* lay wrapped in the folds. A brown bottle marked as a mixture of sugar and salt rested next to a handwritten note in Irish.

Mr. Coleman: I wish I could attend to every sick child in this city, but I cannot.

494

Please instruct the lady to give the patient two drops of laudanum on the tongue every four hours and to administer a sugar and salt mix in copious amounts. I have provided what I can of both. A teacup of burned rice mixed with water consumed frequently should help with diarrhea. If this is indeed cholera, the child is probably already dead. Dysentery can kill too. I wish them luck.

Yours, R. Furey

The note chilled her. What if Mr. Furey was right? If the boy had contracted cholera he might be dead.

She wasted no time in dressing but wondered if she should go to Addy Gallagher's. Declan was at work and couldn't help her; her sister would be furious *if* she found out. Lucinda had already left for an interview as a maid in a newly established Beacon Hill residence. The position had come up in the last two days of their search. Nothing could be done but to deliver the medicine herself.

She took a handkerchief from the nightstand and sprinkled a few granules of the sugar and salt mix on the fabric. At least it might help with the neighborhood's bad smell.

Wrapped in her cloak, Briana struck off with the medicine in hand. The feeling that she had something to do — something useful and good — moved her forward with brisk steps. Warm, murky clouds hovered over the brick buildings and white church spires.

She retraced her steps to Addy's and soon found the recessed doorway near the Christ Church steeple. This time no one was on the steps. Shuddering to think what she might find inside, she hesitated for a moment before knocking on the door.

Muted voices filtered through the door as she knocked again, this time with a firmer hand.

The door creaked open and a gray-haired woman peered around its edge. Years of worry and toil had taken their toll on the aged face. Her eyes were sunken and watery; her forehead lined with shadowy creases.

"I've come to see Addy Gallagher and her son," Briana said to the woman.

"Who's calling?" the old woman asked. "Are you the high-toned lady that Addy told me about?"

"Briana Caulfield." She took out the bag from under the folds of her cloak. "I've come to deliver this to Quinlin."

The woman sneered. "The lazy wretch.

He's feeling better — it's all in his head."
She drew a circle around her right ear with
her finger. "As loony as his mother."

Briana disregarded the slight. "I'd like to
see them, if I may."

"Yes, your ladyship." She beckoned her
inside with a flourish of her hand.

Briana wrapped the handkerchief over her
mouth.

The old woman pointed to a door at the
end of the hall.

The dank, unmoving air smelled of unwashed flesh and human feces, enough so
that she gagged while walking through the
dim corridor despite the handkerchief. She
pressed the cloth tighter over her mouth
and nose to keep from retching. The damp
heat in the hallway was insufferable. Four
rooms, two to the left and two to the right,
opened before her as she passed. She
glanced in each, horrified by what she saw.
Candles threw out a grim light because the
two windows on the dim north side of the
building were shuttered, clouded with dirt,
and cracked from years of use. The gaps
had been filled with old newspaper. Piles of
soiled clothes served as makeshift beds.
Children as emaciated and dirty as those
she had left in Ireland sat atop these jumbled masses as their mothers gathered

around flimsy wooden tables. Mounds of refuse — paper, glass bottles, cans — littered the corners. Briana noticed that there were few men in the house. Most were probably at work or out looking for jobs.

A sickly yellow light appeared behind her, casting shadows on the wall. She turned to find the old woman holding a candle.

"Here. You'll need this," the woman said. "She's near the front of the house under the steps."

Briana took the candle in her left hand, opened the door with her right while clutching the medicine, and moved down the rickety wooden staircase one step at a time. Ghostly faces stared at her as the light moved over them. The candle's feeble rays extended no longer than an arm's length and then dissipated in the vacuous murk of the pit. The faces that watched her were tight and grim with tangled hair. With sullen eyes, they followed her movements — apparitions rising from soiled bedding, or piles of rubbish and bits of straw. No light existed in the subterranean dwelling except for her candle. As she descended, the air thickened with sweat and body heat, smothering her as she walked.

She called out for Addy, and a meek voice answered in front of her. How far away it was she couldn't tell, for, like the flame, the sound faltered in the heavy air.

She stepped on someone's leg, but no one cried out. She called again for Addy and, out of the gloom, a beckoning hand appeared, made visible by the white sleeve of a blouse. Briana followed her under the low ceiling, which eventually transformed into the inverted shape of the steps. Quinlin lay on a bed of newspapers and straw, his face drawn and gray.

"You did come back," Addy said, and sat on the bed next to her son.

"Is he any better?" Briana asked.

Addy shook her head and the candlelight reflected off her red hair. "I don't know. He's able to drink, but he doesn't eat." She grasped her son's hand. "He seems weaker each day."

Briana placed the candle on the floor and knelt next to Addy. "I've brought medicine. There's a note attached from the gentleman who procured it — a man from Roscommon. Follow his instructions. I hope your son gets better." She wanted to touch Quinlin but decided against it. "Is he feverish?"

Addy covered her son's forehead with her palm. "His skin is cool and dry, but he doesn't respond to me." She lifted her hand and sat back on her heels. "Bless you for all you've done. You shouldn't have come. It takes courage . . . to remember others." In the candlelight, her eyes flickered with grateful appreciation.

"I hope someone would do the same for me if my child was sick." Briana's eyes had slowly adjusted to the dark. She looked at the women and children who peered out of the gloom. They reminded her of rats emerging at dusk in search of food. Somewhere in the room, water dripped down the wall.

"You have no light?" Briana asked.

"Candles aren't allowed because of fire."

"But above?" Briana protested.

"They have windows," Addy said, gazing back at Quinlin. "They can get out. We can't."

Briana shuddered at the thought of a fire breaking out in this dismal cellar. The tragic picture that formed in her mind was too terrible to imagine. And what if a fire broke out above? Everyone in this room would be trapped. There was only one way out — up the stairs.

"You and Quinlin should leave as soon as you can," Briana said.

"No," Addy replied with a firmness that surprised Briana. "I have to stay."

"Why?"

"That's my business." Addy turned away from her, and the distance between them suddenly grew cold. "Thank you for your kindness, but you should leave me to my business. It's not good for you to be here."

"All right."

When Addy turned, her eyes sparkled with tears. "For your own good, you shouldn't come here." She paused. "Perhaps, I can visit you — and bring Quinlin with me — when he recovers." She took the bag from Briana and held it close to her heart. "I'm not going to let this out of my sight. Let me walk you out."

Briana said good-bye to Quinlin, who had never acknowledged her presence, and followed Addy up the stairs to the front door. She blew out the candle and handed it to the old woman, who stood near a crowded room. Addy opened the door, and the air flowed over them. Looking out on the dilapidated homes, muddy lane, and the thick overcast seemed like a blessing compared to the crypt below. Briana lowered her handkerchief, fanned the folds of her cloak, and breathed freely again, gulping air into her lungs.

She was about to wish Addy good-bye when a portly man appeared at the stoop as if by magic. Briana recognized him but

501

couldn't remember his name; she knew he was one of the brothers who had stopped her and Lucinda when they had disembarked from the *Warton.* His round face and ruddy complexion were burned into her memory. He had offered to escort them to a brothel until Declan had thrust himself into the conversation.

Addy ignored the man until he spoke.

"Where have you been?" he asked with all the authority of a master speaking to a slave. He paid no attention to Briana other than to give her a quick glance as he sidled up.

"My son's been sick," Addy replied with disdain.

The man scowled and then spat into the mud. "That's no excuse. The boss won't like to hear that one. There's so many of you crammed in that house, somebody could care for the little swine."

Addy bristled and straightened like an arrow. "No one touches my son except me. Let me make that clear." Accenting her words, she added, "I'll be back when he's well."

"Always full of spark, Gallagher," the man replied. "That's why the men like you." He smacked his lips and pulled a fat cigar from his jacket pocket.

Addy's face turned crimson underneath

her red hair. She gave Briana an exasperated look and turned away.

"You owe money," the man continued. "It's only right, our fair share." He struck a match and puffed heartily on the cigar until it was lit. "See that we get it, or we'll have to come looking for it." He reached up and tweaked Addy's cheek. She spat on his hand as he pulled it away. The man laughed, shook the spittle off his fingers, and left.

Addy sighed and watched him trundle down the dirt lane, straddling one of the deep furrows carved by carriage traffic.

"I'm sorry you saw that," Addy said. "He's a pig."

"I've met him before," Briana said. "When my sister and I got off the boat, he was there, waiting to take us to . . ."

"No need to be coy about Mr. Carson," Addy said. "It's no secret to many people what he does. I work for him . . . well, I work for his boss, whom I never see." She pushed back her hair and leaned against a ramshackle railing. "After my husband died, I had no choice. I couldn't find work — none that paid well enough to support me, let alone my son."

Briana nodded. "I understand." She shuddered at the thought of doing the same if she had a son and no means of support.

She was certain Addy had done everything she could before turning to that profession; however, if such was the choice, America was not a good place for any Irish immigrant to call home.

"I should be going," Briana said. "I hope Quinlin gets better. Please let me know. You can always send a message to the Newton on Beacon."

She left without offering an invitation to visit and doubted whether she would ever see the woman again. Sorrow bubbled up as she thought of the woman's circumstances and her turn to prostitution to keep herself and her son alive. By the time she reached the end of the lane, she had decided to keep Addy's profession a secret from Lucinda, who would probably look upon it with disdain.

She was about to cross Hanover Street when a man whistled at her. She spied him on the opposite corner and then turned away, not wanting to give him encouragement. He whistled again and then struck out after her on foot. Briana spun in a frantic search for a policeman, but there were none to be seen. However, pedestrians and peddlers crowded the sidewalks while carriages rattled down the street. She doubted anything serious could happen as long as she was so exposed to the public. She strode to the next corner, but he caught up with her there as she waited for the cabs to pass.

He was slim and wore a suit of Continental fashion and a rather high black hat in a style that Briana had never seen before. His face flushed pink from sprinting after her, and his eyes examined her as if he had something important to say. Like her first meeting with Declan, she had an immediate reaction to this man — but this time it wasn't favorable.

The stranger was older, maybe a little less than twice her age, with a pleasing face but one she felt she couldn't trust, like that of a fox. He padded next to her, his breathing forced from his exertions. Briana suspected that she could beat him to the top of the hill above Lear House even though she was carrying a baby.

He bowed stiffly and then spoke in Irish: "I saw you coming in a hurry from the neighborhood. Are you all right?"

"What business is it of yours?" Briana replied.

"County Mayo," he said. "Do you speak English?"

Briana nodded, keeping an eye out for the nearby street vendor selling vegetables from a cart in case she needed help.

The man broke into English with a smile. "How wonderful. You're what I've been looking for."

His assertion drew her distrust; his clothes and manner of approach aroused her suspicions.

"I'm certain I'm not what you're looking for," she replied, turning her gaze once again to the street and the chance to weave through the carriages.

"Can you add and subtract?"

She tightened the drawstrings of her cloak. "Do I need to call for the police? I don't even know your name."

His brown eyes softened, and he bowed again. "Pardon me, but I'm rarely wrong about those whose demeanor has captured me. You look like an intelligent woman, confident and assured. You're what I seek." He took off his top hat and cradled it in his arms. "Again, pardon me. I am Romero Esperanza."

The name certainly wasn't Irish, and it was so foreign sounding she couldn't imagine what a man called Romero Esperanza could want of her. Lucinda might have recalled such a name from reading one of her European novels. "Should I know you?" Briana countered, thinking back on her dismal luck with employment.

"Hardly. I'm certain we haven't met, but I run a business near here and I'm looking for a woman who can run my office and keep books. I have a select clientele of Irish and English customers." He looked down at her abdomen, which showed through the cloak's fabric. "If you'll pardon my frankness, you need a job off your feet."

She thought of Addy and wondered if this was the same sort of misguided attempt to snare another woman. Not trusting the stranger, she said, "Thank you very much, Mr. Esperanza, but I'm sure whatever you have to offer isn't for me." She stepped into the street, waiting for a carriage to pass by.

"Please take my card . . . in case you change your mind," the man called out after her. "I can pay you ten dollars a week."

That offer stopped Briana. The man came up beside her, smiled, pressed his card into her palm, and disappeared down Hanover Street the way he'd come. She looked at the card. It gave his name, the business address, and a title, *Purveyor of Fine Goods.* She clutched the card in her hand and hurried back to the boarding house.

"Ten dollars a week?" Lucinda squealed at Briana's tale of meeting Mr. Esperanza, even though Briana's news had diverted attention away from her own.

"And I'm thrilled you got the job," Briana said, "and, selfishly, for us both."

Her sister looked at the business card and then placed it on the desk. "Ten dollars a week! I can't believe it — that's two dollars more than what I'll be making, and I was thrilled to get it."

"What's the family's name where you'll be working?" Briana asked.

"The Carlisles. They have money." Lucinda picked up the card again and studied it. "*Purveyor of Fine Goods.* I wonder what that means."

Briana grabbed her hairbrush from the table. "I have no idea, but perhaps Declan knows who the man is. Let's go down to supper."

"Yes, let's," Lucinda said. "For the first time since we've arrived, I feel like I have an appetite. I'll tell you all about my meeting." She clasped her hands in a thoughtful manner. "If all works out, I may even have a place to live at the Carlisles' home."

"Really?" Briana brushed her hair, suddenly dispirited by the idea of not sharing a room with her sister, her only ally in the city.

"Never fear, dear sister. I would never

leave you to suffer at the Newton on Beacon."

"Perhaps I *should* look into Mr. Esperanza's offer," Briana said.

Her sister playfully swiped at her shoulder. "Perhaps you should. 'Never look a gift horse in the mouth.' "

Laughing, Briana put down the brush and escorted Lucinda to the stairs, where they sauntered down together, feeling much like sisters again.

Declan Coleman arrived as they were eating breakfast the next morning. He was wearing his work clothes, as he always had except for their first meeting on the wharf. Briana escorted him into the dining room, after assuring the young woman on the desk that he was a friend, and offered him a seat at their table. When Lucinda spoke of her coming employment, Declan's eyes shone with excitement only matched by the storyteller.

"The Carlisles," he marveled after Lucinda finished. "They're nearly as wealthy as the Cabots." Declan told them about all the new homes being built on Beacon Hill, including the one for the Cabots.

Finally, he came to the reason for his visit — to inquire about the medicine he had delivered. Briana recounted her visit with Addy and Quinlin but made no mention of the unexpected appearance of Mr. Carson.

Declan frowned and gazed at the table, his mood shifting from one of congenial conversation to sadness. "I'm sorry to hear about the boy. Life is so unsettled now — it's the main reason my wife and I have not had children. We find it hard enough to live on our own, let alone with extra mouths to feed. Why bring a child into the world when it's destined to die?"

Lucinda gasped and straightened in her chair. "But what about the Church, and our Lord's proclamation to 'go forth and multiply'? You do believe those words, don't you?"

He leveled his eyes at Lucinda, and a fire simmered underneath his cool gaze. "I beg your pardon, but hang the Church. You have no children to care for. Wait until you do — wait until one of them is sick or dying — then you'll find I speak the truth."

Lucinda lifted her napkin and dabbed it against her lips but said nothing.

Briana broke the awkward silence, thinking of her own child and how she and Rory had taken precautions that failed. "My sister meant no harm, I'm sure. She was only trying to understand your way of thinking.

Isn't that right, sister?"

Lucinda nodded and added in a low voice, "This is not the place for such talk, but I do know I will care for and protect my sister when her time comes to deliver."

Declan dropped his defenses and smiled. "I'm sorry. I had no right to speak to you like that. But it enrages me to see children die when there is so little we can do about it. We Irish are stifled at every turn. It's as if our lives don't matter — in our home country and here in Boston. We suffer no matter where we go, and I'm tired of it." He gathered his hat from his lap and stood up. "Excuse me, but I must get to work." He looked at Briana. "I sincerely hope the medicine helps and the boy lives."

He was about to say good-bye when Briana stopped him with a question. "Have you ever heard of a man named Romero Esperanza?"

Declan looked puzzled. "No. Why?"

"He stopped me on the street and offered me a job. He wanted to know if I spoke English and could add and subtract. The card he presented said he was a 'Purveyor of Fine Goods.' He offered me ten dollars a week."

He put on his cap, his face colored by Briana's words. "I assume you declined his offer?"

She folded the napkin on her lap and peered up at him. "For the moment."

"A man who offers ten dollars a week to a woman he's never met is up to no good. I'll check around and let you know if I find out something. In the meantime, I'd avoid him." He doffed his cap, wished Lucinda good luck with her work, and left.

After breakfast, Lucinda was in such a good mood she suggested that the two of them walk the city. They spent the sunny day wandering the banks of the Charles River, exploring the adjoining streets where every new building promised a life of wealth and ease. The construction, the bustle, the clack of the carriages and whinny of the horses energized them both, but as she walked, she found herself thinking of Rory, wondering what he was doing thousands of miles away, and with a pang of jealousy imagined the thought of another woman in his arms. After all, she had "noticed" Declan Coleman. Any woman in her right mind would be attracted to a handsome and kind man. What if Rory was missing her so much he had to find solace in another woman? Her eyes grew misty. Lucinda stopped her and asked what was wrong. Briana told her that the baby was making it uncomfortable to walk. After lunch at a small café, they returned to the house so Lucinda could read and Briana could rest.

True to his word, Declan left a note at the desk that evening, which Briana picked up.

My Dear Mrs. Caulfield: Mr. Romero Esperanza is famous for all the wrong reasons. The goods that he purveys, according to my boss, are unsavory. They include liquor, bets, and payments from English gentlemen for protection against Irish thugs and, sometimes, the services of women. The Carson brothers may work for him. I'm glad that you were able to leave him without obligating yourself. Any job offer from him could result in disastrous consequences. Not wanting your sister to be alone in her employment, I inquired on your behalf at our company. We may need an assistant to our bookkeeper. The pay is not nearly as much as Mr. Esperanza offered, but it is, at least, wages offered without stipulation. Please call tomorrow morning at this address:

Briana crushed the note to her chest and

breathed a sigh of relief. She had hoped and prayed that she would be able to find work, up until the time she delivered her child. With Lucinda and her working, the future looked much brighter. She bounced up the stairs, eager to tell her sister the good news.

CHAPTER 18

Rory and his father-in-law had slept the
night of the eviction in the sodden debris of
the cottage. Constructing a shelter meant
cutting what few branches they could find
and placing them over the shattered timbers
to make a lean-to that offered scant protection against the elements. Fortunately, it
hadn't rained the day of the destruction.
The constable and the dragoons camped
nearby to make sure no one tried to break
into Lear House or rebuild their homes.

Breaking into the manor had been on
Rory's mind, and, in fact, Brian had mentioned it as well, but it was impossible with
the dragoons still on the estate. If he and
Brian could hold out longer than the soldiers, they might be able to get into the
manor.

By the next morning the skies opened and
the rain came down in cold sheets. Rory
clutched the crumbling sod of his cabin and

squeezed the mud through his fingers. It dripped in a slimy mess down his hands to the ground. The sight of his home awash in ruin enraged him. He wanted to wring the constable's neck and those of the men who accompanied him, but such desperate thoughts of revenge would do no good. The Maguires had been rendered ineffective as well. Saving their families' lives rather than skirmishing with an armed force was foremost on the remaining men's minds.

So Jarlath and his wife and son decided to walk to Dublin. Rory and Brian would try their best to find work at Westport. They strapped their meager possessions to the sides of two ponies, leaving the other three animals to fend on their own. They had no choice, and Rory doubted that the two work horses and the other trotter would be there if they ever returned to Lear House.

Brian shed a tear as they looked down from Carrowteige upon the desolate and abandoned manor.

They spent a cold, rainy night shivering in the hills near Carrowmore Lake before stopping the second night with his brother and family in the crumbling home of Frankie and Aideen Kilbane. The house bore little resemblance to the first night Rory and Briana had stayed there: The walls were stripped to the bare stone and sod, and the thatched roof had split, letting the unrelenting rain fall into the back room. Nothing of use remained — every pot and pan, any of the Kilbanes' personal belongings, had been plundered. They managed to light a turf fire and eat a meal of warm mush. Despite the rain, Rory sheltered the two ponies as best he could in the other room.

The adults knew the Kilbanes had been murdered, but the story had been kept from Jarlath's son. As night fell around them, even with familiar company sleeping nearby, Rory sensed the murdered couple watching him, as if their souls still lingered on the land that had been their home.

The next morning, under a leaden sky, Jarlath and his family said good-bye. Jarlath decided to retrace their steps north on the trail to Bangor, then head west to Ballina and the three-day journey on foot to Dublin. Brian gave Jarlath as much money as he could, saying it should last them for a month in Dublin in a decent lodging house.

Rory tried to keep the tears from falling but was unsuccessful as he embraced his brother and family. Except for the occasional trip to Westport or separate forays into the heath surrounding Lear House, they had never been apart. The parting time was bitter. Brian put a steady hand on his shoulder.

Filled with anger at God, the government, and the English, Rory fell to his knees as they walked away. Instead of three confident, healthy individuals, nourished by the land that had borne them, Jarlath, his wife, and son stumbled away, thin, black-clad figures as colorless and bland as the muddy trail upon which they trod. A feeling of dread, like the hand of Death, fell upon him as his brother and family disappeared over the top of a hill. He suspected he would never see them again.

That day, Rory cleaned out the Kilbanes' fire pit and gathered berries and nettles for Brian to eat. They each had a water pouch. With the recent rains there was no scarcity of it to fill their stomachs. He wandered through the brambles far into the swampy land to find the last of the summer blackberries and edible roots. Everywhere he looked, the muddy prints of those who had gone before him were set into the bog. Many others had scoured the area as well.

That night there was little to say as they sat around the turf fire. After stewing the berries and roots in a tin cup he found behind the house, Rory stepped outside and looked up at the breaking clouds. A crescent moon splashed silvery light upon the road and across the land as far as he could see. The tranquility, the silence that surrounded him, pleasures that would have normally delighted him filled him with a building panic. His heart raced as fast as his mind. The silence goaded him — he must do something about their situation, something drastic, or he and Brian would die.

He found his father-in-law slumped against the wall, staring into the fire pit. With his balding pate, the feathery wisps of gray hair that flicked in the wind, the deep-turned mouth, Brian looked old beyond his years. The man was dying before his eyes. What could he do to keep him alive? He stuck his hand past the door to gauge the wind. Cold prickled upon his arm despite his shirt. Summer was passing into fall. The sharp, frosty smell in the air convinced him that the winter would be long and hard. How would they survive?

A man who called himself "Orange" arrived at the door the next morning. Rory judged him to be about his age, but surprisingly he was stouter than most men who roamed the countryside. His hair was almost the same color as his name. A rather rotund body added to the apt description. His clothes were well worn but looked as if they had been mended by someone with a flair for the needle. Rory wondered if Orange was a deserter from the dragoons, or even the English army, because he was well fed. The man seemed jolly enough, of a pleasant disposition with his greetings, but Rory was curious about his intentions.

The man did have news, however, and, once spoken, Rory's estimation of him softened.

Orange called him to the road, away from Brian, and lit his pipe. "Have you heard of the Maguires?" he asked as he puffed, his lips smacking against the stem. The whitish smoke encircled his head and then bounced away on the wind.

Orange asked the question with an innocence that confused Rory. Was he asking because he didn't know about the group, or was he trying to get Rory to admit to his own participation? He took another moment to judge the man and then decided to tell him that not only had he heard of the Maguires, he was a member.

The man guffawed and slapped him on the back before announcing, "Good to see a fellow brother for the cause. Praise be to God to send us more like you than the soldiers who keep us from our rightful food."

"You look as if you haven't missed many meals."

Orange patted his stomach. "I'll take that as a compliment to my resourcefulness."

"Where are you headed?" Rory asked. He was full of questions for Orange, who seemed content in his role to tease him with bits and pieces about the Maguires.

Orange tilted his head, then turned as if on the lookout for prying ears. Spotting none, he continued, "Blacksod Bay. A ship will be in tonight. We need men aplenty to carry back supplies."

"You're going to raid a ship?" Rory asked. "What if it's armed?"

Orange opened his coat and pulled a pistol from the waistband of his pants. "We'll be armed too."

Rory stifled a laugh because he knew that a group of men armed with pistols would be no match for a heavily armed English ship. There might even be cannon onboard to shoot them out of the water. He knew Blacksod Bay — about a half day's walk to the northeast from the Kilbanes' cabin.

If he decided to take part in this scheme he'd have to backtrack on the trail he had taken since leaving Lear House. He won-

dered where the ship would be docked —
in the bay, off the coast between Achill and
Belmullet, near the islands to the west of
the peninsula? Inishglora lay off the coast.
The island was known as the burial spot for
the Children of Lear, who had flown there
after their banishment ended. They had
crumbled to dust when they returned to human form. The thought had its own ironic
amusement, for, in their own ways, Rory
and Brian were crumbling to dust along
with thousands of others who didn't have
food.

"What's in it for me?" Rory asked. "I get
no pleasure out of killing other men." He
considered the suspicion cast upon him by
Sir Thomas's shooting.

Orange rubbed his stomach. "Food. Your
share. All you'll need to keep you and your
father" — he pointed to the cabin — "alive
for months. Who else in Ireland can offer
you that? You'll find only disease and death
in the poorhouse. The relief projects aren't
any better. Do you want to break rocks, as
well as your back, for half-pence a day only
to find there isn't food to buy?"

Everything Orange said made sense. They
would be lucky if they could find work in
Westport, and if they did, Brian would be
unsuited for the hard tasks he might be as-

signed. He had doubts about his own strength in a weakened state, let alone his father-in-law. He needed to take drastic measures to survive. What choice did he have? It didn't take long for him to make up his mind.

"Give me an hour," he told Orange. "I have a few things to do before I can join you."

The man smiled, displaying a crooked front tooth. "Give me your hand," Orange said, and extended his own.

Rory shook it and then headed to the cabin to tell Brian he would be gone for at least a day, maybe more. "I'm going to get food," he told him.

Brian raised his arm slowly, the bone showing underneath his skin. "Who is he?"

"A Maguire who promises us food."

His father-in-law's mouth stretched into a tight frown revealing his teeth and gums. "I don't like them, Rory. Is this dangerous? What will happen to me?"

Rory knelt before him and took his hands in his. "Stay here. Someone has to watch over the ponies." He hated to leave Brian, but staying might mean death for both of them.

He and Orange started off after making sure

that Brian was settled into the cabin for the next few days. Rory gathered what few roots and edibles he could find in the bog, filled the water bag, and left the tin cup behind. There was plenty of peat for the fire. He loaded his pistol, gathered his own supplies, and said good-bye with a promise that he would return with food before they headed to Westport.

Soon he and Orange stepped off the road that would have led them to Bangor if they had continued. Orange pushed onward, cutting across the low bog lands that surrounded Blacksod Bay. The big man followed a trail in the sodden earth stamped with footprints of the men who had trod before them. The path, dotted with tussocks, allowed them to cross over the low marsh and inlets that cut into the land. They stopped in the mid-afternoon for a smoke, which Orange shared with Rory, and a bit of stale bread and cheese that the man pulled from his kit.

Night was falling when they finally stood on the western edge of a spit of land that cut into the bay. Thirty men had camped at the site, and Rory was surprised to find that Connor Donlon was one of them.

"A sight for my sore eyes," Rory said, and hugged his friend. Connor offered him a drink of poteen. Rory guzzled the drink, which set his parched throat ablaze.

"What have we gotten ourselves into?" Rory asked him. His friend motioned, and he followed him down a path away from the fires.

"Most of these men are Maguires," he said. "I see you met Orange."

Rory nodded. "I've been so consumed with my family that I've thought little about them."

Connor poured another drink from a flask. "We don't know how many men are on the ship, or if there are soldiers, but we do know they have food. Our Irish goods go out to England while Indian corn comes in from the government and then goes to the depots, where it disappears. We're cutting out the middle men." He pointed across the bay to the small islands to the west. The stars peered through the deep twilight that inked the clouds to the east. "The ship is past the islands about ten miles out."

Rory was astounded. *Thirty men, ten miles out in canoes?*

Connor read his mind. "Two men to a *curragh* with enough room in the middle to haul whatever we can take."

Rory looked back at the fires, which had been carefully concealed by hillocks. In the flickering light he saw men stripping and donning women's dresses to conceal their identities. Others took off their shirts and smeared mud on their faces and chests. He grabbed the cup from Connor and drank another helping of poteen. The liquor hit his head and gave him a surge of confidence. As strange as the whole evening seemed, he, like the other men, was ready to loot the ship. "Are we armed?" he asked his companion.

"As much as we can be," Connor replied. "We have a few pistols and rifles to keep us protected."

"Then we should be off," Rory said under the influence of the poteen, which had undermined any rational thinking about tactics.

"As soon as the heavens make our way clear." Connor pointed to the sky. The clouds parted, revealing a lacy fabric of stars. "It's beautiful, isn't it? A perfect night to plunder." Connor laughed and then faced Rory. "How is Briana? I heard she and Lucinda traveled to America. I hoped they might make the ship."

The euphoria induced by the poteen shifted to melancholy with Connor's question. A sudden vulnerability washed over him, unmasking the thin veil covering his heart. "Thank you for letting us know, but I've heard nothing yet. I'm confident the *Warton* docked in Boston, because I'm sure any bad news would have traveled to Ireland by now. Beyond that, I don't know. I'll be lucky to receive a letter by the spring. I hope Brian and I last that long. How did you know she had left?" He found his fists clenched by his sides.

"Hardly anything escapes the notice of a mad poet," Connor said, referring to Daniel Quinn. "He ran into a couple of Mollies in Westport in one of his drunken fits and spilled his guts — literally. As they lifted him off the ground, he was muttering about our devilish landlord, Brian and his daughters escaping to America. Word travels fast."

"More than Quinn's mouth is a problem," Rory said, recalling the information he had given to the constable about the shooting at Lear House. "I think he may have been the one who shot Blakely. The poet's nowhere around here, is he?"

Connor snickered. "Quinn? Shoot Blakely? Maybe he's not as crazy as I thought. I may have to shake the poor bastard's hand." He turned the flask upside down, and nothing came out but a few silvery drops. "Quinn would be around if he knew there was something to drink. Most likely he's holed up at The Black Ram or the public house in Castlebar. He doesn't have the mental resources or the money to take his leave from a pub."

They talked about Connor's wife and children, who were safe with relatives in Bangor, although the family was struggling as well. Connor had agreed to go on this mission to get food for them. A low whistle carried on the wind, a signal that it was time to leave.

They returned to the fires and helped the men carry the *curraghs* from the shore to the bay. Rory took off his shirt and spread mud over his face and chest. Connor checked both their pistols and pronounced them ready for use.

Orange and another man, a farmer from Ballycroy, led the way. "Quiet as we go." He pointed to a pile of knotted ropes. "When we get to the ship, a few of you spritely lads will have to scale the side or climb the bowsprit rigging to take our visitors by surprise. One man will remain below to help load the cargo." He looked toward the purple horizon. "It's a far way out, on the other side of Blackrock, but we can make it. Thank God for calm seas. More than your back will ache tomorrow if providence is on our side."

The men loaded the rifles and ropes into the canoes and muttered quick prayers. Rory and Connor took their places in a *curragh* near the middle of the flotilla. Orange raised his hand, and his companion shoved off.

Soon they were pulling hard and following the lead of several canoes cutting through the wind and swells. Neither man talked, but Rory thought, as his arms powered against the waves, that Orange had a strange idea of what constituted calm seas. The trip back, if everything went well, would be much easier. The cold saltwater showered over them as they cut across the bay toward the small island of Duvillaun More. The mountainous form of Achill rose out of the blackness to the south.

Rory was happy that his old nemesis, Connor, still retained much of his strength. His back to the wind, his friend flexed and strained from his place in the front of the canoe. With their synchronized exertions, they soon found themselves near the front of the raiding party. Sweat poured down Rory's body — his body heat and the layer of mud negated any ill effects from the chilly waters.

A large stretch of deep, choppy water opened before them after passing by Duvillaun More. The tiny spit of Blackrock lay in front of them. Rory looked back to see several of the party languishing behind. Then the clouds closed above them for a time, thrusting the canoes into utter darkness. When the heavens opened again, scattering starlight over them, the ship, dusky in its outline except for the folded white sails, rocked on the waves.

"A mackerel sky and mares' tails make lofty ships carry low sails," Connor said. Rory barely heard his words over the wind. The vessel was a lofty wooden ship, a three-master anchored off the western side of Blackrock. A ship showing no light meant the crew had taken to their beds below. No lanterns bobbed on deck, and Rory was happy to see that it was a true smooth-sided merchant vessel devoid of cannons.

The lead canoes held back so the others could catch up. After what seemed a long wait bobbing over whitecaps, the last of the party was in place to raid the ship.

Orange and his companion pulled their canoe next to one containing two young men who, upon his signal, climbed the lines and scurried like galley rats up the bowsprit rigging with the knotted ropes looped around their bodies. Seconds later, the ropes dropped to the waiting raiders.

Connor agreed to man the canoe to keep it from floating away. The pistol tucked into his waistband, Rory climbed fist over fist up the rope until he was able to propel himself over the side to the deck below. Soon fifteen raiders stood onboard the ship looking for any sign of the crew.

Several men brandishing pistols sneaked to the hold doors and, after flinging them open, descended belowdecks. In less than five minutes, a crew of seven and the captain appeared up top in their nightshirts and breeches. They were English, and while they stood tall and proud near the bow, they were no match for the eight firearms pointed their way. That left seven men, Rory included, to unload what they could from the hold.

Orange's stout companion assumed command of the raiders, instructing the men who scurried through the ship lighting lanterns and taking stock of the goods. A line of men heaved the heavy bags of Indian corn to the deck. They were lowered into the *curraghs* by the ropes. Several slipped from their harness and splashed into the sea, bringing forth a volley of curses from Orange.

The true bounty, however, came in the form of dried meats, cheeses, wine, firearms, and other luxury goods afforded the English crew. Rory admired a fine silver sword and a bag of other silver pieces that were passed his way before being lowered to a canoe. In less than an hour, the canoes were loaded and ready to depart.

"Stay put for fifteen minutes or we'll fire upon you," the stout man told the captain and crew before clambering over the side.

Rory scrambled down the knotted ropes with the others and took his place opposite Connor, the corn resting in the middle of the canoe. The two young men tossed the ropes to Orange and took off for the bowsprit rigging. Rory watched as they swung down from the deck, descending the lines like monkeys. They pushed off from the ship and were soon sailing fast over the waves toward their destination on the eastern side of the bay.

"Get down," Connor screamed.

Rory ducked. He didn't see the flash, but he did hear the percussion as a pistol was fired in their direction.

A shriek carried over the waves. The Mollies fired back, and the English crew scattered about the deck. Soon carried by the waves, they were beyond the range of firearms.

The large man bent over Orange, who

doubled up in pain. Connor swung the canoe toward them. Their leader had been struck in the left shoulder by a ball. His blood spread in a large black splotch down his jacket.

"Do you need help?" Rory called out to them.

Orange lifted his head and screamed, "No, damn it. Onward!" He grabbed the oar with his right hand and, uttering curses and crying out in pain, rowed as fast as he could.

Soon the canoes were past the island and on their way back to the camp. With the wind at their backs, the waves picked up their canoes and thrust them toward the coastline. They had completed the raid and were now safely in shallow waters, away from the revengeful reach of the English ship.

Orange stumbled from the *curragh* and collapsed on the beach. Two men held the large man down while Rory stripped his jacket from him and ripped open the shirt where the ball had blown a hole.

"Connor, get me a lamp and gather my shirt," Rory ordered. Connor called out for a lantern and ran to get the clothing. He returned with both and knelt next to Rory.

The ball had lodged in Orange's shoulder. Rory could see its smooth, circular form surrounded by bloody flesh in the yellow light.

"You're in luck," he told Orange. "It didn't even hit the bone. Good thing you're built like a bull. Steel yourself, this is going to hurt." Rory dipped his hands in cold saltwater and returned to the man. He dug his fingers around the ball and popped it out with a thunk. The wound bled profusely after a sharp cry from Orange. "Get seaweed for a poultice," he instructed Connor.

He placed the stringy green leaves over the wound and bunched his shirt across Orange's shoulder and back before knotting it in the front.

"Thank you, my friend," Orange said with a grimace. "There's a place in heaven for you." Many men offered poteen. Orange lifted himself from the sand with his right arm and hobbled toward a smoldering campfire. Rory and the others followed.

"Sleep well tonight, my fellows." Orange collapsed on the heath. "Tomorrow we have the hard work of securing our food. We'll work out the distribution plans on the new day. Keep the fires low so we don't give away our position to the English." He instructed two men to keep watch for the night and then patted Rory on the back and turned him aside. "I'll make some special arrangements for you," he whispered.

Rory waded a few yards out in the chilly bay and washed the mud off his face and chest. Then he and Connor left the others and settled in a hollow away from the beach. The stars blazed overhead in a glorious display of sparkling light, and Rory wondered, as he had many nights, how his wife was faring in Boston. He pictured her in a warm, comfortable room, eating fine food and laughing with ladies from high society. She was attired in a beautiful blue dress, her neck adorned with a pearl choker and her finger showing a glittering diamond ring. He wanted the best for her, now and always. The dream burst when he woke up shivering. He was without a shirt sleeping next to Connor on the cold ground.

He found a lookout and was able to secure an old gray blanket to wrap around him. This time when he closed his eyes he found his thoughts had changed. Now he saw Brian, his mouth drawn and cheeks sunken, crying out for food. He brushed a tear from his eye because he knew that dream was much more real than what he had envisioned for Briana.

Briana started her job as a bookkeeping assistant at Peters Building Trades several days after Lucinda began working for the Carlisles. The office was on Charles Street at the south end of Beacon Hill, not far from the boarding house. As fall deepened, Briana was happy that she hadn't far to walk on cold and rainy days.

The pay was half what Mr. Esperanza had offered as a "purveyor of fine goods," but the job required little physical effort other than filing papers, making ledger notations, and conversing with Irish workers who had questions about their jobs or wages.

The owner was a tall, lean man who, despite his strict fourth-generation Boston heritage, was a Quaker with a good heart and an equal love of humanity. He told Briana he was happy to help the Irish in any way he could, even involving himself in relief efforts in Ireland and working with the Irish Immigration Society in Boston. Mr. Peters had made her feel at home from her first day on the job and, after noticing her wedding ring and her pregnancy, made sure her chair and desk were comfortable. She couldn't have been happier when collecting her weekly pay.

Lucinda was less enamored of her job, although it paid more. It did not include, as she had hoped, accommodations for them both. She often complained about the "poor wages" and "backbreaking work" she had to perform. Briana refrained from reminding her sister about the housework she had done almost single-handedly most of her life. Lucinda had never had to work hard at serving or cleaning in Ireland with Briana in control.

Despite their new positions, they still found themselves on the fringes of Boston society, branded as immigrants who had little to offer. "Isn't it wonderful, what the Carlisles do for the poor," a snobbish lady had told Lucinda as she handed off her wet coat. As her sister described it, had she acted upon her anger that day she would have lost her job.

One evening in late October, a chilly rain swept in from the north. Mr. Peters had offered to escort Briana home to the Newton on Beacon in the dismal weather. Briana happily accepted his offer, and the two set off toward the boarding house as night fell. Mr. Peters's umbrella buckled in the rain. He tossed it aside and grabbed her by the waist to make sure she didn't slip in any of the fast-developing puddles.

She skirted the water and slick cobblestones, keeping her eyes down as she walked. A crowd had gathered near the boarding house door, and Mr. Peters brought her attention to it. A woman lay sprawled on the walk, her legs splayed into the street. Several men and ladies bent over her.

Briana's heart raced in a sudden burst of panic. What if it was Lucinda? But as she drew closer, she saw the woman wore a dress of plain gray fabric. Mr. Peters quickened his step, and soon they had joined the others.

She peered down at the mangled face, the swollen and bruised eyes, the split lips that gushed blood down her chin. The woman looked at her and gurgled in a raspy voice. "I made it. . . . I've come to see you."

"Addy!" Briana knelt beside her and lifted the woman's head from the sidewalk. Addy screamed in pain from the raw and bleeding slit across her neck.

"Take care of my Quinlin," she managed to gurgle as crimson bubbles formed over her mouth. Then her eyes closed.

"Keep her still," Mr. Peters said, and straightened his tall frame. "I'm going for a doctor."

Briana nodded and ran her hands through Addy's wet hair. "Hold on. Help is on the way." She lifted the woman's hand, which was sliced across the knuckles. "Who did this?" Addy didn't answer. "Tell me who did this?" She grasped the bloody fingers.

A woman from the boarding house whispered, "Let her pass, miss. She's done for, and agitating her soul won't help."

She didn't care what the others thought. They didn't know Addy; they didn't know how hard the woman's life had been since she had left Ireland.

Addy motioned for Briana to bend close to her face. "You saw him. . . . He'll kill my Quinlin."

The woman gasped, death rattled across her chest, and her head fell limp in Briana's arms. The rain pattered on Addy's face, washing the woman's blood onto Briana's hands. She lowered her to the brick and swiped at her blood-stained fingers. Seldom had thoughts of revenge entered her mind, but had she carried a pistol she would have shot the man whom she believed killed her friend — one of the Carson brothers.

The crowd dispersed, and Addy lay on the sidewalk, the rain pooling on her flimsy dress. Mr. Peters arrived a few minutes later accompanied by a police officer and a doctor, who, after a quick examination, pronounced Addy dead.

Briana reached out for Mr. Peters's hand, too shaken to stand on her own.

"Did she tell you anything?" the officer asked.

"Yes," Briana replied, her mind whirling. "She wants me to take care of her child."

The agitated policeman sighed. "I mean, about the murderer."

She wanted Quinlin away from the house in case one of the brothers tried to get to him. "One of the Carson brothers — I don't know their names. Her boy, Quinlin, lives near Christ Church. Can you protect him?"

"Is he Irish?" the officer asked with a disdainful tone and shifted on his feet. "We don't have the time to go chasing after Paddy, and if I know the neighborhood, the bog burners will protect him to within an inch of their lives."

Briana wanted to slap the policeman; she was getting nowhere. A sudden exhaustion swept over her.

"We'll go first thing in the morning," Mr. Peters said. "I'll send a man tonight to keep watch."

The officer took Briana's name and address and then turned his attention to the body. "Her throat's been cut," he said to the other officers who arrived in a horse-drawn police wagon.

She wiped her hands on her blood-stained dress and gave Mr. Peters the directions to Addy's house as best she could, for she had no street number.

Mr. Peters shook his head. "Come to the office tomorrow morning when you can. Now go inside before you catch your death."

She thanked him and shuffled inside after a last look at Addy. A crowd of women stood near the front desk giving her looks of horror mixed with disbelief. She slowly climbed the steps to her room, stripped off her dress, and washed herself in a chilly bath.

Briana sat shivering under two blankets when Lucinda arrived about eight. Her sister had seen the leftover blood stains on the walk and rushed to her side.

"Are you all right?" Lucinda asked. "What happened? I heard a woman died."

She collapsed in tears as she told her sister the story. Quinlin, she hoped, would be rescued in the morning after one last night in that terrible house.

Chapter 19

"How on earth do you suppose we will support this child?" her sister snapped at breakfast the next morning.

"I heard the same words when we helped Father O'Kirwin feed the poor," Briana replied. "Remember the boy I saw die at Lear House? His face haunts me to this day. I'm not letting that happen again."

"Yes, but how many others did we save?" Lucinda said with raised voice as she buttered her toast. "How many of those unfortunate people lived? We have enough worry with Father and your husband."

The other ladies in the dining room threw disparaging looks their way.

Briana slammed her hand on the table. "If we saved one life for one day, I'd say we'd done our Christian duty."

Lucinda rolled her eyes. "I had hoped that your flames of charity would be extinguished after all we've been through." She tossed the toast on her eggs and looked at the food with disgust. "You've ruined my appetite and I have to be at work in a half hour. You only have yourself to blame for ruining my day." She got up from her chair and pointed a finger at Briana. "And I forbid you to go to that house and bring home a child. He can't stay here. Think of your baby — and us! Don't be a fool!" She took a sip of tea and swept up the stairs, leaving Briana alone at the table.

She sighed and rested her head in her hands while trying to think of a solution. Not to be undone by Lucinda's threat, she formed a plan of her own. She remained at breakfast until after her sister left for the Carlisles'. Then she took a warm bath, got dressed, and walked to work. The day was windy with grayish clouds that stretched over the city like a curtain. Her unborn child kicked on nearly every step she took during her brief walk to the office. She rubbed her tender abdomen and wiped the sweat from her face. A few steps later she was chilled to the bone by the breeze.

Mr. Peters was behind his oak desk at the rear of the building when she arrived. She tapped on his door, and he waved her in. He directed her to sit in the chair across from him. A lamp burned on his desk, shedding some light in an otherwise somber room with no windows. The floor-to-ceiling bookcases crammed with architectural plans and business ledgers exacerbated an already oppressive space. Briana was glad she worked near the front of the building, where some light entered through a small window.

"Were you able to hire a man to stand watch?" she asked after she had seated herself.

"Yes, and before you ask, I've already talked to my wife about what we might do to help Quinlin." He cleared his throat and leaned back in his chair. "I don't usually discuss such matters with my staff, but knowing the severity of the situation and having a soft spot in my heart . . ."

Joy filled her despite the sunless office. "Thank you, Mr. Peters."

He waved a finger in the air. "Let me caution you — my wife and I can't adopt the boy. We're much too old for that."

She was flabbergasted because she had never thought of asking him to adopt Quinlin. "Oh, no. I only wanted to ask if you could board him for a few days until I can get my sister used to the idea of fulfilling Addy's wish." She wondered if Rory would object to her adding a family member. There was no way to know.

"This is your sister . . . Lucinda?"

Once again, he surprised her. "How do you know my sister's name?"

"Through a man we both know — Declan Coleman."

Of course, it made sense that Declan, who got her the job, would tell Mr. Peters of their history and situation. "I only asked because Lucinda is so protective of me — sometimes too much so."

"In some ways, Boston is a small town," he continued, "particularly within the Irish community." He picked up a pencil and twirled it between his fingers. "So you wish to save this boy and, I take it, your sister may not have the same feeling."

He understood perfectly. "We'd have to find a place to live other than the boarding house. We've been so busy with our new jobs, we haven't had time to look for other housing; in fact, Lucinda found out only recently that a room we had planned on taking at the Carlisles' didn't work out. In fact, we've considered moving in with Mr. Coleman. He asked us when we arrived in Boston if we might want to board in a spare room."

He straightened, his black suit accentuating the appearance of a stern figure. "So, how do we solve this problem? The workday has begun, but I could be convinced to leave my desk for a few hours to rescue a child."

Briana rose from her chair, overjoyed by his offer. "I'll take you there."

"You may lead me, but you will remain outside as I search for the boy. Let's think of your child as well as Quinlin."

She wanted to kiss the man who was behaving toward her like a protective father. She doubted that even her own father would have been as understanding as Mr. Peters. She rubbed her stomach — the baby seemed more settled now — then buttoned her coat and led the way out the door.

As they snaked their way through the crowded streets, Briana spotted the man she had encountered the previous month. Smoking a cigar, Romero Esperanza stood watching them from his position on an opposite corner.

She tugged on Mr. Peters's coat sleeve, and he looked her way. "Do you know that man — the one in the coat and round hat with the broad brim?" She cocked her head to the right.

"I've seen him but never had the pleasure of his acquaintance," he said, and clucked his lips in a disapproving manner. "Nor would any woman who values herself."

"He offered to hire me, but I declined."

"You were wise to refuse his offer." He glanced over his shoulder at Esperanza. "Look at him — dressed in that expensive overcoat and gambler's hat. Smoking a cigar on the street. Ha! From that alone you can surmise he's devoid of any moral fiber. I *can* tell you that there is an element in Boston that works for evil. They try to dress it up, but their business is the business of rogues. The farther away he is from you, the better."

Briana took a last look back at the man, who continued to gaze at them. She shivered and thought of Addy's connection to the Carson brothers. She wondered if there was a connection between the brothers and Esperanza because of the man's shady dealings.

Soon they were in the narrow lane that led to Addy's house. Mr. Peters put on a brave face, but Briana could tell that he was appalled by the derelict condition of the homes, the drunks who slept in the doorways and small alleys, and the disgusting smell of the slops.

"Wait here," he told her when they arrived at the door. The same old woman whom Briana had seen before answered Mr. Peters's knock. The putrid odor of the house washed over them — a noxious mixture of unwashed flesh, excrement, and rotten food.

"What do you want?" the old woman asked in Irish. She picked at one watery eye and then dragged a finger through her gray, matted hair.

Mr. Peters looked at Briana expectantly.

"We're here to pick up Quinlin Gallagher," Briana replied in her native tongue.

The woman attempted a smile, but her snaggletoothed grin turned it to a sneer. "The lazy, good-for-nothing boy is down below, sleeping like he usually does. He played sick for a while, but he's as healthy as a horse, the little beggar. He cried this morning because his mother hadn't come home." She spat on the step. "In her line of work, she didn't come home plenty of times. You'd think the brat would be used to it by now."

"What is she saying?" Mr. Peters asked, his patience with the old woman running thin.

"She said Quinlin is a wonderful boy and she would be happy if he were taken to a good home." She blushed a little from her lie, but there was no need to upset her employer with a literal translation.

"Then let's get to it," Mr. Peters said, pushing toward the door.

The woman stopped him with her arm.

"What's this about? Is he from the police?"

"No," Briana said, "he's Quinlin's . . . uncle. Addy Gallagher is dead."

The woman spat again, this time at Briana's feet. "Ha! She got what she deserved. Uncle, my ass. He doesn't even speak Irish. I don't care who he is as long as he's not from the police. I've got enough trouble in this house. He'd do me a favor taking the boy away. Without a mother, he'll be out on the street."

Briana gestured toward the door. "Go ahead," she said to Mr. Peters. "This lovely woman will take you to him."

Mr. Peters pursed his lips and squinted into the darkness, his face twisted with trepidation.

The door closed, and Briana turned to watch the parade of people winding their way down the street. Women carried baskets of laundry tucked under their arms. Where they were going to wash clothes, Briana wasn't sure. A few grubby children rolled the remains of a fractured wagon wheel up the muddy byway. After hearing the children's excited laughter, she looked down at her belly and imagined her own child playing with other boys and girls — but not in these conditions. Would her child play in Ireland along the cliffs above Lear House?

America had food, but so many times she had longed for her native land. A few men also passed by, but they seemed defeated, as broken as the children's wagon wheel as they trudged along with haggard, bearded faces. Had liquor overtaken them, or was it America — a country not as welcoming as they had imagined?

The door creaked open behind her.

Mr. Peters stood with a handkerchief clutched over his nose while a pale Quinlin shivered in front of him, clutching a muslin bag tied together with a topknot. The old woman hovered behind them. Mr. Peters ushered Quinlin down the steps to the lane, lifted the handkerchief from his nose, and replaced it in his pocket. "I've never seen anything so disgusting," he complained, and gulped in deep breaths of fresh air.

The old woman laughed as if she understood his words, then said in Irish, "Glad to be rid of the brat. He carries that rag with him everywhere." She closed the door in their faces.

"He'll spend the day with me at the office, and when I get him home, he'll get a good scrubbing in a hot bath," Mr. Peters said.

"He may not like it." Briana studied Quinlin, who stood as lethargic and defeated as the men she had seen earlier. She wanted to tell him about his mother but doubted her own strength to do so considering the boy's condition. A painful stab of pity and sorrow cut through her. "Do you mind if I take the rest of the day off?" she asked her employer. "I need to clear things with my sister."

He placed his hands on Quinlin's shoulders. "Please do. I'll see you tomorrow. Let's not go into details until after he's had a chance to settle in tonight."

"Of course — I think that's best," Briana said, relieved by the delay of telling the boy about his mother's murder.

They walked back on the same route, even spotting Esperanza speaking with two women in a carriage a block from where he had been. Once again, he followed them with his gaze.

"A most disagreeable chap," Mr. Peters commented.

When they reached the office, Briana knelt before Quinlin and said in Irish, "Please mind Mr. Peters. He's a good man, and he's going to make your life much better."

The boy, his ragged clothes stretched across his thin body, asked, "When is my mother coming to get me?" His pale blue eyes flickered under his tousled red hair.

"We'll see," she said, holding back tears.

The boy brushed his sleeve over his face. "Something bad has happened — I know it. When my father died, Ma told me that bad things happen."

"We'll talk tomorrow. I promise." She got to her feet and blew a kiss to Quinlin. "Please mind Mr. Peters."

The boy gave a shy nod and looked down at the bricks underneath his feet.

A profound sadness darkened Mr. Peters's face as he opened the door. "Come inside, my dear boy," he said. "Come inside."

Lucinda wanted to hear none of it.

She might as well have been a stone wall, Briana decided.

"We can't afford to keep him," her sister kept repeating as they got ready for bed. "Besides, we'll have to uproot our lives."

"Uproot?" she asked incredulously. Her sister wasn't resisting a move; after all, Lucinda had considered moving in with the Colemans. Quinlin, she was certain, was the point of contention. "We have a few bags to pack. They've offered their spare room, and I'm sure it will be reasonably priced. You've a good hand with boys; after all, you've worked with three of them for two years."

"Yes, my good hand extends to their bottoms if they get out of line." Her sister continued to sputter about money and the "inconvenience to the family."

Briana turned out the lamp. "You'll feel better about it in the morning."

"I *will* not." Lucinda crawled into bed and pulled the blanket over her head, unwilling to discuss the matter further.

Bright sunlight streamed in their window the next morning, but the oak floor was cold on their feet.

At breakfast, Lucinda continued her silence, brushing off any overture to discuss Quinlin.

She waited a few minutes after her sister had left for work and then put on her coat. She had never seen such a brilliant blue sky — a sign of cold New England air. As she walked to the building trades office, Briana wondered if other arrangements might have to be made for the boy. Perhaps Mr. Peters would know a kind family who wouldn't mind taking in the child. Otherwise, as the old woman said, he would be condemned to a life on the streets, or end up in an orphanage. She blanched at the thought.

Mr. Peters was already in his office when she arrived. She hooked her coat on the rack and made her way through the dim hall. As usual, his desk lamp cast a yellow glow across his face. He smiled when she tapped on his open door.

"Come in, come in," he said in a cheerful voice. "It's a wonderful day."

Briana was less enthusiastic about the morning, and failed to return his smile.

"No luck?" he asked, ascertaining the cause of her displeasure.

"She wouldn't discuss it."

Mr. Peters opened the center drawer of his desk and pulled out an envelope. "Perhaps this will change your sister's mind." He pushed it across to her.

Her fingers brushed against the paper. She was unsure whether to open it.

"Go ahead," he urged.

The thick envelope weighed heavily in her hands. She opened the flap and gasped. It was filled with bank notes and silver.

"Don't bother to count it," Mr. Peters said. "Slightly more than two hundred dollars in currency and coin."

Briana closed the flap and pushed it back across the desk. "Your generosity overwhelms me — but I can't accept this."

"It's not a gift from me. The money belongs to the boy."

"What?" She slumped in the chair, astounded by the news.

"The 'rag' he carried with him all the time

held it — a hidden money box of sorts," he said. "I did manage to get out of him — in broken English — that his mother had saved it. As far as I can work it out, they were planning to go to Pennsylvania to live with her husband's brother, who is working on the railroad." He lowered his gaze. "That would lead me to believe the murder might have something to do with this money."

She believed he was correct in his assumption. If Addy was holding back money and the Carson brothers found out about it, they would come after her. After all, she had seen the threat with her own eyes. It made sense; still, she felt it unnecessary to disclose Addy's occupation to her employer. He had probably guessed anyway.

"How is Quinlin?"

"He seems a fine boy, in decent health, thanks to you. He's over what seems to have ailed him, and he mentioned you by name. A shy lad, but eager to learn, I think. He spent half the night looking at Audubon's *Birds of America.*" He clasped his hands and looked at her with sadness. "He needs to be told about his mother."

Sadness coursed through her.

"My wife is bringing him here this afternoon. Perhaps you can tell him then."

The time would never be right, but she

knew Mr. Peters was correct. The sooner the boy knew the truth about his mother, the sooner he could grieve and heal. More than ever, she needed Lucinda to agree to take in the child.

Briana fidgeted through her work, barely able to concentrate on the tasks before her. A short time after two in the afternoon, Mrs. Peters, fashionably attired in a high-necked cream silk dress and accompanied by a young servant girl, accompanied the boy to the office. They exchanged a few pleasantries before the woman turned him over to her.

Quinlin, still pasty white from his months of living in the cellar, squirmed in his new set of breeches, shirt, and jacket. The blue coat accentuated his pale complexion and red hair. Briana led him to a quiet room adjacent to Mr. Peters's office, where they both took a seat. A grimy window threw a murky light into the room.

The boy wasted no time in asking, "Where is my mother, and what happened to our money?"

The bluntness of his question startled her — it seemed a world-wise inquiry from a child of five or six, as she had judged the first day she met him. "How old are you?"

she asked.

"My mother gave me the bag on the ship for my seventh birthday." His eyes narrowed. "She told me to keep it by my side, for it holds a treasure. Where is it?"

"Your money is safe," Briana said, surprised at his age. "Mr. Peters, who fed and clothed you last night, removed it while you were asleep and placed it in an —"

"My mother told me there was more than two hundred dollars!"

She leaned forward and grasped his hands, a lump rising in her throat. "This is so hard for me to say, Quinlin . . . but your mother isn't coming back." She paused, studying his face and holding back tears. "Your mother's dead."

He stared at her; then his tears began to flow, silently, in large drops down his face. The boy registered no other emotion except a sob, and he withdrew his hands from hers. He looked beyond the door, into the hallway, and said, "I don't want to go back to that house."

"You won't have to," Briana said. "I promise." She wiped a tear from her own eye and thought of Lucinda working at the Carlisles' only a few blocks away. If only her sister could see the boy now, trying to act so grown-up in the face of his mother's death. How could she make her sister understand that Addy Gallagher was a mother who wanted the best for her son, just as their father wanted the best for them?

Mr. Peters knocked on the door and entered with the envelope. "I wanted him to see this," he told her. "I can keep it in the company safe until you need it. I imagine he wants to know where his money went."

"He's already asked," Briana said, and handed it to Quinlin so he could inspect it. The boy opened the flap and thumbed through the bills with a slight smile, as if the money was his personal friend. He then closed it and watched them as they conversed in English.

"I'll talk to my sister this evening," she continued. "We have to save — despite this money — still, I see no reason to stay at the boarding house. It'll be more of a walk to work from South Cove, but the exercise will do me good. Can he stay a few more nights with you, at least until I can get the room straightened out?" She looked up at the kind face of her employer, who stood as stiff as a bog oak plank.

"Of course," he said. "I wish you the best of luck with your sister. Perhaps Lucinda will want to stay on at the Newton on Beacon, but I wouldn't wager on it." He ruffled the boy's hair and then left the room.

She turned to the boy. "Mr. Peters is going to keep your money in the company safe and take care of you until I can get a new home for us." She coaxed the money from him, placed it on her lap, and folded his hands between hers. "This is what your mother wanted — it's what she asked of me, and I'm going to honor her wishes."

The small, pale fingers grasped hers, and her heart swelled with joy because she knew that Addy was watching over both of them.

Quinlin seemed to sense something too, for his small voice cracked. "My mother told me that you saved me from dying." He threaded his warm fingers through hers. "I never had a chance to thank you."

She hugged him as her tears spilled down her cheeks. "You're welcome."

Lucinda left her shift at the Carlisles' in a foul mood. Another young woman in their employ had sent a message saying she was sick with a cold and wouldn't be at work. Therefore she'd been expected to clean and wash and help in the kitchen, taking on many extraneous duties in addition to her regularly assigned work.

The night was cold and the heavens seemed without stars as she trudged down

Charles Street. The wind whistled past her ears and threatened to pull her hat off her head and fling her coat from her body. She held on to it with one hand and with the other grasped what objects she could to keep from losing her balance on the uneven brick walk.

Out of the corner of her eye, she happened to catch sight of three men standing in a dark alleyway. There were many such hiding places nestled among the narrow streets of Boston, and she had learned to keep her keen attention on them now that fall had shortened the daylight hours. She couldn't see their faces, but their presence provoked a tingle of fear along her spine. She could feel their eyes upon her.

As if to confirm her fears, one of the three — a large man wearing an overcoat and a muffler that concealed half his face — emerged from the shadows and kept in step behind her. She pushed harder into the wind, but at another narrow alleyway he grabbed her from behind and shoved her into the dark passageway.

She balled her fists and pummeled his thick chest. "What do you want?"

He pressed against her. She was on the verge of screaming when cold metal pressed into her neck.

"I'd be quiet if I were you, little lady, or you might end up dead." The man's voice was masked by the cloth over his mouth, and she could see little of him in the dark.

"How dare you touch me," she said. "Let me go."

His hand smacked her cheek, causing her to see stars. The right side of her head slammed against the rough brick wall.

"I told you to shut up," the man said. "Next time . . ." The knife pressed deeper against her neck. "All we want is the money that's ours. Simple as that. We know you live with the woman who took the boy away. Addy Gallagher had money that belonged to us. Deliver it to the old woman where Addy lived by tomorrow night — and don't go to the police — otherwise . . ." He grabbed a lock of hair that protruded from under her hat and with a flick of the knife sliced it off. The man shoved the hair into her hand. "A little souvenir to remind you of what you have to do." He pushed away and strolled out the way he had come.

Lucinda brought her trembling arms up to her chest and placed her hands over her throat. Her legs buckled against the wall, and she slid down to the damp earth. It took several minutes for her breathing to return to normal; still, her legs refused to move.

Finally she clawed her way up the wall and forced herself to the street. A few men walked by without a look as she brushed the mud from her coat. She tucked her hair under her hat and walked to the boarding house, a trip of a few minutes that seemed like hours. She passed a policeman on the way but kept her distance in case the man who had assaulted her was watching.

The eyes of the young woman working at the desk widened when she walked in. Lucinda said nothing but continued up the stairs to the room.

When she opened the door, Briana was sitting on the bed. Her sister gasped and ran to her side, barraging her with questions. Before she recounted her encounter with a man she was certain was one of the Carson brothers, she took off her coat and walked to the bathroom at the end of the hall. There, the looking glass over the sink reflected the red finger marks on her left cheek from the blow and the bleeding scrapes on her right from striking the wall. She threw cold water on her face and tamped down her anger, for had her sister not gotten involved with Addy Gallagher their lives wouldn't be in danger.

CHAPTER 20

"We are marked women!" Lucinda retrieved the lock of hair from her coat pocket and threw it on her bed. "This is what we have to look forward to — a fate like Addy Gallagher's." She drew a line across her throat with her finger. "This is where *he* put the knife. This would never have happened had you stayed away like I asked." Lucinda collapsed on the mattress.

Her sister was right — Briana had not foreseen the trouble her compassion for Addy and Quinlin would cause.

She rose from her bed and sat beside her sister. "I'm sorry. Let me look at you." She turned her sister's face gently toward her. Her left cheek still bore the red discoloration from the man's fingers. The scrapes on the other side of the face were superficial, but Briana was certain they stung. "There's ointment in the medicine chest in the bathroom. I'll get it for you before we go to bed."

The picture of Addy's body, her throat still bleeding from the wound, floated through Briana's mind like a feather blown from a seabird. The visage horrified her, but there was a strange finality to the image as if fate had intervened between them. But what would be the reason for their meeting? To alienate her sister? To save the boy? The answer wasn't clear.

She traced her fingers across the bruises on Lucinda's face as the specter faded. "I'm sorry for the trouble I've caused. I thought I was doing what was right." Now she wasn't so sure. Even the bank notes could be a problem if they didn't deliver them to the old woman. She rejected that idea, because the thought of giving up the money — for all their sakes — was too much to bear. "We must go to the police," Briana urged.

Lucinda harrumphed. "Yes, but they won't be able to watch us twenty-four hours a day, and, I suspect, they will care even less what happens to us or the child when they find out that Addy was a . . ." She shook her head. "It's too sordid."

"You might change your mind when you hear what I have to say," Briana said, and told Lucinda about her meeting with Quinlin and the money that he had carried out of the house.

Lucinda's eyes brightened when Briana came to the boy's treasure.

"See, we must go to the police," Briana said after she had finished her story. "Now is the time to move in with the Colemans. The Carson brothers know we live here."

"Many times I've cursed the day I came to America. Many times I've thought I should have stayed in Ireland, or traveled to Manchester and thrown myself at the mercy of Sir Thomas." Tears trickled down her cheeks. "Now this attack." She looked down at her trembling hands, revealing a sad vulnerability that touched Briana.

"We've had our differences, but I love you." Briana leaned against her sister's shoulder. "We'll be stronger together than apart with your help and comfort." They hugged each other with a vigor Briana had not experienced for many years.

"Do you think we should move?" Briana asked.

"After tonight, I'm in agreement," Lucinda replied, and dried her tears. "The money does make things brighter . . . for us *and Quinlin.*"

"Oh, thank you, sister! I'm sure it's the

right thing for us." She raced to her bed and pulled down the blanket. "There's so much to do!"

A string of tasks ran through her head. She would contact the police and Declan Coleman, pack, get the boy, and move into a new home. She would have to take another day off from work, but she was certain Mr. Peters would understand. Certainly the Carlisles would allow Lucinda at least part of the day off in light of the attack. The immensity of it all was enough to set her nerves jangling.

As she pulled up the blanket, her sister asked, "Aren't you forgetting something?"

Briana rolled over toward her sister with a puzzled look on her face.

"The ointment," Lucinda said with a grin.

She rolled out of bed, honoring her promise to her sister, certain that tomorrow would be a better day.

The police sergeant sat with them in a secluded corner of the drawing room at the back of the boarding house. He took notes in a small book and nodded and hummed as Lucinda told her story. He was of Scandinavian descent with a bushy blond mustache and muttonchops, tall and wiry, but with a florid face, indicating he spent a great deal of time outdoors.

The casual approach of the sergeant's questioning about the attack shifted when Lucinda mentioned the Carson brothers as possible suspects. Neither of them had mentioned the murder of Addy Gallagher. The officer looked around the room and then stopped writing in his notebook.

"What's the matter?" Briana asked. "Something bothering your hand?"

"The Carson brothers are well known to me and the district force," he said with a note of disdain. "I'm sure you must be mistaken."

"Oh," Briana said, anger causing her voice to rise. "Is that why no one has questioned me about Addy Gallagher's murder? She died in my arms from a brutal beating and a knife wound to the throat after being threatened by the same man who probably accosted my sister — yet the Carsons are fine, upstanding men?"

The sergeant frowned, closed his notebook, and lowered his voice. "Addy Gallagher was a woman of ill repute, and that, ladies, is putting it delicately. It would be wise for both of you to go on with your lives and let the district police investigate both crimes."

"Investigate?" Briana asked. "It appears

that it would be wise for us to keep our mouths shut and remove ourselves from the whole affair. Am I right?"

The officer's lips curled into a smirk. "You seem to be a smart lass."

The hackles rose on Briana's neck. It was one thing for her to be called a "lass" in Ireland but another to be addressed so in Boston by a son of Nordic immigrants.

Underneath the bruises and welts, Lucinda's face flushed crimson. "And if we are to keep our mouths shut, how are we to protect ourselves if the police feel these men can do no wrong?"

He placed his notebook and pencil in his uniform pocket and glanced about the room to see if anyone was eavesdropping. "I would say that twenty-five dollars would ensure your protection, and I'm certain the Carsons would feel the same about staying out of your way. Such good men wouldn't want their names besmirched by unsubstantiated charges of assault . . . and murder." He leaned back in his chair and smiled.

The choice was clear. The Carsons and the district police were quid pro quo, and it would do no good to pursue accusations they couldn't prove. For their own safety, they would have to comply with bribery and get the money from the safe. "Meet me outside the Peters Building Trades at three this afternoon. You'll get your money." Briana didn't want the officer to know the money was being held there.

Lucinda's eyes widened, but she said nothing.

"Good, I'll consider the case closed," the officer said. He rose from his chair and bowed slightly. "Good morning, ladies." He tipped his hat. "I'll see you at three, Mrs. Caulfield."

After the officer left, Lucinda turned to her. "I can't believe we have stooped so low." She shook her head in disgust.

The whole affair was obvious to Briana. "It's all about money, isn't it — here in America, in Ireland, and the English government with their hands-off politics?"

Lucinda folded her hands as a thoughtful look crossed her face. "You're right, as much as I'd rather deny it. Why isn't more being done to help Ireland? Why did Addy Gallagher have to die? It is all about money."

Briana rose from her chair. "You have a job to go to, and I must make arrangements for us to move to the Colemans'."

Lucinda stood, moved a hand across her bruised face. "*We* do need each other."

She hugged her sister. "See if you can get the afternoon off, or at least leave early. It's time we left this boarding house. We've only a few days left in the month anyway." She laughed. "I think the Newton on Beacon will be happy to be rid of us."

"I think you're right." Lucinda grasped her hands. "By the way . . . twenty-five dollars well spent — let's hope."

A flurry of arrangements took up her day.

Briana was able to reach Declan Coleman through Mr. Peters. Declan was thrilled to know that they would be moving in, because his sisters were unable to book passage from Ireland. Their rent would help with household expenses in South Cove. The sergeant arrived outside the office promptly at three to collect the money, which she took from Quinlin's bank notes, along with extra for a cab, promising herself to pay it back to the boy. The officer assured her that the Carson brothers would leave them alone because he had secured their "safety after a mutual agreement."

She left work early to pack their things and then informed the proprietress that they would be leaving after dinner. The woman was unconcerned because she now had the rent paid on a room she might let before the end of the month.

Lucinda arrived at the boarding house at

four, and after dinner they loaded their belongings in a carriage, picked up Quinlin from the Peterses, and headed to South Cove.

The Colemans greeted them at the door of their modest brick building. Her hands strained with her bags, but her exhaustion was temporarily overcome by the hope of a new start. Mrs. Aletha Coleman, a short, pretty woman of Greek descent with a narrow face and long black tresses, showed them around the house.

To Briana, the home seemed a welcoming fortress. After climbing up a set of wooden stairs at the entrance, a narrow hallway opened up before them. The first floor held a sparsely decorated living room with a cheery wood-burning fireplace, while a second room on the rear served as their bedroom. An outside alley led to the kitchen below the first floor. The room contained a coal-burning stove and an old maple dining table, and the space smelled of smoke and spices. Outside, a wooden privy stood against the brick wall.

Aletha led them to the second floor — their bedroom, with two single beds and a rectangular sack stuffed with straw that would serve as the boy's bed. The fireplace was stoked with birch logs, which sent out a warm and welcoming light. A small desk and chair sat near two windows at the front of the room.

The Colemans soon left them, but not before saying the kitchen was theirs to use when they wished, as was their living room. Declan indicated that if their privacy became an issue, the boy might have the third floor, which was currently used for storage, until his sisters arrived in Boston next spring.

"Well, what do you think?" Briana asked her sister after the couple had gone downstairs. Quinlin curled up on his bed and watched the logs crackle in the fireplace.

"It's not Lear House," Lucinda said, "but I think it's a dream come true." She rubbed her hands over her arms and shoulders, luxuriating in the warmth of the fire. "How I wish Father — and Rory — were here." The smile she had worn moments earlier disappeared. "I've hardly had time to worry about them, but when we sit in such luxury, I can't help but think about them."

"I feel the same way," Briana said. The house was grand compared to the conditions her husband and father might be living in at this moment in Ireland. She looked glumly into the fire and tried to think of something to cheer her. One positive thought struck her, though not exactly a happy one.

"I didn't tell you what I saw this afternoon," she said to her sister.

Lucinda eagerly looked her way.

"I went inside and watched from the window when our police sergeant left," Briana continued. "He was so brazen about it."

"About what?" Lucinda asked with a studied gaze that lighted upon her.

Briana lowered her voice to keep Quinlin from hearing. "He walked to the corner of the green across the street — perhaps he thought I couldn't see him, for he was partially hidden behind a tree — but he gave the twenty-five dollars to a man we know."

"One of the Carson brothers?"

"No — Romero Esperanza. It was Romero, all right — wearing the same gambler's hat and tailored overcoat. He must be the Carson brothers' boss. Addy said she'd never met the man, but it makes sense."

Lucinda shuddered. "Well, let's hope that's the end of it and we never see any of them again."

Briana walked to the fire, stood beside it, and rubbed her hands in its warm rays. "There are only two people I want desperately to see again, and you know who they are." She supported herself against the fireplace mantel and slid to her knees because it was hard to maneuver with a swollen belly. The light played over her in flickering shadows as she sat on the boy's bed and stroked his red hair. It needed trimming, that is, if he would allow her to do it. He curled up beside her. She snuggled against him and wondered how Rory would feel about adding an older son to his name.

Another thought on her mind was writing a letter to her father, and thus to Rory. She doubted it would get to Brian before March or April, but the idea reinforced her hope that they were both still alive. When she put pen to paper, she would have much to tell him.

Clouds lingered over the campground the morning after the raid as the sun struggled to cut through the overcast. The Nephin Beg range lay dark in the eastern shadows. Orange and some of the Mollies inspected the grain and goods that remained in the *curraghs.* Others prepared to offload and transport the rest by hand or in makeshift barrow carts to a sympathizer's farm near Geesala at the northeastern tip of the peninsula. Rory chose to go with the latter because he needed to get back to Brian at the Kilbanes' cottage.

Orange outlined his plans for the goods while sitting on the damp plank of a canoe as the men ate plundered meat and cheese. His once-ruddy complexion had faded to ashen with the pain of his injury. Although no doctor, Rory worried an affliction might strike down the large man because of the wound's proximity to his heart.

"We'll take the canoes north until we reach the shore near Glencastle. We can't risk suspicion from the Constabulary at Belmullet. Those of you going that way can make arrangements for what you need. The rest will be stored and buried at the farm near Geesala." He paused, placed his thick right hand over the wound on his left shoulder, and grimaced in pain. Orange sputtered a bit and then continued, "The silver we'll convert to cash when we can sell it safely, and we'll use that money to buy food in any way we can. Every man will get his fair share either at Glencastle or Geesala. Each of you will get rations of meat and cheese. But for now, we must let the goods remain in hiding for a few days. Anyone who believes he's entitled to more and sets out to get it will pay the price." He waved his pistol and pointed to the still smoldering fires. "Clear the grounds and let's be off before the English send the dogs after us."

The men scurried about, dousing fires, obliterating footprints as best they could, and gathering belongings so that few traces of their presence remained. Three hours past dawn, Rory and Connor watched as the men shoved off and headed north over the slate-colored waves of Blacksod Bay.

Rory wrapped the blanket he had slept in around his shoulders and secured it at the waist, his shirt gone to bind Orange's wound.

He, Connor, and eight men dragged the heavy sacks across the muddy heath for more than an hour until they arrived at the farm. The sympathizer, a bearded old man named Coyle, gave them water and then muttered and stomped around his stone barn, the hiding place for the stolen goods. He and Connor supervised the placement of the grain sacks under the barn's hay ricks while the divided silver pieces were buried outside in a box near a tussock.

After their tasks were complete, Rory headed out with Connor after telling Mr. Coyle that he would return with his father for grain in a day or two. Connor left him at the crossing of a small stream to continue on to his family in Bangor after pledging to return for his share of the grain and money. They said good-bye and wished each other luck.

Rory headed across the heath as the wind freshened from the bay. Streams of silvery clouds pelted him with bursts of rain. He was soaked to the skin when he arrived early in the afternoon at the cottage near Bally-croy.

He called out for Brian, but there was no answer.

He stepped inside the gloomy cottage. The smell of roasted meat filled the room, but the odor was gamier than pork or beef.

Brian lay against the wall, his back to the door. Rory didn't know whether he was dead or alive. A spit of wood hung between two branches over the smoldering turf pit. On it were the remains of a rat and a bird skewered head to tail. They had been partially eaten.

"Brian," Rory called out in a panic.

The man stirred, gazing up at him with fear in his watery eyes, and then rolled toward the pit. He muttered and thrust out his scrawny arms.

He couldn't understand his father-in-law's mumbled words, so he cradled Brian's head in his arms. The man's mouth opened and closed in shallow breaths.

Rory kissed Brian's forehead and cried out, "Don't die. Please, don't die."

Sir Thomas sat at the oak desk in his library reading the document brought by his solicitor, who was seated across from him. The rain pelted the window behind him in pearly drops and ran down the panes in streaks like silvery shoals of fish. The fireplace crackled on the north wall, penetrating the crepuscular light provided by the weather. As usual, a brandy glass rested not far from his right hand.

The solicitor, a man of upper-class means who dressed the part in stiff breeches and a satin waistcoat, stared at Sir Thomas with a pinched expression. The man knew better than to interrupt while his client was reading an important contract.

The last page seemed so much gibberish that Sir Thomas skimmed through it before lifting his pen. Before he signed, he said, "All appears well. Can you guarantee it?"

"Certainly, sir." The man bowed his head in an obsequious gesture. "All you need do is sign your name."

"The sheep will be delivered on time?"

"By April of next year, after the worst of the winter but hopefully before the spring lambs are calved." The solicitor smiled. "That way the estate can take advantage of extra stock, for our contract is for fifty of the beasts."

"And the men who will oversee this business have been hired?"

"Yes, sir." He tapped his fingertips against one another. "I'm assured that the two men are fine representatives of the business. Your agent — I forget the name — has been released and will not be part of this." It was as much a question as a statement.

Sir Thomas stared at the solicitor. Their kind was puffed up but necessary. He had often wondered whether he could trust the man, who seemed to sense this thought and leaned forward in his chair anticipating a question.

"Brian Walsh — he is no longer under my employ."

"Then everything should be settled." The man tipped his glasses back on his nose and folded his hands.

Sir Thomas dashed off his signature, sealed the document, and handed it back to the solicitor, who placed it in his valise. He rose from his chair and said, "The first payment, according to the contract, is due within a week, the second upon delivery of the animals to the estate in Ireland."

"You shall have it." Sir Thomas rang the small bell on his desk. His valet appeared almost immediately to escort the man to the door.

He turned his chair toward the fire so he could watch the flames and, to his right, the rain as it drenched the house. Shortly, the solicitor's coach disappeared down the drive into a foggy torrent. He was alone in the library again with only his man and the housekeeper for company, and they, on these depressing fall days, were not much help in lifting his mood. They were, after all, only servants — as expendable as everyone else in his life.

A sharp pang stabbed his heart, and he likened it to the sadness he sometimes felt when he was a child while still in the company of his mother and father. But he had no right to be sad, he told himself. He had everything a man could want — except for the love of a woman.

His thoughts turned again to Briana. Every day he shut her out of his mind, but the concentration, the effort to rid her from his thoughts, only worsened the problem. She appeared before him when she was least wanted or expected, often dressed in fine silks, Parisian shoes, and powdered face, looking more lovely than any woman should dare.

He, alone, could lift her from poverty, if only she would accept his offer. The Walsh family, and the beggar of a husband, had nothing to offer. *Why is she stubborn? Why won't she listen to reason?* The loneliness, the emptiness of his grand life, shattered him. Not even his mistresses could force her from his mind. *Could it be I have no concept of love?* His parents were strict disciplinarians, and although they touted their love for him he rarely felt it in his mother's cold kisses and his father's unemotional handshakes. A few women had professed their love for him, but the feeling he got was one of anxious fawning for his riches rather than any true affection.

He rang for his valet again, and when the man arrived he ordered, "Gather my coat and bring the carriage around. I'm going into the city." The man bowed and turned away.

Soon the carriage was at the front door, his man holding the umbrella over his head as he escorted him down the walk. "I'll be dining at home tonight," he told the valet. The carriage door closed. He raised the shade, settled in the leather seat, and watched the dripping landscape roll by.

Sir Thomas knew where the carriage was headed, and the driver did as well. They had both traveled many times to a grimy stone building near the banks of the River Irwell. There he would take comfort in the arms of a particular woman, one of the many who worked there. His chosen lady would rid his mind of Briana at least temporarily, along with his worries of what might become of Lear House if the grazing scheme failed.

That afternoon, as he lay with the woman and ran his tongue over her powdered neck, he saw Briana again and knew he must make a trip to Ireland in the spring to see how Lear House was faring. Perhaps, if he was lucky, she would be there.

Rory spent the evening attempting to feed his father-in-law from the plundered rations and drying his damp clothes. Brian was in no condition to make an arduous trip on the turf ponies to a city where there might not even be a bed.

He threw out the rat but kept the bird, which had been partially eaten. With a trembling hand, Brian pushed away the small portions of cheese and meat from the rations Rory had carried.

The fire needed peat for fuel. After it was stoked, he gathered fresh water, boiled it, and washed Brian's body with a dry swatch cut from the blanket he'd worn.

He had been away only for one night. His father-in-law had declined so much in twenty-four hours, something must have gone wrong. Maybe the meat had been bad; or worse, perhaps he had contracted the fever. Brian was too weak to talk, however, so any discussion would have to wait.

He went to sleep that night with the blanket covering both of them and the pistol at his side. His sleep was fitful because the ghosts of Frankie and Aideen never seemed far away, staring through the window, peering out from the flames.

The sun broke through the clouds the next morning with intermittent splashes of light on the green heath. Rory was happy to see that the rain had moved on, although the wind cut in from the bay and the sharp air bit at his exposed chest. He washed in the clear rivulet behind the house. Although the Kilbanes' bodies had long been removed by the Constabulary, the bath sent chills down his back, and not just from the cold water. He imagined the bodies looking up at him with staring eyes from the spot in the bog where he had placed them.

He was eager to depart the crumbling cabin. His body sagged from exhaustion, yet his limbs had been jolted by the cold. Rubbing his arms, he hurried inside and stoked the fire.

Brian stirred, lifted his head, and gazed at Rory with the look of one who has awakened from a long sleep. A spot of color had returned to his cheeks, but despite that good sign, deep lines cut into his cheeks like furrows, his sunken cheeks as hollow as a cave.

"You're back," Brian whispered.

"Yes, I've been back since late yesterday afternoon. Don't you remember?" He offered Brian the now-cooled boiled water he had transferred to the flagons. The water slid out of the tip above the man's lips and dribbled down his chin.

Brian brushed the water away. "I don't remember anything after supper on the night you left. I ate some of the mush — the pain turned my stomach, and I felt light-headed like I was walking in a dream."

Rory drew back the blanket and looked at his father-in-law's breeches. "You need to wash off. I'll scrub your breeches and dry them out. You can wrap up in the blanket until then."

"You don't have a shirt," Brian said.

"It's a long story," Rory said. "I'll tell you later. Eat some of this meat and cheese, if you can."

Brian nodded, his sorrowful eyes taking in the cabin.

Rory agreed it was a sad sight — the empty rooms, the split thatched roof in back that let in the wind and rain, the house stripped to its sod and stone walls.

"I want to go home," his father-in-law said abruptly.

Rory knelt before him. "We were going to Westport to look for work." He felt as if he were talking to a child.

"I want to go home. I want to be near my wife."

"We have no home," Rory said, and remembered the stones that marked the communal graveyard at Carrowteige. There, Brian's wife was buried. He didn't want to hurt the man, but he needed to be reminded that there was nothing to go home to.

"Yes, we do," Brian insisted. He took a piece of cheese, placed it on his tongue, chewed, and swallowed. "Lear House."

"We'll be arrested," Rory said, thinking his father-in-law had lost his mind.

"Not if they don't know we're there." Brian rose and propped his back against the wall, moaning in the process that all his joints ached from his illness. "The house will save us — it must," he said after he caught his breath.

Rory thought for a moment while holding his tongue. Lear House was a more comforting option than trying to find work in Westport — if jobs were available at all. There would be furniture, blankets, towels, and shelter. It was an easy enough task to break in. The more he thought about it, the more he liked the idea.

Because of the early nightfall, they could light fires in the kitchen, when the smoke wouldn't be seen, and he could cook the meals he had earned through the raid. There might even be clothes to wear, courtesy of Sir Thomas. They were about the same size, although he was broader at the shoulders. The Master wouldn't show his face until the spring at the earliest. They might have to dodge the Constabulary, but if they kept their eyes and ears open, they could make a go of it.

"I'll consider it," Rory said, trying not to give in immediately. "You need to rest until you're well enough to travel."

"Tomorrow," Brian replied, "I'm going back whether you do or not." He smiled at Rory, and the decision was made.

CHAPTER 21

December 1846

Not one district officer had come to question Briana about Addy Gallagher's death since the sergeant had taken the money. Lucinda convinced her that avoiding the police was wise, especially since she could offer no evidence other than Addy's enigmatic words as she was dying. Only one time in the past month had she seen Romero Esperanza, and that was far down Charles Street as he darted into a building. He appeared not to notice her.

Her pregnancy made it hard to venture about. As it turned out, there were plenty of Irish where she now lived. Much of the time she took a carriage to work, particularly when the weather was sloppy. Lucinda accompanied her when she could.

October slipped into November and then early December, and she and Lucinda settled into a routine at the Colemans'.

Their days were spent at work — Briana at the Building Trades, Lucinda with the Carlisles. Mrs. Coleman watched over Quinlin while her husband and the women were at work. True to his developing spirit, the boy moved to the third floor in mid-November, calling the space among the boxes and crates his own special place. Briana granted him permission on the condition that he study English and whatever else Mrs. Coleman saw fit to teach him.

After workdays, everyone savored happy evenings in the kitchen with generous servings of meat, potatoes, and vegetables, much of it provided to Declan through the generosity of Mr. Peters. These suppers were bittersweet because they reminded her how much she wanted a home for Rory and her growing family.

By mid-December, pine and evergreen boughs appeared on doors and in shop windows. Her thoughts turned to Christmas. Briana had written several letters to Rory indicating their new address at the Colemans' but decided not to mention Addy Gallagher's death, the boy, or the attack upon her sister. Those developments would be an additional burden upon him in an already trying time. She preferred to keep an optimistic outlook.

The postmaster had no idea when her letters might arrive in Ireland. Any sailings, now that winter was on the horizon, might not be until late March at the earliest. Also, she addressed them, as planned, to *Rory Caulfield, Lear House.* Where her husband and father might be was unknown to her. She took the chance that they might be delivered to the general store if the manor was deserted.

Rather than lighten her spirits, the holiday dragged her down with memories of Christmases past when the family was together at the estate. It was all she could do to concentrate on her work and to keep her mood lifted when everyone was gathered for supper. As the winds deepened in Boston to a cold she never thought possible, she wondered if she would ever see her husband and father alive again. What if Rory and Brian never had the chance to see the child she carried? How could she live with herself if they . . . ? It was too distressing to think about.

Those were the dark questions that occupied her mind the evening of December fifteenth as she climbed the drafty stairs to the second floor. She opened and closed the door quickly to keep out the wind sweeping up the hallway. Flames flickered in the fireplace, but the pleasing warmth didn't alleviate her innate sadness. Outside, a light snow coated the brick buildings and window frames a frosty white. She shivered, dressed in her nightclothes, and crawled into bed.

Lucinda came into the room a few minutes later. "You don't look well, sister," she remarked, and drew close to her bedside. She put her hand on Briana's forehead and then took it away. "You're burning up. I don't think it's wise for you to work tomorrow in this weather." She looked out the window. "And it may get worse."

Briana drew the two blankets on her bed up to her neck. Her bones ached, her joints hurt, her stomach rolled with a queasiness she hadn't experienced since the voyage to Boston, and her nose felt stuffy.

Lucinda lit the oil lamp on the desk and took out a sheet of paper and pen. She began to write as Briana shivered in bed.

Intrigued by her sister, Briana forced herself to ask through chattering teeth, "What are you doing?"

"I'm composing a letter to Father," Lucinda explained, and then turned back to writing.

"I've written them many times," Briana said.

Her sister turned once again, this time with a frown on her face. "I know. But you may have the grippe with your baby nearly due, and Father and Rory deserve to know."

"That's comforting," Briana said, and rolled over to face the wall.

Lucinda's words drifted over her. "I also want to wish them a Merry Christmas. This may be the last chance I get."

She lifted her head and said, "I think about them every night at dinner. You think about them, too, don't you?"

"Yes," Lucinda said, her head outlined by the yellow glow of the lamp.

She understood what her sister meant by "last chance" — she had pictured the same horrible consequence of the famine — Rory and her father dead. The cold enveloped Briana, and she couldn't stop shaking. She closed her eyes and tried to sleep as the pen scratched across the paper.

Rory sat in the kitchen at Lear House, drawing near to the stove, which provided the only warmth in the manor. From the shuttered library came the sounds of books being thrown about, of the desk chair scraping against the floor. Irritation crawled over him — after all, he had saved Brian's life, had kept watch on him while his father-in-law could barely sit on top of the pony. He had lugged three bags of Indian corn from the farm near Geesala and then loaded two on his pony and strapped one to Brian's; he had sheared off the padlock to the kitchen with an ax; cleaned the rat droppings from the stove, table, and cabinets — all for one simple request: Brian was to keep away from the windows, be quiet and calm, and make the best of their tenuous situation.

Instead, Brian raved like a madman. It was not an easy time. The weather had been brutally harsh — snow had fallen in October — the cold and damp seemed to come from the ashen sky in relentless waves. The house sucked the heat away from them into its dark recesses. Rory longed for spring days when he could take a walk with Briana, perhaps see his brother off for fishing in Broadhaven Bay; but in Lear House he was imprisoned with his father-in-law, living like hermits through what promised to be a brutal winter. He was tired of watching for every step, listening for the sound of hooves that might signal the Constabulary or the dragoons come to drag them from their illegal haven, or worrying that smoke rising from the chimney might send a signal at night to the uninvited. He had no fear of the few remaining villagers, or those farmers who might wander back to the estate, because they knew Lear House's history and could be trusted to keep a secret. Perhaps he could even aid them as well, if circumstances permitted. Outsiders, however, were a different story. They might unintentionally send out an alarm.

He leaned back in his chair, put his feet up on the table, and pulled the sleeves of one of Sir Thomas's sweaters over his hands. The landlord had so many, Rory imagined he was in a goods store in Dublin the day he and Brian had rummaged through the Master's clothes. It gave him great satisfaction to see the two of them standing in front of the upstairs looking glass clothed in such finery.

The landlord was soon relegated to the attic of his thoughts as he peered through the dark east window, which looked out upon the shattered remains of the tenant farms. The panes rippled with rain and blocked what little was left of the view; only the closest of the sodden mounds were visible through the glass. Rather than think about sunny days and warm clothes, he was much more concerned with how he and Brian would get through the winter with dwindling supplies and a madness that preyed upon his father-in-law. His actions reminded Rory much of what he had witnessed in Daniel Quinn. He couldn't help but think it was a madness born of malnutrition, desperation, and loss.

It had taken him days to come to terms with the stillness they had experienced on the road back to Lear House. Was there a living creature stirring? Had they all been eaten — the birds, their eggs, the hare, the grouse, the berries, the roots . . . ? When they'd crossed the river at Bangor, Rory had expected to see people — Irishmen and women — like he was used to seeing on trips to Westport, but the village seemed deserted, as if those who lived there had been eaten by the earth itself. He cringed at the sight of a few dogs along the side of the road. In fact, he felt so sorry for one, he had wanted to coax him to Lear House, but he had nothing to feed any unnecessary animal. The hairy mutt soon joined others feasting upon a corpse partially frozen to the ground.

They had spotted dead along the trail that bordered Carrowmore Lake — not whole bodies but fragments, hands wrenched in the air, naked feet extending from ripped breeches. They passed by the sickening sights numbed by the fact that there was nothing they could do.

On the outskirts of Carrowteige, they came across the hut of a woman whom Rory knew by reputation only. Rumors had swirled that many lonely men and even Sir Thomas had taken refuge there on occasion. The hut had been leveled — the woman missing, perhaps buried under its remains. At the house of an elderly husband and wife, no such supposition was needed. The tangled bodies were intertwined with the sod and rocks, their home their burial mound. Carrowteige was as silent as any village they had traveled through. Through that deserted and deathly landscape, they had arrived at Lear House.

A book banged to the library floor, and Rory cringed. Anger coursed through his body, and he fought to quell it. Brian was ill and not to be blamed, but the older man's outbursts risked revealing their hiding place.

He left the kitchen, shutting the door to keep in the heat. His father-in-law was sitting at the oak desk, the ledger books piled so high that only the top of his head showed in the dim light.

"Come to the kitchen," Rory said. "It's warm." He looked at the disorderly desk, shaking his head. "Remember your promise." He might as well have been talking to a two-year-old.

"Why can't I make sense of these books?" Brian asked. "There should be plenty of money. Sir Thomas shouldn't be angry with me." He paused and placed his hands on a stack to his left. "Where's Lucinda — she has a head for these things."

Rory moved behind him. Brian had pulled a pair of satin breeches and a silk evening jacket over one of the landlord's white nightshirts. The sight of the balding man dressed so made him chuckle despite the pathetic situation.

"Don't you remember where Lucinda and Briana are?" Rory asked calmly.

"They should be inside," Brian said. "It's dark and they'll get the switch if they don't come in soon."

Rory put his hand on Brian's shoulder. "They've gone on a trip, but they'll be back," he said, attempting to mollify his father-in-law. Sadness swept over him as he watched the man paw at the books and then fiddle aimlessly with the pen.

Brian rubbed his temples. "When did they leave? Where are they?" His eyes grew moist. "Please come back," he said to the air.

Rather than confuse him, Rory replied, "They've gone to find work, and as soon as they do, we'll join them." He knew his father-in-law would forget what he'd said by tomorrow.

Brian looked at the shuttered window with an expression of disbelief and then turned to Rory. "A trip? Where are they?"

He was about to guide his father-in-law into the kitchen when a knock on the front door reverberated through the hallway. He put a finger to his lips, skulked to the library door, and peered around its edge. Through the narrow strips of glass surrounding the entry, he observed the dark form of a man lurking in the murk. A shiver raced up his spine.

His father-in-law darted past him into the hall, the silk jacket swirling around his body. Before Rory could stop him he was at the glass, his nose pressed against the window. He put his right hand against the pane as did the figure outside. Brian turned, his eyes blazing with delight. "I know him . . . he's a friend."

The man outside the window was Daniel Quinn. Rory had not seen him since the night at The Black Ram at Westport, but his tipsy, happy appearance at that time had disintegrated to something akin to a skinny, bedraggled dog.

"Let him in," Brian ordered, and shook the door handle, not remembering that it was padlocked from the outside.

Rory didn't know what to think as he listened to his father-in-law plead on behalf of the poet. Daniel Quinn wasn't an outsider, but neither was he a villager nor tenant farmer. Upon hearing his poem in the public house, he had wondered about Quinn's mental state. His suspicions about the poet's hand in Blakely's shooting had never abated. He had informed the constable, and now he had the poet in hand. If he was able to get Quinn to confess, he could clear himself. But could he be so callous? He'd have to think twice about sending a man to prison or transport. Blakely, whom he had no love for, had fled to the luxury of his Manchester home leaving the tenants to suffer. In this case, real justice had only nicked the owner.

On the other hand, he had pledged to help people, and Quinn was certainly someone who needed aid. Perhaps the poet could be of service. His father-in-law needed someone to look after him, especially on the days Rory might travel to Belmullet or Glencastle for his remaining shares of plundered supplies.

"My dear friend," Brian repeated as he clawed at the glass. He turned on Rory and spat at his feet. "You are unkind, sir!" It was the first time his father-in-law had ever spoken harshly to him.

Rory shrugged it off, knowing that the man was not himself, but he knew the mood would turn foul if he didn't let the poet in. Quinn might also hold a grudge against them if he was denied entry. He remembered the poem at The Black Ram recited in jest to the English sailors. A poet's revenge could be fatal.

Rory drew close to the window. "Come to the back — the kitchen door."

Clutching at his satin breeches, Brian raced to the kitchen.

Rory followed, still uncertain whether he had made the right decision. He waited for the knock before opening the door.

Daniel Quinn, shivering, his clothes shredded and soaked, stumbled past the door. His curly, once-black hair had turned almost gray, washing out an equally dreary face; his eyes sat like lifeless black rocks in their sockets. The poet gasped and teetered toward the warm stove.

Rory feared the man might die on the spot. Brian knelt over Quinn as if attempting to retrieve a memory from deep in his brain. It came to him after a few minutes, and he repeated the word "poet" many times without a flicker of recognition from the quivering man.

Rory rushed upstairs for a towel and then returned to strip the wet clothes off the poet. As he fumbled with Quinn's jacket, the end of a smoking pipe protruded from a pocket, but it was a glint of light off metal that caught his attention. He opened the pocket to find the flute the poet had played at The Black Ram. He had only seen one other like it in his life — at the home of Frankie and Aideen Kilbane.

The Carlisles were kind people of privilege who embraced their place in Boston society and had a keen understanding of the servant's role in their home as well. Therefore, Lucinda was expected to be at her station on most days, even when Briana's condition worsened. She had ingratiated herself to Mrs. Carlisle with the promise that she would be happy to tutor their young son in numerous subjects before he started private school. Mrs. Carlisle took this offer with kind skepticism at first but soon realized that her employee had much to offer as a governess.

Lucinda had also come to respect the kindness, the hard work, and the dark-haired beauty of her landlady, Mrs. Coleman. The young woman would sit with Briana during the day, not only tending to her needs but schooling Quinlin and attending to the wants of her working husband. She became a saint in Lucinda's eyes, one to whom she would be forever grateful for her attentions to Briana and the boy.

As the days progressed toward Christmas, Briana's illness took a turn for the worse. What at first had seemed like a bad cold, or the grippe, turned into days of fever, drenched bedclothes, parched lips, and pleas for relief. Declan enlisted the help of Mr. Furey, the Irishman who had dispensed the medication to cure Quinlin, but the tinctures, the potions, and the powders did little to help Briana.

After a grueling night of serving at a festive party to mark the holiday, Lucinda asked Mrs. Carlisle for a few days off after the last of the guests had departed.

"What is this about?" The lady pressed her hands firmly against the waistline of her plaid taffeta dress.

"I've told you of my sister," Lucinda said. "She's been gravely ill for days now, made even more so by the fact that she carries a child." Her eyes clouded over as she thought of Briana's damp face, her hair plastered to the pillow in wet strings. She didn't want to distress her mistress with details that might be too delicate for her employer's stomach; on the other hand, she wanted Mrs. Carlisle to understand the severity of the situation. "She's had trouble eating and sleeping. I fear most for the baby."

"I had no idea," the woman replied. "Why didn't you come to me sooner?" She took a step back from Lucinda and withdrew her handkerchief from her sleeve. "Let the others finish tonight. Please do take the time to nurse your sister, but let us know of her progress." She covered her mouth with the cloth. "We know of a doctor who may be able to help."

"I'd be most grateful for your consideration," Lucinda said.

"Dr. Scott," Mrs. Carlisle replied almost immediately. "I'll send him to you tomorrow morning."

Dr. Jonathan Scott arrived at the Colemans' shortly after one the next afternoon. Lucinda heard the door open, as well as the whoosh of the cold draft up the stairs. She opened the door of their second-floor room and peered down at the landing, where Mrs. Coleman was helping a man with his overcoat, umbrella, and bag while he wiped the muck from his calf-high boots. It had rained during the morning, turning what snow was left on the streets into a cold slush.

The doctor was not the man she had imagined. She had expected an aging, balding gentleman of bristling manner with unkempt facial hair and muttonchops. Instead Dr. Scott was a young man, probably in his midthirties, with a full head of brown hair, a finely trimmed mustache, and a light beard. From her first impression, she ascertained that he was confident, assured, but not boastful and ready to take on a challenge. Certainly, the health of her sister presented one.

His light blue eyes met her own as he climbed the stairs. Mrs. Coleman followed to facilitate the introduction. He failed to grasp her hand, possibly for some medical reason related to germs, but conveyed his pleasure upon their meeting with a slight smile and nod of his head. Mrs. Coleman went back downstairs, where she was keeping watch over Quinlin.

The formalities over, Lucinda led him to Briana's bedside.

The doctor pulled up the desk chair and sat near the bed, studying her sister for several minutes. He placed the back of his hand upon Briana's forehead and then withdrew it. Finally, he asked, "How long has she been like this?"

"For several days now. Her illness has gotten progressively worse." Briana attempted to turn in bed but instead cried out in a long moan. The blood drained from Lucinda's face. She had never felt so alone — not even on her way to England in her years as a governess, or crossing the Irish Sea and landing at Liverpool, or taking the carriage to Manchester to work for people she had never met in her life. In those times, she had always known that her father and sister would be waiting for her at home — at Lear House. Her sister, the only family she had on American soil, was ill and, as far as she knew, could be dying with her unborn child inside her. The possibility of that tragedy struck her like a blow to the heart.

The doctor rose, lifted the sweat-soaked blankets from Briana, and circled his hand first around her wrists and then her ankles. "What treatments has she received?" he asked after completing further examination.

Lucinda lowered her gaze, suddenly feeling ashamed that she'd had to leave her sister alone while she worked.

He must have sensed her distress, for he said, "I know you work for the Carlisles. The lady of the house told me that you had been exemplary on nearly all occasions and that you are quite educated. It's rare to find so talented and indispensable a . . ." His face flushed.

"Servant?" She blushed as well, embarrassed by her profession. "On *nearly all* occasions?"

He shook his head. "I'm only conveying the message I received — I meant that you do not have time to properly care for your sister while you discharge your duties. Mrs. Carlisle is aware of your situation and wants to help."

Had it been another day, she might have sparred with the doctor, telling him how many times she had wished to be anything but a servant in Boston, anywhere but in the employ of a wealthy American family. The Carlisles carried on with hardly a care in the world while her own family had sunk into poverty because of a potato blight. It was degrading to talk about, but Briana's health was more important than challenging the doctor.

"I wish I could tell you more about her treatments; perhaps Mrs. Coleman can." She sighed and wrung her hands. "I know she's been given teas, ointments, warm sponge baths, cold compresses at night to soothe the fever. Nothing seems to help."

The doctor eyed her, as if taking her in from head to toe. "When is your sister's baby due?"

"Next month, sometime after the New Year." She got the distinct impression that he was looking at her as if she was an equal, something she had rarely experienced from men. The feeling was refreshing, even soothing. Her own brother-in-law thought of her as nothing more than a sophisticated upstart, a pretentious social climber.

The doctor turned away and, strangely, inched around the room studying the windowsills and baseboards. At the corner where the north wall met the front of the house, he stopped and bent down. Straightening, he motioned for Lucinda to come over.

"Look." He pointed to the dusty intersection of the floor and wall.

She saw nothing at first, until she leaned in and stared into the corner.

"They're mouse droppings," he said. "The little creatures can be nasty, carrying all kinds of diseases. Your sister may be suffering from an illness carried by vermin."

"I've never seen a mouse here." She had observed plenty of them at Lear House, particularly in the months following the onset of the blight.

"Have the landlord look for holes. They must be plugged, the mice eradicated."

She nodded. "That's fine, but what of my sister?"

His face stiffened, yet still retained the compassion he'd displayed. "I'll do everything I can, but your sister is in a precarious state. Since traditional methods have failed, I may have to try a new approach — with your permission, of course." He lifted his bag, which he had placed in front of the bed. "I'm afraid I have nothing here that might help her except willow bark tea, but at this late stage of her pregnancy I don't think that's a wise idea." He paused. "I saw a boy downstairs. He lives here?"

Lucinda nodded.

"Keep him out of this room. Children are more susceptible, and, by their nature, they spread germs."

"Whatever you can do for my sister," Lucinda said, her voice wobbling. "I can't bear the thought of losing . . ."

He took another look at Briana. "I understand. I'll return tomorrow morning with a serum I hope will help. We should know if it's successful within twenty-four hours. In the meantime, make her as comfortable as possible." He bowed.

Lucinda opened the door and walked down with him to the landing. "Thank you again, Doctor."

He smiled, pulled on his overcoat, and gathered his umbrella. "I'm happy that we met, but I'm sorry it was under unfortunate circumstances. Perhaps tomorrow will be a better day."

"I sincerely hope so," she said.

As he grasped the door handle, Lucinda stopped him. "I'm sorry, I did mean to ask . . . in England all jobs are based on references and education. Where did you get your degree?"

He appeared unperturbed by her question. "Harvard." His eyes twinkled with unabashed pride. "Until tomorrow." He descended the steps and disappeared down the slushy street.

Harvard? Harvard. She had heard the Carlisles mention the university often with delight in their voices. She climbed the stairs thinking that she could do much worse than meet an attractive doctor from Harvard.

Dr. Scott returned to the Colemans' before eleven the next morning. What he withdrew from his medical bag frightened Lucinda because she had never seen anything like it. The vial of red liquid had the thickness and color of blood, but it shone purple at the bottom and pink at the top as if it contained three liquids not yet combined.

"How is she today?" he asked.

"Little changed," Lucinda said. She had hoped to look better for the doctor than she did. There hadn't been much time for primping while caring for her sister. Perhaps he would excuse her unkempt hair, the plum-colored circles under her eyes, the wrinkles that rumpled her dress. "I was awake much of the night," she said, and smoothed her hands down the fabric.

"I'm hopeful that won't be the case to-night and thereafter." He sat on the bed and then withdrew a strange-looking apparatus.

"What is that?" she asked, awed by the hollow needle and tubing that he held in his hand.

"Is she coherent? Can your sister speak yet or take water?" He shook the capped vial until the liquids combined in a purplish mix, held it up to the light of the window, and then pointed to the needle. "This is something new to medicine, in fact, invented by an Irish doctor recently. I've just started working with them. It injects medicine under the skin. As I warned you yesterday, there's no certainty in what I'm doing, but we have few choices."

"Please, do what you must." Still eyeing the needle, Lucinda replied, "Sometimes she comes around, and I get some soup or water down her, but then after a few minutes she goes back to sleep breathing heavily and moaning."

The doctor shook the vial again. "This comes from the blood of a woman who has exhibited similar symptoms, yet she recovered from her illness. We don't understand why, but often the fluids of one who has returned to health can aid the sick." He grabbed the tubing. "I'll need your assistance. If your sister was aware of her surroundings she could drink the serum — it would taste terrible — but as she is she might choke to death. We can't take that risk."

He uncapped the vial, inserted the tubing over its opening, and then attached the needle to the other end. Holding the apparatus so the liquid couldn't escape the vial, he sat on the bed next to Briana. "Hold her right arm firmly while I administer the serum."

Lucinda knelt by the bed and held Briana's arm while the doctor tapped the skin for a suitable vein. "Her blood vessels are thin. She's dehydrated. This may take longer than I like . . . be prepared for some blood."

He leaned forward, again testing the arm before deciding on a spot. He wiped the tip of the needle with a cloth, elevated the vial so a bit of the serum squirted out, and then stuck the sharp point into Briana. Her sister moaned and shifted in bed, but her resistance was so feeble she could muster only a clenched fist.

"Good." Dr. Scott raised the vial higher. "Hold on while I squeeze the tubing." He ran his fingers down its length as the serum drained from the vial. He continued to do so for several minutes until it was empty and only a pink film remained on the glass.

He withdrew the needle and placed the cloth over Briana's arm. A bright red spot blossomed upon it. He dropped the apparatus into his bag and pressed his hand over the wound. Soon the bleeding stopped.

He rose from the bed and looked down on his patient. "It's out of our hands. We can only hope and pray that God takes pity on her body."

Once again, Lucinda found herself overwhelmed. Calling upon God was fine, but what if He decided to call her sister to heaven? The loss would kill her, as well as her father and Rory. She burst into tears.

The doctor drew her close and put his arms around her. Lucinda collapsed against his chest, breathing in the warmth of the man. She drew back, startled by the strange electric power coursing through her body. He withdrew as well.

She wiped her tears and started for the desk. "I'll get your fee."

He gathered his bag. "You needn't. The Carlisles have found it in their hearts to take care of everything. Your gratitude should be shown to them. I will call tomorrow — after a prayer for a positive outcome."

She started to follow him to the door, but he stopped her. "I can find my way out." He bowed his head. "Good day." He descended the stairs and was soon out the door.

Lucinda returned to Briana's bedside and prayed over her. Oddly, her sister seemed more at peace than she had been in several days.

Cheered by her observation, she rested on her own bed only a few feet away, and soon the warmth and crackle of the fireplace lulled her to sleep.

Briana awoke during the night with a terrible moan. Her eyes fluttered open, and she jumped with fright, for she was unaware of where she was. Everything in the room was in focus: The dying embers from the fireplace cast an orange light on the ceiling, the windows were glazed with frost. She turned her head to see Lucinda sleeping. It was as if she had awakened from a fevered dream that had lasted years. She shifted her body, and her fingers clutched bedding sopped with sweat. When she touched her forehead, perspiration cooled her fingertips.

"Lucinda?" The name came out in a hoarse gasp. She called it again, but there was no answer. She lifted herself on her elbows and looked across the room. She sensed a familiarity about a house with two windows. They faced west toward the setting sun, but the room was dark now; her bones ached, and her stomach was knotted by cramps. She reached for her belly and found the round swelling. *What? A child.* Memory came flooding back — Boston, a boarding house, a family. What was their name?

Needing to relieve herself, she swung her legs over the bed. The cold wood smarted against her feet, and she lifted them back to the bed. She blurted out her sister's name again several times.

Finally, Lucinda stirred and then leapt from her bed. "My God," she exclaimed, "our prayers have been answered."

Briana's foggy mind was in no state to talk of prayer. "I need to go to the privy," she said.

Lucinda leaned over her. "It's too cold to go outside. I'll get the chamber pot."

Briana lay back while her sister fetched the pot from under her bed.

She lifted her night clothes and moved herself onto the cold porcelain as her sister turned away. When she was done, Lucinda cleared the pot and then sat next to her on the bed.

"How long have I been sick?" Briana asked.

"Days — longer than you've ever been before." Lucinda clutched her hand with warm fingers, almost hot to the touch. "I feared the worst, but a kind doctor administered a serum that helped you get over this awful illness." Tears glistened in her sister's eyes from the embers' dying light.

"I remember you writing a letter at the desk. I grew hot with fever, and then everything seems a blur."

"You hardly spoke . . . but don't worry about that now. You must rest and get better. The Colemans will be glad to know you're recovering. Everyone's been so worried."

Colemans. Of course. The fog was beginning to lift, the room, the house coming into focus. "Can you bring me a glass of water?"

"Of course. I'll get it." Lucinda grabbed

her coat, for the path to the kitchen would take her outside through the alley.

She drifted off only to awaken to Lucinda's soft touch on her shoulder. Her sister stood over her, water cup in hand, like a guardian angel who would nurse her back to health.

The recovery was slow, but Briana soon was able to walk a few steps, converse, and eat meals, which Mrs. Coleman delivered to her room. She met Dr. Scott the morning after the fever broke and was impressed with his manner and his devoted attention to Lucinda. Before leaving, after a promise to continue his visits, he referred to Briana as "his miracle." The next day, Lucinda returned to work at the Carlisles' with a pledge to give many thanks to her employers.

Each day Briana grew stronger, and on Christmas she was able to join her sister, Quinlin, and the Colemans in celebrating the holiday. Declan had paid for a large turkey, and all of them feasted on the meat, squash, and potatoes prepared for the occasion. She had always loved the taste of potatoes and the various ways she could cook them in Ireland, but this year the sight of them turned her stomach and brought up bitter memories. She picked at her helping and then spooned them to the boy. How hard it was to be happy on this day when all she could think of was her husband and father! Were they cold and starving? She'd received no letters and had no communication with anyone who might know them. What if they were — ?

She blanked out the thought and concentrated on getting well for her baby. The time was coming soon and she wanted to be prepared, both physically and emotionally. Worry could wait until after her child was born. In the meantime, she needed to eat and rest.

Mr. Peters paid a surprise visit on Christmas Day, which cheered her. Her employer dropped off a present for Quinlin — a large tin soldier — and told Briana that he wanted her to take several months off after the birth of her child. Another job would be waiting at the building trades office if she chose to come back. "And I hope you do," he added.

"Push," Dr. Scott prodded. He spread her legs apart until she thought she would split open.

Nothing much mattered, because her body shuddered with pain, as if she had been lowered into a fire pit. None of the preparations seemed to matter: The ointments, the salves, the compresses on her head were of little use against the agony banding her belly like hot iron. The room she had lived in for weeks faded in a white haze.

Lucinda sat bedside, facing her, and clutched her hand in an unrelenting grip.

"Breathe," the doctor ordered, and expanded his own lungs with air. "It shouldn't be long now." He stuck his head under the sheet that covered her legs. "I can see the baby's head. Keep pushing. Steady . . . steady."

She gulped air and pushed again. A fiery pain shot in a line from her belly to her brain and then something snapped, and after one excruciating moment her legs trembled and then relaxed, quivering upon the bed.

A baby's sharp cry split the air, and the doctor yelped with joy.

Delirium swept over her as her body sank into the mattress.

"It's a girl," the doctor announced after emerging from under the sheet. He wrapped the baby in a towel and handed her to Lucinda. Briana reached out for her child, and Lucinda obliged her wishes before carrying the baby to the washbasin to bathe her.

The doctor sat next to Briana. "She's a beauty."

At 2:32 in the afternoon of Tuesday, January 5, 1847, under the care of Dr. Jonathan Scott, Shona Caulfield was delivered into the world. The baby weighed less than the doctor would have liked, but otherwise he pronounced the girl in good health.

After the bath, Briana held the little one in her arms as the birth was announced to those waiting outside the door. Mrs. Coleman cheered, and a timid smile broke out on Quinlin, who had been dismayed that he might be thrown out of the house because of the new arrival. Briana had assured him that no such measure would be taken because she had grown to love him, along with the memory of his mother.

The baby had fine red hair and blue eyes like her father. Still, she retained characteristics of her mother, long of limb with a delicate nose and cheekbones. The girl lay against her mother's breast, warm and contented, as the birch logs blazed in the fireplace. Spits of snow filled the air, but Briana didn't care. Her daughter was born in America, and it was a blessing. She had now fulfilled her promise to Rory to keep the baby safe from harm. Briana cradled

Shona close as the others left her in peace with her child.

In the quiet, she looked down at her daughter's face and then out the window at the thin, flat clouds. In the spring, she would travel with Shona to Ireland to bring her father and Rory back to America. Her daughter had been born, and it was clear what she needed to do. Shona's father deserved to see his child and his wife. She and her baby would survive the famine.

CHAPTER 22

Rory wished Brian Walsh could write a letter to his daughters, but the task was like asking a child to plow a field. His father-in-law grew worse by the month, often wandering about Lear House in his nightclothes, or even undressed, seemingly unaware of where he was. Rory couldn't write well himself, so, against his better judgment, he relied on the poet, who had taken up residence, to be his scribe.

The depressing winter carried on after a bleak Christmas with more snow than he could ever remember. It swirled high upon the manor walls, coating them with a thick layer of white. Sunlight was rare, as clouds swept in from the Atlantic blanketing Carrowteige in thick layers of fog and, sometimes, freezing rain.

Rory found it necessary to open the library shutters during the day to let in light, lest they all go mad from the dark. The insipid winter illumination was the only distraction from the gloom they experienced daily. The miserable weather had one noticeable advantage: It kept others away from Lear House.

On the rare days of decent weather, Rory traveled to Glencastle and then to Belmullet to post letters, avoiding Carrowteige when possible. This tactic was of some cost to the pony, who occasionally struggled through forearm-high snow. Many times he dismounted from the poor animal until he was able to find a trail tamped down by other riders. The two remaining ponies barely subsisted on leftover cooked meal and the sprouts of heath grass Rory could gather. The other animals had disappeared during the time Rory spent with Orange.

Daniel Quinn and Brian remained at Lear House — a less-than-ideal situation but one that was necessary, for his father-in-law and, to some extent, the poet were in no condition to help him procure food. Quinn, attired in Sir Thomas's clothes, embarked on walks for hours after sunset, at times in the worst weather, and Rory often hoped that he might take an accidental plunge off the western cliffs. Quinn was another mouth to feed. But always, a few hours before bed, the bedraggled poet would show up grumbling about the state of man and the inclement weather. Quinn showed an increasingly morose and moody side as Brian regressed into childhood.

On one of his trips to Glencastle, Rory visited Orange at the sod farmhouse where he was staying. The big man shook his hand heartily and offered him a mug of poteen. Rory welcomed the chance to have a drink with sane and pleasant company. They sat around the warm turf fire.

"You've come for more of your share?" Orange asked.

Rory raised his mug, signaling his assent.

Orange patted his left shoulder. "You saved my life. I have extra meal for you, as I promised, and a reward." He pulled three pounds from his pocket and handed it to Rory. "Use it wisely, for the well is running dry." Orange pointed to the single window where the sun's feeble rays streaked into the house. "Did you know the relief projects are running in this bitter weather? Women and children are taking over for dead husbands. They get half-pence a day for freezing their toes off while breaking rocks for new roads. Then they drop dead by the side of the road and are buried in a snowbank. They'll thaw out in the spring." He half laughed and downed some of the liquor. "The works can take their coins and shove them up their ass. They'll transport me out of Ireland before I'll give them my body and soul."

"I can't work," Rory said. "My father-in-law is going mad . . . and Daniel Quinn has made his home at Lear House. I've my hands full."

Orange pulled his pipe from his pocket, stuffed the bowl with a plug of tobacco, and lit up. "So Quinn is staying at Lear House. I'd watch out for that one. He may be as crazy as your father-in-law — maybe dangerous, depending on your liking."

"What do you mean?" Rory asked, knowing what the man implied.

"I heard stories told by English sailors at Westport." He puffed on the pipe, sending balls of smoke into the air. "Some say Quinn shot an Englishman and the only thing that stopped him from killing him was his poor aim. More's the pity."

"I heard the same from his lips." Gooseflesh prickled up his arms, and he thought back to the time at the bay when Noel had shown him and Connor how to shoot the pistol. Quinn had watched from the dunes and had disappeared shortly after. The poet had been staying with Brian at the cottage the night Sir Thomas was shot. "Blakely told the constable to come after me, but there was no proof I'd fired the pistol."

The large man's forehead furrowed into rows of flesh. "Did *you* shoot him?"

"No." Rory took a sip from his mug. "I'm not a murderer."

Rory wondered if the poet had killed the Kilbanes too. He was certain Quinn had stolen the flute from them. Suddenly, it seemed the connections were too clear-cut to be coincidental. The poet's actions were coming into focus and, stunned, Rory wondered if the man might try to kill him and Brian as mad and desperate as he might be for food and money. What if Quinn was ransacking Lear House at this moment looking for the pistol? He brushed these suspicions from his head. He had to remember that his feeling about Quinn was a supposition, not a fact. It was a stretch to identify the poet as a murderer. Perhaps one day he would have the courage to ask him.

Orange offered him a puff from his pipe, which Rory declined. The big man cocked his head. "Yes, I'd say you've got your hands full. I'd watch my back if I were you." He patted his wound.

"I've told the constable, but I can't turn in the poet while we're living illegally in Lear House," Rory replied. "I'll bide my time."

"Your secret is safe with me, brother," Orange said.

They talked for some time about the Mollies, with Orange revealing the rumors of a burgeoning plan to assassinate Queen Victoria. *A plot to kill the Queen — better they take on the Prime Minister and Trevelyan.* The treasonous madness was descending around him like a smothering shroud, and he felt powerless to stop it.

Before they said good-bye, Orange asked about Briana and whether Rory had received any word.

The hour hand moved past one. He hoped to be back at Lear House before dark. He strapped two sacks of meal to the pony's side, pocketed the money in his bag, and struck off. The pounds were an added surprise from the sale of the silver pieces. He wished he had remembered to take his pistol on this trip and vowed never to forget it again.

When he arrived at Lear House, Rory found his pistol untouched where he had stashed it behind books in the library. Still, he slept uneasily for the next few nights. Brian, Quinn, and he made their beds in the kitchen to take advantage of the stove's warmth, but Rory kept one eye open to track the poet's movements at night. Nothing out of the ordinary occurred.

The wind continued to howl from the northeast through the winter months, dropping a barrage of snow and rain upon the manor. Rory, in spirit, thanked Orange daily for the meal, because the store on the bay stood silent and shuttered with nothing to sell. The pounds he had been given were useless.

Quinn earned his keep by daily collecting the peat that had been cut and abandoned by the tenant farmers. The poet also washed and clothed Brian, who was able to do little as his mind grew weaker. Food grew scarce again by late February, and Rory resorted to a scheme he would never have considered in better times.

The wind quieted one day in late March as the sea fog rolled in from Broadhaven Bay — a rare event when Rory could smell the ocean brine in the air. He dressed in the landlord's hunting jacket and boots, taking gloves along, and gathered a hammer, several wooden stakes, and a long, sturdy length of reed rope.

From Lear House, he walked east, past the gully and the fresh water spring that ran toward the bay. The fog hung in thick veils across the heath, but when he gazed upward he could sometimes see the white disc of the sun skirting above the clouds. Better climbers than he had been lost in the fog, sometimes tumbling to their deaths off the cliffs. Benwee Head was particularly dangerous, for its sheer face jutted so high above the sea that no man could survive the fall. But today he needed food and hoped the fickle sun would guide his way.

He stopped near a yellow line of rock that led down the cliff face to the sand below. Seabirds often made their nests in the area and he was counting on finding them, or their eggs. He remained optimistic, peering down the cliff face into the misty haze, despite Quinn's protest that it was too early for mating season. When the fog parted, he spotted lines of foam running from the bay to the shore; the waves broke gently as opposed to those crashing violently in winter gales.

He withdrew the stakes from his bag and hammered the wood into the turf, trying several times to secure them through the frosty layers of bog. After testing them, Rory was convinced they would not fail. He looped and knotted the rope several times around the wood, gripped it with his hands, and leaned at a precarious slant to see if the stakes would hold his weight. They did.

The cliff awaited him. The area he had chosen was steep, but rock striations jutted out at angles. His legs would buttress his descent.

He put on the cloth gloves, tied the rope around his waist, and took a deep breath. First he dropped three yards, then four, then six, until he was eight yards down from the precipice. Small rocks tumbled from the face, through the fog, to the sand. They were lost in the mist, as he would be if he fell. He would surely die, and it would be days, maybe weeks, before anyone would find his body washed up on the beach.

He gripped the rope in his right hand and the outcrops with his left, dropping another yard down the cliff. The rope was almost at its end.

A hand's length away in a hollow sat a black-legged gull that looked at him with indifference as if it had never seen a man before. Rory rocked to the left toward the bird, and, after uttering a shrill cry, it launched into the air with ease, sailing on broad wings until it disappeared in the fog. He smacked against the cliff face, close to the nest. It was littered with downy feathers, and the remains of a few cracked eggshells lined the sides, but there were no fresh eggs or chicks — as Quinn had predicted. He cursed himself for making such a foolish trip. Another hollow, to his right, with no bird in sight, yielded the same result.

His hands ached and his stomach roiled with hunger as he climbed the slope, praying that his footing would hold. When he came within reach of the cliff top, he grabbed the peat with clawed hands, dragged himself across the wet turf, and then collapsed on his back gasping for breath. What could he do now?

He collected the gear and cut across the bog until he came to the trail leading down to the bay. The waves streamed in like they did at the cliff. He hoped to find something to eat, but there was nothing on shore. Neither a dead fish, nor mollusk, just a smooth coating of sand. He was drawn to a rocky point where seaweed with long, brown stems undulated in the surf like strands of hair. He pulled one up from the cold water and realized he was hungry enough to eat it.

The seaweed tasted bitter, smelled like brine, and had a stringy consistency unlike anything he had ever eaten. Rory had soaked it in a bucket, scoured it with his hands, and then boiled it. After supper, his stomach churned and he fought to keep the fibrous mess down. Quinn refused to eat it, preferring to dine on day-old mush. His father-in-law sipped the seaweed broth, took a couple of bites of the meal, and then wandered off to the library, an overcoat flapping against his thin frame.

Quinn helped Rory clean the pots and dishware. When they were close to being done, the poet looked at him and said, "He's dying, isn't he?"

Rory looked up from his drying and threw the towel into the pot. For the first time in days Quinn had said something that made sense. Perhaps the poet wasn't as crazy as he thought. "I don't know. Brian is suffering from a madness I can't explain. It reminds me of what happened to Mrs. Haughan five years ago. She hung on for a long time."

Quinn stoked the fire. "He's always been a friend to me — many times when others would look away. Yes, Brian Walsh was always a kind man." The poet rubbed his hands over the warm stove and then put them to his face as if he was about to cry. "I don't want him to die. Let someone else die in his place."

Rory sat at the table. Except for the light of one candle, the kitchen swam with shadows. "I don't want him to die either, but he's in God's hands." As soon as the words left his mouth, they struck him as spineless, an attempt to rationalize an illness over which he had no control. But for more than a year, all life in Ireland had been in God's hands. There was no other way to understand what was happening. Anger burned within him as he contemplated how tenuous life had become. Why *did* God place this plague upon the land? Why was he ripped apart from the woman he loved? There seemed to be no end to the madness of life, the destructive horror of existence. As the foul mood swelled within him, he blurted out, "Did you shoot Sir Thomas Blakely?" *There. It's out now.* He had said it and a feeling of relief mixed with dread spread over him.

Quinn turned, his face layered in shadow by the candle; his features stern but his manner calm.

He rose from his chair and lurched toward the poet. Quinn would have no chance to overpower him if he struck first. His anger at the poet, and the world, spurted out of him. "Where did you get the flute you play? Did you murder the Kilbanes?"

Quinn held up his hands, signaling Rory to keep his distance, and rushed to the kitchen door. "I'm going to find Brian. He needs help." He disappeared into the dark hallway.

Rory followed the poet determined to get answers; instead, he found Brian slumped over the library desk. His father-in-law was asleep, not dead, and sputtered questions as Rory lifted him from the chair as if he were carrying a newborn. "Where am I? Who are you?"

The questions pierced his heart as he carried Brian to his straw bed near the stove.

Saying nothing, Quinn soon reappeared, sat on his own bed, and held one of Brian's hands.

The gesture moved Rory — there was still humanity left in the poet despite what crimes he may have committed in the past.

"You won't answer me?" Rory asked.

"There's no need — what's done is done," the poet said. "The past can't be changed."

"But the constable believes I shot Blakely. You could clear my name and I could go to America."

The poet studied him with eyes encircled by darkness. "And go to prison myself or be transported. I've heard that the cell is better than the way we live. I only want justice . . . wrongs to be righted. When I'm through helping my friend, you'll get your answers."

Quinn wouldn't solve the mystery. Rory would, as he told Orange, have to bide his time. He lay down on his bed next to his father-in-law.

Quinn continued to stroke Brian's hand until the candle flickered out.

A few days later, after his temper had cooled and his mind had regained some peace, Rory asked the poet, "Will you help me write a letter to Briana? I must get it to her soon."

"Do you know where she lives?" Quinn asked.

"No, but I'll hold the letter until I find out. Then, I'll post it. . . . If I don't write now, Briana may never see her father alive again." He lowered his gaze. "I don't want that to happen."

"Tonight, then," the poet said. "We'll write the letter together."

That evening, Quinn retrieved paper, pen, and ink from the library. They sat at the kitchen table, the poet writing in Irish as Rory dictated his letter. The sturdy rock walls of Lear House protected them from the wind and damp as the candle glowed soft and yellow. For the first time since he had seen Orange at Glencastle, he felt as if he was doing something positive to lessen the fear that surrounded him. However, in the letter, he could reveal only so much.

My dearest Briana,

I hope this letter finds you holding our child, and both of you in good health. Daniel Quinn is writing my words and he may embellish it with my blessing, but, above all, I want you to know how much I love and miss you and our child, whom I'm certain is at your side. Both of you fill my thoughts every hour.

Know that I am well and have been able to find food and shelter through my own resources, but the days grow more treacherous as each one passes. Your father and the poet are currently in my care and we have been able to survive the winter at Lear House. We look forward to spring and the hope of a plentiful harvest for Ireland this summer. However, that will not come about on the estate. All have been ejected and have had to make their own way.

Of more pressing news, it pains me that I fear your father has not long to live. I understand that you and Lucinda now have a life of your own, but I know that he would love your company as much as I, and, perhaps, it would strengthen him to see your loving faces. I also long to see our precious child, but a journey may be too hazardous for the newborn.

God speed, my love, come what may. I will never leave your father's side as I know your wish would be to see your father well again. I pray your letters will come soon, so that I may write to you in Boston.

Your loving husband,
Rory

Quinn read the letter to him several times before Rory pronounced it ready to post.

Two days later, nearing April, he carried the letter to Belmullet to buy any food he could find. The pony stumbled along, weak from its own scarce foraging, and several times he was forced to dismount and walk beside the animal. When he arrived, he was happy to see the masts of a tall ship in the harbor. A line of wet, bedraggled people waited on the quay. Many had no shoes. They sat huddled around their bags, waiting to board the ship. A sailor told him the vessel had sailed from Liverpool and was soon to return to Quebec to pick up a load of lumber harvested in North America. The news cheered him as he made his way to the post office.

"Have you anything for Rory Caulfield?" he asked the postmaster, a bent old man who had seen many days in the building.

The man looked him over and then said, "Rory Caulfield of Lear House?"

"Yes."

The man's eyes flashed. "There's no one at Lear House — at least there's not supposed to be, from what I heard. Everyone was ejected."

"That's true, but I'm Rory Caulfield and I'm hoping to receive letters from my wife in Boston."

The postmaster turned and thrust his scrawny hand into a wooden letter box. He withdrew a pack bound with string and faced Rory. "I was holding these until Mr. Caulfield turned up. They've been here for less than a week."

"May I post a letter to Boston?" Rory asked in a rush. "I've got money for a stamp."

"The ship departs in a few hours," the man said. "It sails to Quebec first, but I imagine the letter will get to Boston in three weeks, maybe sooner, if the vessel isn't quarantined because of illness onboard."

He hadn't considered that thought, but looking at the miserable crowd ready to board, quarantine seemed a real possibility.

Six letters were bound with the twine. He snapped the string and looked at the white envelope on top. It was from Lucinda, who had carefully put the South Cove address in the upper left corner. He ripped it open and skimmed it quickly to make sure the numbers on the envelope matched those in the letter.

"Would you do me a favor and write the post address on this," he said to the man. He withdrew his letter and handed it to the man, who, with a grumble, granted his request.

"It's going to cost you since it's going by sea and then most likely by land."

"It's a grave matter and needs to get there fast. If I could send it on wings I would."

The postmaster laughed and shook his head at Rory's imagination.

Rory paid for the stamp and left with the Boston letters. He still needed to find food for Lear House and for the animal. Saving the pony was the most important thing he could do, but he couldn't wait to get home and have the poet read the letters to him.

The sound of Lucinda's footsteps rushing up the stairs startled Briana from her reverie. Her sister flung open the door with breathless excitement. She waved a letter above her head. "It's from Rory!"

Nothing could have brightened an early spring day more than a letter from her husband. Leaving Shona upon the bed, she rushed to her sister, her excitement bubbling up. "Let me see!"

Lucinda held the envelope in front of her, and Briana reveled in the handwriting. Of course Rory couldn't have written the letter himself, but it didn't matter — the important fact was that a letter from her husband had been delivered to Boston. He was alive!

But what if it was bad news? She collapsed on the bed and caressed Shona as if the love for her child might dissipate her fear. "Read it to me," she told Lucinda. "I'm too nervous to look at it."

"I'm the same," her sister said. Lucinda's hands trembled as she placed the letter on the desk and stepped back.

"Bring it here and we'll look at it together."

Lucinda picked up the letter, trudged toward the bed as if her feet were made of lead, and sat next to Briana. With a trembling finger, her sister lifted the flap, withdrew the stationery, and read aloud.

Stunned when the last word faded, they both slumped on the bed. A deep sadness soaked into Briana, while Lucinda, crest-fallen, gazed at the floor. Briana cradled her baby close, not thinking much about the soft squirm of the infant. They were silent until Quinlin, in the care of Mrs. Coleman downstairs, let out a childish guffaw, which echoed up the stairs.

"What are we to do?" Lucinda asked. She folded the letter and returned it to the envelope.

"I must go to Ireland," Briana said without hesitating, "on the first ship I can book passage."

Her sister's eyes narrowed in disbelief. "Madness. Utter madness. Rory says that Father's time is limited, and he may already be —"

"Be what?" Her protest came out louder than she wished, for the baby was asleep; surely her sister could see that at least one of them must go. "What are we to do?" she asked. "Wait until everyone is dead before we can deliver the money to save them? It will be too late for Father and Rory if I don't go. We can't let that happen."

"You can't travel with Shona," Lucinda said. "What of the voyage, the weather, the famine."

Lucinda's objections only cemented her resolve. "Shona will be better off with me.

I'm not leaving her in the care of a wet nurse. I promise you that I will protect her." She ran a finger around her daughter's chubby pink face. "We have the money to bring them here. I'll find food, and I'll protect my child." She held out her hand to her sister. "Father and Rory need us."

Lucinda only shook her head. "I think it's the most foolish action you've ever contemplated, and you've done some ill-advised things in your life."

Briana looked past her sister to the sunlight splashing upon the brick building across the lane. The wind shook the still-naked branches of the lone maple that rose from the sidewalk. Puffy white clouds breezed across a sterling blue sky.

A sudden calm descended upon her, putting her at ease despite her sister's objection. "No, I have to return to Ireland. Rory and Father need me." She walked to the window with the baby and looked to the bright western sky. "I'll bring them back to America."

"Your optimism never ceases, does it?" She got up from the bed and stirred the embers in the fireplace. Licks of flame sprouted under the birch logs. "It may sound selfish, but I don't want to leave my job. Quinlin needs care, and someone has to pay the Colemans. I don't want to lose our room to another tenant."

Briana stepped toward her. "You know that all I've ever wanted is for all of us to be together. For so long I thought our family could only find joy at Lear House, but now I think we could be happy here. If you can find it in your heart to look after the boy, I, and Addy, would be most grateful." She smiled. "But there's another reason you should stay on, sister. . . . Your suitor."

Lucinda's eyes brightened and her cheeks flushed at the mention of Dr. Scott. "I would hardly call him a suitor. We see each other now and then."

"Now and then! You've seen the good doctor at least twice a week since Shona's birth, and I don't think there's any disputing that he cares for you."

Her sister came to her side. "Am I not allowed? Am I to remain a spinster for the duration of my life because my sister is married?"

"No, of course not. I believe your life is here in Boston. Why return? You've never been as fond of Ireland as I have."

Lucinda sat at the desk, folded her hands, and sighed. "I suppose you're right. My job with the Carlisles is not one to sniff at, and they have been more than kind to us. And

Mr. Peters has given you free rein at the trades office, so there's no reason you can't leave." She lowered her gaze to the inkwell and paper on the desk. "I am fond of Dr. Scott. I think he values my intelligence rather than my beauty, though. You were always the pretty one."

Briana stood behind Lucinda. "You are beautiful, my sister, but you've lavished your affection upon one man who doesn't deserve it."

Lucinda reached back and grasped Briana's hand. "Then you shall go and I shall remain here, awaiting your return with Father and your husband." She got up and embraced her.

"It will be for the best." Shona wriggled in her arms. "Now we must find a ship to take me home."

Three days later, Briana had booked a reservation on a commercial steamer that had resumed Atlantic passage now that spring had blossomed. Mr. Peters was able to convert enough of Quinlin's bank notes to Irish currency for the voyage over and passage back for three people when he heard that Briana was going to take care of her father. He assured her that when she returned, a position would be waiting for her at the Building Trades.

It took only a day to pack what she needed for the baby and herself before she began her good-byes.

The boy clutched at her dress and cried from the steps of the house in South Cove the day she departed. Lucinda assured him that Briana would one day return to Boston. Her last memory of her American home was Lucinda, Quinlin, and Mrs. Coleman standing on the steps while patches of sun fell on their shoulders. She settled in the carriage seat with Shona in her arms, her bag packed with provisions. The open sea and the lurking specter of the famine awaited.

CHAPTER 23

"What's going on?" Quinn peered through the kitchen window one morning in early April, looking east toward the hill that rose toward the village.

Rory, always keeping the Constabulary in mind, rushed to his side. A line of white dots descended the rise and then split apart as two black specks skirted around them.

"Sheep, by God," Rory said with a sense of wonder. "Sir Thomas is bringing in what he promised." The animals' muffled bleats sounded through the window.

Quinn turned, a fearful look in his eyes. "They'll eject us from the house."

"Not if they don't know we're here," Rory said. "Keep quiet. They can't get in if we bolt the kitchen door." He adjusted the flue on the stove so the fire used for breakfast would die and the smoke would cease to rise through the chimney.

It didn't take long for the sheep to find

their way through the destroyed tenant farms. Soon they were grazing on the turf around the potato ridges. The two men accompanying the animals called off their black-and-white dogs with a series of sharp whistles, and the flock settled across the land in a listless pack. The burly men leaned against the ruins of a sod wall, smoked their pipes, and ate from their packs. Rory didn't know where they had come from. He knew most everyone who remained in the village, and these men were not from Carrowteige. Most likely they were hands hired by Sir Thomas to herd the sheep, purchased from another landowner, to the grounds of Lear House.

Throughout the afternoon, the men worked on building a crude fence of stone and turf around the central grazing area. The work and the enclosure caused Rory no alarm; however, two other prospects did. First, what if the men explored the exterior of Lear House and found the unchained kitchen door? Second, the animals' appearance might mean that more sheep and other workers would follow.

Their discovery at the manor would be imminent. That disturbing prospect left him shaken. If they were arrested, which by law the owner had every right to do, they would spend time in prison or be transported to another country. If they left Lear House, they would be homeless with few available possibilities for shelter. Perhaps the Molly sympathizer at Geesala, where they had stored the grain and silver, would take them in, or the farmer at Glencastle where Orange had been hiding might welcome them. But in these times with everyone struggling, options were scarce.

In either case, arrest or abandonment, the letter he had posted to Briana that listed his address as Lear House might mislead her. If she arrived to find no one at the manor, they would miss each other altogether, or she might assume the worst — that he and her father were dead.

By sunset the men, apparently pleased with their work, left the sheep and walked up the hill with their dogs. Rory suspected they had somehow procured lodging with one of the villagers. How long would it be before the men knew they were living in Lear House?

The setting sun broke through the clouds and cast long shadows across the turf. Now and then a bleat from one of the animals penetrated the window. How delectable a lamb feast might be to a starving stomach. It also might mean a rope around his neck.

Starvation or hanging, either manner of death would be a dismal choice.

For the next few days, the men watched over the sheep even when the rain poured down upon them. Rory had little sympathy for them but found his heart in his throat when one circled the manor grounds.

He closed the kitchen shutter as the man started toward them. He had time to herd Quinn and Brian into the dark hallway. The back door creaked and shook, but it held firm. Certainly the man noticed that the door was not padlocked from the outside, unlike the front door. He cupped his hand over Brian's mouth until he was sure the man was gone. He and Quinn breathed a sigh of relief and debated whether to leave under cover of darkness the next evening.

That night, an awful crack, like the breaking of bone, awakened Rory.

Quinn started as well, calling out Brian's name. He was the first to get to the man's side in the hall. "He's bleeding," he called out to Rory, who sprang from his bed. "He's hit his head."

Rory lit a candle and found Quinn hunched over his father-in-law. A gash on the left side of Brian's face spewed blood on the floor. He returned to the kitchen, dipped a cloth in a bucket of fresh water, and then instructed the poet to apply it against the wound while he went for towels. He found them in the bathroom upstairs.

They wrapped Brian's head in cloth and carried him to his bed. His breathing was shallow, his face a sickly white in the yellow candlelight.

"Oh, God, make him well," Rory entreated, his voice tinged with sadness. There was no doctor to go for, nothing to do except watch and wait. He looked down at the bloodied head of his father-in-law and prayed that Briana was on her way to Ireland.

Quinn muttered a prayer over his friend's body and then repeated the words, "There's no justice in this world."

They watched over him as the night turned to day.

The Atlantic had been cruel on the voyage to Liverpool, and, much of the time, Briana was locked in her cabin in dizzy solitude with Shona. The steamer shivered and moaned across the waves but made good time because of the westerly gales. Even the channel crossings stabbed at her tender stomach; food was plentiful but hard to keep down because of the turbulent seas. Shona adapted to the waves. The ship's motion often rocked her to sleep.

Briana touched Irish soil at Belmullet for the first time in eight months when she completed the final portion of her journey. Her legs wobbled a bit as she walked along the quay. A kind porter took pity on her, carried her bag, and secured a carriage for her journey to Lear House. A thousand questions tormented her as she stared out the cab window with Shona mewling in her arms. Nestled in the carriage, the baby was the least of her concerns at the moment. What would come after she reached Lear House? Where would she go if Rory and her father weren't there?

The landscape shifted into the familiar greenish brown hills of the bog. The silence that fell upon the land when the plague burst forth still remained. Nothing moved, no bird sang. The eerie feeling made her skin crawl.

Dreadful memories burst into her head when the carriage crossed the shallows where she'd seen the first starving family so long ago. As she looked out at the rushing blue waters, her heart pounded with a hopeful excitement that, ahead, she would find her husband and father. Uttering soothing words, she lifted Shona to the glass so her daughter could glimpse the land Briana loved.

Her joy was muted, however, when the carriage rolled through Carrowteige. The once tidy homes had fallen into disrepair, and some had even been destroyed. No one walked the streets, no one stirred in the silent windows.

The carriage topped the ridge, and she looked down upon Lear House and the grounds where the tenant farms had once stood. She gasped, her breath fleeing from her lungs. The homes had been reduced to muddy mounds. Lear House still stood looking out over the bay like a rock fortress, but its windows were shuttered, the manor as silent and deserted as the village. Sheep grazed on lands once occupied by hundreds of farmers, but no men tended the animals.

She clutched Shona and a tear dropped from her eye. The destruction was worse than she had imagined.

The coachman stopped in the lane leading up to the entrance of Lear House.

"Are you sure this is the right place?" he asked as he lifted her bag from the carriage.

"Very sure," she replied. The wind cut around her, ruffling her skirt. She breathed in the clean freshness of the air and took in the broad expanse of the bay. How she had missed her home!

"It's grand, but it looks empty to me," he said. "I'd hate to leave a lady stranded, but I must return to Belmullet."

"Would you mind waiting a few minutes? I have the return fare if need be."

"Of course. It'll give me a chance to water my horses."

"The cistern is up the hill." She covered Shona with her blanket and walked to the front door. The rusty padlock and chain that hung from the gate covering the front door looked as if they hadn't been touched in months.

Briana skirted the east side of the house, following the carriage as the driver urged his horses up the hill. She spotted something — the figure of a man — moving behind the kitchen window, behind a shutter that looked askew.

When she turned the corner, he was standing there, his hands clenched at his sides. She rushed to him, but he thrust out his arms, begging her to stop.

Rory stepped toward her. "I want to be sure this isn't a dream. I want to know that you and my child are real." He brought his hands to his mouth.

She stopped. The baby cried in her arms.

He ambled like an old man, his frame

thinner, much more fragile than when she had left those months ago. Above his clasped hands and the growth of beard, his weary face showed thick creases. But it was *Rory,* and her heart leapt with joy. He was alive!

He stumbled against her and collapsed at her feet. She knelt beside him and covered his face with kisses, her tears flowing.

"Your daughter," she said, and handed the baby to him.

Rory cradled her in his arms, parted the blanket covering her, and looked down lovingly upon his daughter's face. "What's her name?"

"Shona."

"A beautiful name." He pulled his daughter close and sobbed into the blanket.

"I'm home," she said. "And I'm never leaving you again."

The driver appeared by her side. "So this is the right place."

"Yes," she said. "I'll be staying."

Briana never heard the carriage leave as she and Rory melted into each other's arms.

Daniel Quinn's voice finally broke their embrace.

They slept upstairs in Blakely's bed behind a closed door. They lay against each other, savoring their precious time together, freed from carnal needs, with their daughter safely settled between them. There was another reason they clung to each other. Sorrow. Brian Walsh had died three days earlier.

Rory had dug a shallow grave next to Brian's wife the night after the death. Quinn had helped him place the body over a pony, which Rory led to the community graveyard. After much sweat and tears, the deed was done. Father O'Kirwin, still at the post across the bay, wasn't notified, for Rory wanted no attention drawn to Lear House. So his father-in-law went into the ground without the benefit of the priest's prayers. Rory stood looking at the bare earth high on the hillside. The rain came in off the Atlantic as he made his way back to the manor.

Rory took Briana to the gravesite the morning after she arrived. Shona was bundled against her mother's warm bosom. Slate-colored clouds swept in from the Atlantic. The wind buffeted them as they stood by the spaded earth.

"We almost left Lear House after he died," Rory said, "but something told me stay."

"I'm glad you did," she said, and pulled her shawl around her shoulders and head. "I don't think he would have liked America.

He'll be happier here, buried next to Mother."

"He didn't suffer much after the fall," Rory said. "His spirit had already been broken. . . ."

"By everything," Briana said, and turned her back to the wind. Her tears had already been spent when she learned of her father's passing, but now she trembled at the thought of Death touching her with its cold hands. She was tired of thinking about the famine, tired of remembering the bodies along the road, the starving children, the men and women of County Mayo dressed in rags with nothing to eat and no hope for the future.

Now that she was back in Ireland she understood clearly what America had to offer. With her father gone and Lear House shuttered, there was no reason to stay. For all she cared, the poet could make his residence at the manor. As much as she loved her home and her country, the birth of her daughter had changed her thinking. Shona was three months old and deserved more than Ireland could offer.

She turned and snuggled against Rory, using his body to block the chill, the baby pressed between them.

"Could you live in America?" she asked him.

He gazed down the hillside at the jumbled remains of the farms, the grazing sheep, the shepherds, and was silent for a time before he spoke. "My brother and his family are gone, and our friends are scattered to the four winds." He stopped, his voice choking, and then spaded the earth on Brian's grave with his hand. He rose and kissed her. "As much as I don't want to believe it, there's nothing to keep us here. Shona and you are more important to me than any country."

She returned his kiss, and they walked down the precarious trail on the west side of Lear House, taking care not to be seen by the men guarding the sheep. As they neared the kitchen door, she said, "You saved my mother's crucifix. I'm returning it to her."

That afternoon she sneaked out of the house and carried the crucifix to the graves and placed it as a marker. "Dust to dust," she said, knowing that within a few years it would crumble and disintegrate on the turf.

Late that same day, Rory was the first to spot the carriage hurtling like a crow over the top of the hill. The black coach traversed the slope with haste, making a speedy descent toward Lear House.

"Close the shutters," Rory shouted to Quinn as he dashed past him on his way to find Briana upstairs. The stairwell was dark, but he knew it well enough to find Blakely's bedroom. There, Briana lay with Shona on the bed as the muted light of day filtered in through the slats.

"He's here," Rory shouted. "It has to be him."

"It can't be." Briana jumped from the bed, leaving the baby concealed by the blankets. She peered through the slats, hoping to see the carriage. "He's at least a month ahead of schedule. What's he doing here?"

"The sheep, I suppose. Gather Shona and get to the kitchen. If there's trouble, get out the back door fast and we'll meet at the general store."

She picked up the child and wrapped her in the blanket. "And what am I to do if Sir Thomas shoots you on sight — run to the bay with the baby? Madness. I'll remain here. He wouldn't harm a child."

"You'll do no such thing. Get in the kitchen and be quiet." He retrieved the bag containing the pistol and ammunition from its hiding place in the bedroom, having removed it from the library. It would do him no good unless he threw it at the landlord's head, for the weapon was neither loaded nor primed.

Clutching the bag, he led Briana and the baby down the stairs.

"It's the devil himself, isn't it?" Quinn asked when they entered the kitchen. His hands were behind his back. "You can't fight the devil — only remove him from your soul. He'll make short work of us." He revealed his hands — in one he clutched a butcher's knife.

Briana skirted the three straw beds on the floor and found a seat at the table. "Are you mad, Quinn? Put that knife down. He's not going to harm us. I'll see to that."

Rory gave her the eye and stuck the pistol under his shirt so it rested between his stomach and the waistband of his breeches. "How will you arrange that?" Thoughts of Sir Thomas lusting after Briana burst into his head. In some ways, Briana's maturity and beauty had blossomed with mother-hood. What would Blakely want from them now that they had been discovered?

"By reasoning with him," she said.

Quinn dropped the knife on the table beside Briana.

The crunch of carriage wheels in the lane echoed through the hall. For a few minutes, they remained frozen in the kitchen while they listened as trunks scraped against the slate terrace. Then the gate rattled, the chain dropped, and the door opened.

Sir Thomas stretched out his arms until he found the draped hall table. The landlord was framed in the light — three men followed him into the house, all equally as blind as they waited for their eyes to adjust to the dark.

The landlord dropped his greatcoat on the table and shouted a few orders to the men. They dragged a large trunk and two cases into the hall. Sir Thomas turned his head toward the kitchen door, stopped, and took off his gloves. "So, it is true." He edged down the hall, choosing his steps carefully. "Sometimes I find it hard to accept rumors, the words of underlings, but I will learn to pay more attention to gossip. I should have known better than to doubt their word over a trespasser and a man who wants me dead."

Quinn opened the shutter, flooding the kitchen with light. The landlord, attired in a black waistcoat, breeches, and boots, stood with his hands planted against the door frame. "So you've all come to greet me — the poet, the beauty, and the man who tried to kill me."

"I've never shot anyone, nor taken anything that wasn't freely given," Rory said, holding his spot. "We're here because we have no other home — and no place to turn to."

Sir Thomas laughed. "Well, I suppose that is true if you haven't been charged with theft or murder, but knowing the inept Irish Constabulary . . ." His eyes lighted upon Briana and the baby she held in her arms. "Oh, the beauty has a child — I doubt from immaculate conception." He said those last words with a sneer born of rage.

Rory could take no more insults. He lunged at the landlord, but the man sidestepped him and knocked him to the floor with a blow to his back. The pistol jabbed his stomach, and he grimaced in pain.

Briana, clutching Shona, rose from the chair. "How dare you strike him! He's weak from hunger."

"I've every right to strike a trespasser — even string him up — if there was a decent tree in this God-forsaken country." Sir Thomas ordered two men to pick Rory off the floor. "Allow me to introduce my herders," he told Briana. "They're the ones who told me that someone was living in Lear House." He put a finger to his lips. "Villagers can be secretive. No one — not one — would tell them the names. But, I suppose,

I shouldn't be surprised."

The men dragged Rory from the floor and plopped him in a chair. His head ached, but his pride had suffered more. What had happened to the man who had defeated Connor in the town square? He was weak now, barely able to throw a punch.

The landlord leaned toward Briana, breathing in her face. "Let me see the child."

"You've been drinking," Briana said.

"That reminds me," Sir Thomas said. "There must be a glass buried somewhere in these cabinets." He ordered his driver to get brandy from the coach. "Yes, I've been drinking since I got off the ship at Belmullet. What a miserable country. I'm here for a few days, only to make sure the house is secure and my flock is in place." He wagged a finger in Briana's face. "I was wrong about the house."

The driver returned with the brandy and excused himself. "Let Constable Davitt know that I have uninvited guests," he shouted after the man. "Be back in three days, or be damned," the landlord ordered.

"Would you like a drink, my friend?" Sir Thomas said, and sat next to Rory. "It may be the last you take before I have you arrested. The constable will know by morning, and by tomorrow afternoon you may all find yourself in prison." The herders chuckled as they sat on the straw beds.

He wanted to shoot the landlord between the eyes, but his rage turned to sorrow as he realized he could only grovel before Sir Thomas. "I would like that drink."

"Rory?" Briana cautioned.

"Pour us all a drink," the landlord said to Quinn. The poet needed no prodding, since it had been several weeks since he had partaken of liquor. He rushed to get the glasses.

"Would you like one, my dear?" Sir Thomas asked Briana. She shook her head.

Quinn put three glasses on the table, and the landlord poured the brandy.

"Now we're getting somewhere," Sir Thomas said. He pushed back in his chair and put his booted feet on the table. "A toast to your health." He raised his glass and snickered. "Poor choice of words."

Rory took a swig of the brandy. It burned his gullet but fortified his courage. "Arrest me, but leave my wife out of it. Quinn had nothing to do with trespassing either. He's here because he cared for Brian Walsh."

"How is the old man?" Sir Thomas asked with a wicked grin.

"My father's dead," Briana said coldly.

The landlord's smirk faded. "Starvation?"

"No," Rory answered, "but it might as well have been. He died from a fall — he was weak from hunger."

"I liked the old man." Sir Thomas paused and lifted his glass. "But I have nothing to do with the law or what is done to lawbreakers. I wish I could do more, but it's out of my hands."

"As it is with all the English," Rory countered.

The landlord swiped at his boots and then put them on the floor. "I suppose it would do no good to cast you all out in the night — especially a child — so you can stay in the kitchen on one condition."

Rory's stomach fluttered from the effects of the brandy. "What's that?"

"A simple request, really. That you watch me eat my supper." Sir Thomas pointed to the two large cases at the end of the hall. "I don't think there's enough food for everyone." He rose from the table. "I'll be upstairs stoking the fire. And tonight I'll sleep soundly behind a locked door." He grabbed the brandy bottle and started down the hall, but before climbing the stairs he opened his waistcoat, withdrew a pistol, and held it up to the light. "And I'm armed."

He enjoyed eating the dried meats and fruits

in front of them. He was particularly generous with the herders who were acting as bodyguards of sorts during supper.

There were beans in the crates as well, which Briana offered to cook in exchange for three plates of them.

The woozy impact of the brandy opened his heart for a time, and he allowed them the beans and some scraps. The poet was particularly grateful for the handouts and consumed them greedily. Briana took the food as well and coaxed her sulky husband to eat after he had initially turned down the offer.

It served them right. After all, they were the ones that had broken into his house, used what they could, made it their home — although, from what he could tell, they had stolen or damaged nothing except the clothes the men had commandeered for their own use. He could never wear them again. But the wine and liquor he had stashed behind a false back in his wardrobe was untouched — a good thing with the poet in the house.

He asked Quinn to help him cart his trunk and the two cases upstairs so he could keep an eye on them. The poet obliged, although the look in the man's eyes made him uncomfortable despite the presence of his pistol concealed under his jacket. Quinn seemed to be searching for something, for what he couldn't be certain. He couldn't wait to be rid of him. The poet was another that would be out of the house by tomorrow night if the driver completed his task of contacting the constable.

The fireplace had warmed the room by the time he had dismissed the herders and was ready for bed. He took off his clothes, slipped into a nightshirt, and drank the last of the brandy. He was alone again. Even the village woman who had given him comfort had disappeared. He had seen the jumbled remains of her home as the carriage passed by.

Another bottle was concealed in the wardrobe — the one that Brian and Rory had received from the sea captain on their trip to Westport. He lifted the wood panel, grabbed the half-empty bottle, and returned to bed. His pistol lay hidden under his pillow. Perhaps he wouldn't need it, but one could never be sure with the ruffians sleeping below.

He fell into a hazy, dream-filled sleep until he was awakened by a baby's cry. The front door scraped open and then closed. From his bedroom on the front of Lear House, he heard the infant's wail.

"Shut up, shut up," he cursed to the air. He threw on his coat, leaving it open over his nightshirt, wanting to end the incessant cry. Before he fled down the stairs, he swigged another gulp of brandy, believing it to be his last of the night.

Briana, rocking the baby in her arms, stood at the bottom of the stone steps leading into Lear House. The front door stood open behind her. The wind plowed off the ocean in strong gusts, sending broken clouds shooting across a nearly full moon. On the bay, whitecaps sparkled in the shimmering light.

Shona was wrapped in her white blanket, which flapped wildly against Briana's body. The child wasn't used to Ireland or the loss of her comfortable bed in Boston and had been cranky since supper. Rather than use the back door, Briana had walked to the front, as far away from the kitchen as possible so as not to disturb her husband or Quinn. They were trying to catch what sleep they could with so much to think about. She found it hard to sleep as well. What if Rory was arrested and carted away by the constable tomorrow? She couldn't bear the thought of her husband in prison. Rory and Quinn's diminished strengths would be put to the test if tomorrow was their only chance to escape.

She jumped when a hand touched her shoulder.

She turned to find Sir Thomas behind her looking bedraggled, anger firing in his dark eyes.

"The child woke me up," he said, "but I was dreaming of you." He swayed toward her.

"I've no control over the cries of a three-month-old," Briana said. "Besides, you've had plenty to drink. I doubted you would hear anything." She stepped away from him. "Maybe a walk by the bay will calm her down. She doesn't like this place."

"No." He grabbed her by the arm. "Don't go. Let me look at you."

Briana pulled away from him, eager to distance herself from the landlord.

He soon caught up and walked beside her. "Why is it certain women adore money and privilege above all else and others can't be bought for any price? You're among the latter."

"I'm flattered," Briana replied, "but you're well aware of my reason. He's sleeping in your house."

Sir Thomas lifted the blanket covering Shona's face and squinted in the moonlight.

"She's as pretty as her mother."

The wind roared overhead as they descended to the beach. The surging waves added their own deafening crash as the moon appeared, casting their shadows across the sand.

"This is how the legend got started, isn't it?" Sir Thomas yelled into the wind.

At first, Briana was unsure of what he was getting at, but a spit of fear bit into her. *The legend of Lear House — the children of Lear?* She clutched Shona tighter to her breast.

"She was jealous of her husband's children," he shouted, "so she turned them into swans to swim the oceans for nine hundred years. She got her wish — and a husband filled with grief."

He whirled and grabbed Shona from Briana's arms.

She screamed, but her cries vanished in the fierce wind and booming waves.

Sir Thomas ran down the gentle slope to the bay with the baby in his arms.

She stopped, numb with fear, as the landlord stepped to the water's edge, the waves surging at his feet, holding the child above his head like a sacrificial lamb. His greatcoat fluttered in the wind; his nightshirt rippled against his body.

A voice behind her yelled, "Put the child

down, English bastard."

Quinn brushed past her and stopped a few yards from Sir Thomas. He held a pistol in his hand, aimed at the landlord.

Sir Thomas lowered the child, and Briana ran to him.

"Who is that?" he asked as he handed Shona to her. "What's he doing?"

She seized Shona and ran back to Quinn. "Don't, you'll hang," she shouted at him.

"I missed once, but I won't miss again," Quinn yelled. "I'll make sure they never find the body. The sea hides its victims well." He shook the pistol at the landlord and cocked his head toward Briana. "Go to your husband and tell him what I've done for Brian Walsh."

"Don't kill him," she pleaded.

"Go!"

Briana ran to save the life of her child. She looked over her shoulder to see Sir Thomas advancing in drunken steps toward the poet. A pop sounded in the air, and a brief flash lit the dunes. She knew what had happened.

Sir Thomas Blakely was dead.

EPILOGUE

As he had many times before, Quinn disappeared by daybreak. He had not come back to the house after the shot had been fired. In those early hours, Rory and Briana searched Lear House and found nothing but the landlord's bags and the two crates of food. However, the landlord's pistol was missing and couldn't be found. In the morning, they took what provisions they could pack, along with their funds. Rory turned the ponies out with the sheep before leaving the house.

They ran into the herders as they ascended the hill toward the village and told the men that they were leaving upon the owner's orders and that he had gone to bed the previous night asking not to be disturbed. In another two days the carriage would return from Belmullet to an empty house. The constable, if he came at all to arrest the trespassers, wouldn't arrive before late afternoon. They would be far away from Carrowteige by then. They planned to avoid the Constabulary, but if detained, they now knew the truth.

Briana looked back at Lear House as they topped the hill. Everything had changed and the world was different. The sun burst forth for a moment on the manor, brightening it to a silvery gleam on the green heath. As far as she knew, she would never see her old home again or the land where she was born. The house and its owner were dead.

As they walked, Rory asked her if she thought Quinn had murdered the Kilbanes. She replied that Quinn's hatred for the English and the landlord, particularly after Brian's death, fueled his rage against Sir Thomas. Perhaps he had stumbled on the Kilbanes' cottage after their murder. Quinn had no reason that she could think of to kill the couple.

When they reached the river where the villagers said good-bye to their loved ones, they held on to each other — Shona strapped to Rory's chest — and waded through the shallow waters scalloped by rippling whitecaps. The wind whipped against them and reminded Briana of her walks along the cliffs she was leaving behind forever.

They hoped to make Bangor by nightfall and find Connor and his family. If not, they would find shelter and then make their way to Dublin, where it would be easier to book passage out of Ireland than in County Mayo. In Dublin, they would book passage to Liverpool and then America.

She shed no tears as they walked along the road near Carrowmore Lake, the Nephin Beg rising up brownish green in the distance. The walk to Dublin would be long and hard, but a better future awaited them. Her sister, Quinlin, and the Colemans would be their new family, in a home of their own making. Rory's love would guarantee a home no matter where they lived.

For the first time in many months her soul was filled with hope and peace.

AUTHOR'S NOTE

In late July 2017, I stood near Benwee Head looking out over the North Atlantic as plump opalescent clouds dumped a chilly rain on my head. The temperature was about 58 degrees Fahrenheit, but a buffeting wind off the water made the brisk air seem much colder. To my right, the Stags of Broadhaven rose from the ocean in their jagged formation. Few visitors had ventured forth on this wild and windy day to the cliffs west of Carrowteige, Ireland, known for their breathtaking views from the numerous walking trails traversing the boggy headlands.

The experience was one of many sobering moments I experienced in Ireland while doing research for *The Irishman's Daughter.* I had eaten a full breakfast at our hotel in Westport; grabbed a snack at the Ballycroy National Park visitor center about halfway in our travels; and, upon arrival, even purchased a to-go lunch at the local village store. I wasn't hungry, neither was I cold, when the rain clouds raced in from the Atlantic. When the elements became too harsh I retreated to the warmth of the rental car. I was lucky to have the comforts afforded me that day. I had to remind myself that this was July — the weather was murky to say the least — the climate not exactly hospitable even for the height of summer. I imagined how hard it must have been to eke out a living on the heath in 1845, and, in the following years, to survive The Great Hunger.

Several days earlier, we had stopped at Strokestown Park in County Roscommon for a visit to the Irish National Famine Museum, where I was able to visit with John O'Driscoll, the General Manager. The museum is sobering in itself, now housed on the grounds of the former estate of Denis Mahon, a landlord assassinated during the famine years. The terrible facts about the famine are displayed in Strokestown, but my conversation with Mr. O'Driscoll confirmed something that had lurked in my mind since I had begun my research for the novel.

The Great Famine is often relegated to the dustbin of history. It's not extensively discussed in Irish schools. Young people know it happened, but their lesson on it might be a page or two in a textbook. In fact, discussion of this almost incomprehensible disaster has been so late in coming that the famine museum didn't officially open until 1997, 152 years after history tells us the blight began.

The Irish suffered for three reasons during the Great Famine: pain, shame, and truth. *Pain* from their losses and *shame* for not being able to stop the famine's natural course by any means, either through scientific or governmental remedies. The *truth* of the matter was that the suffering population could do little about the famine through its own efforts. Planning to avert a disaster really didn't enter the minds of the starving. They *reacted* as best they could. I liken it to modern-day preparations for a nuclear war. Few of us construct fallout shelters, hoard supplies, and plan for a postnuclear apocalypse. Mostly we understand that there is little we can do in the face of such a horrific and devastating occurrence.

One might think that writing a fictional account of the famine would be an easy task. Take a natural disaster, throw in pain and suffering, and somehow get your heroine to survive. But the famine is a difficult beast to conquer. The laissez-faire politics of the time, though seemingly simple, led to complex debates and crippling governmental standoffs in England and Ireland. Landlord, agent, and tenant relationships were byzantine and codified but were, in their own way, haphazardly circumvented by the growing Irish population. The laws of ownership, conacre, rent, and farming collided with the nascent methods of the industrial revolution. The life that made Ireland's population swell prior to the famine, thanks to the nutritional benefits of the potato (the average adult ate ten to fourteen pounds a day; yes, you read that correctly), was diminishing cataclysmically under new and unforeseen circumstances. Ireland would be irreparably altered by the famine, including a devastating population loss that hasn't recovered its mid-1840s number to this day.

According to most sources, nearly 1 million people died, possibly more, and an equal number emigrated from Ireland, with huge numbers leaving for the United States and for neighboring England and Wales. Most of those affected were poor and from the most densely populated Irish-speaking districts in the west, where death or emigration were common. Thus, the Irish language and other cultural aspects endemic to the region were diminished by this disaster. These people with little education, no money, with an overarching reliance on the potato, had no escape plans, no manner of removing themselves from the disaster other than through starvation or emigration.

Another of the sobering moments I experienced came when I fully realized the famine's immense devastation. The famine pots used to serve soup still exist on the grounds of Westport House as a silent reminder of efforts to save a starving population. The outlines of the potato ridges that failed the people during those years still line the County Mayo hills. How can an author accurately portray the horror of that time without overwhelming the reader? It's a tough task. Page after page of misery and gloom would swamp all but the most dedicated. But, in reality, poverty, death, and misery were what the Irish suffered. What little hope there was came in the form of friends, neighbors, and relatives looking for a miracle in their struggle to survive.

I chose to set the book in Carrowteige, a lovely village on the northwest coast of Ireland because I wanted a certain "romance" for the novel emboldened by a wild Atlantic setting. Lear House is, of course, fictional. However, the setting around it, as portrayed in the novel, is not. Because the Irish landscape changes from county to county and the crops and farming methods differ by location, I have taken some fictional liberties with those aspects. Despite that fact, I have attempted to be honest about The Great Hunger, drawing not only from history but the lives of my characters. Authors sometimes take criticism from readers for ratcheting up the stakes to what appears to be "no way" or "that couldn't possibly happen" moments, within a fictional context, but that's what drama is about. Briana Walsh and her family are subjected to dire circumstances, but I've included nothing in *The Irishman's Daughter* that I felt was out of the realm of possibility. As always in my historical fiction, I've attempted to meld tragedy with hope.

Many thanks go out to Evan Marshall, my agent; John Scognamiglio, my editor at Kensington, for his steadfast vision; and my readers, Bob Pinsky, Michael Grenier, Heidi Cote, and Lloyd A. Meeker. Special thanks go to John O'Driscoll of Strokestown Park House and the Irish Heritage Trust, and Treasa Ní Ghearraigh of "the old school" in Carrowteige for her valuable historical and environmental insights regarding most everything about Carrowteige and County Mayo. Also of invaluable assistance were my manuscript editors, Traci Hall and Christopher Hawke of CommunityAuthors.com. Their combined efforts made this book possible.

ABOUT THE AUTHOR

V. S. Alexander is an ardent student of history with a strong interest in music and the visual arts. Some of V.S.'s writing influences include Shirley Jackson, Oscar Wilde, Daphne du Maurier, or any work by the exquisite Brontë sisters. V.S. lives in Florida and is at work on a new historical novel for Kensington.